PRAISE FOR *PHOENIX ISLAND*
WINNER OF THE BRAM STOKER AWARD
FOR SUPERIOR ACHIEVEMENT

"Fast-paced and thoroughly engrossing—I could not put it down!"
—Lissa Price, internationally bestselling author of *Starters*

"*Lord of the Flies* meets Wolverine and *Cool Hand Luke*. A tribute to the indomitable human spirit that challenges the mob and chooses values over expediency."
—F. Paul Wilson, *New York Times* bestselling creator
of the Repairman Jack series

"Fast-paced, exciting . . . This action-packed novel combines adventure with extreme violence. . . . Dixon's page-turner will keep readers of all ages enthralled."
—*Kirkus Reviews*

"An unusual premise makes Dixon's thriller debut a welcome series kickoff. . . . The pacing and smooth prose will have suspense fans waiting for the next book."
—*Publishers Weekly*

"100% great!"
—*Cemetery Dance* magazine

"A thrilling adventure story."

—*Philadelphia Weekly*

"A fast-paced read on its own terms, gritty, grim, sometimes unrelenting, but always with an underlying theme of hope. Odds are, you'll want to see what happens next."

—Blogcritics

"A crazy fun ride to read . . . Packs quite the wallop."

—The Hub (YALSA)

"*Phoenix Island* is one of those rare books that stay with you. I couldn't stop thinking about it long after I had read it. I loved the characters, the action, and the world."

—Tripp Vinson, executive producer of *Intelligence*

"Fantastic . . . superbly suspenseful . . . unpredictable and frightening. Welcome to the next big thing. *Phoenix Island* will blow you away."

—Mark Sullivan, *New York Times* bestselling author of *Rogue*

"Dixon brings Carl's world to life with an entrancing mix of color and violence that will leave readers weary, yet desperate to turn another page."

—The Daily Quirk

DEVIL'S
POCKET

JOHN DIXON

GALLERY BOOKS

New York   London   Toronto   Sydney   New Delhi

G

Gallery Books
An Imprint of Simon & Schuster, Inc.
1230 Avenue of the Americas
New York, NY 10020

First Gallery Books trade paperback edition August 2015

GALLERY BOOKS and colophon are registered trademarks of Simon & Schuster, Inc.

For information about special discounts for bulk purchases, please contact Simon & Schuster Special Sales at 1-866-506-1949 or business@simonandschuster.com.

The Simon & Schuster Speakers Bureau can bring authors to your live event. For more information or to book an event contact the Simon & Schuster Speakers Bureau at 1-866-248-3049 or visit our website at www.simonspeakers.com.

Interior design by Davina Mock-Maniscalco

Manufactured in the United States of America

10   9   8   7   6   5   4   3   2   1

Library of Congress Cataloging-in-Publication Data is available.

ISBN 978-1-4767-3866-6
ISBN 978-1-4767-3871-0 (ebook)

This book is dedicated to my wife, Christina,
who always believes in me, and also to my mother,
Doris Dixon, who didn't live to see me publish . . .
but who never doubted that I would.

My undying love to you both.

If you're going through hell . . . keep on going.

—Unknown

And when you gaze long into an abyss, the abyss also gazes into you.

—Friedrich Nietzsche

That age produced a sort of men, in force of hand, and swiftness of foot, and strength of body, excelling the ordinary rate and wholly incapable of fatigue; making use, however, of these gifts of nature to no good or profitable purpose for mankind, but rejoicing and priding themselves in insolence, and taking the benefit of their superior strength in the exercise of inhumanity and cruelty, and in seizing, forcing, and committing all manner of outrages upon everything that fell into their hands; all respect for others, all justice, they thought, all equity and humanity, though naturally lauded by common people, either out of want of courage to commit injuries or fear to receive them, yet no way concerned those who were strong enough to win for themselves."

—Plutarch, *The Lives of the Noble Grecians and Romans*

ONE

GUARDS STEPPED ASIDE, and Carl strode into Training Base One. New recruits stood in ranks near the loading bay of an equipment shed, their freshly buzzed scalps shiny in the bright sunlight and streaked red by the clipper blades. The formation vibrated with fear.

Drill sergeants lurked, scowling.

At a glance, Carl noted injured sergeants—split lips, bloody noses, the red *O* of a bite mark on one forearm—and a massive kid sitting on the ground with splayed legs and his back to the loading-dock wall. The kid stared straight ahead, looking stunned, holding his nose.

Had this huge newcomer gotten into it with the sergeants? No. He wasn't restrained, and no one was eyeballing him. Not him, then—someone else.

Bang-bang-bang.

The metal shed door rippled with impact. It sounded like a mule was trapped in there, kicking its way out.

Someone had knocked it with the big kid and the cadre, and now they had him locked up in there.

And Carl knew in his gut who it was.

Dubois. The exact individual Stark had sent him to "check on"—Stark saying it the way he said so many things, giving Carl an order but not really explaining it.

Carl, of course, had agreed. During the six months since he'd surrendered his freedom, he had played the willing apprentice. Soon, he would have what he needed to burn this organization to the ground, but for now, he continued to play his role.

The loud pounding stopped, and muffled shouting started in the shed, curses and threats.

Drill Sergeant Rivera saw him and came away from the formation, smiling. They shook hands, Carl genuinely happy to see the man. The other drill sergeants eyed Carl like they might a Bengal tiger. Now the recruits were staring, too, their eyes going from Carl to the drill sergeants and back again to Carl.

Good. Let them wonder. Let them fear.

"Freeman," Rivera said. "Glad to see you."

"You, too," Carl said, speaking casually with Rivera—a sharp contrast to the contempt with which he habitually addressed other sergeants. "What's the sitrep?"

Rivera glanced toward the metal door. "We got a bobcat caged up in there."

"His name Dubois?"

Rivera tilted his head. "How'd you know?"

"Is he armed?" Carl asked.

Bang. Bang. Bang. The pounding started up again, hard as hammer blows.

Rivera raised his brows. "Sounds like he picked up something."

"Well," Carl said, "I guess I better go in."

"Your call," Rivera said. "I'll send these kids back to the barracks and keep a couple of drill sergeants here. Martinez worked on a CERT team, cell extractions, all that."

"No," Carl said. Even without thinking the problem through, he knew the answer. Strange, the way he understood things so intuitively now—a phenomenon that had nothing to do with the chip in his head and everything to do with Stark, the man constantly lecturing about leadership. "The recruits need to see this. And I'll go in alone."

Rivera hesitated only for a fraction of a second—even with his rapid processing and accelerated powers of observation, Carl barely caught the pause in his old drill sergeant's eyes—and then nodded. "Lima Charlie, Freeman. Whatever you say."

They climbed the stairs to the loading dock, drill sergeants stepping aside for them. Toppled chairs and electric razors lay on a many-colored carpet of freshly shorn hair. Feeling the hot sun on the back of his neck, Carl recalled his own day on the loading dock, Campbell trying yet failing to save his dreads.

Campbell.

Reflexively, Carl pushed his friend from his mind.

"Watch out," Rivera said. "Dubois looks like a Chihuahua, but he fights like a pit bull."

Inside the shed, muffled threats and curses joined the pounding. Carl glanced at the shaking door and wondered what was so special about this guy that Stark wanted Carl to check on him. Well, he'd find out soon enough. He motioned to Rivera and another soldier, and they unsnapped hooks at the base of the rolling metal door.

The banging stopped.

Probably waiting just inside, ready to clobber me, Carl thought, but this, of course, was of no real concern now that the chip was a part of him.

When he lifted the door a few inches, Dubois's voice called from farther back in the shed, "Come on in, boys. I got something for you."

Carl opened the door the rest of the way.

The kid stood maybe thirty feet away, looking small yet

sturdy beneath a flickering fluorescent light. He had a grin on his bloody face, a broken mop handle in one hand, and the tall black pompadour of an Elvis impersonator. Ridiculous.

Carl stepped forward.

He and Dubois stared silently at each other. The light buzzed erratically overhead, and Carl smelled clean linen, a scent strangely out of place in this tense moment.

Dubois began pacing back and forth, slapping the stick in the palm of his hand.

Considering the damage the kid had done outside, Carl had expected someone bigger. And considering Stark's interest, he'd expected someone more impressive.

Dubois strutted, eyeing Carl.

He didn't look afraid. Carl had to give him that much. What he looked like, Carl thought—the guy rugged but short, maybe five-five—was a fighting rooster. He even had the comb, all that tall black hair piled on top of his head.

Turning to the sergeants, Carl said, "Close the door."

One of the soldiers started to protest, but Carl's glare stopped him. Rivera hooah-ed, and the door rattled down.

When Carl turned back around, Dubois had closed half the distance and stood there grinning. From a gash in his hairline, blood streamed down the middle of his forehead and forked at the bridge of his nose, drawing twin lines of crimson to his jaw. Between the hair, the grin, and the oddly symmetrical blood, he looked like a psychotic clown.

"Come to see the sideshow, boss?" Dubois asked with a country twang.

"Something like that," Carl said, keeping his voice flat.

Dubois rolled his head atop his shoulders, a classic prefight gesture. "Guess you're the breaker, huh?"

"Breaker?"

"You know, the resident skull knocker. You look like a breaker."

Carl guessed probably he did. People back in Philly wouldn't even recognize him. Several months ago, when he'd first arrived on Phoenix Island, he was five foot nine and weighed 152 pounds. Now he was six foot two and 205. During his time here, he'd been beaten and burned, sliced and shot. Add to this bulk and these scars his crooked fighter's nose, his battered knuckles, and his Phoenix Forcer uniform—boots, cargo pants, tank top, and beret, all black, save for the flaming red phoenix on his chest—and yeah, he must look like the resident enforcer. "What if I am?"

Dubois took up a batter's stance. "Then you got your work cut out for you, buddy."

"Relax," Carl said, and raised his hands. "I came to talk, not fight."

The kid looked doubtful. "This ain't my first square dance, boss. I heard that one before."

Keep him talking, Carl thought. "You been a lot of places like this, ones with breakers?"

Dubois grinned, and Carl saw he was missing a tooth not too far back on one side. "They been sending me places like this since I could tie my shoes. I tell them, send me someplace with a revolving door, because they won't keep me long, either. Shoot, I don't even bother unpacking no more."

Carl let a smile come onto his face, figuring he'd ease the tension. Stark told him to check on the kid, not crush him. What was so special about Dubois, anyway? So far, he seemed like one more 150-pound knuckle-tosser, fearless, sure, but the streets were full of kids with big mouths and bad haircuts. "Well," Carl said, "you better plan on staying here a while. How old are you?"

"Sixteen and a half."

Same age I was when I came here, Carl thought. "My name's Carl Freeman."

Dubois straightened, lifting his chin. "Texarkana Reginald Dubois."

He pronounced it *Doo-bwah*, but what really caught Carl was the first part. "Texarkana?"

Dubois tensed with the question, and Carl thought, *His whole life, he's been carrying that name around like a* KICK ME *sign taped to his back.*

"It was my granddaddy's name," Dubois said.

"I thought it was a place," Carl said.

Anger flashed in the boy's eyes. Whatever potential Stark saw in the kid, this hair-trigger temper would likely ruin it. "It is a place—*and* a name, kind of like Washington. You ever hear of anybody named Washington before, genius?"

Carl said nothing, picturing not someone *named* Washington, but rather someone *from* Washington. Someone with beautiful gray eyes and a streak of white in her hair . . .

Texarkana Reginald Dubois ran a hand over his pompadour, seeming to relax again. "People call me Tex. Hey, you got a cigarette?"

Carl shook his head.

Tex sighed. "Figures. Probably all out of beer, too."

"Yup," Carl said. "So what happened out there?"

Tex snorted. "See, I got a problem with people trying to push me around."

Me, too, Carl thought, but said nothing.

Tex shifted the mop handle to one hand, leaned on it like a cane, and nodded toward the door. "You see that boy out there, kid about eight feet tall, built like a gorilla?"

"I think so," Carl said, remembering the enormous recruit slumped against the wall.

"Well, old King Kong's been riding me since we climbed onto that bus back in Mexico. Hitting me in the back of the head, saying he'd never seen a white boy with an Afro, stuff like that." Tex ran a hand gently over the thick mane like someone caressing a beloved pet. "I tried to ignore him, stay out of trouble, but then he started getting the other kids going, too. You don't stand up then, someday you have to fight them all."

Carl nodded, picturing it: Tex with his funny hair and his strut, not even five and a half feet tall, and with that country twang—exactly the type of guy some big, mean kid would push and push. He remembered his own start on the island—Davis, Decker, Parker . . . all of them pushing—and how difficult it had been, holding back.

Tex laughed. "We was formed up out there, waiting on haircuts. I knew what I had to do. Didn't say a word, just turned around and gave him the old Texarkana haymaker right between the eyes." He demonstrated, throwing a looping punch in the air. Not the greatest technique, but fast, and he shifted his weight with it. A strong punch. "Knocked him on his butt. He just sat there, blinking, and I told myself, 'Texarkana, you got to fix this old boy right now and fix him good enough that everybody'll leave you alone.' So I grabbed him by the ears and put the knee to him."

Carl let the hint of a smile creep onto his face. "The drill sergeants didn't like it?"

Tex spat blood and grinned, one of his front teeth red. "Didn't seem to, the way they hollered and put the boot leather to me."

Carl laughed. Against all odds, he actually liked the kid. His guts, his sense of humor.

Tex said, "I knocked a couple of bulls down, too, but there sure was a bunch of them. They shoved me in here and locked the door, so I picked up this mop, broke off the handle, and here we are." He shrugged, looking at the makeshift weapon. "Look, buddy," he said, some of the tension going out of his muscles. "What are we doing here? You come to dance or fight?"

"I'm here to see you," Carl said, and remembered Stark saying the same thing, a long, long time ago, when Carl was locked in the sweatbox, waiting to die. "We don't have to fight."

Tex nodded. "Guess I don't need this anymore, then, huh?" And he tossed the mop handle across the room.

Good, Carl thought. Stark would be pleased that he had defused the situation.

"Say your name was Carl?"

"Right," Carl said.

"Had a cousin named Carl," Tex said. "Guess I still do, though I ain't been home in so long, it's hard to say. Given his habits, he might've gone to his reward in heaven by now."

Carl said nothing. *Let the kid talk*, he thought. *Make him comfortable.*

"He was a snake handler, my cousin Carl, you know what I mean?"

"Not really."

"Ballsy, man. It was a church thing, back in the mountains. Pentecostal. Gospel of Mark and all that. The kid fourteen years old, leading the congregation, standing up there on this little, old, nailed-together stage, handling rattlesnakes as big as your leg and speaking in tongues." He let out a stream of garbled nonsense that degraded into laughter. "You a snake handler, Carl?"

"Not me," Carl said.

"So . . . let's get this straight," Tex said, squinting one eye.

"What are you, the *man* around here? I see the way the bulls act around you. They're wearing the boss hats, you're half their age, and they still do what you tell them."

"No," Carl said, "I'm not the man, but I guess you could say I'm the man's man."

"The man's man, huh?" Tex said, and spat on the floor again.

"Look," Carl said, "you relax a little, I might be able to help you."

Tex nodded thoughtfully. "Truth be told, I reckon I could use a hand right about now."

"All right."

"Hey," Tex said in a soft voice, his eyes looking hopeful. "You reckon I really gotta get my head shaved?"

"Your grape," Carl said.

Tex squinted. "My what?"

"Your grape," Carl said. "That's what they call your head around here. Might as well get the lingo straight. And yeah, they're going to shave it."

"That right there is the worst news I had all day." He whistled and ran a hand once more through his thick hair. "But I suppose, when in Rome . . . get your grape shaved."

Carl laughed. "Pretty much."

A look of concern came onto Tex's face. "What are they going to do to me, Carl? One guy kept talking about a sweatbox, and I'll tell you right now, I can't hack small spaces."

"Don't worry," Carl said. "I can make this go away. No sweatbox, and a fresh start."

Tex whooped and clapped his hands. "You *are* the man!"

Carl smiled, but picturing Stark, he said, "No, trust me . . . when you meet the man, you'll know it." He turned and crouched, reaching for the door handle. "He's the most—"

And then he was ducking, rolling sideways, his body reacting automatically before his conscious mind even registered the footsteps racing up behind him. Tex's boot slammed hard into the metal door, right where Carl's head had been, and the shed filled with insane laughter.

"Wake up, boss!" Tex shouted, leering at Carl through wild eyes. "Almost took your grape off with that one!"

He almost had, too. A kick like that could've broken his neck. Rage leapt up in Carl as hot and fast as a flame, and then he was smelling ashes again.

Tex raised his fists. "Come on then, Carla. Let's see what you got. I do love to fight!"

Carl advanced slowly and silently, outwardly calm. He'd been nice to Tex, helped him, and the second he'd turned his back, the kid had tried to take his head off—*would* have taken his head off if it weren't for the chip.

Rage roared, demanding retribution. *Control it*, he cautioned himself.

Tex backpedaled to the far wall and picked up the broken mop handle.

Carl walked toward him, arms loose at his sides.

Behind him, the door rattled open, and men's shouting filled the shed.

"Come on in, boys!" Tex shouted. "The more the merrier!" And he swung the makeshift club with a *whoosh*.

Without even looking in the soldiers' direction, Carl stuck out a palm. "Stand down."

He walked toward Tex, saying nothing.

"You can't sweet-talk Texarkana Reginald Dubois," Tex said, and charged, raising the mop handle overhead like a chopping ax.

For Carl, the world decelerated as the chip worked its magic.

Tex swung the stick in slo-mo. Carl slid easily under the attack and drove an uppercut into the kid's stomach.

Tex dropped to the floor, gasping. The broken handle clattered away.

Seeing the traitor crumpled at his feet, Carl braced himself for the red wave. For the chip had done more than make him faster . . .

His eyes found the sharp end of the broken handle a few short strides away, and the beast within him demanded he drive the pointed end into the exposed neck of the sucker-punching thug lying helpless as a sacrifice before him.

Carl's body took one step in that direction, but he gritted his teeth and stopped himself. *No*, he told himself, fighting the rage that lived within him now like a dark twin. *Don't do it, don't give in*. When that didn't work, he thought, *Remember Sanderson*.

The memory slapped him hard with its sun and sand and screams, allowing him to wrestle his rage temporarily into uneasy submission.

Tex stirred. "Punch," he gasped, "like a girl."

"Shh," Carl said. He plunged his hand into the thick black pompadour and lifted Tex's head. "Nap time."

The strike was short and sharp, a palm heel to temple, and Tex went instantly limp, snoring the way some guys do when they get knocked out.

The dark twin within Carl roared, and Carl stepped back, afraid that if he lingered even briefly, he would pick up that broken handle. He turned to discover Rivera and the others staring at him with fear and awe.

"Toss him in the sweatbox," Carl told them, "but first, shave off that stupid hair."

TWO

THE GIRL CALLED MARGARITA sat in the hard plastic chair, alternately toying with her long blond ponytail, which remained as strange to her as her new face, and drumming her fingers on the edge of the desk.

This place reminded her of a police station interrogation room. Small and cold, with block walls painted white and a camera mounted high up in one corner. A sparsely furnished space—just two chairs of blue plastic and the table between them, its surface an empty span of nondescript Formica, save for the low divider running across its middle, so you could see the head and shoulders of the person sitting opposite you but nothing below that.

Not that anyone was sitting across from her now.

Half an hour she'd been waiting. Another test? Probably. Often, she felt that *everything* here in the SI3 Bunker was some kind of test.

She pictured Bleaker somewhere behind the camera, watching her and taking notes with that little recorder of his. *The subject exhibits signs of impatience*, she could imagine him reporting—and the scene was purely imaginary, not visionary, a distinction of some importance here among the Bunker Bots—*shifting of position, eye rolling, finger drumming . . .*

She stopped drumming her fingers and turned her attention

instead to the magazines stacked beside the desk: dog-eared issues of *Sports Illustrated*, *Time*, *Reader's Digest*, and, strangely
enough, *Bird Talk*. Did Bleaker have birds? She could imagine
him tending small, bright birds—finches, perhaps, or canaries—
keeping them warm and safe and well fed but never, ever letting
them out of the cage.

Or perhaps Crossman had donated the *Bird Talk* back issues,
the man secretly an unlikely avian enthusiast. It wouldn't be
finches for Crossman, though, and no canaries, either. He would
keep hawks, falcons, maybe a bald eagle.

The magazine atop the stack was not *Bird Talk* but *Time*.
On its cover, a handsome middle-aged man in a tie and tweed
waistcoat smiled warmly, surrounded by a dozen beaming children displaying a diversity of ethnicity and regional garb. *Person
of the Year*, the cover announced, *Payter Oaks: Lord of Orphans*.

Of course, she'd recognized Oaks without the caption. He
was the most famous orphan in the world, a rags-to-billions
philanthropist, every orphan's hero.

And of course she was an orphan . . . wasn't she?

Yes, she told herself. *You're an orphan, a recent orphan.* She
pictured the faces of her parents—*Jaime and Rosalinda*, she reminded herself—from the file sitting back in her room. *You miss
them*, she told herself, and remembered Crossman frowning at
her. *Miss them*, he had hissed. *Tears, tears . . .*

The door opened at last, and Dr. Bleaker came in, tall and
stooped and smiling apologetically, wearing not a white jacket but
a light green button-down, wrinkled and untucked, the sleeves
rolled up to reveal flesh as pale and soft-looking as cave fungus,
making her wonder how long he'd been a Bunker dweller. She'd
go insane if she stayed here long, feeling all that stone and

steel—a mile of it—pressing down from overhead. Thankfully, she was leaving soon.

Too soon, in fact. Which was why she needed to hurry.

"Sorry I'm late," he said. "I was stuck in another meeting."

"No problem," she said, and forced a smile. She liked Bleaker—compared to most of the Bunker Bots, he was positively warm and fuzzy—but her growing impatience made it difficult to be anything more than perfunctorily polite.

He settled into the chair across from her with a characteristic sigh and began unpacking his valise.

Now he'll ask me how I slept, she thought, and Bleaker said, "How did you sleep?"

"Fine," she lied, pleased with her accurate prediction, which of course had been a product not of precognition—*how SI3 would love that!*—but of pattern recognition. *How did you sleep?* was the question Bleaker always asked as he unpacked his things, what passed as small talk between the pair.

Right now, she wasn't in the mood for small talk or routine. Right now, she wanted to *learn.*

They had already hashed out all the ground-floor stuff, and no matter how amazing it was, they were crawling when she needed to sprint. With only days until her departure, she needed to learn remote viewing *now.* "Are we moving on today?"

Without looking up, Bleaker said, "Moving on?"

Bitterness rose in her. "I need you to teach me. I know all this stuff. I need you to show me how to range."

Now he did look up, frowning. "I'm sorry. I know this must be frustrating, but we have to be certain. Until the foundation is finished, there's no use building a mansion, now, is there?" He lifted his frown into a less-than-convincing smile.

She leaned forward, palms flat on the table. "All right. Let's get this over with."

"Okey doke," Bleaker said, and produced a deck of playing cards with blue paisley designs on the back.

She had seen the cards before. Many times.

Sitting up straighter, she said, "Can't we move on to something new?"

He raised a pale, soft-looking hand and patted the air. "Patience. First things first."

First things first. Of all the maddening phrases in the world . . .

Bleaker smiled as he positioned the cards—three as always—fixing them side by side into a thin groove atop the dividing wall between them so that she could see only the backs of the cards and he could see only the faces. He looked at the cards, looked at her, and nodded. Then he thumbed his digital voice recorder to life and started speaking, recording the date, time, location, and their names: Dr. Travis Bleaker and Margarita Carbajal.

As always, hearing *Margarita Carbajal* jarred her, and for the first time, it struck her that the pleasant, habitually tardy, maddeningly repetitive man sitting across from her almost certainly wasn't actually named Dr. Travis Bleaker.

She wondered further: *Am I even looking at his real face?*

Had Bleaker—or whatever his real name was—also had extensive facial reconstruction surgery? Was that a requirement here in this supersecret bunker? Could be. After all, she had needed work after what they euphemistically referred to as "the accident," but she hadn't needed half of what they'd done. They'd left her with a beautiful face, but it wasn't *her* face. In fact, her own mother, had she still been alive, wouldn't even recognize her now.

"Shall we begin?" he asked her.

"Let's try something new, something harder."

He gestured toward the divider. "The cards first."

"How many?"

"How many what?"

"You know," she said. "Cards."

"You mean how many *correct* cards."

"I never miss."

"You did once."

"I was hurrying. That doesn't mean anything."

"It means everything."

"How many *correct* cards, then?"

Bleaker tidied the cards unnecessarily. "We'll see."

"How many?"

Now he looked at her. "Do you really want me to set a number?"

"No," she said. "But if I do well, can we please move on to something new?"

"Probably," he said, "if there's time—but for now, push that out of your mind. Focus."

Oh, I'll focus, all right, she thought. She had to blow through these so they could move on to something new, something important, before Bleaker ran off to another meeting.

"You know the drill," he said. He tapped one card and raised his brows.

She stared hard at the blue paisley pattern, focusing her eyes and mind like knobs on a microscope. Seconds later, the blue design faded, and she was looking at the ghost.

Ghost was her word, not theirs. A ghost was the flip-side image, which she saw as if she were sitting in Bleaker's seat rather than her own. Not that she was seeing through his eyes; that wasn't her particular talent. The ghost was in her head, a *simulacrum*—and that *was* their word—conjured by her mind, a representation of data her brain was receiving via some quadrant to which she had no direct access.

That part of your brain, Bleaker had told her when they first started working together months earlier, *is like a database with no querying language. In time, it will all be open to you.*

She believed him. The data was all there, all whole, in her mind, even if she couldn't access it yet, just as game show prizes—cars; toaster ovens; trips for two to Aruba, airfare included—were all real, all whole, before the smiling host pulled the curtain aside. Some part of her brain knew exactly what was hidden behind the curtain. It just wasn't very good at sharing that information with her *conscious* mind yet.

The ghost was faint and blurry and not at all like the actual flip-side of a card. Bleaker said with time, that would change—*could* change—and she would be able to see a hidden object as if she were actually looking at it, would even be able to study its details. But for now, looking at the ghost was like studying a card doodled by a child and half-obscured by heavy fog.

Come on, she thought, pushing hard with her mind. *Let's have it.*

A twinge of pain in her forehead.

You're pushing too hard, trying to see it too quickly, she cautioned herself, then gritted her teeth and pushed even harder.

Pain solidified, a thrumming wire at the center of her brain, making her squint.

Through the thinning mist, she saw a triangle with no base—a *chevron*, she thought, another of their words coming to her—and the pain-wire vibrated faster, generating heat.

An involuntary grunt escaped her, but still she pushed, and

the ghost grew more distinct, another triangle visible to her now, this one solid, black. . . .

"Ace of spades," she blurted, and realized she was shaking from the effort and the pain.

"Margarita views an ace of spades," Bleaker told his digital recorder. "Correct."

Of course it's correct, she thought, and pinched the bridge of her nose.

Bleaker smiled approvingly. "That was fast."

She nodded, thinking, *Too fast*. She'd pushed too hard, and now she needed ibuprofen and a nap. But she faked a smile and said, "Next one?" Instantly, she knew she'd put too much chirp into her voice, and for a flickering instant, she feared Bleaker would see through her, guess her pain, and stop the exercise, but he only nodded, pointed to the second card, and lifted his brows.

She stared at the card, and—*oh, crap*—the line of fire in her head thrummed, vibrating like a plucked piano wire.

Deal with it, she told herself. *You've dealt with worse pain. Far worse.* She settled back into her seat, trying not to force this one, waiting . . . waiting . . .

Minutes later, slick with sweat and gripping the table with white knuckles, she said, "Eight of diamonds." It was a tremendous relief, like breaking the surface after nearly drowning, and the hard-earned ghost washed away.

"Margarita views an eight of diamonds," Bleaker recorded. "Correct."

"Now can we move on to something new?" she asked, doing her best not to show her intense pain. "I got them both right—and in half the time it normally takes me."

Bleaker shook his head. "Not yet."

"Why?"

"You're close," he said. "We have to be sure."

She closed her eyes, struggling against her pain and frustration. When she opened them again, Bleaker indicated the third card and raised his brows.

She took a deep breath, leaned forward, and pushed.

The jack of hearts came to her quickly—but at a price. As Bleaker recorded her success, she shuddered, weak with effort. The thrumming wire in her head glowed red-hot now. The room around her had gone wavy, and her stomach did a slow, greasy roll.

"Now?" she asked.

He looked at her.

"Are we done with stupid cards?" she asked.

He shook his head. "You're doing very well, but we're not ready to move on yet. First things first."

She slammed her hands on the desk. "You heard Crossman. I have days, not weeks . . . *days*. Then I'm gone."

Bleaker looked uncomfortable. "When you come back, then."

"No," she said, and it was all she could do not to scream it. "I told you I would do all of this *if* you taught me to see."

"And we will."

"I meant *now*," she said.

"Don't raise your voice at me," he said. His own voice remained maddeningly calm and patient—the voice of a man meant to study glacial melt.

"I can't wait any longer," she said. "I have to see. I have to know."

"We must follow protocol."

She told him where he could shove his protocol. "Tell Crossman I quit."

Bleaker stood, his mouth a straight line, and left the room.

She called after him weakly—it was the best she could manage through her pain and exhaustion—but he didn't even look back.

Great, just great.

She let her head fall forward onto the desk. There were no tears, only pain and fatigue and the leaden weight of failure and long frustration.

You blew it, she told herself. *Pushed too hard, too fast, and blew it.*

Out of spite, she pushed again, hard, this time at nothing at all. The line of pain in her skull gave a sharp twang, making her hiss, and then something changed. . . .

Sitting there with her forehead pressed to the desktop, she could *feel* the room around her. Some part of her mind for which she had no name reached with invisible hands and touched the walls and floor, Bleaker's empty chair and the staring camera. She could feel the Bunker itself, a mile of stone and steel, crushing down on her like the world's heaviest coffin lid.

Then she felt something else—or rather *someone* else—in motion, coming closer. It would have been amazing, were it not for her crippling pain and despair. She could actually *feel* someone approaching out in the hall, could even feel the stiff manner in which he walked. Bleaker, offended, coming back to tell her to pack her bags, she was out of the program. . . .

But when the door opened and she lifted her head, it was not Bleaker coming into the room but a lean, hard-looking man in a navy-blue suit, staring at her through cold blue eyes she knew all too well.

Director Crossman dropped a sketchpad and pencil onto the desk. "Dr. Bleaker tells me you're playing hardball."

She nodded. Even that small motion cranked the pain and summoned nausea from wherever it had tenuously retreated.

"Okay," Crossman said, and spread his arms. "You win. We're moving on."

She glanced at the pencil and pad and shook her head. "I've been drawing for weeks."

And she had. Only *drawing* wasn't the right word for what she'd been doing. Like ghosting cards, this new form of drawing, in another place at another time, would have been mind-blowing.

They would give her pencil and paper and tell her to sketch an object. First, it was a brick. Then an archery target, circles inside of circles. Then a basket of fruit, a vase of flowers. She'd drawn them perfectly—only it hadn't really been like drawing.

Trying to draw from imagination, she was stuck with the same so-so doodling ability she'd always had, but if she sketched a *real* thing, all she needed to do was begin—a single line would do—and the rest was a matter of position and proportion, one line or curve in relation to others, and these lengths and distances and angles she could *feel* with more accuracy than she could see. And as she felt these facets, her hand moved, marking the paper as if guided by the very thing she was sketching.

Truly amazing—but again, she'd already learned this trick.

She crossed her arms. "I told Bleaker. Teach me something new, or I quit. No mission, no nothing."

Crossman's smile was icy. "He made that clear. Do you really think I'd be here otherwise?" He turned and opened the door, and she was certain she'd overplayed her hand, but instead of marching out, he called into the hallway.

A muscular boy around her age stumbled into the room. Or

at least she *thought* he was her age—it was difficult to say with the sack of red cloth covering his head.

Seeing his broad shoulders, perfect physique, and big hands, hope sprung up and soared within her—but then crashed down as she *really* saw him. He was too tall. His shoulders were broad yet not broad enough, just as his hands were large yet not large enough. . . .

"Map him," Crossman said.

"What—draw him?"

Crossman shook his head. "Map him. Sketch his face."

"You mean the"—she was about to say *mask*, but that wasn't accurate—"hood?"

"I mean the face," Crossman said. His own face looked absolutely serious, even impatient. "Focus. Look through the hood, beyond it. View his face like a landscape. Move over its contours. Map it."

"I don't—"

Crossman scowled. "You wanted progress. This is your chance."

"I," she said, starting to protest, meaning to tell Crossman that he was crazy—this wasn't a step ahead, it was a mile's jump forward—but then she reconsidered. She had to know. Even if she split her head in half, she had to try. "Okay," she said. "I'll give it a shot."

He nodded and stepped aside.

The boy stood five feet away, still as a statue, save for his breathing.

All right, she told herself. *Focus.*

For a second, she just sat there, staring at the red hood, careful not to push too hard, telling herself, *Don't burn out. Not now. This is it. Take your time.*

Her eyes blurred with the pain in her skull.

So stop trying to use your eyes to see him, she thought, and when she closed her eyes, the ghost appeared.

It was like flying over a land obscured by fog. She could sense topography behind the cloaking mist, could feel it, she just couldn't see it. . . .

Push harder, she told herself, growling as flames filled her skull, the pain so severe that her gorge rose.

The mist swirled, and—yes!—she glimpsed a line, there and gone, like a ridge of stone seen from an airplane through a quick break in rolling cloud cover.

His nose?

No, she corrected herself. *Don't guess. Don't put yourself into this. See the lines. Feel the truth. Don't imagine him; map him.*

Breathing through her nostrils, she concentrated despite the pain and nausea, and when the line came once more into view, her hand moved, sketching. She did not think about what she was seeing—did not try to name the part—nor did she check what she was drawing.

And suddenly she *was* drawing. Her hand moved faster and faster as she explored the boy's face, not actually *seeing* it but *sensing* its contours, her mind reaching out like the fingers of a blind person reading a new acquaintance's features. Inch by inch, she moved away from the first line, and as her hand sketched, she slid into something like rapture, her mind and body reading and recording with seemingly no thought of her own, no interpretation. The ghost disappeared entirely, and there was only the feel of his face, the truth of every line and curve and angle. Her hand moved faster and faster until she felt dizzy with the speed of it all, a kind of pressure building and building within her until her head snapped back and her eyes opened and she was fully aware of herself, the room, the boy in the red hood, Crossman looking at her through narrowed eyes, and the absolute fountain of pain and nausea gushing within her.

Before her was an incredibly detailed, almost photographic sketch. She'd seen none of it while drawing—a true forest-for-the-trees moment—but now she leaned back and saw the whole thing, not a forest but a face, a good face, a face that would have been handsome, very handsome, if it weren't for the pain and the nausea. . . .

"Well done," Crossman said, offering a rare smile. He lifted the red hood, revealing the exact face she'd just sketched: the black bangs, the dark soulful eyes, the bright smile, and dimples, everything accurate down to the scar splitting one eyebrow. "Allow me to introduce your boyfriend."

"My . . . boyfriend?" she said, a tornado of pain whirling all through her now, spinning down out of her head, dipping into her stomach then lifting again.

"Yes," Crossman said. "Your boyfriend, Julio."

Julio stuck out his hand and stepped forward, saying something that she never heard . . . because at that moment, the girl now known as Margarita Carbajal squeezed her eyes shut and vomited all over Julio's outstretched hand.

THREE

BREAKING FROM THE JUNGLE, Carl stepped into the bright sun beating down on the stone ridge that ran like a spine across the center of Phoenix Island. Glancing left, he saw the sheer cliff and felt the old fear, faint now in its power over him.

He paused for a moment, struck as always by the beauty of this elevated vantage point, the island sprawling greenly away toward the sparkling ocean that defined the limits of his world. Straight ahead, the rocky ridge led to the apex of Phoenix Island, atop which Stark's silhouette blocked, punched, and kicked as if engaged in combat with invisible opponents. Carl's eyes, so different now that the chip had become a part of him, focused, drawing Stark into clearer detail until it was like looking through binoculars—or, he thought, the scope of a high-powered rifle—and he could make out the snarl of concentration, the determined eyes, even the sheen of sweat glistening on the shaven head.

Carl had wondered, when he'd returned to the empty hangar and found Stark's invitation to the train atop the mountain, what they'd be doing. Now he knew, and it came as no surprise: more kata, more choreographed combat, every move practiced to perfection. Stark believed in repetition.

Stark spotted him then, broke form, and beckoned, calling, "Come on up, son, and give me your full report on Recruit Dubois."

Carl climbed up to the flat peak and delivered his full report in five words: "Feed him to the sharks."

Stark laughed. "Outstanding. But I'm surprised to hear this from you. Certainly you know that anger is defeat."

True enough—Carl had often used opponents' anger against them—but sometimes *feeling* was stronger than *knowing*. Sometimes rage trumped truth.

He had always struggled with his temper, but rage was different in him now. Stronger and more demanding, manifesting within him another Carl, one capable of horrific things—like that day early in his apprenticeship, when, out of the blue, he'd snapped on Sanderson and nearly beaten him to death. Since that nightmare afternoon, he had been on guard against his rage. Was the chip trying to reprogram him into a killer? A terrifying notion . . .

"He's a punk," Carl said, feeling only *normal* anger now. "He acted all friendly. Then he tried to take my head off."

Stark scooped up a small stone and flung it out into the open air.

Carl tracked it, his eyes autofocusing as the rock dropped in a spinning plummet toward the canopy, and he felt a curious unease, as if the little stone might suck him into its wake, pull him once more into the void that had almost killed him several months earlier, when boys now dead or beneath his unofficial command had hunted him with spears and knives and guns.

"Of course," Stark said, turning to him with a dangerous smile, "if you're serious, I'll see that he's shark food within the hour."

A tempting concept—Tex had tried to kill him, after all—but Carl knew Stark meant it. He shook his head.

"In that case," Stark said, "I believe I'll keep him around."

"What's so special about him?" Carl said. "He's just one more psychopath."

Stark nodded slightly. "Psychopaths can be useful in their own way. Besides, I believe there is more to Texarkana Reginald Dubois than meets the eye."

Carl kicked a stone across the flat summit but not hard enough to send it over the edge. The sun was very bright up here, very hot. With barely a thought, he dialed back his body temperature.

"Your idealism blinds you," Stark said. "It's neurotic and foolish, even dangerous, for a leader to evaluate someone on only his worst trait."

"Maybe I'm not a leader, then."

"You'd rather be a follower?"

"Maybe I'm not a leader or a follower," Carl said. "Maybe I'm just me."

Stark seemed to consider this. "Whether or not you wish to lead, people will follow you."

Carl started to say more but reined himself in. Anger had already loosened his tongue. He couldn't allow it to ruin everything, not after six months of pretending to be Stark's loyal apprentice, six months during which he'd hated himself for bumbling around like Hamlet, waiting, waiting, waiting. . . . But what choice did he have? If he acted rashly, if he rebelled or fled the island, someone would call the mainland, and one of Stark's monsters—dressed, perhaps, as a nurse or an orderly or even a doctor—would enter Octavia's room and press a pillow over her face, and . . .

No. He couldn't strike until he was certain of total victory, and for that, he needed access to Stark's computers: his documents, the location of Octavia's hospital, video clips of training exercises and Phoenix Force's atrocities, and the ability to contact government agencies. However he gained access, he needed to do so quickly. Stark had temporarily halted chip implantation, wanting time to study Carl's progress prior to chipping others. Once he flipped that switch, there would be no stopping him. What havoc would hundreds of chipped, combat-experienced, and fanatically loyal Phoenix Forcers unleash on the world?

Stark was bent on destroying civilization and blasting humanity back into the Stone Age. In this twisted future, hobbled survivors would worship a new Olympus: Stark and his pantheon of genetically and technologically augmented gods. It didn't matter to Carl that he was slated to play Apollo to Stark's Zeus. He didn't desire power. He wanted only to stop the madman and save Octavia.

Stark stooped again, this time picking up not a stone but a handful of loose grit. He let dirt and pebbles sift slowly from fist to palm, seeming to study each fragment. "Tell me," he said. "What is the most valuable trait a soldier under your command could possess?"

Carl thought for a moment—Stark valued many traits, including bravery, composure, intelligence, strength, and endurance—then said, "Training."

"Training is indeed valuable, even indispensable, but no," Stark said. He lifted his palm and blew, expelling a gritty cloud and leaving only a few larger chips of stone. "The most valuable trait is loyalty."

"Loyalty?" Carl didn't bother to keep doubt out of his voice. As a mentor, Stark didn't mind questions. He was more concerned with answers.

"Loyalty."

"More valuable than training? More valuable than guts or strength or brains?"

"Yes," Stark said, and tossed away the remaining chips. "A loyal soldier will go to his own doom on his commander's whim. A disloyal soldier will doom his commander on his own whim."

"Fair enough," Carl said, "but if you're a good leader, can't you assume loyalty?"

Stark snorted. "Start assuming loyalty, son, and you won't lead long."

Fine by me, Carl thought.

Stark said, "Until very recently, civilization valued loyalty above all other traits. Consider a samurai's loyalty to his emperor, a knight's loyalty to his king, or the gallant loyalty of those poor Confederates serving under Pickett on Gettysburg's fateful third day."

Carl nodded. They had covered a lot of military history over the last six months.

"This modern age of self-worship would have us discard honor for individuality, but reverence for loyalty—and a corresponding loathing of disloyalty—stretch all the way back to the very roots of Western civilization. Certainly the Greek myths prove this. And what of Dante? Have you finished his *Inferno*?"

Carl shook his head. "Not yet." He could read very quickly now—two pages every ten seconds or so, one eye reading one page, the other eye reading the opposite—with absolute retention, but that only worked for straightforward material: handbooks, simple prose, and, thanks to the way his mind now processed notation, chess manuals. He was still stuck, however, with his own vocabulary, so trying to read Dante's *Inferno* was like trying to run through chest-deep water, every line an Olympic length. At this point, he'd struggled through enough to understand the gist: Dante's tour of hell's nine circles, with sections of each ring reserved for sinners of a specific stripe.

"Spoiler alert," Stark said with a smile. "Dante's hell is much like the Greek underworld. Asphodel, Styx, it's all in there, and the Greeks' idealized punishments live on in the *Inferno*'s *contrapasso* . . . poetic justice in scale with sin. Outside the gates, Dante saw those who had done neither good nor evil in life, fated in death to mill eternally in limbo, but Virgil led him down through the circles, past pagans and adulterers, gluttons and suicides, lower and lower, the punishments growing ever more severe the deeper Dante descended, until at last they arrived at the lowest, the most severe level of hell."

"The ninth circle," Carl said.

"Not a lake of fire," Stark said, "but a lake of ice, the lake itself tiered, with its lowermost level known as . . . ?"

Carl shrugged.

"Judecca. Named for . . .?"

Carl could only shrug again.

"Judas."

"Like the cow?" Carl asked. Stark had told him of how, when nervous herds scheduled for processing wouldn't enter a slaughterhouse, workers would introduce a trained "Judas cow" that would mix with the herd, then lead the way up the ramp. Cows, being cows, would follow. At the top of the ramp, just before the conveyor belt that would suck incoming beeves to their bloody deaths, workers would divert the Judas cow. By that time, the herd would be pressing hard from below, and the cows in front would stumble forward into the factory of death.

Stark laughed. "Not exactly, though if beasts faced the abyss, Judas cows would undoubtedly belong in the lake of ice. Judecca was named for Judas Iscariot, the betrayer of Christ."

"Oh," Carl said, feeling stupid.

"The lowest level of hell was reserved for the treacherous," Stark said, "and Judecca itself was reserved for the absolute worst sinners, those who had betrayed their *benefactors*."

"Oh," Carl said again, not liking the direction of this discussion.

Stark turned and surveyed the sparkling ocean. "Loyalty is the central pillar of humanity, society, and goodness. And as a leader of men, no matter what the outside world would have you believe, loyalty is the most valuable currency. Instill it in your troops, and you will march to victory. Forge on without it, and you and your men are so many cows on a conveyor belt."

"Okay," Carl said. Like much of what Stark said, this all made sense without telling the whole story. Before he could sort this out, Stark continued.

"Look past men's flaws. Earn their loyalty, and you'll convert liabilities into assets."

Carl said he understood and for the hundredth time, imagined pushing his own "benefactor" off the mountaintop.

Stark turned to face him. "Do I have your loyalty now, son? Can I trust you?"

These questions hit Carl like a stiff double-jab, not just because they rocked him out of his traitorous thoughts but also because Stark had never mentioned Carl's loyalty, not once in the six months since the duel. Carl had unfailingly played the role of committed protégé, but with these questions, he had to wonder— had Stark, too, been acting?

Reacting with a counterpuncher's composure, he opened his mouth slightly and furrowed his brow, conveying, he hoped, mild shock and a shade of indignation. "You know I am. You know you can."

"Good," Stark said, staring directly into his eyes. "That's good, son."

Seconds passed. Stark stared. Carl felt like a man entering airport security with a knife in his pocket.

Stark gestured toward the ocean. "In that case, I'm sending you away."

Oh no, Carl thought, *not Zurkistan*. Many times, Stark had suggested Carl accompany Baca and Z-Force to "get his feet wet"—a phrase they both understood meant killing—and each time, Carl had declined. He was willing to endure this place for however long it took him to overthrow the organization, willing to suffer, willing even to act with contempt and cruelty, but he refused to become a murderer. He might surrender his life, but he wouldn't sell his soul.

"Your first combat mission," Stark said. "Everything on the line."

"But our training together," Carl said, reeling. "You're teaching me so much, and—"

"Don't look so distraught," Stark said. "It's not Zurkistan."

Carl relaxed a little, but the phrase *combat mission* still echoed in his mind. "Where, then?"

A playful light came into Stark's eyes. "I don't know."

"You don't know where you're sending me?"

"No—I only know what you'll be doing once you get there."

Carl waited.

In the distance, gunfire rattled faintly.

"Fighting," Stark said, and his smile widened.

"Fighting?" The word could mean so many things. "Boxing?"

Stark shook his head. "The Funeral Games."

Funeral Games? Carl thought. A vaguely familiar, overtly unsettling phrase . . .

"Named for the ancient Greek tradition, of course," Stark said. "The modern Funeral Games is an annual underground tournament held at an undisclosed location and hosted by the Few, a small group of enormously wealthy elitists who happen to love blood sport. One-on-one, mixed martial arts, ten million dollars to the winner. You will represent Phoenix Island."

Carl's mind whirred. Was he actually leaving Phoenix Island?

Stark laughed. "You look stunned. Hefty prize, eh? But as usual, we don't care about money. We care about honor. Speaking of honor, you have proven a perfect apprentice: apt, diligent, durable, and *loyal*."

"Thank you," Carl said, thinking, *If he could read my mind . . .*

"Phoenix Force idolizes you, and the cadre fear you . . . and yet, you have no official title. Win this tournament, and that will change. How does '*Lieutenant Commander* Carl Freeman' sound?"

"Wow—I . . . really?"

"Really," Stark said, putting a hand on Carl's shoulder. "This is your big moment, son. As lieutenant commander, you will be second-in-command here, and whenever I need to travel, I will leave you in charge."

"That would be awesome." Carl didn't need to fake a smile. This was it, the opportunity he'd been waiting for, exactly what he needed to topple Stark. Second-in-command would mean access to computers. "Thank you."

"Don't thank me yet," Stark said, giving his shoulder a friendly shake. "A soldier must earn his commission. You've put in your time and duly impressed me, but to earn your promotion, you must win the Funeral Games."

"Okay," Carl said. For this opportunity, he'd fight anybody.

Surprisingly, a thrill of excitement shivered through him. "Who do I fight?"

"Whom," Stark corrected.

"Whom do I fight, then?"

Stark spread his hands. "Does it matter?"

"No," Carl said, but it did matter, possibly very much. Over recent months, he had mastered MMA, and the chip made him incredibly fast, accurate, and devastating. During sparring, he destroyed Phoenix Force and consistently bested Stark, even holding back, but this was different. As every boxer learns early, sparring isn't fighting, and the gym isn't a tournament.

"Competition will be rather fierce," Stark admitted. "Teenage fighters who've trained their entire lives. Some come from places like Phoenix Island. Others exist in the shadowy world of underground fighting. A few dwell year-round in temples and dojos, leaving only to defend the honor of their chosen discipline. Do you accept this challenge?"

Carl hesitated for a fraction of a second. What was he getting into? Excitement had abandoned him—but determination remained. "I'll do it," he said. "I'll fight."

"Fighting isn't enough," Stark said. "You have to win."

FOUR

"BACK WHERE IT ALL BEGAN, eh, son?"

Looking at the wavering air above the black macadam lot, Carl said, "Square one."

His memory of that first day on Phoenix Island remained clear—Parker taking his medal and pulling him out of formation for front-back-go; all the drill sergeants shouting, calling him an individual, calling him Hollywood; Davis glaring at him before collapsing—and he was glad he had experienced that day before the chip. With time, pre-chip memories could still fade like old photos left in the sun. Now his eyes and mind worked quickly, taking in so much detail during any experience that new memories forever retained the sharp clarity of high-def footage.

Most of his life, the past returned to him foggily: things people said, their facial expressions, smells, certain details that stood out to him. Now his recall was like watching a film clip. He could even freeze the frame in his mind and *search* the remembered moment for details he hadn't consciously registered while living it. If, for example, he and Stark had a conversation, he could draw it up later in such vivid detail that he could look away from the memory-Stark and identify items he hadn't even consciously registered during their real-time talk. Amazing.

But perfect recall could be an awful thing, too, and he was

glad the ghost of his arrival on Phoenix Island might one day fade to mist.

Stark turned his head toward the blazing sun, which flashed along his mirrored aviator sunglasses. "Close to eleven," he said. "The chopper will arrive soon."

"I'm taking a helicopter?" Carl said, and his stomach hopped with excitement. He'd never ridden in a helicopter before.

"For the first leg of the trip. After that, who knows? The tournament moves each year, and its location is absolutely top secret." Then with a grin, he added, "Even *I* don't know it."

Carl smiled, no acting necessary. He was finally leaving Phoenix Island.

Hearing an engine, he turned and saw an approaching jeep. The driver could have been anyone, but the passenger was easily recognizable even from this distance: Agbeko.

"Ah," Stark said, "the heavyweight."

"Heavyweight?"

"Did you think you were the only fighter representing Phoenix Island?"

If he had to travel with someone, Carl was glad it was Agbeko. They'd had a strange relationship—to say the least. They had started as fast friends, but Agbeko had ended up shooting Carl in the face with a rifle shortly before Carl saved his life *and* beat him into unconsciousness. Strange, indeed. But since the duel with Stark, Carl's friendship with Agbeko had surged again, becoming a high-stakes relationship with no parallel in polite society. Agbeko would gladly risk his life for Carl, yet Carl also knew that if he ever revolted against Stark, Agbeko would kill him without hesitation. The hulking African was absolutely, blindly loyal to the commander.

The jeep dropped off Agbeko and left. Agbeko approached,

huge and grinning. "What is this? Please tell me, Commander, that my brother Carl will be fighting beside me."

"So he will," Stark said.

"Hooah!" Agbeko bellowed, lifting Carl from the ground in a crushing hug. Releasing him, Agbeko held out a massive fist. "Pound it, my brother."

They pounded it, just as Carl had taught the gigantic soldier.

"But why did you not tell me that Carl would also be fighting?" Agbeko said, draping his heavy arm across Carl's shoulders.

"Can't a commander surprise his troops from time to time?" Stark said, beaming. "The tournament has three weight classes. Agbeko, you're our heavyweight. Carl, you're our middleweight. Ah—and here comes our lightweight now."

They turned, and Carl saw another jeep approaching.

"It will be Ladrido," Agbeko said.

Carl started to nod—the little Filipino wasn't very bright, but he could scrap—until his eyes did their focusing trick, bringing the jeep and its passenger into close-up view. So close that Carl could see, even at this distance, not only the boy's great height and dark, scowling face, but also the teardrops tattooed beneath his eye.

"Davis?" Carl said, and instantly regretted it. A rare slip, after months of disguising the true boundaries of the chip's abilities. After all, the less impressive Carl's new abilities seemed, the less likely Stark was to immediately restart chip implantations.

"Good eye, son," Stark said, and stared down at Carl through mirrored lenses. His smile was gone. "Very good eye, indeed."

"But, Commander," Agbeko said, oblivious of the tension between Stark and Carl, "surely Davis is too heavy for lightweight."

Stark nodded. "Indeed he is."

Carl watched the approaching jeep, happy to break stares with Stark. How could he have been so stupid?

But he knew the answer, didn't he? Shock. For months, he had assumed Davis was dead. The last time Carl had seen him, the former gangbanger wore cuffs. That had been at the duel with Stark, where Davis, Sanchez, and Octavia's friend Tamika had cheered for Carl from the sidelines. Carl had assumed that Davis, who had turned some kind of ethical corner when Carl stood up to Decker and Parker, had refused to take part in the barbaric hunts. Having not seen Davis, Sanchez, or Tamika since the duel, he'd further assumed that they had finally participated in the hunt—as prey. A logical assumption here on Phoenix Island. How, then, was Davis still alive?

As the jeep pulled up, Carl saw the reason: a *third* teardrop.

Davis had relented. He had killed someone—and thereby saved himself.

A wave of disappointment crashed over Carl. But he caught himself. *You have no room to judge him*, he thought, *not after the things you've done here . . . and the things you haven't done.*

Davis rose, looking skeletal. His eyes, which seemed unnaturally large in his emaciated face, raked the trio, settled on Carl, and narrowed slightly. Then he faced Stark and came to attention. "Specialist Davis reporting for duty, Commander."

Specialist? A rare rank, reserved for people with highly developed proficiencies . . .

"At ease, Davis," Stark said. "You know Carl, I believe, and this is Agbeko, team heavyweight. Careful with that handshake, Agbeko. Davis will need his hand in good working order to patch you up during and after the fights. He will be your cut man and medic."

Cut man and medic? Davis? It made no sense.

Davis nodded at Carl, his eyes distant and . . . what? Suspicious? Angry?

"But, Commander," Agbeko said, "if Davis is our medic, who is the lightweight?"

Wondering the same thing, Carl looked at the driver, a sergeant named Plonski, a tough guy nicknamed "Hammer" but far too big for lightweight. Where was Ladrido?

Plonski turned, yelling into the backseat.

A head popped up from the backseat of the jeep, saying, "Woo-ee, we there already?"

It took Carl a second to recognize him without the hair. Then he turned to Stark and said, "No way. You can't be serious."

Texarkana Reginald Dubois hopped out of the jeep and swaggered toward them, his beaming face cloudy with bruises. "Which of y'all do I fight first?" Then, seeing Carl, he said, "Well, if it ain't the snake handler. You ready for round two?"

To Stark, Carl said, "He'll ruin everything. He's out of control. He's completely   "

Stark raised a fist, not a threat but an order. Carl stood down. Unreal, absolutely unreal . . .

"You must be the head honcho around here," Tex said, addressing Stark.

"Indeed I am."

"Heard you needed a real fighter, so I hopped in the jeep."

"Good of you to make time for us," Stark said, smirking with obvious amusement. "Specialist Davis, I suspect you met Recruit Dubois on the ride over."

"Yes, Commander." Davis gave Tex a hard look and spat on the ground. "We met."

Tex slapped Davis's arm as if they were old buddies. Davis

tensed. "Bygones be bygones, doc. Who's Mount Kilimanjaro over here?"

"This is Agbeko," Stark said. "He's second-in-command during your trip."

Tex jerked a little during the handshake, and Carl smiled inwardly, seeing Agbeko's huge forearm muscles ripple as he crushed the smaller kid's hand.

Gesturing to Carl, Stark said, "And of course you're already acquainted with the mission leader, Carl Freeman. You'll do as he says during the trip, hooah?"

"Hoo-friggin'-ah, boss man. Old Chatty Cathy and me did the gear-shed shuffle, but no hard feelings. Right, pal? We buried the hatchet so deep you couldn't find it with a backhoe." Extending his hand toward Carl, Tex said, "Put it there, old buddy."

Before Carl could even decide whether to shake, Tex jerked his hand away and smoothed it over his shaven head. "Oh—too slow!"

Carl's fists ached.

Tex patted around his bald dome for a second. "Sure do miss my crowning glory."

Carl heard a helicopter approaching and turned to Stark. "May I talk to you in private?"

"No need and no time," Stark said. "I've made up my mind, and you have your orders. Now, you men listen to Carl, do what he says."

"Hooah!" Agbeko sounded off, solid and willing.

Davis nodded almost imperceptibly, staring straight ahead.

Tex whacked Carl's shoulder. "Old Carl's my main man! His wish is my command."

"Good," Stark said. "Should anything happen to him, command goes to Agbeko."

Should anything happen to me? Carl thought. This was a tournament, not a battle.

"And should anything happen to Agbeko, command goes to Davis," Stark said. "If anything happens to Davis, well . . . you'll figure it out, Dubois."

"Sure thing, boss," Dubois said, grinning wide. "I'm a resourceful son-of-a-female-dog."

Stark smiled. "So it would seem," he said, and again, Carl had to wonder what Stark saw in Dubois. The commander was many things—some great, some terrible—but he wasn't stupid.

The helicopter *thwup-thwup-thwup*ped overhead and banked, curling around and descending toward the landing strip. At Stark's insistence, Carl had memorized decks of "scout cards" and could now identify countless military vehicles by silhouette alone. This was an American Black Hawk—though American only by manufacture, he realized, noting its lack of flag, insignia, or identification.

Shouting over its noise, Stark said, "The warbird will carry you to your next destination. From there, you will likely travel a great distance. Could take days, even weeks. Hooah?"

Carl and the others hooah-ed, Carl thinking, *Weeks just to get there?*

"From this point forward, you'll be known by numbers," Stark said. "Carl, you're Fighter 19, hooah?"

"Hooah."

"Agbeko, you're Fighter 20."

Agbeko hooah-ed.

"Dubois, you're Fighter 18."

"Yeah!" Tex shouted. "How about we switch that to Fighter 21? I'd rather drink than vote!"

"Davis," Stark said, turning to the tall, stone-faced boy. "You're Medic 8."

Davis nodded.

"I won't wish you luck," Stark said. "While warriors acknowledge luck, we never count on it. You *must* win this tournament, hooah?"

"Hooah!" the fighters shouted. Davis shifted his weight and looked toward the helicopter.

"I'm counting on you," Stark said, looking at them each in turn, until his mirrored shades faced Carl. "There is more riding on this tournament than you could imagine."

Yeah, Carl thought. *Like the entire world.*

The copter door slid open, revealing a man wearing faded green coveralls, a black helmet, and sunglasses like Stark's. The pilot, who could have been this man's twin, stared straight ahead. The man in the doorway saluted Stark. Stark returned the gesture and faced the boys.

"Agbeko, you've been on a chopper before. Take point. You others, approach at a ninety-degree angle, straight at the door, and keep low. I'd hate to see you lose your heads." He made a chopping motion across his throat and smiled. "Wait for the crew chief's signal."

The force of the blades was intense. Squinting into the wind, Carl studied the spinning blades. To normal human eyes and brains, the motion of copter blades, like the movements of small birds on the ground, appeared choppy. The eye couldn't keep up. Thanks to the chip, Carl could now fully appreciate the speed—and smooth movement—of birds and blades alike.

The crew chief beckoned.

Stark patted Carl's back. "To victory, son." Then, to the others, he said, "Go, men—and remember: with your shields or on them!"

Agbeko ran forward, keeping low, and Carl mimicked him, running low with squinted eyes and gritted teeth until he hopped up into the Black Hawk.

The crew chief shouted, "Pack it in!"

Agbeko dropped onto a bench seat and started pulling together the belts of an elaborate harness.

Carl watched and imitated, pulling a *V* of belts over his head. He was lifting another belt up between his legs when Tex slammed into him from the side.

"Sorry, boss!" Tex shouted over the roar of the blades and immediately started belting himself in—smoothly and quickly and without even glancing toward the others. How did Dubois know what to do?

Whatever. Carl pushed it aside, excited and jumpy, like a kid buckling into his first roller coaster.

He'd just finished snapping and snugging his five-point harness, when the crew chief shut the door and said, "Belt in tight. We're flying map to the ground."

Agbeko started re-cinching his belts.

"What's he mean," Carl shouted, "map to the ground?"

Before Agbeko could answer, the helicopter rushed upward, lifting into the air like the world's fastest elevator, and leaving, Carl felt, his stomach back on the ground.

Tex shouted, Davis looked like he might hurl, and the copter shot forward in a curving arc that gave Carl one last glimpse of Phoenix Island. Down on the ground, sunlight winked off Stark's mirrored shades, flashing up at them like gunfire.

FIVE

"FEELING WARMER, RITA?" Julio said, pulling her against him.

She gritted her teeth. Margarita wasn't her real name, and yet she was so sick of being under this guy's arm that even his use of the diminutive "Rita" annoyed her.

She wanted to say, *It's* Marga-*rita*, and then shove him away.

But she didn't push him. Not now, not in this unbelievable cold.

The wind blew fiercely, blasting the group of perhaps one hundred hikers with ice and snow, stinging her eyes and lips, the only parts of her directly exposed, thanks to her parka, ski mask, and mittens. From this high ridge, mountains spilled away in a jagged chain of rocky peaks swirling in windblown snow. Far below, beyond the point where the mountains met the leaden sea, a shattered peak jutted, steaming, from the dark water, blurring the air over it with billows of roiling heat.

A volcano, she realized, and instantly wished it would erupt. In this cold like she had never known, she would risk anything, everything, for warmth.

A week of travel by train, boat, and bus had carried them over thousands of miles to this place, what felt like either the southernmost tip of South America or even farther down the globe into Antarctica. They'd been walking for hours, ever since the mountain road had grown too steep and icy for the buses. The men in gray-and-white camo had marched them the rest of the way up the mountain, where they had begun their long hike across this snowy ridge trail, buffeted by icy winds, spectators to a landscape both beautiful and terrible.

With the constant gales, the snow was thin, but ice made the trail treacherous, and it was a miracle no one had slipped and tumbled into one of the chasms flanking the path. At least she didn't *think* anyone had fallen. With the howling wind, it would be hard to hear someone scream.

If an underground fighter falls in the mountains, she thought with an inward grin, *and no one is able to hear him, does he make a noise?*

Enough, she scolded herself. *You're loopy from cold. Keep it together.*

Then, at last, they reached . . . *something.*

The trail ended at an enormous metal door set into the cliff of sheer stone that was the flat and battered face of the final ascent to the only peak rising above their position. Painted in gray-and-white camo not unlike the winter camouflage of the overseers, the door was big enough for an airplane hangar. Overhead, someone had immaculately chiseled words into the stone: LASCIATE OGNE SPERANZA, VOI CH'INTRATE.

"Is that Italian?" Julio asked, speaking not in Italian or English, of course, but in Spanish. They were supposed to be from Mexico, after all.

"Latin, I think," she said.

Right now, she didn't care if it was written in Swahili. She just wanted the door to open and allow them inside. Even if the space beyond the door turned out to be a refrigerator, it would beat standing in the icy wind, with snow blowing all around.

The fighters and trainers, vaguely ghostlike in their white

parkas and white ski masks, hunched in huddles of mostly threes and fours, though a few groups seemed, like Julio and she, to be comprised of only two members: one combatant, one trainer. They shivered, grumbling in dozens of languages, and flicked glances beyond their groups, so many packs of freezing wolves, snarling incoherently as they waited to enter the den. Between these groups circulated the men patterned in gray and white. She didn't need her viewing skills to know the bulges at these men's sides were firearms. Pistols, probably, or maybe submachine guns. In the end, did it really matter?

So far, no one had shouted, much less drawn a gun, and yet the firearms disturbed her. After the things she'd seen over the course of her not-quite-eighteen years, she didn't think that would ever change.

The mountain gave a metallic *clank*, and the overseers backed people away from the heavy camouflage door, which rumbled slowly upward with a grumbling, grinding complaint.

Yes! Finally!

The roar of approval rendered all linguistic differences momentarily inconsequential.

"Come on," Julio said, steering her with his arm.

Annoyance leapt up in her again. She didn't need him telling her where to go, and really, wasn't it safe to say they'd made the boyfriend-girlfriend thing clear enough? They'd been in constant physical contact, Julio either holding her hand or draping his arm over her shoulders, since they had donned their parkas and ski masks, come off the steamer, and joined the others.

An overseer moved forward, and lights snapped on, illuminating the tunnel.

She wasn't sure what she had been expecting to see behind the massive gate—a cave, perhaps, or maybe a crude alcove outfitted with burning barrels over which they might warm their hands—but whatever she might have expected, she never could have imagined the reality unfolding before her now.

It stopped her. It really did.

This was no crudely chiseled chamber but a huge tunnel of polished stone, with a set of glimmering train tracks at its center and, waiting there, a shining engine and three passenger cars, bright and new and almost incomprehensible.

No, not a train, she corrected herself. *A subway.*

A subway tucked away inside a mountain, a million miles from the world. No trash, no graffiti, just gleaming rails and bright lights shining down on the burnished silver train cars.

Overseers beckoned them inside.

Fighters surged forward, momentarily forgetting the distance they'd been tending, as they gawked and laughed and shouted.

She advanced with a laugh of her own, feeling the temperature inside the tunnel—not warm, exactly, but also not the frigid air through which they had hiked all day.

The men in camouflage asked in Spanish and English and several other languages she could not understand that the athletes please move quietly forward and enter the trains.

"This is unreal," she said, and Julio nodded, apparently struck speechless by the spectacle.

When they reached the train, he stepped aside and motioned for her to enter first, making her wonder again if he really was some kind of macho gentleman or just a consummate actor. She grabbed the rail, hauled her snowy boot onto the first step, and felt his hand on her back, boosting her, as if she needed help, as if she were either a small child or an old woman.

Whatever, she thought, and entered the train.

The passenger car shone just as brightly inside as it had out, everything new and polished and well lit.

Something like reverence came over the fighters, who moved slowly down the aisle and spoke in whispers as they chose their seats.

She and Julio sat down beside each other, and Julio slid his hand onto hers.

She barely registered his intrusion as the question came into her mind.

Who would build a brand-new subway here in the middle of nowhere?

The train had obviously never been used before, and since every tournament location was destroyed at the conclusion of the Funeral Games, none of this would ever be used again.

The time, effort, and money that would go into creating all of this within a mountain in this wild and inhospitable land—all for a single event—was mind-boggling. Like carving a goblet of purest diamond, then smashing it after the first sip. Who thought that way? Who had that kind of money, that kind of power?

Then came the shiver—one of those ironic shudders that come not from cold but when a long period of cold is finally broken—and she realized she didn't care who had built the train or why they'd done it. At least not yet. For now, she was just happy to escape the wind and extreme cold. She would engage Nancy Drew mode after she'd thawed.

There was a chime, and the doors slid shut.

"Here we go," Julio said, his excitement plain.

Something clunked and hissed beneath the car, which gave a slight lurch, then started moving, sliding smoothly ahead. They built speed rapidly. The tunnel dimmed, angling downward, and the train flashed along underground, the occasional light flickering by like yellow passing hyphens on a highway.

As the train gained speed, its passengers seemed to thaw, chatting excitedly and laughing again, their eyes bright within their ice-crusted white ski masks.

In that moment, she thawed, too . . . or at least her brain did. Masks.

She could have slapped herself for not thinking of this earlier, but she'd been preoccupied by the brutal cold, trying not to fall to her death, and fending off Julio's constant hugs and pats.

All these masks represented a perfect opportunity to test her new —and soon to be crucial—ability. She took a deep breath, hoping . . .

"Feels good to sit down," Julio said, and started rubbing her thigh. Despite his thick glove and her heavy parka pants, she wanted to bat his hand away.

Don't, she told herself, remembering Crossman's warning: "All of this falls apart if you're not a believable couple. Why else would this fighter bring along a second-rate cut man?"

"Cut *woman*," she had said.

Crossman had spread his hands. "High-stakes stuff, lady. If you're not believable . . ." It was funny, the way somebody like Crossman, with his close-set predator eyes and hawk nose, could imply life-or-death stakes simply by trailing off.

Once he'd explained the stakes and accepted her demands, she'd agreed to play the role. Now, sitting here with this stranger pawing her, she hoped she hadn't gotten in over her head.

She closed her eyes, drawing her nose full of air, trying to focus. She smelled the sharp new-vinyl smell of the seat in front of her, and thought of school buses, an absurd idea here in this place that had never known schools or children. The train slid steadily deeper into the stony ground, and she could feel the enormous bulk of the mountain range rising overhead. They were shuttling along beneath the saw-backed main range, hurtling onward toward . . . what?

The ocean. They were angling downrange toward the ocean.

Another thought to block. Outward geography, like Julio's intruding hand, was merely a distraction now. She needed to map nearer topography—the landscape behind those masks.

She focused on a ski mask in an adjacent row. The boy's red patch read 18. Otherwise, he looked like everyone else, except his leg bounced continuously and he *never* stopped talking to his teammates.

"Not just a cheerleader," she heard him say. "The *head* cheerleader . . ."

She wished she were back in the lab with pencil and paper. It would be easier to sketch him—but that would be an obvious mistake here.

Don't push too hard, she reminded herself. Puking in a ski mask would be decidedly unlovely. She cleared her mind, letting go of the boy's shaking leg and nonstop blabbing and even that red 18.

She closed her eyes, and almost instantly, an image—the curve of his cheekbone, she thought—came into her mind. But it struck her then that it would do no good to map his face so closely. Without her sketchpad, she had no way to reproduce the simulacrum. She needed to try something new, needed to pull back, gain a point of reference, and see not just the trees but the forest. Her mind's eye drew back with a dizzying tilt, and a familiar line of fire shot across her skull. This time, it was there and gone—a fierce but fleeting laser pulse—and she could see the rough outline of the boy's face.

Amazing.

The image was blurry and unsteady like her old card ghosts, but she found a rhythm, dipping back in to pat around with her mental hands before drawing back out, and after several repetitions, she drew him into clearer focus.

A shaved head. Close-set eyes. A small pug nose. He needed a shave.

"This is really something, huh?" Julio said, and squeezed her thigh.

Her connection to the masked stranger broke instantly, and the laser beam of pain sizzled again through her skull.

"Shut up," she said, and batted his hand away.

"What? I—"

"Stop," she said. Some part of her mind cautioned her, remembering Crossman's warnings, but she zapped it immediately. Real girlfriends got mad at their boyfriends sometimes. *If anything*, she thought, *I just improved our cover.*

Julio crossed his arms and slumped away from her.

Good.

Her head pounded steadily now, and she felt a little sick, but it was still nothing like she'd experienced during that first session back in the Bunker. She was getting better, stronger. Mapping still hurt and often left her feeling sick and shaky, but less so every time, and she was getting faster, too. Returning her attention to the adjacent block of seats, she focused not on Fighter 18 but the guy sitting silently across from him.

Fighter 19.

She closed her eyes, ignoring the throb building like a drumbeat at the center of her skull—*my parietal lobe*, she told herself, remembering part of Bleaker's explanation—and the fog cleared quickly, bringing the angle of a strong jaw sharply into view. She pulled out, swooped back in, and scaled upward, moving as smoothly over his features as a traveler over familiar ground, the face coming clear to her as effortlessly as remembered topography: the scowl, the crooked nose and high cheekbones, the eyebrows intersected by thin scars.

She could have screamed, could have laughed, could have shouted his name . . .

But in that thunderclap moment, she instead pulled back and sat staring not at the simulacrum but at the red patch, the 19 there, with her heart pounding and her mind reeling.

It couldn't be true . . . but it was.

It was *him*. . . .

It was Carl.

SIX

AS THE TRAIN SLOWED, Carl noticed the others dropping hoods, removing mittens, and peeling off ski masks. *Must be warmer here*, he realized, and dialed his temperature sensitivity back to normal. He removed his mask and mittens and unzipped his bulky parka. The train came to a gentle stop.

Fighters pressed against their windows, murmuring with excitement. Carl felt frustrated—from his aisle seat, he could see nothing—but the train gave a mechanical hiss, and guards motioned toward the open doors.

Tex whooped, Agbeko grinned, and even Davis looked less displeased. Still no smile from the emaciated medic but a look of something like relief. Whether from the warmth or the long trip coming to an end, Carl didn't know and wasn't going to ask. For the several days they'd been traveling—going by copter, horse cart, container ship, bus, on foot, and finally onboard this train—Davis had utterly stonewalled Carl, avoiding eye contact and answering only in quiet monosyllables.

Everyone stood, filling the aisle with that strange politeness so common in fighters, and filed slowly off the train. This was the first Carl had seen these people—*my future opponents*, he thought—without ski masks, and yet they were familiar to him, as types. Boys with scarred faces, drawn and angular from cutting weight and cloudy with fading bruises that bespoke the brutal training they had endured in preparation for this event.

Across the aisle was the couple he'd dubbed "Romeo and Juliet." He'd noticed them during the long trudge across the mountains, largely due to the long blond braid that had hung from her ski mask. She was the only obvious girl in the bunch—he thought he'd noticed a couple of others but couldn't be certain—and she'd spent the whole time attached to her boyfriend, the two of them jabbering away in Spanish. What a stupid idea, bringing your girlfriend to work your corner. Between rounds, a trainer needed to work as calmly as a machine. How could these two possibly put their emotions on hold once the blood started flowing?

Filing off the train, Carl's own *whoa* joined the fighters' chorus of awe. An incredible space opened before them. The tracks ended at a high-domed concourse of polished stone that reminded Carl of New York's Grand Central Station.

Older men in good suits appeared, moving singly among the fighters and attaching to groups. A trim silver-haired man in a wine-dark suit came toward Carl's group. Offering a slight, somehow proper smile, he said, "Team Phoenix Force."

It wasn't a question.

"My name is Kruger," he said. He was spotless in every way: perfect suit, perfect hair, perfect posture. "I will be your personal steward here at the Cauldron." He shook their hands, giving each of them a subtle bow, and a "very pleased to meet you, sir"—his accent not quite English, but not Australian, Irish, or Scottish either. Similar yet different from all of them.

Addressing Carl last—the guy with a good grip, a *remarkable* grip for his age—Kruger said, "And you, sir, would be the team captain if I'm not mistaken."

Carl said that he was, and Tex said, "Don't remind him, Jeeves. Goes to his head."

Carl ignored him. Tex had been a constant annoyance, but he hadn't disrupted things nearly as much Carl had feared. He'd started and quickly lost a fight with Agbeko, and had almost gotten them killed on the container ship by talking smack to a guy with dead eyes and an AK-47, but in the end, he'd done no significant harm. Yet.

Stewards were leading teams away. At the end of the concourse, a group including an impossibly tall fighter with an oddly shaped head rounded the corner and disappeared into an adjacent hallway.

"Follow me, please," Kruger said. He walked in step with Carl, matching strides, just ahead of the other Phoenix Forcers, speaking to Carl but loudly enough that the others would hear him. "Here at the Cauldron, we will make every effort to erase the discomfort of your arduous travels."

Directly in front of them, yet another tall fighter—this one a middleweight, Carl thought—had shaved an urban skyline into the short hair on the back of his head. New York City, Carl realized with a surge of happy recognition. Despite their famous sports rivalries, New York and Philly actually had more in common than apart. They weren't really enemies. They were like two brothers who went at it hard when they tossed the knuckles. Carl figured he'd say something, but then the guy raised his fists overhead and shouted, "Yeah! Red carpet for the king!" and Carl recognized his voice as that of the loudmouth who had trash-talked the whole hike here.

The red carpet led them down the center of the hall and around the corner into a wide corridor of exquisite beauty. Walls of polished white marble veined in gray rose from floors tiled in matching stone, arching high overhead in a vaulted ceiling spangled in chandeliers that winked and twinkled in the upper gloom like constellations of candles and cut glass. The fighters followed the red carpet past ornate fountains and lush flower arrangements that filled the air with summery sweetness.

Incredible, Carl thought. *Like a king's castle.*

"As you are most likely already coming to understand," Kruger said, no doubt noticing Carl's amazement, "the Few spared no expense in welcoming you."

The procession rounded a corner into a corridor flanked in fine tapestries and slowed to take in the massive bronze statue dominating the center of the hall: a rugged guy with a fighter's build and a battered, bearded face, sitting leaned over with his thick forearms on his muscular thighs, his head turned toward one shoulder, as if someone was hailing him from behind.

Calling him to the ring, Carl thought, seeing the guy's boxing gloves . . . then corrected himself. No, those weren't gloves. Not waiting to draw closer, he sharpened his vision, drawing into view the stone hands mummified in thick wraps with weird rectangular blocks over the knuckles. Padding? No—it looked more like armor plating.

"The Boxer of Quirinal," Kruger said, gesturing grandly. "A replication, far larger than the original 330 BC statue, made to scale for this space. Historians believe him to be the great Greek boxer, Theogenes, who won well over a thousand matches, most to the death."

A thousand fights? Carl took in the thick neck and heavy shoulders, the lean, muscular torso and small waist, the powerful yet not over muscled arms and boxy puncher's fists capped in metal. *A thousand . . .*

"Old boy looks like he took a few to the face, that's for sure," Tex said.

True enough. Feeling mesmerized, Carl noted the flattened nose and misshapen cauliflower ears. Surrounded by heavy scar tissue, the shadowy, indistinct eyes stared from a face displaying neither concern nor anger, only power and grim resignation, the face of a man who had traversed and transcended both fear and malice to dwell in the heart of fighting itself. This was a man, Carl realized, connecting to the statue in an unexpectedly visceral way, who neither wished nor feared to fight.

Carl felt close to the bronze giant, felt the connection that is art's ability to jar people from their automaton lives—and yet did not understand it as such. He knew only that he understood this ancient warrior and felt a secret, long-suffering pain radiating from those dark eyes. He wished he could stay to study the statue and explore this strange yet undeniable kinship, but Kruger was pulling them along again.

He led them down the hall and around another corner. Teams stood at the end of this hall, which looked out over an open space, like the mouth of a cave opening onto a great canyon.

"Gentlemen," Kruger said, "I give you the arena."

Beyond the cluster of murmuring fighters, the corridor ended—no more walls, no more ceiling—but the tiled floor continued, becoming a balcony that jutted into the most breathtaking space Carl had ever seen: a vast cavern as big around as a professional sports complex, a rock-walled shaft hundreds of feet in height.

He moved forward, past fighters who stood with their heads leaned back and their mouths open, struck dumb. Walls of stone rose up and up, lit by rings of fluttering torches. Between torches, dark squares stared blankly out onto the great shaft. Higher up, the rings of torch fire grew smaller as the circumference tightened. Far above—three hundred feet? Four hundred?—where a far-flung ceiling might have capped the space, a crack opened onto a dimming patch of open sky.

Amazing.

Forgetting his team, Carl continued on to what he now realized was a wide set of stadium-style bleachers, several tiers of bench seating encircled by a red railing and suspended high up one rock wall of the vast chamber. He descended to the rail and stared with amazement.

We're inside a volcano, he realized.

He remembered standing atop a high peak, away from which the mountain chain had dropped in a jagged line to the ocean. A short distance out in the water, a cone of dark rock, its craggy sides mottled in ice, jutted from the bruise-colored sea like a broken fang, wide at the base and tapering not to a point but to a shattered peak out of which wavered a column of steam.

The Few turned that volcano into this arena.

From these bleachers, they would watch the tournament. He looked down—and had to look again.

Far below, the cavern floor was . . . incomplete.

What looked like an Olympic running track hugged the wall, ringing the entire circumference of the chasm in several lanes of red. At its center, the shaft tumbled away another fifty feet to oily darkness spangled in torchlight: a great subterranean lake at the bottom of the volcanic caldera. Across the center of this vast open space, in a line parallel to Carl's vantage point, a bridge spanned the gap, connecting one end of the track to the other, and at the center of this, on an elevated circular platform, was the octagonal fighting cage. Over this, suspended by almost invisible wires, cylindrical spotlights shone down, illuminating the octagon.

From this height, the strange incomplete lower level—with its surrounding track, central bridge, circular ring platform, and large empty spaces—looked like a gigantic, two-spoked wheel. The rubberized red track was its oblong tire, each span of the bridge was a spoke, and the octagon and the circular platform on which it stood were the hub.

"Marvelous, isn't it?" Kruger said, joining him now. Beside him, Agbeko grinned. Davis leaned back, looking profoundly uncomfortable. Tex gaped, silent at last.

The rest of the teams were coming onto the balcony now, taking seats.

Carl sat on the lowest row. Kruger and the team sat beside him.

The dark squares between the torches were windows, Carl realized, windows looking out from rooms built inside this mountain, and he was staggered by a sudden understanding of the facility, the place like a towering hotel built around the shaft of a volcano, circular floor stacked atop circular floor, the entire thing tucked away from the world inside a mountain in a frozen wasteland.

Incredible.

They would fight at the center of the "floor," suspended high above the subterranean lake. His eyes flicked to one end of the bridge, where, just beyond the track, he saw a wide opening like the ones out of which professional football players entered a stadium. Overhead hung a red bunting. Glancing to the other side of the arena, he saw the opening there and the blue bunting hanging over it and understood.

A long ring walk, one fighter coming out of the red side, one out of the blue, and meeting in the cage at the center.

His heartbeat spiked a little, imagining it.

"This place," Agbeko said, still beaming, "is amazing."

"A staggering feat," Kruger said, a note of pride in his voice. "Years in the making. As I'm certain you've already pieced together, we are in the heart of a remodeled volcano. Geothermal activity powers the entire facility. The electricity, the torchlight, the heating, all of it is powered by the volcano itself."

Carl nodded. Impressive—but crazy, too.

The Few had tunneled through a remote mountain chain and under the ocean, installed a working subway, and converted a volcano into a fight venue. Disconnected improbabilities—money, materials, workers, secrecy—tumbled through his mind in a gust of dismay.

That's when he realized he didn't like the Few.

He'd been so excited to leave Phoenix Island, he hadn't given much thought to them, but now he knew he disliked them.

Why spend millions, perhaps billions, when for *far* less, they could have secured secrecy, comfort, and world-class competitors?

But the Few—and suddenly their name made perfect sense— liked to show off.

In Carl's experience, anyone who needed to impress others— whether it was a fighter showboating for a crowd, some kid in lockdown bragging about stuff you knew he never did, or gang-bangers flashing cash and bling—lacked heart.

No, he didn't like the Few.

Directly across the chasm, slightly higher up than these bleachers, an ornate semicircular parapet overlooked the cage. Carved vines inlaid with gold twisted up its marble balusters, interrupted in places by heavy bunches of grapes that twinkled in the torchlight. Gems, Carl realized. Golden vines and gemstone grapes.

Beyond the rail rose three semicircular tiers. Three marble

chairs cushioned in crimson sat empty atop the lowest level, two waited on the second, and what could only be called a throne, given its great height and gem-encrusted surface, dominated the final tier. Behind all of this, crimson curtains separated the balcony from whatever lay beyond.

That's where the Few would sit to watch the fights. He was sure of it. Their opera box . . .

High up one sidewall hung a massive black panel . . . an enormous television screen.

"Look at the bird," Tex said. He pointed, his arm sweeping sideways.

"Where?" Carl said, and then spotted it. The dark bird, almost invisible against the stone wall, climbed in a looping ascent. Round and round the great shaft the bird circled, spinning faster and faster as it rose, until it reached the top and fired like a bullet into the sky.

"The Krebs hawk," Kruger said. "Birds of prey that fish the sea and nest here, within the Cauldron." He spun a finger, then poked the air. "Centrifugal force."

Then another group was coming onto the bench beside them, led by a steward speaking a guttural language Carl could not understand.

Their lightweight, a short cocky-looking guy Carl disliked instantly, strutted in front, side by side with the trainer.

"Phoenix Island, correct?" said the trainer, a familiar-looking man with black hair, a goatee, and dark, intense eyes.

Seeing him, Carl felt a pang of unease. Who was this guy?

Agbeko rose, smiling. "Lieutenant Commander Ba—"

"Stop," the man said, and made a cutting motion with his hand. "No names. I am the Z-Force trainer, and these are my champions."

Then Carl had it. Z-Force. Zurkistan. And his mind finished Agbeko's slip: Ba-*ca*. Lieutenant Commander Baca, the high-speed psychopath he'd seen slaughtering innocents in green nightmare footage from Zurkistan.

"I am Fighter 20," Agbeko said, as they shook. Gesturing to Carl, Agbeko said, "This is our team captain—"

"I know who he is," Baca said, turning to Carl with glittering eyes. "The commander's beloved apprentice, the legendary Carl Freeman."

"Thought you said no names," Carl said.

"Ah, yes, no names, no names. How foolish of me," Baca said, feigning remorse and doing a poor job of it. "Perhaps I was awestruck."

"Perhaps," Carl said.

Baca did not offer his hand. Carl didn't either . . . and didn't bother to stand.

"Enough small talk between camps," Baca said. "After all, we may be brothers in war, but we're enemies in peace, hooah?"

Agbeko hooah-ed, but Carl and the others just sat there, Carl studying the man, noting the quickness of his eyes, the alertness there. Stark had once called Baca the personification of the OODA loop. Observe. Orient. Decide. Act. Rapid, decisive execution . . .

"What's up with your boy?" Tex asked, nodding past Baca to the Zurkistani lightweight, a fireplug of a guy, who scowled at them with the menacing contempt of a fighter accustomed to inspiring fear. "He looks constipated."

Baca said something in Zurkistani, and the lightweight snarled. Behind him, the middleweight laughed, but Carl barely noticed—as he'd spotted the Zurkistani heavyweight. The guy was shorter than Carl—maybe six foot, maybe not—but thick as a gorilla . . . and still wearing the white parka and ski mask. He stood staring out into the chasm, seemingly oblivious to the entire conversation.

"Big boy must be a couple cans short of a six-pack, huh?" Tex said. "Nobody tell him they got the heat on in here?"

"Fighter 47 does not care about heat or cold," Baca said. "He is impervious to both pain and comfort. Suffering is nothing to him. He lives only to fight."

"Well, la dee da," Tex said, standing now. "I don't live to fight; I live to win."

"All right," Carl said, wanting to avoid trouble. "Take it easy." He laid a hand on Tex's forearm, but the smaller boy shook free.

Baca didn't even seem to notice Tex, looking instead at Agbeko and saying, "I have some advice for you, Fighter 20: forfeit."

Agbeko, obviously uncomfortable, trapped between respect for a superior officer and his duty to Phoenix Island, shook his head. "I will fight till the end, sir."

"Please reconsider," Baca said. "You're a good soldier. I'd hate to lose you to this . . . game." Then, turning to Tex, he said, "I will, however, enjoy watching my lightweight still your tongue."

"Talk's cheap, boss," Tex said, and cracked his knuckles. "Your boy wants to rumble, we don't have to wait for the bright lights. We can settle this right now."

The Zurkistani fighter stepped forward, understanding the moment if not the language, but Baca raised a hand, and the scowling boy backed off immediately. "And you," Baca said, turning to Carl. "We will see if you are everything Stark claims."

Carl stared at him with no expression on his face.

"I suspect," Baca said, stroking his goatee, "that you lack the necessary killer instinct."

"We'll see," Carl said, understanding Baca's meaning. As Z-Force's head honcho, Baca likely knew that Stark had tried and failed to recruit Carl for missions.

"Yes," Baca said, "We will. And then—"

That's when everything went dark, and explosive booms filled the arena.

SEVEN

BOOM...BOOM...BOOM...

Heavy thumps pulsed in the darkness, as rhythmic and foreboding as a monster's heartbeat.

BOOM...BOOM...BOOM...

With every beat, crackles of purple light flashed across the gigantic television screen.

BOOM...BOOM...BOOM...

A woman's face filled the screens.

No more booms, no more crackling light, just the woman, her image very large and bright and crisp in the darkness of the volcano. She was coldly beautiful. Her bright blue eyes stared from a pale face crowned in red hair pulled tightly back.

She smiled down at them without warmth.

"On behalf of the Few," she said, her voice coming from all directions at once, "I welcome you to this year's Funeral Games."

Fighters applauded in the darkness.

In his peripheral vision, Carl could see stewards leaning close to their groups, interpreting.

"We are honored by your presence," the woman said, her voice as precise and austere as her features. "You have traveled great distances to join us. Welcome to the world's greatest sporting event."

More applause.

She waited on-screen for them to finish, then said, "Forty-eight of the finest fighters on the planet, representing countless disciplines and arranged into three weight divisions of sixteen competitors, with ten million dollars going to each champion."

All along the walls, fire huffed from the torches, there and gone, punctuation of flame, and the fighters erupted once more into applause.

Carl just waited.

Ten million dollars was an inconceivable sum—but he wasn't here for money.

"To win your weight division," the woman said, "you will need to defeat four opponents in as many days."

Murmurs went through the teams.

Four fights in four days? Carl thought. A brutal schedule, but so be it. At least he had the chip and Vispera's blood virus, which had changed Carl's blood, raising his endurance, enhancing his performance, and greatly accelerating his rates of recovery and healing.

"You will fight in the cage," she said, and lights over the cage snapped to life, illuminating the octagon. "Three-minute rounds with one minute of rest in between, until one competitor surrenders or can no longer continue."

Wait, Carl thought. *There wasn't a set number of rounds? No wins by decision? Only knockouts and submissions?* An absurd idea. He'd fought guys who could take a baseball bat to the head and keep coming. No decisions meant . . .

"Anything goes," the woman said, the phrase odd in her precise voice, "other than eye gouging, biting, or strikes to the groin."

Strikes to the back and the back of the head and neck were legal? Kicks to the knee? That was crazy.

"Like the fighters of the ancient Greek Funeral Games," she said, "you will wear the cestus." Then she was gone from the screen, replaced by a gigantic fist. Leather straps encased the wrist, crisscrossed the hand, and stretched in three bands across the knuckles.

A simple, brutal design.

The woman's voice said, "The cesti provide wrist support and knuckle protection while still allowing sufficient hand flexibility for grappling."

And they turn our fists into sledgehammers, Carl thought. Cold went through him. There was no cushion beneath the leather. Punches would be devastating. The rawhide would open cuts.

The woman returned to the screen. "From here, your stewards will provide a brief tour of the facility and escort you to your rooms, allowing you to make yourselves more comfortable prior to this evening's weigh-ins. The tournament will begin tomorrow. Again, we thank you most graciously for your participation in this year's Funeral Games and applaud your courage and fortitude. We do hope that you enjoy our hospitality and encourage you to call upon your personal steward for any needs that arise."

The TV died, and the lights came on.

People are going to get hurt here, Carl thought, and suddenly very real to him was the whirlpool of violence into which he was about to descend. *People are going to die here.*

Then a thought wrapped in leather struck him hard: Stark had known. He had known the rules and conditions.

Why are you so surprised? he asked himself, and instantly responded, *I'm not.*

A chill rippled through him like one of Stark's dark chuckles.

Carl had to fight, had to win—but with these merciless rules, the rage-beast clamoring inside him, and his knuckles encased in leather, how could he win without killing?

EIGHT

KRUGER PRESSED THE LAST BUTTON not marked with a red
X, and the elevator started its silent climb toward the fifth level.

During the tour, they had explored the arena, the locker
rooms, multiple training facilities, and a sauna area. They had
skirted a kitchen, where the good smells of cooking food had almost driven Carl insane, and visited an infirmary where Tex told
Kruger to book space for his opponents and where Davis finally
perked up, scanning the first-aid supplies with bright eyes, his fingers passing over tools and tubes and bottles like the fingers of a
pianist warming up on a grand piano. For an instant, Carl thought
a smile was going to break onto the eternally grim face, but then
Davis had turned and nodded, satisfied if not necessarily pleased.

Carl was impressed. Not just by the facility, which was absolutely amazing, like a five-star hotel combined with a cutting-edge
sports and entertainment complex, but also by their tour guide.
With his perfect suit and manners, Kruger could have been a butler for the queen of England. How had he ended up here?

Even as Kruger pointed out occasional doors marked in red
X's, explaining that these were strictly off-limits, he managed to
sound both authoritative and apologetic. No entrance, no excep-
tions, and sorry very much . . .

The elevator dinged, its doors opened, and Kruger gestured
for the team to exit.

"The residential level," the silver-haired steward said. He led them down a curving hallway carpeted in crimson and painted cool blue. Beside each door stood a small table adorned with an arrangement of fresh-cut flowers. Their sweet floral scent suffused the air.

Somewhere around the next bend, others approached, speaking loudly in . . . what? Spanish? Not Spanish, but something similar. . . .

The other team appeared, three smiley guys who looked like triplets, save for their remarkable differences in size, all of them ruggedly handsome with bronze skin, thick necks and rounded shoulders, dark hair shaved close, and the cauliflower ears of experienced wrestlers. Seeing Carl and the others, they smiled, all three of them at once, and Carl couldn't help but smile and nod, and they nodded back and were gone. Grapplers of some type. Probably jujitsu guys. Maybe Brazilian. Good guys, good energy, confident and strong, not mixing up the fights with the moments in between. A rare type here, a rare type in the world. Most people couldn't fight without hatred.

Carl hoped he wouldn't draw their middleweight. In boxing, you could fight anyone, even a friend, and it was okay. Here, though, with the cesti? He hated the idea of shattering those friendly smiles.

"Fighter 19," Kruger said, and Carl realized they were stopping.

"Yes?"

Their steward pointed toward a glass square mounted beside the door. A red light glowed at the center of the glass. "Press your right thumb into the identification pad, please."

Carl did.

The red light turned green, something clicked faintly, and

the door slid smoothly open, disappearing into a pocket in the wall.

"The door will recognize any of your thumbprints," Kruger said, inviting them inside with a sweep of his well-tailored arm. "Gentlemen, welcome to your quarters."

Carl stepped into the foyer. "Whoa."

Agbeko stood beside him. "This is magnificent."

Tex cursed appreciatively, and even Davis emitted a low whistle.

The room was like a ritzy Las Vegas suite out of the movies, with bright paint and framed artwork and high ceilings and columns instead of walls. To the left, the foyer flowed into a large carpeted area with soft-looking couches and recliners facing a huge television. Farther back, a chandelier lit a dining area next to a fancy kitchen complete with a stainless-steel refrigerator and a soda machine.

Kruger led them into the carpeted space. "This should be a very relaxing area for you." He entered the semicircle of couches and recliners and pressed a section of wall beneath the massive television screen. A panel slid aside, revealing racks of electronics. "Entertainment central. Thousands of recorded shows and movies, music from around the world, and multiple gaming systems."

"Wonderful," Agbeko said.

"Once the tournament begins," Kruger said, "matches will stream on the lower channels, should you care to enjoy your victories or scout your opponents."

Scouting the competition would be crucial, Carl knew—and not just to study his own opponents. He needed to coach Agbeko and Tex as best he could. Neither would win against top-caliber opponents, but there were considerations beyond winning and losing. He would do what he could to help them protect themselves.

"Now, please follow me," Kruger said, "and I will show you to your rooms."

"We get our own rooms?" Davis asked, that almost-smile coming onto his face again.

"Of course," Kruger said, "each with a private bathroom, as well."

Agbeko beamed like a two-hundred-seventy-pound ten-year-old on Christmas morning.

Upon each of the four doors set into the back wall was a white oval plaque etched in red. "Sir," Kruger said to Carl, and gestured to the ID pad beside the door marked F19.

Carl pressed his thumb against the pad, and the door whisked aside.

"This is your room, Fighter 19," Kruger said, waving Carl forward. "It's only proper that you should enter first."

Carl's feet sunk into the plush red carpet. At a glance, he took in the minifridge, a shelf crammed with books, and a television mounted to the wall. A large bed draped in a black comforter dominated the room. At its center burned the bright red likeness of a bird engulfed in flame.

Agbeko laughed joyously. "The phoenix!"

Yeah . . . great, Carl thought, but outwardly he pretended to share Agbeko's pride and excitement.

"Your wardrobe is similarly customized," Kruger said. He pressed a recessed wall button, and a panel slid aside, revealing a closet filled with black-and-red clothing, each article emblazoned with a burning phoenix and stitched with a red 19.

The Phoenix Island theme continued throughout his private quarters. Black shower curtain, black towels, black drapes covering the room's lone window . . . each with a red phoenix at its center.

Kruger opened a nightstand drawer, withdrew a small box with a green button, and handed it to Carl. "Should you need anything at any time, night or day, press this button, and we will accommodate you immediately."

"Press that bad boy right now," Tex said. "Order me a couple of blondes and a bottle of Wild Turkey."

Carl pulled aside the room's only curtain, revealing a window through which he spied yet another amazing sight: the vast arena of the volcano.

Craning his neck, he could see the balconies and the red track, the black bridge and the octagon at the center of the emptiness that tumbled away to the subterranean lake far below.

"Wow," he said, and meant it.

"Indeed," Kruger said, and the boys crowded around Carl, trying to see. A moment later, their steward called them back into the main suite.

He led them into the kitchen, where Tex ogled the soda machine. "Got any quarters, Kruger? I'll pay you back, soon as I win the ten mil."

The steward offered his subtle butler's smile. "Everything here is free to you, sir, compliments of the Few."

"Sweet!" Tex said, and slapped the Coke button. With a muffled thumping, a red can tumbled into view. Tex scooped it up with a hoot, and everyone froze as he popped the top with a familiar *shuick-hiss*.

Carl could all but taste the cold, sweet soda. How long had it been? Months, a year . . .

Tex leaned back and chugged.

Kruger laid a hand gently on the boy's forearm. "Sir, might I suggest you first verify your weight?"

Tex pulled the can away. "Huh?"

The steward said, "From here, I will take you to the official weigh-in. As team lightweight, you will need to weigh no more than one hundred and fifty pounds."

"Oh," Tex said, and smirked. "No problem, Kruger, my good man."

"Yeah," Carl said. "Don't get DQ'd over a soda."

Tex waved dismissively, said, "You worry too much," and lifted the can again to his lips.

"No," Agbeko said, and grabbed the soda away. "You must have self-control."

Here we go, Carl thought, expecting a punch, a kick, something—but Tex just spread his hands in disbelief as Agbeko dumped the rest of the soda into his own mouth, crushed the empty can, and tossed it into the sink.

"What about self-control?" Tex said.

Agbeko grinned. "Heavyweights do not fear the scale."

Tex released a monstrous belch, Agbeko roared one back at him, and everyone laughed—even Davis, who said, "Neither do medics," and stepped around the hulking African to slap the Sprite button.

Kruger's smile widened a touch. Then he led them into the dining room, where stood a table set for four. "After the weigh-ins," the steward said, picking up a stack of laminated menus from a side table and handing one to each boy, "you will have dinner."

"Sounds good," Tex said. "I'm so hungry my stomach thinks my mouth's on strike."

Carl couldn't believe the menu. Page after page of amazing choices. In the "American Favorites" section alone, he saw pizza, french fries, onion rings, hot dogs, chili dogs, and at least a dozen types of hamburgers.

His stomach roared. Since the chip, he'd lived in a state of constant hunger, and over the last few days, he'd been cutting weight, not wanting to take any chances or play the fool's game of losing the last few pounds the day of weigh-ins. He'd fight a pack of pigs for a bacon cheeseburger.

Still, despite the many choices, he didn't see his *favorite* food.

Davis, who'd been sipping his soda loudly, paused to ask, "We can order anything?"

"You may order anything you like," Kruger said, his smile there and gone, brief and formal as a bow or curtsey.

"How about booze?" Tex asked.

"Of course, sir," Kruger said.

"Got any weed?" Davis asked.

"I'm so sorry, sir," Kruger said, "but we do not."

"Gin?"

"Of course, sir. The bar is well stocked."

"Well, in that case," Tex said, "I sure could use some rum to go with this Coke."

"No," Carl said, picturing Tex and Davis drunk, broken things everywhere, blood on the carpet, security dropping Tex with Tasers, the team lightweight and medic eliminated before the tournament even started. "No alcohol."

"Look, chief," Tex said, turning toward him. "I get that you're the Eagle Scout, but I don't need a den mother, all right?"

"Tell you what," Carl said, remembering Stark's advice to listen to troops and maintain order without crushing all hope . . . no matter how absurd their desires might seem. "We win this tournament, we'll party. Whatever you want, okay? But for now, we're sticking with food."

Tex rolled his eyes, and Davis shook his head.

"If Carl says no alcohol, there will be no alcohol," Agbeko said, but his eyes looked distant, and when he spoke again, his voice sounded wistful. "Though I hope one day to again taste banana beer."

Kruger offered a small frown. "I'm terribly sorry, sir. The bar isn't quite *that* fully stocked."

"Banana beer?" Tex squawked, and burst into wild laughter.

"Oh, it is very good," Agbeko said. "We drank it when we were boys. The men drank so much, their eyes turned yellow."

"That would have been their livers shutting down," Kruger said. Then he smiled, saying, "I must confess that banana beer was a guilty pleasure during my youth."

"Where'd you find the stuff?" Tex asked. "You never did say where it is you hail from."

"No, I haven't," Kruger said. "As to the beer, Africa, mostly. Rwanda. Rhodesia. Liberia. The Democratic Republic of the Congo."

"That is my country," Agbeko said, slapping the table, a wide grin on his face . . . but then the smile fell away. "What were you doing in the DRC, Mr. Kruger?"

Kruger hesitated for a second, neither smiling nor frowning. "I was a journalist."

Agbeko looked at him doubtfully.

Kruger glanced at his watch. "Ah, but the night flees before our conversation. If you select your dinners, I will place the order, and your food will be waiting for you after the weigh-ins."

"That's what I'm talking about," Davis said. "I want a pepperoni pizza."

"I will have the steak," Agbeko said, announcing it like someone might declare political candidacy.

"Order two if you like," Kruger said, and this time his smile lingered longer. "Or even three . . . as heavyweights needn't fear the scale."

Agbeko thumped one of his huge fists on the table. "This is wonderful!"

Carl had to agree. Tacos, pizza, spaghetti with meatballs. If only . . . "Wish they had cheesesteaks. *That* would be wonderful."

"Our chefs are of the highest caliber, and I assure you that their larders are most impressively supplied," Kruger said. "A cheesesteak will be no trouble at all."

"Awesome," Carl said, and had to swallow at the thought.

Tex poked the menu. "Foy grass? What the heck is foy grass?"

Carl looked where Tex was pointing: *Foie gras, complemented with figs and wild mushrooms in a honey-balsamic-port reduction.*

"Foie gras," Kruger said, pronouncing it *fwa gra*, his eyes twinkling with amusement.

"Never heard of it," Tex said. "Got any squirrel?"

NINE

"THIS IS WHERE WE PART WAYS," Kruger said, pressing his thumb into the ID pad of a door marked with a large red X. "Certain you have your bearings?"

"Yes," Carl said. "Thanks."

Tex jerked his thumb toward the door. "Thought those were off-limits."

"Privileges of employment," Kruger said. "Gentlemen." He gave a bow and disappeared.

"I'd like to get in there and have a look around," Tex said. He pressed his thumb into the pad, but the light stayed red.

"Forget it," Carl said. He'd had enough mysteries on Phoenix Island. Here, he wanted to fight, win, and leave . . . and eat a bunch of cheesesteaks. His stomach growled at the thought.

Tex threw a flurry of punches as they walked down the hall. "Let's hurry up and get this over with, boys. Get back to the room before old Stretch drinks all the soda."

Davis had stayed behind. No need for the medic to weigh in.

Heavyweights, on the other hand, had to. They had no upward weight limit, but the Few wanted all fighter weights on record.

Agbeko said, "Our steward was not always a concierge."

Carl looked at him. "He said he was a journalist."

Agbeko's shook his head. "The only white men I ever saw in

the DRC were missionaries or mercenaries . . . and missionaries did not drink banana beer."

"A mercenary, then," Carl said, "like a Phoenix Forcer."

"No," Agbeko said, looking grim. "Not like us at all."

"Shoot," Tex said, "I don't care if he was a nun. Guy offers me a six-pack, he's okay in my book. You know what I'm saying?" He hit Agbeko's big shoulder with a playful jab.

"Be cool," Carl said.

Tex snorted dismissively and bopped along, swinging his shoulders and nodding his head as if to music.

"Control yourself in here," Carl told him.

Tex cocked his head and raised one brow. "I'm fine."

"You're hyped up."

"We're here to fight, ain't we?"

Unless you screw this up and get disqualified, Carl thought, but what he said was, "Yeah, we are. Tomorrow. No earlier. You see Z-Force, just turn the other way."

Tex made a face. To Agbeko, he said, "You ever see somebody worry like this guy?"

Agbeko put a big hand on Tex's shoulder. "Carl is right. We must avoid conflict now. We fight for the honor of Phoenix Island."

"Never heard of the place," Tex said, then jerked. "Ow—easy there, Hercules. You squeeze me like that again, I might not be able to fight."

They turned the corner to see teams disappearing into a room. From within came a muddled burble of voices and a crisp *whap-whap* sound.

"Stick together and ignore trash talk," Carl said. "Save it for the octagon, all right?"

Agbeko hooah-ed, Tex shrugged, and they entered into a

huge, well-lit room with mirrored walls and benches and a warm-up area covered in wrestling mats. Most of the teams were already there, and at the front of the room, people dressed like Kruger appeared to be readying a scale, over which hung an electronic display currently reading 0.00.

On the warm-up mat, a tall, lanky Asian drove a succession of fast roundhouse kicks into a blue foam shield—*whap-whap-whap-whap!*—all with the lead leg, then hitched his hips and pounded a stiff rear-leg kick into the target. Impressive speed and power. Like many kickers, however, the guy leaned back too far and stayed in front of his target. *Jam the kicks and bull forward,* Carl thought, but he couldn't tell if the guy was a big middle-weight or a small heavyweight.

Other than the locker room's bright lights, obvious newness, and absence of bad smells, this was a scene very familiar to Carl. Fighters, mostly stripped to the waist, stood in small groups. Some whispered cagily, like thieves; others laughed and shoved, like drunken sailors on shore leave; others listened to trainers, slipping mock attacks or throwing light punches at outstretched hands, using every second for some sort of preparation. All of them, no matter what their outward demeanor, glanced around, sorting the other fighters, weighing them with their eyes and guessing at potential opponents.

Some were already familiar.

He saw Romeo but no Juliet. Couldn't blame the guy for not bringing her into a room of half-naked guys built like heavily scarred gymnasts.

Romeo looked calm. He stood alone, his eyes drifting over the others but giving nothing away. A middleweight, Carl was sure of that. A few inches taller than Carl. Big hands, but not as big as Carl's, maybe a puncher, maybe not. Wide shoulders but not overblown, like a weight lifter's. Might be quick. He had the dark features of a handsome Mexican fighter: an inch of black hair atop his head; high cheekbones; dark eyes set close to a hooked nose slightly crooked from past battles; with a scar—what looked like the work of a knife—slicing a pale diagonal from his ribs across his six-pack abs. From boxing, Carl knew Mexicans to be tough as nails, aggressive guys with good chins and all the heart in the world. No quit in their bones. Punchers, most of them, but even the guys with cupcake hands came at you, determined to out-throw and out-tough you, every last one of them prouder to be Mexican than Carl had ever been to be any-thing. It was strange to Carl, back in the States, hearing white guys badmouth Mexicans, treat them like they were stupid or in-ferior or something. The majority of Mexican guys Carl had known were hardworking and smart—not to mention bilingual, unlike their naysayers—and most of them, even hard-core crimi-nals he'd known in juvie, lived by a code that gave sense and something approaching honor to their actions.

This guy Romeo, the way he stood, kind of loose, with his toes pointed out to the sides, Carl thought he was more than a boxer. Probably a kicker, too.

Up front, one of the officials near the scale called, "Fighter 47."

There was a commotion near the front, fighters moving aside, and Carl saw Zurkistan's heavyweight, still decked out in his parka and ski mask, step onto the scale.

What was with this guy, still dragging around in his snow gear?

Baca's voice echoed in Carl's mind: *Fighter 47 does not care about heat or cold.* . . .

Tex whistled. "Boy's got shoulders like a trailer . . . and I mean a double-wide."

He is impervious to both pain and comfort. Suffering is nothing to him. He lives only to fight. . . .

The display over the scale flashed three times, then showed 277 in bright red.

Two hundred and seventy-seven pounds? The guy was what . . . five-ten, tops? He was big, sure—huge, even—but 277? Guy must have some dense muscle.

Agbeko stared, chin elevated, eyes serious.

"Woo-ee, buddy," Tex said, slapping Agbeko's arm. "Better you than me."

"Muscle-bound guy like that," Carl said, feigning more confidence than he felt, "just stick and move, and you'll cut him to ribbons." But coming off the scale and swaggering toward the opposite side of the room, Fighter 47, despite his massive bulk, looked loose and fluid, not muscle-bound at all.

Tex laughed. "Check out the ballerina."

Over on the mat, the Asian guy—a middleweight, Carl was almost certain now—stood with his leg high in the air, frozen like a photo of someone throwing a powerful side kick at the ceiling. Not so much as a quiver. Then, using one arm, he drew the outstretched leg—still fully extended in its frozen kick—inward until his knee was flush to his ear, and started hopping up and down.

"Reminds me of my ex-wife," Tex said, and brayed laughter. Teams turned, looked.

"Keep it down," Carl said.

Tex rolled his eyes and gave a sarcastic salute.

Agbeko reached for him, but Tex dipped away and put up his fists. "Hands off."

Great, Carl thought. He'd been worried about Tex getting into it with some other team. Now he was ready to pop Agbeko. "Save it," Carl said, using the command voice Stark had taught him, not a bark—*alphas never bark,* Stark told him—but a low, sharp burst, a six-inch punch of a command. Tex and Agbeko stepped apart.

"Y'all need to loosen up your skirts," Tex said. "I'm fine."

"Good," Carl said. *Weigh in and get out,* he thought, and had to swallow, imagining the smell of fried onions and mushrooms and hot peppers, a cheesesteak oozing grease and sauce, its soggy weight in his hands. . . .

Up front, the men in suits continued the weigh-ins. Teams pressed forward. Despite all that had happened and all that was about to happen, despite his concerns over the cesti, the great stakes, and the daunting task that awaited him after the tournament, Carl felt a familiar lilt in his heart. This was it. The weigh-in. His opponent was somewhere in this room. . . .

Fighter after fighter stepped onto the scale, the administrators calling numbers that made no sense—41, 38, 35—until Carl realized they were summoning the heavyweights in descending order.

When they called Fighter 32, the giant with the misshapen head climbed shirtless onto the scale, looking like he could step straight into the Eagles' offensive line. Easily seven feet tall with skin as bright as Siberian snow, he spread his arms wide, the guy's reach long even for his great height, and stood there nodding, his brow low and heavy, his jaw wide, the thick lips twisted into a brutal smile. The overhead display registered 341, and Fighter 32 flexed, sneering at the crowd. That's when Carl spotted the red triangle tattooed on his shoulder.

Recognition shuddered through him. Stark had told him about this guy—or rather about the triangle, which meant he'd won the triple threat of underground fighting: Tokyo, Marseilles, and Rio de Janeiro.

"Better you than me, Agbeko," Tex said again, and Carl told him to shut up. His gut had tightened into a fist. Tex had a point. . . .

Another heavyweight stepped onto the scale, this one—

"Hey, man, you a middleweight, huh?" someone said, nudging Carl's shoulder, and he turned to find Fighter 13, the tall loudmouth with the skyline of New York shaved into the back of his head, staring down at him with a cocky grin full of gold teeth. "Me, too."

Beside him, a short, muscular fighter flashed his own grill of gold teeth. His hair was cut close, almost shaved to the skin, but he was making a show of brushing it anyway.

Carl read their grins and posture. "All right," he said, and turned away.

"My man here," New York said, "he thought you was a lightweight."

"Wish he was," the guy with the brush said. "Easy work."

Carl said nothing. The tall guy nudged him again.

"You ready? This is the real deal right here, winner take all, you know what I'm saying?"

Carl watched the front of the room, where a huge kid with a red flattop and biceps like freckled cannonballs flexed beneath the red display of 264.

Another nudge. Harder. Almost a push.

"Yo, man. No disrespect, but I gotta tell you," the tall guy said, pausing to fake a laugh. "You don't look like a fighter. You know what I'm saying?"

Another shove, this one hard enough to turn Carl a little. He faced the guy. "We'll see."

The shorter kid showed his gold teeth again and raised his palms, feigning surprise. It was a skit Carl had seen before. Many times.

The tall guy shrugged. "Maybe you're gooder than you look." He put his hand on Carl's shoulder, the guy's reach very long. "Maybe you're gooder than I think."

This really cracked up the short guy.

Tex said something, but Carl shook his head, and surprisingly, Tex backed off.

"Fighter 20," the organizer called, and Agbeko headed toward the front.

The tall guy nudged his friend now, pretending to be serious and doing a purposefully crappy job of it. "Yo, man, yo. Maybe he gooder than he look, right?"

"Too pretty to be a champion," the short guy said.

The tall guy put his arm around Carl. "I like you, man. You funny."

Feeling heat in his face, Carl shrugged off the arm.

At the front of the room, Agbeko weighed in at two hundred and seventy on the dot, a good weight for him.

Now the smaller guy pushed Carl's arm. "I got to tell you, yo. My man right here?" He hooked a thumb toward the tall kid and raised his brows, still grinning that stupid golden grin, and shook his head, the same dumb act Carl had seen in city gyms a hundred times. Part of the game. Thugs trying to psych you out, all loud, lots of laughter, always the challenge, acting friendly but calling you out, too, and Carl had found it best over the years to just hunker down and wait, let the storm of stupidity pass, and then settle it in the ring.

The short guy slapped Carl's shoulder again. "He undefeated, son. You hear me? Undefeated."

Another slap, and Carl felt a grin coming onto his own face, the ache in his knuckles pulsing rhythmically like a sounding alarm . . . a *smoke* alarm . . . and his nostrils filled with ash.

The short guy rattled on, talking about how his buddy knocked everybody out, *everybody*—"You hear me, son?"—and moved to give Carl another cuff, but this time, Carl batted it away.

Time dilated.

The short guy sneered in slow motion, and the tall guy stepped in, saying, "What's up? What's up?" and reaching for Carl, who slipped the hand and stepped in with a pop of his shoulder, bumping the tall guy into the short guy. At the same time, Carl registered their team heavyweight, hurrying through the crowd, snarling—and Carl, seeing this guy had gold teeth, too, laughed aloud.

"You guys all have the same dentist or what?" Carl said, and brought up his fists.

But then, as if by magic, Kruger appeared, pulling Carl away with a quick apology to the other team's steward, who'd materialized at exactly the same moment.

Disappointment flooded Carl—he ached to thump them—but Kruger led him across the room. Tex followed, laughing.

"We mustn't have any of that," Kruger said. "The Few tolerate no violence outside the ring."

"Yeah?" Carl said. "They don't want to miss the show, huh?"

Then the organizer called, "Fighter 19," taking Carl by surprise. They hadn't even finished weighing the heavies yet. Whatever.

He peeled off his shirt, handed it to Tex, and headed for the front of the room.

"Fighter 19?" the organizer asked.

Carl nodded, kicking off his shoes. He pulled off his socks, dropped his pants to the floor, let out the superstitious exhale of every guy who's ever sweated making weight, and stepped onto the scale in his underwear. The display flashed three times and registered 199.9.

When he came off the scale, Tex was there, handing him his shirt and grinning like a maniac. "What was that you were saying about saving it for the ring, boss?"

TEN

CARL OPENED HIS EYES. He was sitting on the still-made bed. His eyes flicked to the bedside clock.

1:11.

He had "slept" for exactly an hour, and no surprise. Setting a mental alarm clock accurate to the minute was a nice convenience, but it was nothing compared to what his mind and body did with the single hour of deep rest he needed each day.

After only sixty minutes of shutdown time—his unconscious state more closely resembled meditation than sleep—he felt better rested and more mentally reconstructed than he had after eight hours of pre-chip sleep. Dr. Vispera had done more than implanted a chip in his head. He'd modified Carl's blood and dumped thousands of tiny chips into his bloodstream, and these had implanted throughout his body, connecting its various systems to the master chip in his brain. As much as Carl disliked the thought of this invasive technology, as much as he resented being used as a lab rat, he very much appreciated needing only an hour's rest per night.

Whenever he needed rest, he simply slowed his breathing and heart rate, lowering them until his heart beat only a few times a minute and his breathing practically stopped.

His stomach growled.

The kitchen is open around the clock, Kruger's voice echoed in his head.

The silver-haired steward hadn't lied about the chefs' excellence. The cheesesteak had been awesome. Sitting there, Carl rewound the memory, savoring the greasy meat and cheese, the fried onions and mushrooms, the sweet sauce, and the heat of the chopped-up cherry peppers.

Full menu at any hour, Kruger had said. *Whatever you like.*

Another cheesesteak, that's what he would like . . . maybe even two or three.

He swept the little box from atop the nightstand, but his thumb hovered over the green call button as another voice came into his head. Not Kruger's this time, but that of his old trainer, Arthur James. . . .

Stay hungry, son. Full belly, empty heart.

He remembered standing in the ring with the old man, remembered Arthur throwing a slow jab, bringing it back low. *Full man gets lazy and gets countered. But a hungry man . . .* He straightened, whipped out a jab, and brought it straight back to his face. *He snatches food out of your mouth and brings it straight back to his.*

Carl tossed the box back onto the nightstand. *All right, Arthur, all right.* As usual, his old trainer was right. Suffering, not cheesesteaks, built heart. He couldn't let comfort make him soft.

A cheesesteak sure would be good, though. . . .

His stomach growled again, weighing in on the debate. Using the chip, he could slow his heart, dim pain, or dull his sense of heat or cold, but he remained at the mercy of hunger.

Well, he just had to distract himself.

He rose and went to the window, drew the curtain aside, and looked out into the arena. Torches flickered only dimly along the walls, but he could make out people here and there—a couple on the bleachers, someone on the track, shuffling along. No one in the octagon.

He needed to feel the ring, to test it. He'd never fought in a cage before. Would the mesh have a spring to it, like ring ropes?

Time to find out.

Beyond his door, the common room was silent. No television, no laughter, no talking.

He changed into the black warm-up suit with a phoenix on the chest and a big red 19 on the back.

The common room was empty . . . and spotless. When he'd gone to bed, the place was trashed—dirty plates and bowls, empty soda cans, chip bags, and candy wrappers everywhere. All gone now. At some point, a cleaning team had slipped in and silently tidied the room.

An oddly creepy moment. The sense of an invisible army working within the walls. . . .

Time to leave. Take a walk, have a look.

He crossed the room and opened the door and stepped from the suite into the hallway. Everything dim and quiet at this late hour. A light sweetness in the air, less floral now, just a subtle richness that reminded him of Atlantic City casinos where the Philly ham-and-eggers fought. Something else in the air, too, a sense of collective anticipation—that strange and pervasive pre-fight restlessness that haunted cheap hotels during long nights on the road, the next day's fight everywhere and nowhere, everywhere and nowhere. This place practically vibrated with it.

That's not the place, he told himself. *That's you.*

He walked down the hall, passing rooms of those he would fight. Behind some doors, parties raged. Thumping music, shouting, laughter. Most rooms, however, were silent—and no surprise there. These fighters weren't high school athletes on a fun and exciting trip; they were hardened warriors arrived at the all-or-nothing moment of their lives. Everything on the line.

He turned the corner and stopped. Midway down the corridor, someone—and Carl recognized him by his height and black hair as Romeo—was leaning into one of the doors marked with a big red X.

Juliet was nowhere in sight.

Romeo pressed the door with one hand and held the other against the ID pad. Not his thumb, though, Carl saw, tightening his focus, but the back of his hand.

A flash of green, a light pop, and the door opened.

Romeo turned his head, checking the hall.

Carl dipped out of sight.

When he peeked again, he saw Romeo disappearing into the forbidden space. The door with the red X slid shut with a soft click, and the hall was empty—as if nothing had happened.

What was Romeo doing?

None of your business, Carl told himself. *Kid pokes around and gets burned, that's his problem. Now vanish before somebody finds you standing here like a lookout.*

Reaching the elevator, he pressed the call button, and the doors slid silently open. He started to press the button for level one, the arena, but then stabbed number three instead. He wanted to say hi to someone before heading to the octagon.

※

"Hello, Theogenes," he said five minutes later, staring up into the battered bronze face.

The hall was dim and empty now, but a cone of brighter light shone down on the massive statue, magnifying the definition of

the great bronze muscles and casting the dark eyes into exaggerated shadow.

Again Carl experienced the strong connection he'd felt when
he'd first seen the statue. *How many times did they call you to
the ring?* he wondered, staring into the shadowy eyes.

What was it that he saw in them?

Numbness?

No. Too much soul there for numbness, and the slightly
downturned mouth suggested not the absence of pain but a bearing up beneath it. A wrecking machine that, having feelings,
needed to repress emotion in order to carry on.

The eyes weren't numb. They were haunted. Haunted, yet un-
afraid.

"How do I do it?" Carl whispered, and his eyes went again to
the blocky fists wrapped in leather and banded in metal.

In a few hours, Carl's hands would also be locked in leather.

"How do I do it?" he repeated.

Theogenes stared back over one shoulder, locked in old pain
and resignation.

Why had the ancient Greek warrior fought? Duty?
Fame? Wealth? Or some higher purpose—to please the gods,
perhaps . . . ?

And why are you *fighting?* Carl asked himself.

All his life, he had fought—but there had always been a good
reason, even if he'd misunderstood his own motivation at times.
He had fought to protect his father, fought for sport, fought for
both hatred and love, fought for his very survival . . .

For what was he fighting now?

For a title that would earn a promotion that would create an
opportunity to . . .

Standing here before this frozen warrior, staring at the great armored fists, his own chain of motivations—no matter how important, ultimately—felt indistinct, tenuous, almost unreal.

What seemed real were the battle-scarred boys sleeping fitfully upstairs—and the brutal cesti he would wear tomorrow.

Not tomorrow, he told himself, remembering the hour. *You're fighting later today.*

The question lingered: *Why?*

This was no boxing match. His opponents would come at him with murder in their hearts. To them, he was a stepping-stone toward ten million dollars.

But he didn't care about money. He cared about stopping Stark, and yet he hated what seemed the only path to that goal.

Within the cesti, his fists would tear flesh and shatter bone. And what if, smelling blood, the dark twin within him gained power? What if it *seized* power?

He remembered Sanderson's pleas for mercy as he'd hit him again and again, wild with rage, insane with wrath.

Knowing these terrible risks, how could he enter the octagon and face people against whom he held no grudge?

It was a night for channeling voices, and Stark's supplied the bitter answer: *The price of progress runs high at times.*

Wavering torchlight gave the vast arena an unsteady gloom. Far overhead, in the upper darkness, drifting clouds mottled a ceiling of moonlight.

Stepping on the rubberized red track that ran round the volcano walls, Carl heard shouting in a harsh language—German, he thought—and saw a flat-faced trainer leaning over the balcony railing, hollering down at the fighter wearing a parka shuffling around the opposite end of the track.

He saw someone else on the balcony, too, someone small, sitting alone at the far end of the benches. She looked up then and, seeing Carl, came halfway out of her seat, raising one hand. Even at this distance, he could see her open mouth, her staring eyes, and the long ponytail of blond hair that curled from the back of her head and across her shoulder.

Juliet.

She froze like that for a fraction of a second, then withdrew her hand slowly, sat again, and turned away.

Thought I was Romeo, he realized, and could have laughed. *She must have lousy eyesight.*

Whatever. Again he considered the insanity of bringing a girlfriend to the Funeral Games. Even if she knew the fight game and doctored cuts like a champ, how would she react when a fist wrapped in leather ripped off half of her boyfriend's face?

Whatever the case, that was their problem, not his.

Romeo was a middleweight. If she weakened him, that only helped Carl.

The guy in the parka shambled past, looking wasted. Hollow eyes in a mask of exhaustion. No sweat, though; this guy had wrung himself dry. If the fighter noticed Carl, he showed no sign of it, just shuffled past, staring dully ahead. The trainer yelled again from the bleachers. The fighter grumbled and spat and then put up the parka hood.

Carl shook his head. Cutting weight last minute for a boxing match was bad enough, but doing it here, with the brutal schedule, fight-till-you-drop rules, and the best fighters in the world? Suicidal . . .

Hope I draw him as my first opponent, Carl thought, and stepped onto the bridge of black glass that stretched away to the octagon.

The bridge was wide and yet, as he strode out onto it, Carl was very much aware of its flat design, its lack of sidewalls or railings, and the terrible emptiness to either side, an unbroken drop of perhaps fifty feet into a black lake twinkling with torchlight. His legs felt a little rubbery with the same illogical fear he'd felt back on Phoenix Island, crossing the stone ridge between mountain peaks—as if the void beyond the edge would somehow pluck him off and away in a kind of vertiginous vacuum. Ironically enough, of course, he had ended up pitching himself off that same ridge. Not something to remember now.

He went to the edge and peered down at the black-water bowels of the volcanic caldera. Torches ringed the walls, and a shore of black sand ran along one side. Nice beach for a vampire family vacation. . . .

He walked the rest of the way to the octagon. A strange moment, climbing the steps of the elevated ring. Old excitement surged through him, his body reacting to seemingly familiar circumstances. His legs had carried him into many rings.

He loved boxing in front of a crowd. One-on-one—with no one to blame if you lost and all the glory to you if you won—two guys matching fists and hearts, chins and brains, giving everything they had to see who could out-think, out-punch, and out-tough the other.

But this wasn't boxing. This was different. Way different. Here, he would face monsters, top-notch fighters sucking down from street weights of 230, 240. They would weigh in at 200 and rehydrate overnight to 225. With ten million dollars on the line, they would use every ounce of that bone and muscle to punch and kick, knee and elbow, grapple and head butt until only one fighter still stood.

Me, he thought. *It has to be me standing at the end.* Even if it meant wrecking people against whom he had no quarrel, he had to win. He could hate himself for it later.

He opened the door and entered the cage. A huge space, maybe thirty feet across. Good. That would give him plenty of room to stick and move if he faced a strong grappler.

He shuffled around the ring. Not a lot of bounce to the floor. Good traction without grabbing at his feet. Not bad. Crouching, he pressed his fingertips into the padding. Thin. Any type of throw or pile driver would be devastating. He lifted into a front bridge, stretched his neck, rolled into a back bridge, arched, then kip-upped onto his feet.

His only concern was the cage itself. Stark had given him a crash course in using the cage offensively and defensively, but Carl had never actually fought in one, and he knew learning about something and doing it were two very different things.

He backpedaled into the cage wall, a chain-link fence maybe eight feet high coated in black vinyl. Not a lot of give to it. He would miss the spring he generated counterpunching off ring ropes.

He moved around the ring, throwing combinations of punches and kicks, tumbling, stretching, and shooting for take-downs against invisible opponents. He kept everything to half speed until the vast arena emptied. No more Juliet, no more shouting trainer, no more delirious fighter, shuffling toward destruction.

For the first time since getting the chip, he was finally alone in a ring. After months of holding back, not wanting Stark or Phoenix Force to know how much he'd changed, he ripped combinations at full speed—several hard punches per second—but the chip had done more than speed up his hands and increase his power. It had accelerated his processing so that he could see and adjust and think in the middle of things, and it had given his body such amazing coordination that he could fire a constant barrage of strikes and still attend to blocking, defensive head movement, and adjusting his angles. That would be key, he knew, against these hulking opponents with sledgehammer fists. This war would be as much about position as punching, as much about angles as kicks, as much about tending the gap as taking shots.

He ripped a lightning combination that ended in a double knee and a hip toss, gave his invisible opponent the ground-and-pound, then popped to his feet and shook out his arms, grinning. He felt *great*.

That's when the clapping started. Each clap was crisp and measured—a single person, applauding slowly. The sound echoed in the vast chamber.

Carl turned a full 360 in the ring, scanning the bridge, the track, and the dark tunnels beneath the buntings but saw no one.

Then he realized the clapping was coming from above.

His eyes flashed to the bleachers. Empty.

Higher . . .

His gaze lifted to the opera box, where a man in a flowing purple robes stood, looking down and clapping.

Carl's eyes focused instinctively, and he could make out within the shadowy recesses of the hood covering the man's head, a wide chin covered in a trimmed beard split by a smile. Above this, a golden mask gleamed in the torchlight.

One of the Few, Carl realized.

The man stopped clapping and his voice, inhumanly deep, filled the arena. "Very impressive, Number 19. Truly first-rate."

"Thank you," Carl said, feeling very small at the center of the ring, at the heart of this hollow mountain.

"I am pleased to have taken this suddenly fortuitous midnight stroll, which you have transformed into a bettor's reconnaissance." The man's voice, both modified and magnified, came from many directions at once, dark and humorous . . . the voice of the volcano itself, a subterranean god that, Carl understood instantly and intuitively, would demand blood sacrifices. "I will wager heavily in your favor on the morrow. But of course attacking is merely half the battle. How would you rate your defense?"

"Offense is the best defense," Carl said.

"Bold words," his interrogator said, "but the gods favor the bold. At least . . . for a time."

Bright light flashed behind Carl, and he turned to see the giant television screen announcing the matchups for Round One. Two stacks of numbers, designated by corner—red or blue. The lightweights scrolled past first. Carl's eyes found Tex's number, 18, at the very bottom of the division, opposite not a number but the word *bye*. Someone had missed weight or missed a flight, and Tex had pulled the longest of long straws . . . a free pass into the second round.

Next came the middleweights, eight matchups, with Carl's coming last. He would fight out of the red corner versus . . .

He smiled grimly.

Maybe you're gooder than I think, Fighter 13's voice echoed in Carl's mind like the ghost of some grammatically impaired parrot. *Maybe you're gooder than I think.*

Count on it, Carl thought, and felt a wave of relief. If there was one guy who would help him to set aside his reservations long enough to do whatever he had to do to win, it was the big talker from the weigh-ins. Carl couldn't have arranged for a better opponent.

"Bet as much as you want," he said, but when he turned back around, the opera box was empty.

ELEVEN

CARL ROCKED, slick with sweat, waiting for it. . . .

"Low-four-double knee," Agbeko called, and extended the Thai pads that covered his hands and forearms.

Carl blasted the pads with a lead leg round kick, snapped out the "four" combo—jab, right cross, left hook, right hand—exhaling sharply with each blow, grabbed the back of the pads like he would grab the back of an opponent's neck, and pulled them down as he drove his knees up, one-two, into the targets.

The combination's *bap . . . smack-smack-smack-smack . . . thump-thump* echoed in the red-corner locker room.

After the combo, he sidestepped. Never hang around, waiting for the guy to fire back. Better to swivel out, see what he gives you, then pull the trigger again or keep moving.

"You're going to kill this guy," Tex said.

I hope not, Carl thought.

So far, the Funeral Games had been shockingly brutal. Broken bones, teeth in the ring, blood everywhere. Faces cut to the bone, heads misshapen with broken jaws and cheekbones. Guys limping on battered legs, hugging broken ribs, puking from concussions. Teams carrying unconscious fighters out of the ring.

You have to win, Carl told himself. But then his mind asked, *Even if it means killing somebody?*

Strips of leather wound around his wrist and crisscrossed his fists, where three bands of leather covered his knuckles, making his hands hard as stones. Made of thicker leather, the cesti would "grip" on impact. Solid punches would cut an opponent's face as the knuckles twisted. These things were straight out of the gladiatorial days. Carl hated them.

You won't kill anybody, he thought, but his mind instantly counterpunched, *What are you going to do, hold back?* The people in this tournament were serious, talented, and hungry. If he hesitated, they would eat him alive.

"Low-low-eight," Agbeko called, and Carl fired like a machine.

"Hooah!" Agbeko thundered.

"You're going to kill him!" Tex repeated.

Davis watched from a nearby chair, frowning.

Carl thanked Agbeko and shook out his arms. He was ready. Physically, anyway.

That's when he noticed the other teams in the locker room. They'd all stopped to watch.

Only Romeo, who was on deck, didn't seem to notice. He stood in a far corner, his back to the room, warming up alone.

On the faces of the others, Carl saw concern, fear, awe.

Good. Eventually, he'd end up fighting some of them. Best to plant the seed of doubt in their heads right now.

Arthur James had always told him to hold back when the other guy was watching, save something to surprise him with, and despite the blistering speed and crashing power Carl had displayed, he was holding back. He would show them more in the ring, feeding that seed of doubt, so it would drink their confidence as it spread within them, growing into a tree of fear.

"I'm good," he said.

Agbeko took off the pads, laughed, and held them up for Carl to see. "Look, my brother."

Carl's strikes had split the leather pads. Stuffing pushed from the tears like herniated intestine.

"I'll tell you what, boss," Tex said. "That gold-toothed dummy is one dead cat." He was grinning like a madman. Earlier, he'd accepted his win by forfeit. The ref had raised his hand, canned applause had poured from the speakers—odd, that—and Tex had taken a theatrical bow. Since then, he'd been all wound up, boiling over with energy, like he was fighting instead of Carl. To his credit, though, he'd stopped messing with his teammates. He was excited for Carl, his loudest fan.

The doors banged open, letting in a blast of loud music, and a voice called, "Fighter 7."

Romeo crossed himself and headed for the door. His eyes met Carl's as he passed.

Carl nodded.

Romeo nodded back.

No words, but they had exchanged what passed for respect between fighters.

Carl hoped the kid won.

The doors opened, and the Gypsy bareknuckle fighters from Ireland came in, cursing loudly. Their middleweight sagged between them like a bloody rag. The tournament was over for him, just like that. Long way to travel for a beating.

Z-Force's middleweight advances, then, Carl thought, remembering the matchups. *Makes them 2–0 on the day*.

Knockouts and submissions had ended most of the fights within three rounds, but one contest had gone ten rounds, another fourteen, and one pair of lightweights had battled for *three hours*. The winner and the loser both left the ring on stretchers.

"Fighter 19 on deck," the voice in the hall announced, and the doors swung shut again.

Here we go, Carl thought, and his gut tightened. *On deck*.

In boxing, *on deck* meant you'd be fighting within minutes. Here at the Funeral Games, though, where fights could end early or last hours, *on deck* just meant you were fighting next.

"That's us," Tex said. "Yeah, buddy!"

Carl peeled off his wet T-shirt and tossed it into a nearby laundry bin. They would fight shirtless and shoeless. Carl would wear only his shiny black trunks with a red phoenix on one thigh and a red 19 on the other.

Davis came out of his chair then, telling Carl to close his eyes, and Carl felt the medic's long, slender fingers reapplying Vaseline over his face.

"Not too much," Carl told him, "or they'll make us wipe it off in the ring." Insufficient grease would be disastrous. Any cut sustained during the first fight would be a terrible liability for the remainder of the tournament.

"I got you," Davis said, smoothing the grease over Carl's brow and the bridge of his nose and across his cheekbones.

Agbeko was behind him then, massaging his shoulders. "How do you feel, my brother?"

"Ready," Carl said. Which was half true. Physically, he was good to go.

"You are a tiger, Carl," Agbeko said.

Carl nodded, his eyes still closed, and pictured the tiger he'd once seen at the Philadelphia Zoo. He'd shown up at feeding time, and the tiger had swiveled back and forth in its cage, awaiting meat, ten feet of growling predator with bright liquid eyes and fluid muscle and a pink tongue lolling out between white fangs.

"You are as strong as a tiger," Agbeko's deep, lyrical voice said.

Carl breathed deeply through his nostrils, feeling the strength in his body and linking it with the memory of the pacing tiger.

"You are as fast as a tiger," Agbeko said, his big hands kneading Carl's shoulders.

Yes, Carl thought. *I am fast and strong, like a tiger, but—*

Then, as if reading Carl's mind, Agbeko said, "You are as *merciless* as a tiger."

Carl nodded. *Be a tiger. Be a tiger now and do this thing and have it done.*

He concentrated on his breathing, picturing his opponent and running through his game plan again. Nail him once, out of the gates, just to test him, but then back off and move, play it safe, see what he had. Adapt. This wasn't about rounds. You couldn't win a decision. You had to stop the guy. Knock him out or make him tap.

Using the chip, he'd rewound his memory of the weigh-in scuffle dozens of times, studying Fighter 13's height and reach and habits, and, as was always the case when he looped a memory, he recognized things he hadn't noticed in the original moment. Chapped lips and ashy skin, signs of dehydration, proof that Fighter 13 had struggled to make weight. Good. Carl would take any edge he could get, knowing that fights between experts usually came down to the accumulation of small advantages.

"Soon as the bell rings," Tex said, "kick him in the hey-now. Show him who's boss."

"You're crazy, man," Davis said. "Low blows are against the rules."

"You want to play fair or win?" Tex said. "They won't DQ him for one foul. These guys love blood. Nail him hard and—"

The doors banged open again, filling the locker room with another blast of loud music and canned applause, and Romeo jogged in, smiling. He had a small cut high on the forehead, near the hairline, but looked otherwise unhurt. There was blood on his fist and feet.

Not his, Carl reasoned. *The other guy's. Good for Romeo.*

"Fighter 19," the voice called from atop the ramp, and they started for the door, Tex in front, like a bulldog on a leash, then Carl, then Agbeko, still rubbing his shoulders and talking to him, the words lost to the music and swelling applause, and Davis at the end, carrying the med kit and corner man's bucket.

"*Bueno suerte*," Romeo said as they passed, and he and Carl bumped fists.

Carl rolled his head on his shoulders, telling himself, *I'm a tiger.*

The doors opened for them, and a man in a black suit waved them forward. Kruger appeared, his signature smile slightly wider as he joined them. Music and loud cheering boomed from speakers, filling the arena. The music wasn't rock or rap, like you usually heard at fights, but some kind of hard classical music with thundering drums and crashing cymbals.

Distractedly, he noticed Juliet on the track nearby, her warm-up jacket splattered in blood. Her big brown eyes stared from her pale face, then looked quickly away.

Must be in shock, he thought, *after cornering her boyfriend's fight.*

He thought there was something strangely familiar about the girl—not her face, but her posture and the way she moved—but then he was past her, and the music dimmed as the coldly beautiful face of the woman who'd greeted them filled the massive television screen, saying, "Fighting out of the red corner, representing Phoenix Island, Fighter 19." She sounded less like a boxing announcer and more like some stuffy tour guide, perfect enunciation and no emotion.

Another burst of music and applause roared from the speakers, and Kruger led them across the track and stopped them at the edge of the bridge.

"Check it out, boss," Tex said, nudging Carl and pointing to the big screen. "You're famous."

It was weird, looking up and seeing his own face on the massive screen . . . the type of entrance reserved for big-time pros. Most amateurs fought in dusty, ill-attended venues packed with folding chairs, and entered to a boom box blasting hip-hop or "Welcome to the Jungle" as assorted aunts and uncles clapped and shouted.

Then his image was gone, replaced by the woman, who said, "Fighting out of the blue corner, representing the United States of America, Fighter 13."

"She don't sound too excited," Tex said.

Kruger's chin lifted a bit higher. "She is consummately professional."

Music and applause returned, and the face of Carl's loud-mouthed opponent filled the screen, glistening with sweat and grease, the eyes hard. So great was the size and resolution of the screen that Carl could make out the whiskers on his opponent's unshaven chin, the scarring over his eyes, the bead of sweat hanging from the tip of his flattened nose.

Kruger motioned them forward onto the bridge, the black glass of which pulsed to life with the amazing trick of special effects that Carl had first noticed during the lightweight bouts. Every time their feet struck the bridge, what looked like bolts of purple lightning flashed and forked along its dark span.

In front of him, Tex shouted something, but the words were lost to the booming music and false applause.

Carl glanced up at the bleachers, where teams huddled apart

from one another. Some applauded. Others merely watched, waiting.

Agbeko's big hands propelled him forward.

And there it was—the old ring-walk tension—and he grinned as excitement and dread chilled his core. Something in him shifted then, an old cog turning once more into position, and suddenly this place, with all its spectacle and strangeness, its light show and canned laughter, no longer mattered.

All that mattered now was the fight.

He threw a short combination, and then they were across the bridge, hurrying up the steps of the elevated octagon and into the cone of bright light shining down from a light suspended overhead. Kruger opened the door, and they stepped into the cage just as the opposing team entered the other side.

The mat felt damp to Carl's bare feet. At least they'd mopped the blood.

Fighter 13 glared across the ring, looking very tall, with arms as long as bullwhips. He had rehydrated since the weigh-ins, putting on twenty, maybe twenty-five pounds overnight, and his muscles looked like they had been inflated by a pump. The short guy with gold teeth was shouting something, but Carl paid no attention and stared back at Fighter 13 with no expression on his face, waiting for the referee to call both teams to the center of the ring.

The music and fake applause stopped abruptly, and the voice of the woman said, "Ladies and gentlemen"—and for the first time, her voice *did* sound excited—"a great honor has been bestowed upon us. All rise and show your respect."

"Oh," Kruger said, sounding surprised. "My."

Looking up, Carl saw men and women in purple robes, their upper faces hidden behind golden masks, sitting in the opera box high above. Seated on the throne atop the highest dais was the bearded man who had spoken to Carl in the middle of the night.

"The Few have entered the Cauldron," the woman said. This was the first time they had appeared in the arena. "Let us honor the Few."

"Everyone bow," Kruger said.

Carl stayed standing as people all over the arena bowed toward the opera box. The Few watched from on high.

Let's go, Carl thought, and threw a flurry of punches in the air. *Time to fight.*

Then the moment was over and the referee's voice boomed across the arena. "Fighters," he said, and Carl walked to the center of the ring, with his team all around him, until he stood toe-to-toe with Fighter 13. "You were given your instructions in the locker rooms," the referee said. "No eye gouging; no biting; no strikes to the groin."

Fighter 13 leaned in, going for the stare-down, like so many other fighters had in the past. Carl just stared dead ahead at the lean, muscular torso and the *Thug Life* tattoo scrawled there. Truth in advertising. A thug like this guy would take Carl's lack of eye contact as fear, as weakness. Good. Let him think that; let him be aggressive. Then, once Carl hurt him, he'd show him his eyes. He knew from past experience that the eyes, timed correctly, could be powerful weapons. Hard stares before the fight meant nothing. When Carl used his eyes, it meant everything.

The ref said, "Stop when I say stop; break when I say break; fight when I say fight. Three-minute rounds until one of you submits or can no longer continue. Any questions?"

Carl shook his head, and the ref sent them to their corners.

"He is very tall," Agbeko said, visibly nervous. "You must get inside his guard."

Carl nodded.

"Knock this punk out," Tex said, grinning. "I want to go upstairs and order a pizza."

"Seconds out," the ref called, signaling that it was time for the seconds to leave the cage.

Turning to Davis, Carl said, "Mouthpiece."

Davis looked sick with worry. That surprised Carl. Davis, the triple murderer, who despised Carl so much he wouldn't even look him in the eyes, nervous for the fight? The tall medic shoved in the mouthpiece and started out of the ring, followed by Tex.

Agbeko hugged Carl. "Work his body. Chop down the tall tree."

Both cage doors shut, leaving only Carl, the ref, and Fighter 13 in the octagon.

Take your time, Carl told himself. *Figure him out; time him. Watch your D*. Then, remembering how quickly rage had engulfed him at the weigh-in, he thought, *And whatever you do, keep the beast in its cage.*

Across the ring, Fighter 13 hopped up and down, snarling and banging his fists together. All of this meant nothing. The guy would stick and move, using his height and reach advantages. Eventually, Carl would stalk him, cut off the ring, and get inside that long reach.

The bell rang.

Excitement whooped in Carl's chest, and he shuffled forward, his fists hard with leather.

Surprisingly, Fighter 13 charged.

To Carl, the world slowed. His mind, working with blazing speed, had time to see Fighter 13's snarl, had time to watch the long lead leg stomping outward, and even had time to feel surprise. The guy was coming straight at him, giving up his height

and reach to rock and shock. Carl stepped outside the kick and
drove a power jab into the *Thug Life* tattoo.

Carl felt ribs break. Fighter 13 hit the canvas, where he
curled into a ball, howling.

Carl waited for the ref to count, then remembered . . . there
would be no count.

"Fight on!" the ref said.

Fight on? The guy was curled in a fetal position.

Carl leaned over him. "Tap or I kick you in the ribs."

Fighter 13 opened one hateful eye, saw Carl meant it, and
tapped the mat.

The ref waved his arms. "Fight's over."

Canned applause roared.

The door clanged open, and Tex and Agbeko rushed into the
ring, shouting. The huge African embraced Carl, lifting him from
his feet. Over his shoulder, Carl saw the Few leaving the arena,
disappearing through the purple curtains at the rear of their
opera box. Last to leave was the bearded man, who gave Carl the
slightest of bows and exited.

Fighter 13's team helped him up, and he limped off, hugging
his broken ribs.

The ref raised Carl's fist in the air, and the television woman
announced calmly, "The referee calls a stop to this bout in eleven
seconds of the first round, a new tournament record. Fighter 19
is the winner."

Mock applause erupted. Overhead, the screen replayed Carl's
knockout blow.

"One punch, my brother," Agbeko said, "and you scored a
knockout in record time."

"Record time, my butt," Tex said, beaming. "I won without
even throwing a punch."

TWELVE

DESPITE THE RECORD SPEED of his victory, Carl had just enough time for a quick shower and a quicker lunch before heading back downstairs to help Agbeko prep for his fight.

Now, after forty-five grueling minutes, the heavyweight's fight was finally over. Carl was hoarse from shouting.

"Should've stopped it," Davis said again. During the fight, he had impressed Carl with his skill and composure, but ultimately, even the best cut man in history couldn't have stopped the bleeding.

For eleven nightmare rounds, the Hungarian fighter had run a stick-and-move clinic on Agbeko, nailing him with leg kicks and blistering jabs and straight rights, tending the gap and never pausing long enough for the Phoenix Forcer to counter. When he staggered Agbeko in the opening minute of the twelfth round, the Hungarian made his first—and final—mistake, squaring with the wobbling Phoenix Forcer and pounding away with a barrage of crushing blows meant to end the fight. He never saw Agbeko's hook.

"You worry about your job, and let me worry about mine," Carl said, keeping his voice low and talking out of the side of his mouth as the announcer did her thing.

"Patch him up, right?" Davis said. "That way you can fight your dog again?"

"Enough," Carl said. "We'll finish this later." He knew it was a mistake, letting Davis question his command even this much, let alone scheduling a follow-up discussion about something that clearly fell under Carl's sphere of leadership, but truth be told, Davis was right. He should have stopped it, shouldn't have let Agbeko take that awful beating.

At the center of the ring, the referee raised Agbeko's hand. The hulking fighter swayed back and forth as if buffeted by the applause roaring from the speakers. His bloodied head hung forward like he was nodding off to sleep.

They helped the dazed fighter down the octagon stairs. Kruger joined them, telling Agbeko he'd fought very bravely.

Agbeko didn't seem to hear the compliment.

"We can't let him go to sleep," Carl told Davis. "He might have a concussion."

The medic pressed another towel to the battered fighter's face. "Worry about your job, let me worry about mine." He dropped the bloody towel into the bucket and scowled at Carl. "Last towel, boss man. What now?"

"Let's get him back to the locker room," Carl said. "Tex, lead the way."

With music and false applause blaring, Team Phoenix Force crossed the black bridge, purple lightning crackling at their feet. Carl stayed in the back, with his hands on Agbeko's sweaty shoulders. He didn't want his friend to stumble off the bridge.

By the time they reached the track, the Russian team had already topped the ramp and stood beneath the red bunting, ready to start the next bout. At their center towered Fighter 32. The red triangle tattoo shone brightly on his pale flesh. Beneath the bony ridge of his low brow, his dark eyes flicked toward Agbeko and then, seeing nothing of consequence, focused once more with burning purpose on the octagon. He banged his huge fists together.

Confidence, Carl thought. *Real confidence.* And then, the truth: *Agbeko wouldn't stand a chance against him, even before what just happened.*

"Step aside," Tex said to no one in particular. "Winner coming through."

Winner, Carl thought. *If that was winning . . .*

Kruger stopped them just before the ramp. "One moment, please."

"Not now, Kruger," Carl said. "I have to get my fighter into the locker room."

Kruger frowned. "This will only take a moment, sir."

"He's bleeding," Davis said.

"Not a problem," Kruger said. "I'll have someone mop it up."

Davis scowled. "That's not the point. We—"

The music stopped, and the coldly beautiful announcer said, "Ladies and gentlemen, please rise for another unexpected honor . . . the Few have returned."

Kruger stood at attention, chin held high, and his bright blue eyes twinkled up at the robed quintet in the opera box as if beholding the face of God.

Carl didn't bow with everyone else. Instead, he narrowed his eyes, bringing the opera box into tighter focus. The bearded guy, smiling, leaned from his throne and put a hand on the shoulder of the masked, blond-haired woman below him. She half turned as he spoke, and the man seated beside her threw back his head with rich laughter.

Cracking jokes while we bleed, Carl thought.

To this point in the tournament, the Few had attended only one fight—his—but he wasn't surprised to see them returning now. Fighter 32 wasn't just huge. His reputation made him the main attraction.

"Fighting out of the red corner, representing Russia," the announcer said, "Fighter 32." Standing at the edge of the bridge, the Russian raised his cesti high overhead.

"Fighting out of the blue corner, representing Zurkistan," the announcer said, "Fighter 47."

Fighter 32 had at least a foot on Z-Force's weird heavyweight, far longer arms, and supreme confidence. *Good night, Fighter 47*, Carl thought. *Sleep well.*

Private conversation and lightheartedness had ended in the opera box. The Few stared down intensely—not, to Carl's surprise, at the Russian champion . . . but at Fighter 47.

"Let's go," Davis said impatiently, and Carl realized with a wave of embarrassment that he'd hyper-focused again—it had been happening from time to time since he'd received the chip—and had been ignoring his swaying friend. He nodded to the medic and pushed his fighter gently forward without waiting for Kruger's permission.

In the locker room, Agbeko straddled a bench, and Davis went to work on the worst cut, which frowned like a red mouth over one eye.

Other teams watched, whispering among themselves.

"Hold your head still," Davis told Agbeko, who'd started that slow nodding again. "Gotta stop the bleeding." He packed gauze tubes into the wound and applied pressure with his thumbs.

Carl watched, feeling helpless. "How's the cut?"

Davis shot him a look of disbelief. "Man, are you serious? *How's the cut?*"

"Can you handle it?"

Davis shrugged, then grimaced as he pulled away the packing

and a fresh stream of blood flowed out. "I'll do what I can. He needs stitches. Lots of them."

Carl watched, thinking, *How would anyone survive this tournament?*

Pointing to the med kit, Davis told Tex, "Hand me that salve. Nah, not that. The yellow one, the coagulant."

Tex cursed, pawing through the supplies. Carl joined in, happy for something to do but not seeing the clotter.

"*Ei*," someone said, and Carl looked up to see one of the cool Brazilian jujitsu guys pulling a yellow canister from their kit. "*Este?*"

Davis nodded. "That's it, baby. Thank you." He clapped his bloody hands, and the Brazilian guy tossed the salve.

Carl nodded. Good guys. Good fighters, too: 2–0, so far.

Out in the arena, the volcano erupted with applause.

"The Red Triangle strikes again," someone said across the room. "First-round knockout."

Moments later, the doors at the top of the ramp banged open, and the Russians hurried into the room, carrying the massive fighter between them, their faces twisted with strain and panic. The lightweight shouted. The middleweight wept. All color had fled the face of the old trainer, who stared down at his champion with a look of stunned disbelief.

Fighter 32 stared back with empty eyes and an open mouth, his head tilted at a nightmare angle.

THIRTEEN

CARL STOOD IN SILENCE among the fighters gathered upon the shore of black sand. The inky surface of the lake winked with torchlight. The arena and upper floors were utterly dark. After twelve bloody hours, the first round of fights was finished. Now the sconces along the glistening stone walls guttered around the lake, dimming everything to gloom.

"Warriors." The voice, inhumanly deep, spoke from all directions. Carl recognized it at once: the bearded man. "The Few salute your valor . . . and value your sacrifice."

Light shone down from above. Carl looked up and saw a giant television screen glowing fifty feet overhead. *It's underneath the octagon*, he realized.

On the screen fluttered a simple flag of three bars: white, blue, and red. Music started then, a national anthem that Carl found stirring despite the foreign lyrics.

"We honor Fighter 32," the voice said, and on-screen the flag vanished, replaced by the scowling face of the Russian heavyweight. "May we all die such an honorable death."

Honorable? Carl thought. He'd seen the fight on replay, during the hours between the tournament and Kruger's summoning them here. There had been no particular honor to the death. Just one guy suplexing the other headfirst into the floor. The only thing you could really call it was *quick*.

"Russia," the voice of the Few said, "has lost a hero."

Someone nearer the water started sobbing.

A hollow thump drew Carl's attention left, to the far end of the lake, where shimmered a ghostly white square—an illuminated doorway in the cave wall, he realized—and a boat trundled forth from the light, slid down a short ramp, and splashed into the dark water. The music played on, and the vessel—it was a sailboat, Carl saw now, with a Russian flag serving as the sail—drifted slowly out onto the lake. Carl saw no one on board, just a dark shape, maybe seven feet long at the center.

That's him, he realized. *That's Fighter 32, wrapped in some kind of shroud.*

He heard a faint creaking sound—the taut straining of whatever hidden towrope was dragging the boat—and that noise triggered the awful memory of another funeral, ropes creaking as his mother's casket was lowered into the grave years earlier. His throat tightened as he remembered that day, remembered the breeze and the sound of the droning preacher, and how hard he'd fought the tears and how he'd cried anyway and how angry he'd been at himself for crying. So absurd now, but true—he'd been furious at himself for giving in and crying, as if he'd let his mother down rather than paying her the only tribute he had left.

The boat stopped at the center of the lake, directly in front of them. Something huffed, and flames leapt up on the deck, encircling the shrouded figure.

For a second, he assumed something had malfunctioned and caught fire, but then he understood. This was no accident. The burning boat was a pyre. Feeling stunned and disgusted, he remembered another of Stark's history lessons. *They're giving Fighter 32 a Viking burial.*

Near the water, sobbing became wailing.

Flames raced across the deck and up the sail, engulfing the entire boat, which glowed blindingly bright at the heart of the gloom.

Averting his eyes, Carl saw a strange sight. Along the opposite shore stood several large black birds, as hunched and gloomily attentive as funeral mourners.

Weird, Carl thought. Though not so weird as the knowledge that a fighter he'd seen earlier this same day, very much alive, was now burning at the center of the lake.

The fire burned fast and hard, the shape at its center growing indistinct, and then the boat was coming apart. The mast tilted and fell in a line of fluttering flame.

Carl could smell it now, and thankfully, he smelled only smoke and nothing else. *Nothing cooking*, he thought, and his stomach gave a slow roll of revulsion.

Poor guy never expected this, he thought, remembering how huge and strong and confident Fighter 32 had looked, walking toward the ring.

Then Arthur James's voice cooed in his head, *Ain't no guarantees in fighting, son.*

The boat sunk slowly, the flames hanging on feebly like the final breaths of a dying man. Overhead, the TV screen, still bearing the snarling image of Fighter 32, faded to black.

Around him, the crowd started breaking apart. Some teams talked as they left, and that didn't seem right to Carl, and when he felt his team looking at him, waiting for his signal, he decided to stand right there until the last flame went out, his own meager tribute to a real person, someone who had been and no longer was, a fighter whose charred and broken bones would lie at the bottom of this dark lake forever.

Someone bumped into him, jolting him from his thoughts. It

wasn't until after she'd offered a quiet apology that he realized she had dipped her hand into his jacket.

A life spent around criminals brought him instantly alert. Had she just pickpocketed him? Before he could calculate the absurdity of that worry—he had no possessions here, not even a room key—his hand closed on the folded piece of paper she'd left in his pocket.

Half turning, he saw her walking away under the arm of a dark-haired fighter.

Juliet.

He pulled the folded paper from his pocket.

Out on the lake, the last remnants of the boat sputtered and died—but not before he read the single word written on the square of paper: *Carl*.

FOURTEEN

AN HOUR LATER, Carl paced back and forth in the kitchen.

The rebroadcast of the three-hour lightweight bout played out its bloody drama on the common-room TV. No sense scouting that one, considering the damage both guys took. Neither would be able to fight the next day.

What you should be doing, Carl told himself again, *is studying the other fights.* Thanks to the chip, reviewing memory segments was usually easy, but no matter how hard he tried, his thoughts kept coming back to the note. The chip had no emotional kill switch. He was stuck being human.

Was it really her?

"You're going to wear a hole in the floor, boss," Tex said.

"Yes, Carl," Agbeko said, a smile on his swollen face. He had recovered remarkably over the hours since his bout but still looked awful. "Please join us."

Carl paused at the edge of the dining room, where Tex and Agbeko sat, drinking sodas and passing a bag of cheese curls back and forth. Their fingertips were bright orange.

Davis's were red. He leaned over Agbeko, still working the cuts. "Keep ice on that."

Agbeko hooah-ed and raised not the ice bag, which sat melting on the table, but the Coke can to his swollen brow.

"No sense stitching them," Davis said, pinching shut and

retaping a cut alongside Agbeko's eye. "You even blink, they're going to open up again."

Tex slapped Agbeko's knee. "How about you keep your hands up next time, huh?"

Agbeko chuckled. "That is good advice. Carl, why did you not give me this advice?"

Carl forced a smile, feeling like he might explode. He needed to prep for the upcoming fights but just wanted to fast-forward the clock to midnight.

"Laugh it up," Davis said. He'd fastened the cut with butterfly bandages and wiped at the yellow goop oozing out between them. "Keep taking punches, you'll lose an eye. Or worse."

Nobody asked what he meant. They didn't have to. For a moment, they were as silent as they had been at the lake, watching the pillar of flame burn upon the oil-black water.

Then she bumped into me, Carl thought, and remembered her hand in his pocket, there and gone, like the girl herself.

Stop, he told himself again. *Push her out of your head for now. Prepare for tomorrow.*

"Lighten up, doc," Tex said, plunging a hand into the cheese curls. "These guys won, remember?"

Nodding toward Carl, Davis said, "He won." Then, looking at Agbeko, "Him, I'm not so sure."

Agbeko, suddenly angry, pushed the medic's hands away. "Why do you say this? Of course I won. Winning is my mission."

Davis stepped back. "Be cool, baby. I'm just saying, you took some shots, you feel me?"

Tex said, "Yeah, your eye's so swelled up, we could blindfold you with dental floss."

Agbeko ignored this and continued glaring at Davis, who

said, "Tomorrow, some other two-ton tough guy's gonna try and take off your head. You ready for that?"

Agbeko came out of his chair. "Are you saying I will quit?"

Carl stepped between them and put a restraining hand on the hulking boy-soldier's chest. He really didn't feel like dealing with this now. Duty and distraction were already playing tug-of-war with his brain. "Enough."

Agbeko glared at Davis but didn't resist Carl. "I will never surrender."

"That's your whole problem," Davis said. "You don't know when to quit. What, didn't you see the funeral?"

Agbeko's voice went low and dangerous. "I am not afraid to die."

"That's it," Carl said. "Sit down, Agbeko. And you, Davis, just drop it."

Davis nodded knowingly, regarding him through hooded eyes. "Anything for the win, right, boss man?"

Carl's face went hot. "What do you mean by that?"

"Nothing," Davis said. "Nothing at all." No apology in his voice. No fear, either.

For a second, they just stared at each other, Carl struggling against his temper, Davis looking down from his great height with loathing and something else . . . contempt, perhaps, or maybe disgust.

Seconds passed.

Then Tex cracked a joke about some guy walking into a room with a sheep in his arms. Everybody laughed, and the tense moment passed. The others went back to their cheese curls and sodas, and Carl retired to his room, determined to clear his head and study fighters until midnight.

It didn't work.

He turned on his TV, then turned up the volume, trying and failing to block out the noise in the common room.

The replay of the long fight finally staggered to its inglorious finish, and the first pair of middleweights—one of whom could be his future opponent—came into the ring.

Focus, he told himself. *Watch now, review the important stuff later.* He needed to learn his opponents' strengths and weaknesses, their traps and techniques, their habits and preferences.

Both middleweights were Asian. The similarities ended there. One Korean, the other Thai. The Korean relied heavily on his kicks, which were very fast—even flashy. The Thai sported a balanced attack, mixing hands and feet with knees and elbows. His kicks were slower, but he turned his hips into them, landing not with his feet but with his shins, targeting the Korean's legs and rib cage.

Beyond the door, Tex shouted, "I told that old boy he could keep his fifty thousand dollars!" and the kitchen erupted with laughter.

Using the chip, Carl dialed down their distracting clamor, but this dialed down his TV, too, making the real problem—his wandering mind—even more obvious. He couldn't stop thinking about Octavia.

The last time he'd seen her, she had been a ruined shell of a girl with empty eyes and unspeakable wounds. While he'd been in a coma, awaiting the operation, Dr. Vispera had tortured her into a catatonic state. Then Carl had surrendered his own freedom so that she might leave the island, receive medical treatment on the mainland, and one day start her life over, free in the world.

How had she gotten here? Why the disguise?

Juliet looked nothing like Octavia. It wasn't just the surface stuff—her pallor, brown eyes, and the length and color of her hair—but her actual face, too, the shape of it, her nose and cheekbones, her lips, everything. Octavia's face had been beautiful in a sweet, soulful way. This new face was still pretty but in a different way. Older, harder.

And yet hadn't he sensed a faint familiarity, something in the way she moved? Yes, he had. Besides, only Octavia could have written that note. But what was she doing here?

Was she working for Stark?

With a ripple of jealousy, he wondered, *And who is Romeo?*

Her boyfriend. That much was obvious, the way they hung all over each other. He represented Phoenix Force's Mexican camp. What was going on?

He unfolded the note, rereading the message inside.

> Dear Carl,
>   I can't believe it's really you. I barely recognized you; you've grown so much. We have so much to talk about.
>   Tell no one about this or about me, okay? Not your team, not the guy I'm with. We have to pretend we don't know each other. It's very important—life and death.
>   Meet me here, where I gave you this. Tonight—at midnight.

She hadn't signed it and hadn't needed to. The handwriting was hers—and he remembered the note she'd given him back on Phoenix Island, which still lay atop the dusty ductwork in the book man's room, next to the fading journal of Eric Flemmington.

Tonight at midnight . . .

What if it was a trap? What if she wasn't really Octavia? Had Stark sent some imposter to test his loyalty?

Cheering surged on TV.

Carl shook free of his thoughts to see the Korean crumpled on the mat, the Thai with his bloody fists raised overhead.

He'd missed it. He'd started thinking about Octavia again, and he'd missed the fight, and now he couldn't study the Thai kickboxer. What if he fought him next?

Get it together, he told himself. *Focus on the fights. You can't count on your teammates to win. It's all on you. You have to win.* Not everyone was going to drop like Gooder-than-I-think. These guys were dangerous. He saw now that the kickboxer had broken his opponent's leg, but Carl had missed the technique, along with any setup or feint. Even the smallest tell—the dip of a shoulder or a habit of the eyes—would be valuable. . . .

But not as valuable as Octavia.

Could it really be her?

It didn't seem possible . . . but the note had used her handwriting and his name—Carl, not Fighter 19—so who else could it be?

No one.

Unless . . .

On TV, the next set of guys he was supposed to be studying entered the ring.

Pay attention.

Out in the kitchen, more laughter. He heard the *dink-dink-dink* of an empty can hitting the tiled floor. Even more laughter.

He and Octavia used to laugh all the time.

Enough, he told himself, and turned off the TV. He needed to study the fighters but couldn't, not like this. A glance at the clock told him he had an hour and a half before he needed to leave for the lake.

Time to dim down, then. It would mean missing an hour's worth of fight footage, but so be it. He wasn't able to concentrate now anyway. After an hour of reordering "sleep," he would be able to focus.

Leaning back against his headboard, he slowed his blood circulation and respiration until his heart barely beat and his lungs hardly cycled. Consciousness dimmed, but his mind's eye still pictured his gray-eyed friend.

He tried to dim deeper, but his mind pictured Octavia laughing.

What was this? He'd never before failed at inducing this meditative sleep. He had to get his act together, had to rest so that he could study these fighters.

But then, instead of sliding into unconsciousness, his mind leapt to an incredible realization that brought him instantly to full wakefulness.

The last six months, he'd been playing the part of the faithful apprentice, biding his time so that he might overthrow Stark.

The real reason he had endured this apprenticeship, however, was to keep Octavia safe.

If the girl he was about to meet really was Octavia, he didn't have to study the fighters. He didn't even have to fight. They could run away from this place together. Tonight.

He hopped up and started pacing again.

They could head back to the world and start over, fresh and free. He could place anonymous phone calls and let somebody else deal with Stark. He could make money fighting, and he knew guys in Philly who could get them fake IDs, social security numbers, everything. A new life . . .

Back and forth he paced, envisioning this incredible possibility, until the clock read 11:45.

Time to go, he thought, *time to see Octavia*, and his heart gave an excited flutter. It wasn't one of those romantic lilts you got when you saw someone you liked. Back on Phoenix Island, they had been very close, and he had really liked her, but she had never been his girlfriend. They hadn't even kissed. All of that was still in him, somewhere—and who knew, over time, if maybe they could get together like that—but for now, the flutter in his chest was simpler than romance. He was about to see his favorite person in the world, a girl he'd feared he would never see again.

He went to his window to check the arena, pulled the curtain aside, and jumped back, startled.

Then he laughed and lowered his fists.

A Krebs hawk sat on his windowsill, staring in at him. It had the size and muscular build of a seagull but a shorter neck and a bigger head, like a crow, and its feathers were ash gray streaked in charcoal. *Volcano camouflage*, Carl thought with a smile, still feeling stupid for getting startled like that.

The bird tilted its head and stared, studying him, then flew away.

Carl laughed and went to the window, where he caught one wide arc of the fleeing bird's looping ascent before it disappeared into the upper darkness. Down below, the arena was dim and empty.

Good. Time to go.

FIFTEEN

AT TEN TILL MIDNIGHT, Carl left his room and stepped into the
noise and flashing light of the common room. Tex sat at the center of the couch with his feet up on the coffee table and his arms
spread out behind him, laughing at some stupid movie with girls
skiing in bikinis. The area around him, strewn with soda cans and
chip bags and candy wrappers, looked like a murder scene—if the
victim was a vending machine.

Tex said, "Checking up on me, hoss? Think maybe I ordered
a case of Budweiser?"

On TV, a couple of grinning dorks raised their brows and
skied after the girls.

"No, I'm going to see if they've posted tomorrow's matchups," Carl said, doing his best to sound casual.

"Suit yourself," Tex said. "Old Tex is going to sit here and
watch the rest of *Snow Bunny Bungalow*." He picked up a sack
of M&M's and tilted a rainbow of candy into his mouth.

"Have fun," Carl said. Stupid move, pounding junk before a
fight, but it didn't really matter how Tex prepped. He was meat.
Fighting spirit wasn't enough. He didn't belong here.

Neither did Agbeko.

Carl had fooled himself for a while, thinking maybe Agbeko
could help bring home the team title, but after today, he knew that
the big heavyweight, despite his strength and heart, couldn't last.

That's why you got so mad at Davis, Carl told himself. *Because you knew he was right.*

But not about that *anything for a win* crap. If Agbeko got into real trouble, Carl would throw in the towel.

Carl stepped from the apartment into the sweet-scented hallway and forgot all about the rest of his team.

This was it.

By the time he reached the elevator, his heart was jackhammering, and he was sweating like a seventh-grader on his first date. He dialed back his heart rate and temperature and felt better at once, though the underlying anxiety remained. Was it really Octavia?

He pressed the *L* button, and a moment later, the doors opened, revealing the vast gloomy space that was the subterranean lake and its beach of black sand. Torches flickered along the rock walls, creating an eerie twilight in this broad and vaulted cavern. With his heart pounding again, he stepped from the elevator.

The beach was empty.

He half expected Stark to come rising up out of the lake.

But there was no one. She hadn't come.

He shivered as an emotional iceberg, huge and indistinct, drifted through his inner darkness. Disappointment came first, cutting through his excitement, but following after was a most unexpected emotion: relief. Why would he feel relief at not seeing Octavia?

Because none of this makes sense, he thought. *Because she can't really be here, and you've known that all along, and this is what it feels like when reality slides back into place.*

Once again, his old enemy hope had sucker punched him. . . .

"Carl?"

He jumped at the voice and turned.

Dressed in black warm-ups embroidered with a green snake, she stepped from the deeper shadows between two torches along the near wall. She looked nothing like Octavia. Her eyes were dark, not gray; her skin was pale, not tanned; and her hair was light, not dark—no trace of white in the bangs—and a long blond braid draped like a serpent across her shoulder. None of these things fooled him any longer.

It was her.

Despite her disguise, he recognized her lean body, the shape of her legs and hips, the bend in her arms, the springy way she rode atop the balls of her feet, and the slight angle at which she held her head. Even more powerfully, in the microsecond that their eyes met, he could *feel* that it was her, a heady sensation that had nothing to do with the chip and everything to do with him, with her, with *them*—as if electrical energy had arced between them.

Octavia.

He tried to speak, tried to say her name, but couldn't seem to make his throat and mouth work.

She stopped a few feet away, smiling.

He smiled back at her.

And there they stood, close enough to touch, both of them smiling yet waiting for something, locked in a strange paralysis he had never anticipated during countless hours spent dreaming of their reunion.

"It's really you, isn't it," she said, and it was more of a statement than a question. "I could feel you coming down in the elevator. Oh, Carl—it really is you."

He nodded, feeling stupid and stunned and happy. "Yeah, I'm really me."

She exhaled laughter then—a kind of a breaking sound in her

voice—and for a second, Carl thought she was going to cry, and he hoped she wouldn't, because if she did, he might start up, too, as strange as that would be.

"And you're really you? You're really Octavia?"

She nodded.

"But you don't look like you," he said. "How—"

"Plastic surgery," she said. "I needed a lot of work after what Vispera did to me, and they asked if I wanted a fresh start. A new identity, a new life, and a new face. I told them yes."

"But your eyes . . ."

"Colored contacts," she said, then smoothed a hand over her long blond braid. "Hair dye and extensions."

"I don't care what you look like," he said. "I'm just glad you're okay." He reached out, and she slid her hands into his, and they stood there laughing and looking at each other.

"When I saw you in the Chop Shop," she said, and paused, as if to gather courage. "I thought you were dead. Even later, when I knew you weren't, it didn't seem possible that you could survive. But I never gave up, Carl. I kept telling myself that you were tough and that you would make it, and I could *feel* you out in the world, and here you are. . . ."

Her voice broke, and he pulled her into an embrace.

She stiffened in his arms. She didn't fight the hug or push him away, but she went rigid and did not hug him back.

This was a surprise. What was wrong with her? Was it Romeo? Maybe this felt wrong to her, like cheating or something, rather than old friends reuniting.

Whatever the case, he broke the hug and stepped back.

She looked at him. "What are you doing here, Carl?"

The question took him by surprise. "You told me to meet you here."

She shook her head. "I mean *here*—the Funeral Games."

"Fighting," he said, thinking, *obviously*. "What are *you* doing here?"

She hesitated—and in that pause, he felt the distance she was for some unknown reason tending, like a fighter controlling the gap.

An unexpected wave of annoyance rolled over him. Why was she being like this? Then he noticed her hands. Even in this dim light, he could see the polka-dot scars where Vispera had burned her.

He touched one of these gently, and she flinched, pulling her hand away as if the wounds were still fresh. A kind of wildness sparked in her eyes, there and gone, fast as a muzzle flash.

"Sorry," he said. "I— Octavia, what happened to you?"

She looked down at the black sand between them. "Months ago, I woke up in a Mexican hospital. No idea how I got there or how long I'd been . . . *asleep* . . . but there I was, skinny and pale and covered in scars, lying next to this pile of crazy drawings, and there was some guy in a suit sitting beside my bed, and—well, I really can't talk about that. Not now, anyway."

Trying to picture it, Carl said, "The suit, was that your boyfriend?"

She looked at him for a second as if she didn't understand, then shook her head. "Don't ask me about him. I can't talk about him or what we're doing. And please, whatever you do, pretend you don't know me, okay? He can't know. Carl, don't make a face. This is serious. I mean it. Please, whatever you do, don't let on that you and I know each other. All right?"

Carl nodded—but then a thought hit him. "Wait . . . Does he hurt you?" His knuckles throbbed at the thought of some jealous head case slapping Octavia. He would kill the guy. . . .

"No," she said, and shook her head emphatically. "Nothing like that. I'm sorry, Carl, but I really can't talk about him. I'll tell you more later, but for now you're just going to have to trust me, and please, please, please don't tell anyone about any of this."

Another wave of annoyance. "Well, if you can't say anything, and I can't ask questions, and we have to pretend we don't know each other, why bring me down here in the first place?"

She pulled back a little, looking hurt. "Why would you even ask me that? I *had* to see you." She stood a little straighter. "I would have said something sooner, but . . ."

He frowned. "Sooner? How long have you known that I was here?"

She spoke quietly. "Since the train."

"And you didn't—"

"You have to understand," she said. "I didn't know if you were *you* anymore."

He laughed bitterly. "Who else would I be?"

Now it was her turn to frown. "You don't look like you. You're so tall and big now."

He shrugged, implying the obvious: *people grow*.

"Then I saw Davis and that huge Phoenix Forcer." She looked away, shaking her head, as if remembering the moment. "I thought maybe Stark was forcing you to fight, and these guys were escorting you, like guards or whatever, but then I realized— you were *leading* them." Now she looked straight into his eyes. "Phoenix Force *hunted* us, Carl. Don't you remember?"

"How could I forget?" he said. "But a lot has happened since then."

"Back on the island," she said, "I knew they might kill you, but I also knew they could never *break* you, never make you one of them. I truly believed in my heart that nothing in the world could make you stop fighting them—but now you're what, the team captain?"

Her voice echoed off the stones.

"Keep it down," he said. "You want guards to come down here, check out the noise?"

She tilted her head, as if to study him from a fresh angle. "What happened to you, Carl?"

"Lots of stuff, but not what you seem to think." Who was she to interrogate him? He'd surrendered his freedom and suffered under Stark just to keep her safe. "I didn't sell my soul."

She raised her hands. "Look, you're mad. . . . I get it. I was scared, Carl. I didn't know what to think, so I decided to wait and watch. I'd probably still be waiting if that guy hadn't died today. Then I had to say something. I had to warn you."

"I can take care of myself."

"Come on," she said, and surprised him by taking his hand.

Part of him wanted to pull away and have this out—but most of him just loved the feel of her hand. Funny how something so simple as touch could defuse anger. They started walking around the lake.

"I need to show you something," she said. "I discovered this place—well, my friend did, and he showed me—but we didn't know what it was until the funeral."

Her friend, Carl thought, bitterness seeping in again. *The mysterious Romeo. Save your questions till the end, children.* He was overjoyed to see her, but she was being so strange and secretive, and her presence here made zero sense. The horrible thought returned to him: Was she working for Stark? Had they brainwashed her, turned her into some type of test?

An absurd thought, of course. He only wished he had a better explanation.

"It's right around here," she said, when they reached the far end of the lake. She led him up the boat ramp to the huge opening in the wall. She pulled him across the threshold, and automatic lights snapped to life, illuminating the immense chamber.

"Whoa," he said.

Dozens of sailboats filled the chamber. They stood in three neat rows separated by conveyor belts that led to the ramp. Each vessel was identical to the one they had watched burn, with one exception: the sails. He saw many flags represented, including at least three Stars-and-Stripes sails. Taken together, the fleet made a profoundly strange sight here at the bottom of this volcanic mountain tucked away from the world.

"Do you see?" she asked.

He shrugged. "I see a lot of boats."

"Look," she said, pointing.

He tracked her arm to the far aisle, where a red phoenix burned brightly against black sailcloth.

"Okay," he said. "A Phoenix Island sail. So what?"

"Correction. Three Phoenix Island sails. Three boats, three fighters," she said. "Don't you get it, Carl? They're prepared to burn *everybody*."

He stared out at the boats, which sat in silence, waiting for their shattered cargo, waiting to burn. Then he turned to her, forcing a smile. "Not us, Octavia. We're not going to burn."

"I know you're a great fighter, but this isn't a boxing tournament."

He shook his head. "I don't need to fight. I came here to win this thing—for *you*. This changes everything. *You* change everything."

She looked puzzled, almost afraid. "You came here to win this for *me*?"

"I did." And he laughed, realizing how crazy this must all sound to her. "I thought if I could win . . . It's a long story—and it doesn't matter. Not anymore. Octavia, this is it. Don't you see? We can run. We can get out of here together—now—and start over."

She was shaking her head.

"Listen," he said. "We'll bundle up, pack a bunch of food and stuff, and walk out the train tracks. It'll be hard, but we'll make it. I promise."

Her mouth opened slightly, and her eyes looked very sad. "Oh," she said, and lifted her hand halfway to him—then let it drop. "Oh, Carl . . . No, I can't do that. Not now. I can't."

"Can't?" He pictured handsome Romeo with his black hair and white smile. "Or won't?"

"Later, Carl. I promise. We'll get out of here together, but I can't run now. I'm into something here. Something huge. If I left now—" A little tremor went through her, and she gritted her teeth, as if stopping herself from saying more required physical rather than psychological effort. "You just have to trust me."

And in that moment, he realized he didn't. It was strange, not trusting her. "You've been asking a lot of questions about me, but I have to say . . . you don't seem like the girl I knew back on Phoenix Island."

"I'm not," she said, and her eyes looked sadder than ever. "I'm not that girl anymore."

He turned and walked away, down the ramp and onto the midnight beach with its torchlight and its black sand still furrowed in the footprints of funeral goers, striding away from the girl who was no longer the girl for whom he'd suffered these long months.

"I know about the chip," she said behind him.

It stopped him. He turned.

"What?"

"I know about the chip," she repeated. "And I know people who can help you."

"Wait . . . how do you—"

They both turned as the elevator doors opened.

"Well, well, well," Tex said, strutting onto the beach with a huge smile on his face. "My roomie the Blue Falcon."

No, Carl thought. *Why? Why now? And why Tex, of all people?*

Octavia stepped away and stood there, smiling and batting her lashes, looking from the ground to Carl and then to Tex. "*Debo dejar.*"

"What are you doing here?" Carl said.

"You didn't come back, I figured maybe you got jumped. Came down to the boards, heard somebody shouting down here," Tex said, and grinned. "You sneaky devil. Why didn't you tell me about this little *mamacita*?"

"We just met," Carl said, and faked a smile that he hoped look better than it felt.

Octavia spoke again, this time using English with an Oscar-worthy accent. "My name is *Tres*." She laughed a little and shook her head—the picture of good-natured self-deprecation—and held up three fingers. "Three. My name is Three. I go now."

"Hey, baby, don't run off," Tex said, and gyrated his hips. "How about a little fiesta?"

Octavia turned to Carl, smiling. "Was nice to meet you," she said, and hugged him.

Carl was still stunned by what Octavia had said about the chip. How did she know? What did she mean, people who could help him? He leaned into the embrace, and feeling her in his arms, he was suddenly and sharply aware that, after having spent months apart, they were separating again. Desperation rose in him. He wanted to ask when he would see her again, but Tex stood close by, leering at them. "It was nice meeting you, too," he said, and gave her a squeeze. "I hope we talk again soon."

Her lips brushed his ear and whispered, "You aren't the only one they chipped that night in the Chop Shop."

SIXTEEN

THE NEXT MORNING, Team Phoenix Force crowded around the window in Carl's room, peering out at the giant television screen, which showed not only the matchups but the tournament brackets. Agbeko had drawn a bye against an opponent too badly injured to compete—an absolute jackpot, considering the Phoenix Forcer's badly lacerated face—and their luck hadn't stopped there. Tex, whom Carl had assumed would be slaughtered in the first round, now looked like he had a shot at actually making the semifinals. His opponent, Fighter 9, was the Japanese striker who'd barely won the brutal three-hour bout, left on a stretcher, and was apparently going to fight again

Carl had drawn Fighter 46 from Zurkistan. *Good*, he thought, looking forward to showing Baca a thing or two. He was in a foul mood. He'd tried to dim down into meditative sleep, but he couldn't stop thinking about Octavia, their awkward reunion, and all the questions it had raised. What was she doing here? How had she known about his operation? And what did she mean, he wasn't the only one who'd been chipped?

Whatever she meant, she was wrong. Stark had suspended all implantations to study and learn from the first successful recipient—Carl—before continuing.

Now, tired and frustrated and angry at himself for not having studied the televised fights, he just wanted to get into the octagon, win his fight, and start over. Tonight, he would focus his mind, study the fights, and prep for the rest of the tournament.

And yet even as his team stood there, talking matchups, his eyes scanned the arena. No sign of her . . .

"I wish that I *was* fighting," Agbeko said.

"You need your head examined," Davis said.

"Of course I wish to compete," Agbeko said, and Carl knew that he meant it. "I fight for the honor of Phoenix Island."

Davis just shook his head.

"Screw honor," Tex said. He was more hyped up than ever now that he had a match.

"Why *are* you fighting, anyway?" Davis said. "What's in it for you?"

"Best things in the world," Tex said, "money and freedom. I win this, they ship me home. Clean record, fresh start, call it whatever you want, boys. Old Texarkana back in the world, free as an otter and ten million bucks in his pocket." He grinned at them, then feigned sorrow. "I'd build Mama a house, but they don't have those up in heaven, so I'll probably just buy a double-wide and a pickup, then blow the rest on strippers and booze." With this, he burst into grating laughter that made Carl feel like knocking him out.

He was imagining his right hand catching Tex behind the ear and finally shutting that big mouth, when he realized Davis had asked him something. "Huh?"

"I asked why *you're* fighting," Davis said, "What's in it for you, boss man? Promotion?"

Carl didn't feel like another go-around with this new, morally superior Davis. "Don't worry about it."

Davis snorted and shook his head. "It is, isn't it?" He laughed bitterly. "Perfect, baby, perfect. You got your head so far up Stark's—"

And then he was pinned against the wall, his shirtfront gathered in Agbeko's big fists.

"Choose your words carefully," Agbeko said, and bounced the medic off the wall.

"Take it easy, big man," Davis said.

"Commander Stark is a great man," Agbeko said. "I would die for him."

"You might get the chance," Davis said, nodding at Carl, "if the climber gets his way."

That's it, Carl thought. He pushed Agbeko out of the way and poked Davis in the chest. "Tell me something—when did you become Mr. Morality? Who are you to judge me?"

"I'm just saying it like it is, man," Davis said. "You're the Phoenix Island poster boy now. All you care about is winning, even if these cats get killed along the way."

Carl resisted the urge to slap the haughty look off Davis's face. "That's pretty ironic, coming from a guy with tattooed tears. I've been meaning to ask—where'd you get that third tear, Davis? Last I remember, you only had two. Now you show up with another one, preaching nonviolence. What's that one for, *saving* a life?"

Davis's face twisted with rage and something else—pain?—and he swung at Carl.

Carl dipped the punch easily, scooped Davis into a fireman's carry, and dumped him onto the floor. He got behind him, locked him up, and slid a forearm under his chin, ready to choke Davis out if necessary, suddenly on point with the paradoxical calm and clearheadedness that came to him whenever combat called.

"Take it back," Davis said in a trembling voice—like they were second-graders going at it on a playground or something—and Carl almost laughed, until he realized something so odd that it was scary: Davis, the hard-time gangbanger with three tattooed tears, was *crying*.

Carl was so stunned, he let him go and backed away.

Shaking badly, Davis stood, wiped tears from his face, and pointed at Carl. "You got no idea what you're talking about. You got no idea what I been through." Then he stormed out of the room.

———⸎———

Tex's opponent limped into the octagon, his entire body purple with bruising. Carl could tell by his hunched posture that his ribs were broken. When the ref called everyone to the center of the ring, Carl focused on the guy's eyes. Yes, he was in pain, and he no doubt knew the odds, but he was also clearly without fear, resigned to both the fight and his fate. Quite unexpectedly, Carl felt a wave of respect for the guy. The Japanese trainer, a hard-looking middle-aged man with a boxy head and a glass eye, gave Carl a sharp nod, his face stony, equally resigned. Carl nodded back, and then the referee told the fighters to touch gloves, the two teams separated, and the corner men left the cage.

The fight lasted less than a minute. Tex steamrolled him. It wasn't pretty, and it wasn't surprising, and Carl was ashamed, during the aftermath, when Tex circled the cage, pounding his chest and shouting, "What now? What now?"

Carl was nonetheless glad his fighter had won. With Tex and Agbeko both advancing to the semifinals, a team title—which had seemed like an absolute impossibility—wasn't entirely out of the question after all. That would guarantee his promotion.

What's in it for you, boss man? Davis's accusing voice echoed in his mind. *Promotion?*

The medic hadn't spoken since their weird fight, other than

to answer questions monosyllabically, but he'd shown up to work the corner, so Carl had let it ride.

During the break between Tex's match and Carl's, the others went upstairs to order food, but Carl went instead to the elevated bleachers to watch fights. At least that's what he told his team. In reality, he spent most of his time looking for Octavia, who never showed. It was maddening, knowing she was here, somewhere, and not being able to talk to her. He felt horrible about their train wreck of a reunion. He was upset at himself for getting angry, but his confusion lingered.

She made no sense. Here they were, against all odds, together again. They really could escape, head back to the world, blow the whistle anonymously on Phoenix Island, and start over.

Not yet, she'd said—and that had pretty much been her answer to everything. *Not yet. Later. Trust me.*

He needed to talk to her.

Down in the ring, the fights played out their bloody spectacle. Most competitors were already visibly injured when they entered, and these bouts proved even more brutal than the first round. Carl saw one lightweight poleaxed by a spinning kick to the back of the head. *Boom* and down. They carted him out, clearing the ring for the next battle, which ended with a broken leg.

When the lightweight matches were over, and the first set of middleweights—a tall Chinese guy without a mark on his face and a burly Turk with the build of a wrestler—entered the octagon, Carl headed down to the locker room to warm up. Agbeko and Tex were already there, waiting, but Davis was nowhere in sight. No surprise. Carl pretended not to notice the missing medic and got down to business.

By the time the doors atop the ramp banged open and the

voice called, "Fighter 19, on deck," Carl had a good sweat going, his mind was focused, and yes, there was Davis, clutching his med kit. Minutes later, the call came, and Team Phoenix Force ascended into the loud arena, where Kruger escorted them once again across the flashing black bridge to the octagon.

Agbeko kneaded Carl's shoulders, telling him, "Remember: you are a tiger, Carl."

Seeing Baca's cocky smile and the obvious confidence of the Z-Force middleweight, Carl cursed himself again for not studying the fights. Then he pushed his anger away. No going back and changing it now, so why beat himself up? Besides, he was ready.

It started like the first fight. The coldly beautiful announcer did her thing, and the ref called the two teams to the center of the ring, where Carl's opponent tried to stare him down and Carl just stood there, looking through him, sweating, and waiting.

"Now we will see how the teacher's pet does outside of the classroom," Baca said, and grinned at Carl.

"You really want to see," Carl said, "come on in after I knock him out, and I'll show you." *Won't take but a minute*, he'd meant to add, but then the ref told them to touch gloves, and the Z-Force middleweight swung his fists, intentionally missing Carl's cesti and smashing his forearms.

Carl shouted and surged forward, smelling ashes, and the teams collided in a shouting tangle of arms, everyone pushing and shoving and hollering until the trainers dragged their fighters to opposite sides. "I'm going to kill him," Carl said. "You see that cheap shot?"

Tex slapped his back. "Smash his face in, buddy."

"Relax, my brother," Agbeko said. "Use your mind. They have goaded you into anger."

Davis tapped Carl's shoulder.

Carl snapped around. "What?"

"Open," Davis said, and shoved the mouth guard into place.

Tex held up a water bottle and raised his eyebrows.

Carl shook his head, bit down on the mouthpiece, and drew air through his nostrils, savoring the ashes of rage. His dark twin cheered. Faintly, some part of his mind fretted, telling him to remember Sanderson—but Carl thought, *Screw Sanderson*.

He was going to wreck this punk. Rocking back and forth, he ripped a furious combination, urging the bell to ring.

But then the announcer said, "Ladies and gentlemen, please rise. The Few have entered the arena."

Carl glanced toward the opera box, where the purple-robed, golden-masked bloodmongers were taking their seats. *Great*, he thought. *This time, I'll give them a show*. He didn't bother to face them or bow or any of that nonsense. He just stared across the ring and knocked his leather cesti together. His forearms throbbed, already swelling from the sneak attack. He dialed the discomfort away, leaving only the pain he could never dim: the throbbing in his knuckles.

The beast within him snapped its jaws and surged against the frail bars of its cage.

The bell rang, and he raced across the ring into a world that downshifted into slow motion. The Zurkistani shot for Carl's legs. Carl swiveled easily aside then waited, smiling as the Z-Forcer regained his feet and rushed again, his fists raised in a high peekaboo guard.

Carl flicked out two jabs, not blasting through the high guard but instead drilling his cesti straight into the Zurkistani's forearms—*crack-crack*—and the punk jerked with pain and skittered away. Carl cut him off at an angle, trapping him against the cage, dipped under a pitiful one-two, and bolo-ed crushing hooks into the guy's ribs.

The Zurkistani winced, dropping his cheap-shot hands to guard his broken ribs. Carl rocked back, creating the proper distance to launch a barrage of punches that would pound the Z-Forcer to mush—but the voice of reason whispered in his mind, cajoling his rage. *Why let him off the hook? Let the punk humiliate himself. Make him tap out and live with the shame forever.* He leaned over his hunched opponent. "Tap or I hit you again. Your choice."

"Carl!" someone yelled, and Carl's rapidly firing mind realized it was Baca, breaking the rules again, saying Carl's name, his *real* name, publicly this time, shouting it, and he heard the magnified echo—*Carl!*—blasting from the speakers for everybody in the whole arena to hear. All of this came to him in a flash of shock and anger, and in that second, the Zurkistani middleweight launched the attack he'd been planning.

Unlike Carl, Z-Force *had* studied the previous night's fights and therefore anticipated—and trained for—Carl's *tap-or-else* ultimatum. The Zurkistani middleweight had surged forward with a stomping kick aimed at Carl's knee.

Thanks to the superhuman reflexes the chip gave him, Carl moved his knee just in time, and his opponent's heel slammed down not on this crucial joint but on his foot instead. He felt his big toe break.

The beast within Carl reared its head and roared.

Unhinged with rage, Carl launched his counterattack, a crushing hook that walloped the guy's skull right behind the ear—*thock!*—and the Zurkistani dropped. He didn't try to break his fall, didn't shout, didn't even convulse, just collapsed into a flaccid pile and lay there, still as death.

SEVENTEEN

OCTAVIA RETURNED TO HER ROOM with great news and a bad headache, and found their gray-haired steward, Valdez, in the hall, talking with Julio, who leaned against the doorjamb.

"Sorry," Julio said. "I won't make the mistake again."

"I'm certain you won't, sir," the steward said. Then, seeing Octavia, he gave a nod and stepped aside so she might enter the apartment. He glanced at his watch and said, "Lakeside services in just under two hours."

Julio said they would be there and reached out to shake Valdez's hand.

"Very good, sir," Valdez said, and then excused himself with a polite bow.

Julio closed the door and sighed. His face was badly bruised, and he looked exhausted. As if fighting back-to-back matches wasn't tiring enough, he'd spent his nights snooping rather than sleeping. He was very dedicated, very brave, and she'd never heard him complain. He had a good sense of humor, too, and despite her early fears—looking back, she realized just how irritable she'd grown during their seemingly endless travel—he had proven a perfect gentleman. In public, he still hugged her, draped an arm over her shoulders, or kissed the top of her head, but in private, he gave her space. He was merely one more actor, playing a role.

He motioned, and she followed him into the dining room.

"What was that all about?" she asked, feigning more interest than she felt. She was so excited to share her big news.

"Got caught on one of the restricted floors," he said, and dropped into a chair.

"What?" she said, shocked.

"I had to try," he said. "I've checked all the lower levels."

Directly after every Funeral Games, the Few blew up the venue, eliminating any forensic evidence. SI3 wanted Julio to find and deactivate these explosives. By the time the Few discovered this sabotage, Octavia and Julio would already have passed beyond the local sat-jammers, escaped the faraday-shielded buses, and fled into the wilderness, allowing agency satellites to pick up their signal. Crossman didn't expect to capture the Few, but he hoped SI3 would arrive in time to secure the Cauldron before the Few could reactivate the explosives.

"Tell me what happened," she said. "Did you find anything?"

"Do me a favor and sit down first," he said with a weary smile. "I'm getting tired just watching you stand there."

She took the seat across from him. "Happy?"

"Ecstatic," he said. "After the fight, when you went to the bleachers, I got on the elevator and pushed the wrong button."

"One with a red *X*?"

"Good guess," he said. "When the doors opened, I was staring at a submachine gun."

"Holy crap," she said. "What did you do?"

He grinned. "Put my hands up."

"Dork," she said, and slapped his shoulder.

He winced.

"Oh—sorry," she said. He'd just fought a knock-down-drag-out fight a few hours ago. What a nightmare it had been, trying to stanch his bleeding. Feeling stupid for slapping him, she rubbed his arm. He was as hard as sculpted marble. "So what did you really do?"

"I pretended to be punch drunk from the match," he said. "Asked the guy was this where they made the food. He gave me the stink eye and motioned with his rifle, and I got out of there."

"If they're watching the elevators," she said, "how do we investigate the restricted levels?"

He propped his elbows on the table and lowered his face into his hands. "I don't know."

"You need sleep, Julio."

He lifted his face, looking more fatigued than ever. One of the bandages had come loose and hung from his high cheekbone. "I don't have time for sleep."

She reached up and gently reattached the bandage, covering the cut there.

He smiled with surprise.

Oh, crap, she thought. Unaware of the malfunctioning bandage, he'd mistaken her handiwork for tenderness—maybe even an affectionate caress. *Set him straight, or let it go?* Considering his battered face and exhaustion, she decided to let him think what he wanted. She'd just have to be more careful moving ahead.

She didn't want to give him any false signals, but she did care for him, or at least *about* him . . . which made her big news ten times better. "I have something that will perk you up," she said, unzipping her jacket. "Ready?"

He grinned slyly. "Oh, I've been ready."

Grand, she thought, realizing her mistake. *So much for being careful.* Pulling the paper from her Windbreaker and unfolding it on the table between them, she said, "Meet Lady Number One."

His jaw dropped as he studied the intricate sketch, which depicted the face of a beautiful woman with angular features and intense eyes. "Amazing. It's really one of the Few?"

She nodded and couldn't help but laugh. After all that had gone wrong in her life, after all the injustice and suffering, it felt *awesome* to have succeeded.

He sat up straighter, suddenly fully awake. "The blond one?"

She nodded again. "I waited in the bleachers until they called the Phoenix Force guy, and then the Few showed up. It was tough at first, tuning in." Of course, she wasn't going to confess *why* it had been so difficult. She couldn't let him know about Carl. Things would be safer for both of them that way.

He grabbed her hand and squeezed. "Tough or not, you did it."

"Not in one shot, though," she said. "The fight ended too quickly, and the Few left the arena, so I had to hang around until the announcer called for the scary heavyweight, the one like a gorilla?"

"Zurkistan," he said. "They like that guy, too."

"Apparently," she said, "because they came back, and I was able to finish the sketch. It was incredible!" She slapped the table, remembering the strange rush that always accompanied successful mapping.

"Did you puke on anybody?" he asked, giving her half a smile.

"Of course not," she said, feigning offense. "I reserve my vomit for special people."

"I'm honored. How's your head?"

"Okay," she said. In truth, it felt like someone was drilling a hole into the top of her skull, but she'd endured worse. Far worse. "I'm getting better, stronger."

He shook his head in approving disbelief. "You're incredible."

"Thank you," she said, and gave a little bow.

He folded up the sketch and handed it to her. "Now hide this. Anybody finds it, we're never going home."

"I'll keep it safe," she said. "Crossman's going to flip."

"He might even smile," he said.

"I wouldn't put any money on it," she said.

"Who cares?" he said. "Thanks to you, SI3 will ID Blondie in about five minutes."

"And if Crossman's right," she said, "the Few will attend all of the remaining fights."

"Exactly," he said, and his bright smile was very handsome. "Which means you'll be able to map the rest of them."

"Which also means," she said, coming to the point she'd been wanting to share, "that you don't have to fight tomorrow." Plan A had always been mapping the Few, but in case she failed, Julio had to win, initiating Plan B. Each champion—and a guest—attended a victory dinner with the Few. At such close range, she couldn't sketch but would easily map—and remember—their faces, which she would later detail to the SI3 version of a police sketch artist.

Julio's face twisted with confusion. "What are you talking about?"

"I have all day tomorrow and the finals to ID the other four members of the Few, *whether you win or lose*," she explained, waiting for him to get it. Guys could be so thick sometimes—especially if they set their heads on something. "This means you don't have to fight him."

Him was Fighter 2, the Chinese martial artist who'd killed his opponent in the ring today. The brackets had pitted Julio against this wrecking machine, with the winner facing the winner of the bracket's other side . . . Carl. She didn't know what to think about her old friend—he had changed *so* much—but she was certain of one thing: Carl would win . . . and not just the semifinals. It was clear, witnessing the way Carl had destroyed his opponent today, that they'd implanted the sigma chip—and that was *scary*. She would never forget the shaky video clip, the hutch of horrors, blood and fur everywhere, the voice calling, *Skiddy?*

Julio looked at her like she had suggested torching a day-care center. "Of course I am fighting tomorrow."

"Wait—is this some stupid *macho* thing?" Her anger rose—magnifying her headache in the process. "I mapped her from across the arena. We don't need to attend the stupid dinner."

"Until you sketch all of them, I fight."

His patient-parent tone only annoyed her further. "But I know I can do it. I mean, I already *did*."

He stood. "You have your orders; I have mine."

She wanted to tell him where he could shove his orders, but two things interfered: her jackhammer headache and the troubling suspicion that he was actually right. She leaned forward and put her head on the table. She could feel him standing there for several seconds, then felt him moving away. She could even feel the space through which he moved: kitchen, hall, room . . . all part of this massive mountain complex that rose above her like some smothering pillow.

Beyond him, beyond the rear wall of his room, her consciousness pushed into the vast shaft of the volcano and spun around the caldera like one of those crazy birds—a dizzying, amazing moment—and then she forced her mind back into Julio's room.

She could feel him moving within it—and could feel the

room around him . . . its walls and floor and ceiling. Panning to the right, her mind swooped through his wall, into her room and out through another wall, this one thicker, with a shaft of emptiness at its center. Then she was through another wall and into the common room of the apartment next door, aware of its space and even objects within it—furniture and . . . yes . . . people moving. No sense of who these people were, of course. She couldn't *see* the space or its contents, could only *feel* them—but she discovered that she could discern their number: two. Two people moving around in the room . . . and, she realized, dilating her perspective, spreading out across the rest of the neighboring apartment, feeling its rooms . . . two other people in separate spaces. One in the kitchen, near the refrigerator, another in a smaller space, off a bedroom, standing there, moving its arms . . . showering?

Her mind dropped to the floor of this small space and slipped into the cylinder there—a drainpipe—and her perception flowed along it beneath the floor, past a union with another pipe, and into the wall, where it entered a wider pipe that ran between levels directly alongside the larger vertical shaft she'd earlier detected. Her mind slid into the vertical shaft, and she paused there, feeling the squareness of it and its dimensions—perhaps three feet by three feet—and knew what it was: an air shaft. With a dizzying dip, she plunged down several floors, the ductwork zooming along, unbroken, then whooshed back up again, past this level, up and up and up, to the top floor of the complex, where it bent and traveled along a horizontal path that branched out in many directions, delivering heat to various rooms in the way that branching veins carry blood to quadrants of the body.

Then she was back in her own body, back in her own head, which she lifted. She called, "Julio, I've got it!"

He emerged from his room, looking cautious. "Don't bother," he said. "I'm fighting."

"Not that," she said, and managed a smile despite the pain crashing like cymbals in her skull. "I know how we can access the restricted levels."

EIGHTEEN

AFTER THE SEVENTH BOAT BURNED, the overhead screen dimmed, the music faded, and the voice of the Few filled the gloomy lakeshore.

"May the Valkyries lift these fallen warriors up to Valhalla, and may the gods fortify you brave survivors who battle on."

As the voice echoed and vanished, the fighters gathered upon the black sand shifted and shuffled and started to move away, murmuring quietly.

Seven boats. Seven *people*.

Carl felt shocked and sickened—and yet relieved as well. None of the pyre-boats had borne the Z-Force flag.

"Well, you boys," Tex said, "I don't know about y'all, but winning makes me hungry. What do you say we head upstairs and order a dozen pizzas?"

"Yes," Agbeko said, and clapped the smaller fighter on the shoulder. They were acting like they'd just watched a pep rally bonfire. With Agbeko, who'd witnessed countless atrocities as a boy-soldier, it made a twisted kind of sense, but how could Tex be so unaffected, so callous? "This is a very good idea—and we will force Davis to eat with us." Davis had refused to attend the funeral, saying if anybody had a problem with that, they knew where to find him. He wouldn't even look at Carl since the vicious knockout that had left the Z-Force middleweight stretched like a corpse on the canvas. "Food brings even enemies together."

"Speaking of which," Tex said, nodding to Carl, "you going to break bread with him?"

"You guys go ahead," Carl said, glancing toward the water's edge and the couple standing there. "I'll be up soon."

"Suit yourself, chief," Tex said, "but don't blame me if Agbeko picks all the pepperoni off the pizzas."

Carl lingered in the gloom, trying not to be too obvious as he stared at Octavia. *Come this way*, he thought. All day, she'd been his single distraction, the only thing that had helped him from replaying the awful *thock* sound his hook had made, slamming into his opponent's head, and from worrying about the Zurkistani's condition. Perhaps illogically, this had minimized in his mind the friction between Octavia and him, making their awkward reunion seem an almost trivial and certainly surmountable problem. But now, seeing her coming this way under Romeo's arm, his recent optimism dimmed, and he felt something else—a twinge of jealousy. They were angling this way. He turned halfway around, pretending interest in the far end of the lake, making it easier for her to slip into his pocket the note he was certain she would have for him.

As she drew nearer, he felt a tap on his shoulder and turned to see Baca grinning at him. Beside him stood the Z-Force lightweight, who had stomped today's opponent to death and had just watched him burn to ash. Now he stood there staring at Carl, hatred burning in his eyes.

Fighter 47, who had also killed again today, was nowhere in sight.

To Baca, Carl said, "What do you want?"

Baca said something in Zurkistani, and the lightweight stalked off toward the elevator.

"He does not like you," Baca said, stroking his black goatee with obvious amusement.

"I'll try to get over it," Carl said. He glanced sideways. Octavia and Romeo were coming up the beach, drawing nearer.

"I wanted to congratulate you on your victory," Baca said.

"Noted," Carl said, just wanting to get rid of the guy.

Baca's eyes glittered. "Aren't you curious about your opponent? During the funeral proceedings, you looked . . . unsettled."

"I got an idea—how about you go find somebody who gives a *crap* what you think?" Carl said, and glanced sideways again.

No.

Striding past, arm in arm with Romeo, Octavia looked up at Carl, then at Baca, then back to Carl—and he hated the fear and disgust he saw in her eyes. Then she looked down, and that was that. She was past him, moving away.

No nod, no note. Nothing.

"She is very pretty," Baca said, still grinning. "Far prettier than Alexi."

"What?" Carl said, feeling jarred. Baca had caught him looking. "Prettier than *who*?"

"Alexi," Baca repeated. "The opponent you so mercilessly dispatched today."

"Look," Carl said, and he felt like screaming. Baca had messed up everything, and now Octavia was stepping onto the elevator, and he most definitely did *not* want to know the name of the Z-Forcer. "I told you, I have nothing to say."

Baca patted Carl's arm. "You and I got off on the wrong foot, but that was all part of the game. I told Commander Stark that all you needed was proper motivation—and you proved me correct."

Carl batted away the mercenary's hand.

Anger flashed across Baca's features, faint and fleeting as

lightning along a distant horizon. "You might even say my actions were *ordained*," he said. "From *on high*."

Ordained from on high? Carl thought—but he wasn't going to play twenty questions. "I'm out of here." And he started to walk away.

"Any parting words for Alexi?" Baca called. "He's in a coma, and I doubt he'll survive the night. You hit him *so* hard."

Carl lurched to a stop. "What do you . . ." And he trailed off, realizing he didn't know what to ask. There was nothing to ask.

Baca laughed. "You'll have your precious promotion."

Carl turned from the Z-Forcer's leering grin and marched onto the elevator.

"Stark will be pleased," Baca called as the elevator doors began to slide shut. "Every Spartan needs his Helot."

As the elevator rose, Carl breathed through his nose and stared at the backs of the other passengers, trying to quell the panic and nausea rising in him. *I doubt he'll survive the night. Alexi . . .*

Other passengers mumbled in an unfamiliar language, making him feel dislocated with them, this place, reality.

What are you doing here? he asked himself.

The elevator stopped on level one, and the fighters who'd been standing in front of him stepped out into the arena.

The doors slid shut. Carl poked the button labeled *4*. . . then stared at the strange panel of buttons. He could spend the rest of his life riding elevators and never see another button panel like this one. An *L* on the bottom, then buttons numbered one through four, and finally four black buttons marked with red *X*'s.

Nine floors, he realized. *One for each circle of Dante's hell.*

Had Stark known about the Cauldron's nine floors? Was that why he'd been emphasizing *The Inferno*? Stark had used Dante to discuss loyalty and betrayal, but the man rarely did anything for a single purpose, and this "coincidence" definitely smacked of his sense of humor.

Stark was everywhere, always, and had been for years, even before Carl had heard of Phoenix Island.

My actions were ordained, Baca had said. *From on high.*

Was it true? Had Stark really engineered everything? Ordered Baca to goad Carl and train the Zurkistani to counter in the way most likely to result in Carl snapping on him?

Yes, Carl believed it.

Because *every Spartan needs his Helot.* For half a year, Stark had been pushing Carl to kill someone—anyone—and thereby accept a baptism of blood into full Phoenix Force membership, just like a young Spartan killing a random Helot peasant and earning military rank.

You'll have your precious promotion.

They had known he would never do it on his own. . . .

Fear and rage, doubt and confusion.

The doors opened and Carl trudged to his room like a dazed fighter stumbling back to his corner after the bell. Had Stark and Baca turned him into a killer?

"Join us, brother," Agbeko called from the dining room, where he and Tex sat with a bag of cheese curls between them, apparently waiting for their pizzas to arrive. Davis leaned against the wall, chewing mechanically and staring dully in Carl's direction.

Carl shook his head. "Not hungry."

Agbeko frowned with concern. "You must eat. You will need strength for tomorrow. The Brazilian is strong."

Don't remind me, Carl thought. He did *not* want to fight the Brazilian. The guy was good—great, even—a submission expert

Carl never could have beaten without the chip. With the chip, though, he knew he could beat him—but he hated the thought of what he would have to do to the Brazilian in the process.

Thock!

"Pizzas'll be here in five," Tex said through a mouthful of orange mush.

"I'll eat later," Carl said, heading for his room. "I'm going to watch the fights."

Agbeko rose, dropping a handful of cheese curls onto the table, and lumbered toward Carl. His swollen eye looked better, but tape still held much of his face together. "Please join us, my brother, and we will watch the fights together." Reaching Carl, he wrapped him in an embrace. "Today is a great day. Phoenix Force is tied for first place in the team rankings."

Carl nodded. Only one other team had advanced all three members to the semifinals: the friendly Brazilian jujitsu guys.

"I understand what you are feeling," Agbeko said, lowering his voice. He put his big hands on Carl's shoulders, squared with him, and looked down with a knowing smile, like a father talking his son through a tough time. "I will never forget the day that I first killed." His smile faded. "It is not something that we should forget."

Carl felt suddenly, inexplicably annoyed. "He's not dead."

Agbeko's smile returned. "This is good," he said. "And no matter what happens, you did this for the honor of Phoenix Island."

Great, Carl thought, and in that hopeless moment, feeling like nothing could ever be right in the world again, he just wanted to tell Agbeko the truth—all of it—not only that he felt no duty toward Stark or Phoenix Island but also that he would like nothing better than to burn the place to ash, that the only reason he was in here, in fact, was to do just that. And as he paused there, impulsively compelled to blurt these truths, but restrained by the knowledge of just how catastrophic the consequences of any such confession would be, a strange thought blindsided him: Agbeko had at some point become his best friend in the entire world. . . .

"Fighting out of the red corner," the announcer's voice said on television, "representing Phoenix Island, Fighter 18."

"Here we go, you boys," Tex called. "Come watch me do the Texarkana two-step all over this loser."

Agbeko nodded in that direction. "Come, my brother. It will be good for you. And after his fight, we can watch the others together, and you can coach us. We need your help."

"Maybe later," Carl said, and he turned his back on them.

Alone in his room, he paced like a death-row inmate.

Alexi, he told himself. *His name is Alexi.*

But then, reflexively as he might dip a punch, he thought, *No, don't think of his name. In fact, don't think of him at all.*

He thought instead of his next opponent, the cool Brazilian, who honestly deserved to win the tournament. He was tough and talented, experienced and well-conditioned, and he'd already shown amazing defensive skills, blocking and evading punches and kicks as he took down opponents, tied them up, found their weakness, and forced them to tap. Carl would have to stick and move, avoiding the Brazilian's attacks and picking him apart with shots. Many, many shots. Unlike the others Carl had faced, the Brazilian wouldn't give him a clean opening. He would have to pound the guy to sirloin.

And if the fight dragged on, Carl would have to battle two opponents: not just the Brazilian but also his dark twin, rage. He might even . . .

No. He couldn't live with that. Wouldn't.

He'd taken this risk to stop Stark and save people, not serve him and kill others. What was he doing here?

How had he ever convinced himself that he could beat Stark?

His anger and frustration swung around to Octavia then. Why was she being so stupid? Why couldn't they just run away?

Because of her big secret—and Romeo, of course. And in his mind, he saw them walking arm in arm past him, saw the look of fear and disgust in her wrong-colored eyes. . . .

Then: Why not just run without her?

He'd been concerned with her preservation for so long, the idea had never even presented itself. But now . . .

He didn't know what she was up to, but one thing was for sure: she was no longer languishing in some Mexican hospital with one of Stark's assassins lurking nearby. Whatever she was doing, she was out in the world and had someone else looking out for her now. She certainly hadn't wanted Carl's help. Hadn't even slipped him another note.

Why not bolt on his own, then? Stuff an equipment bag full of protein bars and water, put on his winter gear, and hike on out the train tracks. Run all the way home to Philly, all the way back to his old neighborhood, Devil's Pocket. He pictured the narrow streets and the playgrounds, the people there, people he knew, his old friend Tommy and Mr. Herrera, who used to walk his little dogs every morning and night, and of course Arthur James. Arthur didn't live in the Pocket, but he did live in South Philly. Lived in a little apartment he'd made in the gym's hot boiler room, where he used to make Carl jump rope when it was time to cut those last few pounds. Just go home, back to the real world, back to a good life, maybe even a normal life. Go underground for a while. Arthur would let him live at the gym. He could get work. At the gym or someplace. Lots of cash in Philly, people paying in cash, living on cash.

Forget Octavia, screw the tournament, spare the Brazilian, and deny Stark ten million bucks and bragging rights. Then, after he got settled in, he could buy a prepaid cell, make some anonymous calls, and let the world know about Stark.

Out in the main room, Tex shouted over the TV and Agbeko roared with laughter. Eventually, they would wind down and head to bed. Then . . .

Carl stopped pacing, went to the closet, and grabbed his parka.

I'm going to do it, he thought. *I'm going to run.*

NINETEEN

OCTAVIA WATCHED AS JULIO twisted his hand before the ID pad, then opened the door with the red *X*. They slipped inside. A light popped on automatically, illuminating a long, behind-the-scenes utility room. She saw pipes and wires, electrical boxes, and a large blue tank.

"Neat trick," she said. "Do you have a chip in your hand?"

"Simpler than that," he said, turning the back of his hand to her and pointing to the base of his thumb. "Skin graft. Only it's not real skin. It's a synthetic patch that captures the thumbprint of any hand I shake."

She smiled. "That's why you're always shaking Valdez's hand."

He shrugged. "Well, that and I have good manners. Come on. It's back here."

She loved the way he kept his sense of humor despite his fatigue. "That's it," she said, thrilled at the sight of the silver ductwork running vertically up the back wall. Her mind had correctly registered its location. She placed her hands on its flat surface, closed her eyes, and focused her mind. At once, she could feel it shunting away, up through floors and branching out and out and out, like the circulatory system of the volcano complex.

She opened her eyes. "I can feel it."

Julio looked at her, no doubt in his eyes, only curiosity.

"It's big," she said.

"How big?"

"It goes all the way to the top."

"Through the upper floors, even?"

She nodded.

"Is it blocked? Any type of gate or fence between the lower and upper floors?"

She closed her eyes again and cast her mind up, along the shafts. She couldn't *see* them—that kind of full-blown remote viewing, which Bleaker expected her eventually to master, wasn't available to her yet—but she could *feel* them stretching along, feel their geography, like riding a blueprint. "I don't think so," she said, and opened her eyes again. "I can't say for sure, but I don't feel anything."

He smiled. "I don't need guarantees."

Working together, they removed the access panel. Warm, sweet-smelling air flooded the small room. She twisted her med-kit penlight to life and leaned into the shaft. The galvanized steel interior shone brightly for the first few feet, then faded, then went black. She could feel the long tumble of that deep darkness stretch away like an empty well.

"You'll never fit," she said.

He moved past her and leaned into the space, gauging its dimensions, then came out frowning. "It's not big enough." He shut his eyes and pinched the bridge of his swollen nose. He looked very tired.

"It's big enough for me," she said, and put a hand on his shoulder. "I'll go."

"No. It's too dangerous."

She fixed him with her eyes, unsmiling. "You really think I'd be here if I needed a protector? Look out. You're too big."

She thought he might protest, but then, looking utterly exhausted, he shook his head.

Good, she thought. *Mission beats macho this time.*

"You don't even know what to look for," he said, not putting much into it.

"I'll just snoop a little. Anything up there says *bomb* on it, you'll be the first to know."

"Look for wires," he said. "Any sign of trouble, come straight back. And be quiet. If you thump around in the shaft, they'll hear you."

"Quiet as a mouse," she said.

Then he wrapped her in a hug.

She pushed against his chest, her face suddenly hot. "No need for that. We're not in public, remember?"

He gave her the tilted smile. "I just wanted to say thanks."

"You're welcome," she said, the feel of his rock-hard chest lingering on her fingertips like a taste. "We're in this together, right?"

"You bet. Hold on a second." He crossed the room, opened a supply cupboard, and pulled out an orange extension cord. Working with impressive dexterity, he twisted and looped the cord. "Step through this," he said, "now this," and once he had the cord wrapped around her thighs, he looped it around her waist and drew it all tight at her beltline. "Snug?"

She tugged, did a squat, and tugged again. "Snug."

"Do me a favor," he said. "Don't fall. I'd rather not test this."

She managed a smile. "Sounds good to me."

He tied the loose end around a metal water pipe, then took the middle of the cord in his hands and around his waist.

"We good?" she asked.

"Good. Belay on."

She took the flashlight in her teeth, stood sideways, and leaned into the duct, pressing her back to the sidewall. She swung her left leg in, jamming it against the opposite wall. Then came the moment of truth. Pushing hard with this leg, she lifted her right leg from the floor and swung it into play, pressing it, too, against the duct's interior.

"Don't let your butt drop below your feet," Julio said.

"I won't," she said. "Duh."

"Just be careful."

She laughed. "No matter how I do this, I don't think you can call it careful." Pressing with her feet, she slid her back upward. Not far, just a few inches. Then she walked her feet up. The key was always keeping pressure on both sides. Shimmy up, walk two steps. It was much easier than she anticipated.

And yet . . .

She hated the way gripping the light in her teeth made her snarl like a cornered animal, hated the unnatural sound of her breathing through that snarl, and hated the constant movement of the light's beam and how it flashed so brightly off the near walls but broke apart and dissipated higher up. Her sweaty fingers slipped against the smooth steel.

Relax, she told herself. *You don't need to see it. Feel it.*

She closed her eyes, embracing the darkness. Instantly, her sixth sense sharpened. At once, she could feel the shaft around her, feel it rising above her and dropping away to . . . what? Some heat source.

Far below, something huffed like a dragon exhaling flame, and warm air rushed past, making her even hotter.

She pictured a massive furnace filled with flames, pictured herself slipping, scrambling for a mad second, her legs hammering into the metal sides, her sweat-slick palms sliding as she tried and failed to stop her fall—a terrible dislocation, the shape of her coming unjoined with the shaft walls—then dropping faster and faster, a brief and jolting jag, as she hit the end of her homemade safety line, a snap, a scream, and her final tumble straight into the flames.

Stop, she told herself. *Keep it together. Feel yourself within the space.* That was the key, she understood, just as it had been back in the Bunker, during parkour lessons. *Feel yourself as an object, moving in relation to other objects.*

There was an architecture to the world—the ever-shifting relationship of things to other things, all the way down to the atomic level. Static and dynamic. Push and sit, pull and sprawl. Trick shots in pool and middle school kids sitting shoulder-to-shoulder with their butts in chairs, typing "the quick brown fox jumps over the lazy dog," and a rain-pierced feather of mist lifting from a mossy stone back in the forests of good old Washington State. Here and now, she became very much aware of the planes and angles of her body and her points of contact with the sides of the ductwork. She made small adjustments, lifting one of her feet an inch higher, spreading her legs slightly, and flattening her shoulders against the steel. She let her hands fall away from the walls. She only needed her back and feet, back and feet.

Slide, step, slide, step . . . up and up she climbed.

At last, she arrived at the junction where horizontal ductwork branched away from this vertical pipe, carrying heat and fresh air to the first restricted level. She brought herself even with this section, leaned her upper body into it, and pushed off with her feet until she was lying on her stomach, completely inside the horizontal ductwork.

To go farther, she had to untie the extension cord safety line, which wasn't long enough. She also took off her shoes—a clumsy affair, especially because she had to be careful not to thump around—and used them to weigh down the extension cord.

Flashlight or no flashlight? she wondered.

No flashlight. It might be seen through the heat vents. Feeling the pipe stretch straight away, she crawled forward as quietly as possible on hands and knees.

Moments later, she arrived at an intersection. The main duct continued before her, but to either side, smaller ductwork through which she could not pass branched off in both directions.

No, she thought, immediately imagining the simple design: the big pipe running between and across floors, the smaller pipes branching off to the rooms she needed to see. But she was learning to ignore her imagination and trust instead her sense of space. She shut her eyes, and her mind trotted off like a hound with nose to ground, and she could feel the path of the ductwork cutting straight across this level. Here and there, she felt the branching away of smaller channels, but the main avenue continued, and occasionally along its walls, her mind detected rectangular patches of grooved incompleteness that she understood at once to be louvered vents opening directly from the main line onto spaces she very much needed to investigate.

Yes, she thought, and moved along on her hands and knees until, drawing near to the first vent, she heard faint beeping sounds—familiar in a way that raised the little hairs along her forearms. She heard voices, too, a woman's voice speaking in the tone of one giving directions and a lower voice murmuring in response.

Moving very carefully, she crept closer.

"This one is ready," the woman's voice said, "and this one as well."

Octavia slid the rest of the way forward, peered through the louvered vent into the large room, and went rigid with terror.

TWENTY

THERE WAS A KNOCK AT THE DOOR, and Carl said, "Come in."
He was expecting Agbeko, but Davis walked into the room with
his med kit, saying he wanted to take a look at Carl's injuries. Carl
took a seat on the edge of the bed, and Davis examined his forearms, then said, "Take off that shoe."

Carl didn't understand for a second. With the pain dialed
down, he'd forgotten all about his damaged toe. He dialed pain
back up, and sure enough—his toe was throbbing in pace with
his forearms. Once again he was struck by the inconvenience of
pain. Other than letting him know something was wrong, it
served no good purpose. He took off his shoe.

There wasn't much swelling, but the toe was already black-
and-blue. Davis knelt and pressed the top of Carl's foot. "That
hurt?"

"No."

"That?"

Carl shook his head. "Only the toe."

Davis stood. "It's broke." He tossed Carl a roll of medical ad-
hesive. "Tape it to the next toe. That's all you can really do."

"Thanks," Carl said. He ripped off a length of white tape and
started winding it around the toes, drawing them together.

"The first teardrop burns," Davis said.

Carl looked up at the dark, haunted face and its tattooed

tears. Hooded eyes stared back at him as flat and lifeless as pennies. There had been no accusation in his voice this time, no taunting. More than anything, he sounded weary.

"I was eleven when I got my first one. Little Leaguer, you know what I'm saying?"

Carl nodded. He'd known lots of kids growing up who'd signed on to some gang's junior division. Half-play, half-business. Sixth-graders trying out gangbanging like other kids might try soccer. *It's geography*, Stark would say.

"How many they burn tonight?" Davis asked.

"Seven."

Three of the day's twelve fights had ended in death. The other four dead had held on from the first day's bouts only to die between the first funeral and the second night's burning.

Davis shook his head. "And there're more lying in the infirmary, waiting to die."

Alexi, Carl thought.

Davis gestured toward the door, the apartment beyond. "Those guys need you."

"They're all right."

"Man," Davis said, and his face contorted, shifting through anger to disgust and finally settling on disappointment. "What happened to you?"

Carl filled with a curious foreboding. Intuitively, he knew that he didn't want to hear what Davis was about to say, and yet, as people so often do in moments like these, he said, "What do you mean, what happened to me?"

Davis said, "Back on the island, when you stood up to Parker? It was *beautiful*, man. I mean, that took real nerve. You knew what would happen, but you still gave it to him. You earned my respect. There's guys would take a bullet to earn my respect, you feel me?"

Carl shrugged. He saw where this was going and just wanted it over, just wanted Davis out of here so he could get this place and Phoenix Island and everything else behind him.

"That's why I jumped in," Davis said. "They locked me up, locked my boys up, then said, Okay, you hunt Ross, we'll let bygones be bygones. Everybody else signed up, but I looked Parker right in the eyes and gave him the same answer you gave him the day they dragged you out of the sweatbox." He demonstrated, raising his middle fingers. "Yeah, that caused me some hard times. Sweatbox, beatings, segregation. Dropped me in Camp FUBAR."

"Where?" Carl had never heard of the place.

"Never got to see Camp FUBAR, huh? Makes the rest of Phoenix Island look like Disney World. Half prison camp, half brainwashing center. Anybody said no to hunting, they dropped them in. Sanchez, Lindstrom, that girl Tamika, and that nervous boy, Soares . . . the one talked all the time about his pet iguana? They worked us, beat us, starved us, didn't let us sleep, tried to get us to turn on each other. Hard time, man. Real hard. Then they'd switch it up, go easy, talk to us all nice, tell us why the hunts were good. Crazy stuff. A few people gave in, went with the program, hunted Ross." He frowned. "That kid had real guts."

"He did," Carl said, and grief woke in his chest. A painful thing. So much easier to block out loss rather than deal with it. "He had real guts."

"They were going to hunt that girlfriend of yours next. Then everything blew up. I heard them shooting at you, man, and they told us if we didn't hunt you, they'd hunt us next. I told them they might as well quit asking. See, I don't just give out my respect. It's real, you feel me? I wasn't going to punk out, no matter what. Then I heard you was dead, then not dead, then they marched us over to the beach to watch the Old Man finish you off."

Carl remembered Davis standing there in handcuffs, and the memory was suddenly very sharp, very real to him. He could feel the heat of the sun, the sand clutching at his feet, and the weight of desperation crushing down on him. With a surge, he remembered the bitter determination he'd felt, too, the way he'd harnessed his fear and gone at Stark.

"Man, I screamed my lungs out," Davis said. "I never thought you'd beat him. Nobody did. He was so huge. But then"—he grinned—"you *did* it. You beat him, man, and I knew right then, everything was finally going to be okay. . . ."

Carl realized he was shaking and sweating. Stark had hunted him, huge and fast, inexorable. But Carl hadn't given in. He'd hung in there and focused his mind, and when he'd finally spotted his opening, he'd gambled everything. His fists throbbed now with the memory of pounding the big skull, and he felt again the jolt that had gone up his arm when he'd knocked the giant warrior unconscious.

Davis's grin died. "But it wasn't okay. They sent me away again. It got worse. Way worse. As they say in church, I *descendeth into hell*. They tried to break us, but the whole time I was suffering, you know what kept me strong? You know what kept me going?"

Carl shook his head.

"You, man. I remembered the way you stayed tough, and I stayed tough, too, and I kept thinking maybe there was a way. . . . But then I finally made it out of there, and who did I see standing next to Stark?" Davis's voice quaked with anger, and his finger pointed at Carl's face like a gun barrel. "You, man."

Davis's words hurt worse than a punch. He didn't understand what Carl had done, what he was doing—or had been doing until now. Nobody understood. . . .

"You sold us out," Davis said.

Carl came off the bed. "You don't know what you're talking about."

Davis nodded toward the parka and snow pants. "Looks like you're getting ready to punk out again."

"Who are you to judge me?" Carl said, and found none of the surly toughness he'd wanted in his voice. "You want to put it all on the table, where'd you get the new tattoo?"

Davis tensed, and Carl wondered if he would break again, run out. But he just stared at Carl with those haunted eyes and said, "Sanchez."

"You killed him?" Carl's heart tumbled. Sanchez was a great guy. Kind, motivated, athletic, decent . . . all the things that got you killed on Phoenix Island.

Davis's eyes dropped to the floor, and he spoke in a low murmur. "Had us in a cage together. We was both weak. Dying. Told us we had one night. Dropped in a knife. Said one of us wasted the other, they'd train him in whatever he wanted. Either that, or they'd kill us both come sunrise."

Carl stared, horrified.

"Neither one of us went for the knife," Davis said. "We just sat there and talked. We'd been through a lot together. He was the best friend I ever had." Then Davis started crying again, only this time, it didn't seem weird. Not at all. Carl knew he should comfort him somehow . . . but he'd never been great at that sort of thing.

"You know how we settled it?" Davis said, and looked up, streaming tears, a hideous grin on his face. "Rock, paper, scissors."

Carl tried not to imagine it and failed. "You won?"

Davis shook his head. "I lost. He handed me the knife and laid down, and I told him I was sorry, and . . . I cut his femoral artery." He patted his inner thigh. "It's supposed to take fourteen seconds to bleed out . . . but it took a lot longer than that, because as soon as I cut him, I threw my hands on it and kept pressing, trying to keep the blood in." His eyes went round with terror. "He was screaming, and blood was spraying between my fingers, and he was fighting me, trying to get my hands off. He just wanted it over, but I held on until the blood stopped spraying and he stopped struggling and I realized he was gone. That's when I heard them laughing outside the cage."

Davis broke down then, sobbing.

For a terrible, frozen moment, Carl stood watching. Then he gave the tall boy an awkward hug. "I'm sorry," he said, but he was feeling more than sympathy. He was feeling rage.

Renewed rage. Rage at Stark, who'd started all this, who'd caused so many innocents to die, and who'd killed the innocence of so many others. Stark, whose island had killed Ross and ruined Campbell and changed Octavia and forced Davis to kill Sanchez. Stark, who had perhaps tricked Carl into killing, too. . . .

Davis sighed. "Guess maybe I thought becoming a medic, I might make up for the killing. Maybe someday, I could head back to the world, be a street doctor, you know? People got no insurance, guys with warrants, gangs—they need street doctors. Guess I thought maybe I could quit taking lives and start saving them."

"That would be good," Carl said.

"You could save lives, too," Davis said, and gestured toward the door, through which Carl could hear his teammates laughing loudly. "Those guys need you, man. Go out there, tell them to shut up and watch. Tell them what to see, what to do tomorrow. Otherwise . . ."

"You can't make a fighter in a day," Carl said. "What you're talking about takes weeks, even months of training. I can't go out there, give them some pointers, and expect them to win."

"I'm not talking winning," Davis said. "I'm talking survival."

Carl glanced toward the bed and felt ashamed, seeing the parka lying there white as a flag of surrender.

"You're driving this car, man," Davis said. "You take your hands off the wheel now, those guys out there are going to die. Reach down inside, find the guy who fought Decker and Parker. Find the guy who beat Stark."

"I'm still that guy," Carl said, and knew in that moment that he would not run, knew that he would not only help Tex and Agbeko but would also do the terrible things necessary to win this tournament. He had suffered so long to keep Octavia safe. Now that she had rejected him, now that she had a new protector, Carl no longer needed to go back to Phoenix Island. No, he didn't need to—he *wanted* to. Anonymous phone calls would no longer do. He was going to go back to Phoenix Island and take out Stark himself. Maybe he wouldn't have to go it alone, though. "We can still set things right."

"Never happen, baby," Davis said. "You help these guys, I spend the rest of my days saving lives, we still won't make it right. We can never be clean again."

True enough, Carl thought, remembering what he had to do to the Brazilian.

"We can never be angels," Davis said, "but that don't mean we got to be demons."

Now, with the deep rage toward Stark filling his nostrils with ashes, Carl felt like a demon—or perhaps an avenging angel.

"I'm going to help them," he said, "but first"—he pointed toward the door—"lock that. I have a *lot* to tell you."

TWENTY-ONE

IN BOXING, one often fights friends. Sometimes, he hurts them. Stops them. Lessens them. Friendships change, losing former ease, but both guys move on.

This wasn't boxing.

And the Brazilian isn't my friend, Carl reminded himself, trying to get his head in the game. The thumping music and false applause certainly weren't working.

The ref called the teams to the center of the ring.

Carl and the Brazilian touched gloves and exchanged nods.

"*Boa sorte, meu amigo,*" the Brazilian said. "*Que vença o melhor.*"

The teams separated.

This is it, Carl told himself. He was about to fight not just the Brazilian but also himself—or, more accurately, his *selves*, the opposite sides of his nature: the explosively dangerous rage always lurking within him, and his equally dangerous reluctance to hurt his opponent.

In the end, he would have to hurt him. Badly. He just didn't want to maim the guy, pound his brains to oatmeal, or kill him.

We can never be clean again, Davis had said, and he was right.

We might not be angels, he had said, *but that don't mean we got to be demons.*

If you destroyed someone good for a cause you deemed good, what did that make you? An angel or a demon? Or did it make you something else, some unholy hybrid of the two? Something like Stark, with his progress at any price . . .

"Be fast like a tiger," Agbeko said. "Stay outside, my brother, and you will finish him."

Good enough advice—the Brazilian's victories had come via choke out and tap out—but easier said than done, without unloading on the guy. He had to wear him down, had to keep sticking and moving, even if it meant a five-hour fight. Eventually, the guy would tire or get frustrated and let his defenses slip. Then Carl would finish him with a hard body shot or a clean, *measured* strike to the head.

"Open," Davis said, and shoved in Carl's mouthpiece. Then he patted his shoulder, looking him in the eyes. Carl had told him almost everything the night before, coming clean about what he'd been doing and what he planned to do to Stark, but leaving out the chip and Octavia. It felt good not to be alone anymore. "All right, baby. You know what you gotta do."

Carl nodded.

Tex said nothing. He'd barely spoken since losing his match. He stared through Carl into the past, back to his own match in this very cage hours earlier. His opponent, an MMA specialist from Haiti, had flattened Tex, taking him to the mat for a little ground-and-pound before forcing him to tap. Tex had lucked out in his first two fights, drawing a bye and a badly injured opponent, but the Haitian had exposed his lack of experience and talent, smashing all that smack talk into his face. To Tex's credit—and to Carl's surprise—he had talked no trash after the fight, made no excuses, and issued no threats. He'd just gone sullen and silent.

Agbeko held out his massive fist. "Pound it."

Carl pounded it—first with Agbeko, then with Davis, then . . . but Tex was already leaving the ring—and then the ref called "Seconds out!" and the rest of his team exited.

Across the ring, the Brazilian bounced. He raised his fists into the air.

Carl shook out a loose combination.

The bell rang.

The world slowed—yet not quite as significantly as it had before. When the Brazilian feinted with a punch and shot for the takedown, he was smoother and faster than anyone Carl had ever faced.

Carl slipped aside, but the Brazilian wasted nothing and was immediately back at him, coming forward in a crouching attack with a high guard.

Carl backpedaled, jabbing, catching his opponent on the hands and forearms, doing nothing to slow his attack.

Keep the fight in the center, he told himself. *Avoid the cage.*

The Brazilian tried a low kick and two punches, but Carl again danced away—jab-jab—staying on his toes, and moved laterally, pleased with the big ring, the space it gave him to stick and move, stick and move.

Patience, he told himself, and dialed back his adrenaline. *Break him down slowly.*

The Brazilian shot again, and Carl felt a flutter of panic as a hand latched onto his ankle.

He twisted and yanked free, retreating once more to the center. Agbeko shouted, "Hit him! Hit him hard!" and false applause exploded as the Brazilian attacked again.

More of the same. Jab-move. Jab-pivot.

Wait for a clean opening, he reminded himself, *and do not get angry.*

As the fight trudged on, the applause dimmed. Carl didn't care. He wasn't here to entertain. He was here to win.

The bell rang.

Carl went back to his corner, where he refused the stool but took a swallow of water.

"Why do you not hit him?" Agbeko said.

"Taking my time," Carl said.

Davis, who knew exactly what Carl was doing, patted his back. "Nice work, baby."

"You are playing a dangerous game," Agbeko said. "Hit him hard and be done with it."

Carl nodded, pretending to take it in.

The bell rang.

The second round played out like the first. So did the third. And the fourth. Carl kept moving, snapping out light punches, connecting mostly with his opponent's hands and arms and shoulders before moving away again. The Brazilian kept hunting him.

He hadn't been challenged like this since his duel with Stark. The Brazilian was fast and tough and disciplined, never giving up his guard or making desperate attacks. Here and there, he surprised Carl by making contact. A glancing punch, an almost-grab, the tap of toes meant as a sweeping kick. But thanks to the chip, none of these really landed, and Carl kept moving, kept peppering him with pitter-pat punches. He'd found his rhythm. It was different than his boxing rhythm, jerkier and with bigger movements—dodges instead of slips, leaps in place of pivots—and he realized that he was evolving, adapting to the sport.

The bell rang.

Carl again refused the stool. Davis told him he was doing great, and Agbeko shouldered the medic aside, urging Carl to punch harder.

Carl's eyes swept the arena. He saw the Few, looking bored in their opera box. *Good*, he thought. *You better settle in.*

"You are letting him get too close," Agbeko said.

"I'm fine," Carl said. He glanced toward the bleachers—and saw Octavia sitting there, looking small and alone.

She came, he thought. *She still cares.*

He sharpened his vision. Octavia was leaned forward, her ponytail gripped in one fist. She stared with complete focus—not at him, but across the arena, at the Few. Strange . . .

The ref called, "Seconds out!" Davis shoved in the mouthpiece, Agbeko repeated himself, and Tex carted the spit bucket out the door.

The bell rang, ushering in the fifth round . . . which went the same as had the first four.

So did the sixth.

And the seventh.

The Brazilian showed neither fatigue nor desperation, but his forearms were red and swollen from Carl's constant jabs. Physically, Carl felt fine—if anything, the rounds had warmed him up, putting his chip and body into even deeper sync—but he was distracted by Octavia, who continued to stare not at him but across the arena.

His back hit something, and he realized he'd unwittingly backed into the cage.

The Brazilian shot for his legs.

There wasn't time to dodge or pivot. Carl sprawled, attempting to jam the attack, but the Brazilian powered through, latching onto Carl's legs.

The bell rang.

"He is getting closer," Agbeko warned between rounds.

"I'm okay," Carl said, and glanced again toward the bleachers. Octavia remained fixated on the opera box. Not so much as a glance his way . . .

"Mix it up in there," a gruff voice said, startling him.

It was the ref, a meaty-faced guy with a mustache.

"No, thanks," Carl said.

"The Few came to watch you fight, not dance."

Rounds melted away, mirroring one another. Carl continued to stick and move; the Brazilian pressed on, maintaining his composure and tight guard; Agbeko demanded harder punches; and Octavia kept staring at the Few.

Toward the end of the fifteenth, the Brazilian stumbled, lifting one elbow, and Carl fired. He was a bit off angle, but the hook still banged hard into the guy's gut, and Carl felt the force of it ripple through his opponent the way a hard punch resonated through a water bag. The Brazilian stumbled again, instantly covering his body . . . and dropping a glove from his head.

Carl twisted, cocking the hook, and the opening was there, but in his mind, he heard again the echoing *thock*, held the punch, and instead shot for the takedown.

He recognized his mistake at once.

On Phoenix Island, he'd come to enjoy grappling, and sometimes, when he rocked somebody during sparring, he would take them down and force a submission just to mix things up, but the Brazilian wasn't a Phoenix Forcer. He rolled with Carl's takedown and kept rolling as they hit the floor, wrapping an arm around Carl and turning him in an amazing kind of midair horizontal hip toss that stunned Carl's fast-firing mind—a real *wow* moment— then slammed him hard into the mat.

And the Brazilian was on him.

Fake applause roared.

Stupid! Stupid! Stupid!

Carl had forfeited his advantages. Out in the middle of the ring, the chip had slowed the fight, allowing him to control the gap, pick his shots, and skirt attacks. Here there was no gap.

The Brazilian moved over him like water, a rushing stream that drove him into the mat, then flowed over him in a flood of simultaneous attacks, the Brazilian's legs and arms, hands and toes, head and torso all working in unison.

Carl tried to roll, to pull an arm free, to turn into him, anything, but the guy was fast and smooth, countering everything and breaking him down flat. This was the nightmare scenario, the thing to avoid at all costs. He'd blundered and plunged headfirst into the world of the submission artist.

He tried everything he'd been taught, but the Brazilian was everywhere. He was on Carl's back, then he swiveled out and pounded Carl's ribs from the side. Before Carl could even react, the Brazilian was on top of him from the front, and he felt a forearm slide across his throat.

Carl grabbed the forearm but couldn't pry it away. Wild with desperation, he bulled forward, but the Brazilian simply went with the push, dropping over backward, pulling Carl with him, and wrapping his legs around Carl's waist. The Brazilian cranked the choke, pulling Carl's head in one direction while pushing his hips in the other. Carl tried to pull free, but the Brazilian had him. The world began to fade, darkening at the edges.

Do something, Carl demanded of himself, but he was stuck. His mind went fuzzy, and the strength flowed out of his muscles. Then he was gone. His consciousness fell forward, arching out of his forehead, dropping like a KO'd fighter toward the mat, where it hit with a ringing clang. . . .

He was facedown on the mat, aware of roaring applause.

The Brazilian was no longer choking him, wasn't even there anymore.

He'd lost. The Brazilian had choked him out, and the fight was over, and now—

"He has to stand on his own," the voice of the ref said, and Carl looked up to see his teammates hovering over him, Agbeko waving for him to stand and follow.

Utterly confused, mind whirling, Carl turned and saw the Brazilian standing across the ring, taking a pull of water, staring Carl's way and nodding at something his trainer was saying.

With the deep conditioning of any boxer who's been there and back, Carl struggled to his feet. Blood flow returned to his mind, and he remembered the clang and understood he'd been saved by the bell.

Agbeko led him back to the corner, took him under the arms, and plopped him onto the stool. Davis dug out the mouthpiece and sprayed water into his mouth and over his head, asking if he was okay.

"I'm cool," Carl said.

"Enough of this game," Agbeko said, his voice panicked. "No more waiting. Hit him hard and knock him out. He is too danger-ous. You can't take these risks."

"You used a contraction," Carl said, smiled with amaze-ment—Agbeko had used *can't* instead of *cannot*—and then laughed aloud, enjoying another of those crazy moments fighters experience when their brains fire on only three cylinders: he'd re-membered the word *contraction*. His book-sniffing middle school language arts teacher would never have believed it!

Agbeko shook his shoulders. "Focus, Carl. You know what you have to do."

"But you never use contractions," Carl said, and even as he

finished the sentence, the humor drained out of him. He shook his head, shedding mental cobwebs, and clarity flooded in.

You're in a fight, he told himself. *He would have choked you out, but the bell rang. And now—*

"Seconds out!" the ref called.

Carl stood.

"Knock him out," Agbeko growled.

His team fled the octagon, and the bell rang, and the Brazilian rushed across the ring.

Agbeko's final words echoed in Carl's mind, and he knew he was right. This guy was too dangerous. He should just . . .

His jab slammed into the charging Brazilian, splitting the man's guard, and knocking his head back.

Carl saw the opening but remembered his hook crushing Alexi's temple—*thock!*—and swiveled away.

He didn't trust himself, wobbly as he was, to land the shot with proper force. He wanted to end the fight, not the fighter.

Take your time, he coached himself, dodging another attack. *Don't let what happened last round make you crazy. Find your rhythm again.*

He was back on his bicycle, spinning away, jabbing, moving laterally, cutting away as the Brazilian closed, and popping him again. Jab to shoulder. Jab to the guard. Double-jab to the forearms. Crisper, snapping shots.

With every exchange, Carl came back to himself. Soon, he had his rhythm.

The Brazilian had finally slowed a little. Maybe he'd exhausted himself during the previous round, or maybe he was just taking a breather, readying for his next opportunity.

Agbeko shouted, demanding a knockout, but Carl, committed to this pattern of quiet brutality, kept pecking away with jabs, tending the gap. *Open up again*, he thought. *Drop that guard*, and then, in what seemed like magical obedience, the Brazilian's hand slipped from his head.

Carl cracked him with a straight right hand to the temple, careful not to put too much onto it. Too careful, he realized, as the punch landed. The Brazilian stumbled but didn't fall. Carl leaned left, meaning to finish things with a hook to the body and—

Wham!

Strong arms wrapped around his midsection. The Brazilian had only pretended to be hurt, drawing Carl to him, and now the guy's shoulder butted into Carl as his foot hooked around Carl's ankle, and Carl was in the air, falling, his mind screaming with full understanding—the Brazilian had him again!—as applause filled the arena and Agbeko bellowed, "No!"

Carl slammed into the mat, a jolting impact that knocked the air from his lungs, and the Brazilian flooded over him. They rolled in a frantic tangle. Carl struggled to a crouch, but the Brazilian had wrapped his legs around Carl's shoulder and waist and clung to his left arm, which he'd locked in a bar across his body. The bar was exerting incredible force on Carl's forearm, and panic flooded him as he felt the bones straining, ready to break. He couldn't move, couldn't get free. He bounced the Brazilian off the mat, but that did no good. There was no way out. He felt his tendons stretching and snapping and knew that the Brazilian could break his arm at will.

The Brazilian growled something in Portuguese, then said, "No escape, *amigo*. Tap out."

He spoke the truth. There was no escape. He had to tap out, or his forearm would snap.

Thanks to the lightning speed of his thinking, Carl understood not just these facts but the larger moment as well, understood in a clinical way perhaps more befitting machine than man the terrible thing that was about to happen, and understood with robotic certainty the sequence of events that would occur after that. His wholly human heart gave one brief pulse of terror, wanting none of it, but he forged on into both disaster and victory, growling, "No."

"*Lamento*," the Brazilian said, and bore down.

Carl *heard* his own arm break—a horrible sound like a broomstick snapping over a knee—and felt his forearm give halfway to the wrist. There was no pain, of course—he had that particular dial buried—but he screamed as convincingly as he could.

The Brazilian released the hold, rolled away, and stood. He, too, had heard and felt the bone break, just as Carl had understood he would. Convinced that the fight was over, the grappler stood, raised his fists overhead, and started for his corner.

But this was no more a jujitsu fight than it was a boxing match, and Carl had understood when he'd sacrificed his arm that the ref wouldn't stop the fight until one fighter tapped, died, or lost consciousness completely.

He popped up and rushed after the unsuspecting Brazilian, who turned just as Carl blasted him. The right uppercut slammed into the Brazilian's abdomen, lifting him from the floor. Then the right fired again, a six-inch punch that spun the guy's jaw and dropped him. Carl hovered, ready to finish the job, but the Brazilian was obviously done, and the ref stepped in, waving his arms.

It was finally over.

TWENTY-TWO

WHEN THEY GOT BACK to the apartment, Carl eventually allowed Davis to take a look at his arm—but not until Agbeko had agreed to a prefight nap and Tex had plopped down in front of the TV with yet another bag of cheese curls. In Carl's room, Davis sat across from Carl, moving his slender fingers carefully over the swollen arm.

Davis looked grim. "You need a cast."

"Nah," Carl said, and took another sip of water, elaborately nonchalant. Sure, the arm was broken, but it wouldn't stop him. He'd mute the pain and deal with the consequences after he'd won the tournament. "I told you guys, it's just a sprain."

"Yeah, well *they* might believe that nonsense, but I heard it, man. It's swollen and hot. You need a cast."

"I can't have a cast," Carl said. "They wouldn't let me fight in it."

"Fight in it?" Davis said. "Your arm is broke, man. The radius, the ulna, maybe both. Time to hang it up."

"You know I can't do that."

Davis just looked at him, working the toothpick side to side in his mouth. "Mess with a broken arm, it won't heal right. Even if it's off a little bit, it'll grow weird, and you'll always have a weak point. Get a little ridge of calcium in there, like a fulcrum, always ready to snap again."

Fulcrum? Carl thought, struck again by how much Davis had learned. *What is a fulcrum?*

"You fight again, break both bones the rest of the way through . . ." Davis shook his head.

Carl shrugged. "I'll keep it safe. I don't need it. Really."

Davis raised his brows, the hint of a smile lifting one corner of his mouth. "Win with one hand tied behind your back, huh?"

"Pretty much," Carl said.

"You fight again, you can't use it; you feel me?"

"Yeah," Carl said, "I feel you."

"Keep it close to your body. No grappling, no twisting, no punching."

"Got you," Carl said.

Davis leaned back, shaking his head. "Man, I can't believe I was barking up your tree back in the barracks. You would've thrown me a serious beatdown."

"Yeah, and then you would've shanked me when I wasn't looking."

Davis shrugged, smiling for real now. "Not out of the realm of possibilities."

"Well," Carl said, "I guess it's good for both of us that we never knocked it." He was glad to have Davis on board. The former gangbanger was already coming up with good ideas on how he could help topple Stark. As the star medic-in-training, he had access to all things medical—including tranquilizers—and no one would question his doling out another round of inoculations when the time was right. Wanting to keep him happy, Carl said, "I only have one more fight, and it's against Romeo."

Romeo's fight had been brutal. He'd fought the Chinese kid, some kind of temple purist who did this whole prefight ritual, then decimated people with explosive kicks. Carl expected the kicker to obliterate Romeo, but Octavia's friend turned out to be a lot tougher than he'd guessed. By the end of the first round, both of them had gone down and both of them were cut. The fight dragged on for six bloody rounds. The Chinese fighter battered Romeo with leg kicks and a devastating side kick to the ribs. By the end of the sixth, Romeo's whole face was red with blood, and he was breathing out of his mouth—a sure sign his nose was broken. Octavia stood outside the cage staring at him, terrified. And then, out of the blue, Romeo jammed a kick, dumped the guy to the mat, and choked him out. Octavia had run into the ring and hugged him as the simulated audience applauded wildly. Epic stuff. Very dramatic. No doubt entertaining for the Few . . . but not good for Romeo.

"I think he busted his hand," Carl said.

"And a rib. You see that side kick?"

Carl nodded. "He might not even show up to the finals."

"He'll show. You two got the same medical condition."

"What's that?"

"More guts than brains," Davis said. "Neither one of you know when to quit."

"Well, I've learned my lesson. I won't drag out this fight," he said, and meant it. Why was it so easy to commit to unloading on Romeo? Was it really a lesson learned . . . or did it have more to do with Octavia hugging the guy?

"Here." Davis dug around in his med kit, uncapped a vial, and handed Carl a pair of fat white tablets.

Carl sipped his water, turning the tablets in his palm. "What are these?"

"Pain meds."

"No, thanks," Carl said, and handed them back.

Davis raised one brow. "That's thing's gotta be killing you."

"No. It's all right."

"No pain?"

"Not really."

Davis looked thoughtfully at the arm. "Tissue must've swelled up around the break. It's holding the bone in place, keeping it from hurting. Once that swelling goes down, though, look out. If the bone gets displaced, the edges of the break can move around, cut meat, tendons, mess you up bad."

"Noted," Carl said. As much as his friend's new abilities impressed him, he really wished he'd stop talking about the risks. He had to fight . . . regardless of the risks.

"If it starts hurting," Davis said, "tell me."

"I'll be fine."

"Well, just remember, there's a fine line between tough and stupid."

Carl laughed.

"Speaking of ignorance," Davis said, "what about Tex?"

"What about him? He lost. Tournament's over for him."

"I'm not talking tournament. I'm talking after. How much do we tell him?"

"Oh," Carl said, getting it. He'd been so consumed, it hadn't occurred to him. "He still thinks Phoenix Island is just some hard-core boot camp for bad kids."

Davis returned the pill vial to the kit and snapped it shut. "He goes back there acting like he acts—"

"He'll get himself killed," Carl said. He'd hated Tex at first, then had borne up under his obnoxious company, but the guy had grown on him. He wasn't all bad, could be kind of funny, and besides . . . no one deserved what awaited him on Phoenix Island.

"How much do we tell him?"

"Good question," Carl said. Out in the main room, the television blared. "Some."

"Not all, though."

"No. He'd open up that big mouth of his and start blabbing."

"So we tell him just enough to keep that big mouth shut."

"If that's even possible," Carl said. "I can't figure why Stark sent him in the first place."

"Kid likes to fight."

"Lot of kids like to fight, and I can name half a dozen Phoenix Forcers who could beat Tex. Makes no sense." Then something occurred to him. Had Stark sent Tex just to irritate Carl, making him more likely to snap in the ring? Somewhere else, with different people, that question would sound like self-centered paranoia, but with Stark . . .

"Whatever, man," Davis said. "We take care of business soon as we get back, we won't have to worry about it."

Carl nodded, doing the math in his head. Another day of fights, then the awards ceremony and the champions' dinner with the Few—he was dreading that—the closing ceremonies, a week of travel back to Phoenix Island, and however long it took Stark to promote him. In a matter of weeks, it would be time to strike.

Davis said, "How you think Agbeko will do?"

"The Somali's tough, but he's pretty banged up, too."

"True," Davis said, not looking convinced, "but that Somalian kid can *punch*."

"So can Agbeko. And he's fresher." Considering the remaining heavyweights, Agbeko had lucked out. On the other side of the bracket, the Brazilian heavyweight, a submission wizard, was slated to fight Z-Force's monster. "The Somali's going to come straight at him. If Agbeko sticks to the plan and works his angles, he'll wreck him."

⚜

Agbeko didn't work his angles.

He and the Somali knocked it toe-to-toe for two rounds, both of them whaling away with bombs and taking heavy shots, their heads jolting and jerking, faces coming apart, neither one of them giving an inch until Agbeko finally landed a comic-book uppercut that threw the guy off his feet and ended the fight.

The canned applause had never played louder.

After they had guided him back to the locker room and sat him on bench, Agbeko turned his ruined face to Carl. "Did I win?"

"Yes," Carl said. Thanks to heart, superhuman endurance born of Dr. Vispera's blood virus, and a lucky punch, Agbeko had won the fight, but along the way, the Somali had scrambled his eggs.

"Did you win?" Tex said, giving him a *what are you crazy* look. "You knocked him out, old buddy."

Agbeko hooah-ed weakly. He looked like he'd smashed face-first through a plate-glass window. "That is good."

Davis wiped the blood from Agbeko's eyes and peered into them with a flashlight. Then he tucked the light in his pocket and told Agbeko to follow his finger.

Agbeko didn't seem to hear him. His head started drooping and nodding like it had after the first fight.

Carl repeated Davis's directions.

The battered fighter lifted his chin slowly. His eyes fluttered and tracked after the medic's moving finger.

"You boys knocked it *man style* out there," Tex said, his

voice throbbing with enthusiasm. "Then—whammo!" He threw a wild uppercut in the air. "You see his eyes roll back in his head?"

"Was Commander Stark happy?" Agbeko asked, his voice sleepy.

Davis shot Carl a look that managed to mix concern and accusation, then told Agbeko to hold his head still so he could staunch the bleeding.

Carl pushed on Agbeko's chest, straightening him. "Sit up straight. Take a few deep breaths."

The massive chest rose and fell, rose and fell, covered in blood.

"You fought bravely," Carl said, and patted one sweaty shoulder. "Stark will be proud."

Davis worked his magic, a look of angry concentration on his face as his fingers deftly cleaned, closed, and covered wounds.

When the medic started mumbling about how Agbeko couldn't fight again, Carl pulled him aside. It was his job, not Davis's, to break the news, he explained in whispers. If Davis suggested it, Agbeko would never forgive him.

"All right," Davis said, "so long as we're clear. He can't fight again. Either you tell him or I do."

"I do," Carl said. Agbeko wouldn't like it coming from him, either, but he respected the chain of command. Of course, the mission orders had come from Stark, not Carl. . . .

<hr>

When the fifth pyre at last broke apart atop the black water and its fire died and the Brazilian anthem honoring their departed heavyweight faded, Carl closed his eyes. *Let it be over*, he thought. *Let that be the final boat.* It was not a prayer—given the things he had done here, he felt he had forfeited that right—but a desperate plea delivered unto that false deity, hope.

Another boat trundled forth onto the lake as a new anthem moaned and clashed like a funeral dirge underscored with martial percussion. Carl let his head roll back and beheld the black flag fluttering on the screen overhead, a yellow lightning bolt twisted into a Z at its center.

All the air went out of him.

When Alexi's image came onto the screen, Carl looked away, filled with dread and sorrow and remorse.

The boat drifted toward the center of the lake, and the inhumanly deep voice intoned, "We honor Fighter 46 of Zurkistan."

Not Fighter 46, Carl thought. *Alexi.*

The boat burst into flames.

Carl closed his eyes. *I killed him*, he thought—and the fatal hook looped again and again in his mind—*Thock! Thock! Thock!*—with the merciless vividness of the chip. This wasn't remembering; this was *reliving* . . . and he knew he would spend the rest of his days reliving that awful moment. *You stole his life.*

But no. It was—

Thock!

. . . Stark and . . .

Thock!

Baca . . .

"May we all die such an honorable death," the voice of the bearded man said.

Thock! And Carl could see Alexi's skull give beneath the punch, could feel the bone crunch beneath his knuckles. . . .

He opened his eyes to see groups drifting through the gloom, coming away from the black lake. Oddly, he felt both paralyzed and restless. *What have I done? What have I become?*

He felt a hand settle lightly on his shoulder and knew it was Davis. Davis, who understood, who had been forced to kill as a child and who'd proven a far better person than Carl—though that was laughably faint praise now, wasn't it? Carl had killed not by accident, not in self-defense, not even for justice. He had killed out of rage. He had *murdered* the Zurkistani.

"Poor Alexi," a voice said—not Davis, after all—and the words burned like acid. He turned to see Baca and his smaller fighter. No sign of Fighter 47, who had killed yet again today. The lightweight glared at Carl, teeth bared, tears streaming down his face. He sputtered something in his guttural tongue.

"I . . ." Carl trailed off, unable to even finish the sentence.

Baca's face was serious now, not taunting or goading. "You did what you had to do. Now it is over. And you at last have your Helot."

"That's not how it happened," Carl said. "That's not what I wanted."

"Semantics and philosophy," Baca said. "In the end, the results are identical. Alexi is gone, and you'll have your promotion. Unless, of course, you lose to the Mexican." He smiled wolfishly. "Then, I believe Stark will send you to me. We do have a vacancy on Z-Force now."

"Never," Carl said.

Baca turned to Agbeko and put a hand on the African's shoulder. "Now, soldier . . . I do implore you: forfeit."

Agbeko, despite a face nearly mummified with bandages, had returned to full consciousness. He shook his head.

"This isn't good," Baca said, with a pained expression. "Fighter 47 is unstoppable. Even I cannot stop him. He is pure, unrelenting force, incapable of mercy. He lives to kill."

"I am not afraid," Agbeko said.

"A true soldier," Baca said. "No wonder Stark values you so highly."

Agbeko straightened slightly, his chin lifting.

Baca said, "The commander would not want to lose the pride of Phoenix Force."

"I have my mission," Agbeko said without hesitation.

"You've already completed it," Baca said. "You won your bracket and brought glory to the organization. When Stark sent me Fighter 47, he had no idea how the killer would . . . evolve. Otherwise, he never would have sent you here. He never intended this as a suicide mission."

In a strange turn of events, Carl found himself agreeing with Baca, wishing Agbeko would see the man's logic. Someone bumped him in passing, but it barely registered, he was so riveted by the exchange.

"But that's exactly what this will become if you fight tomorrow," Baca said, "a suicide mission. Especially given the championship cesti."

"What are you talking about?" Davis said.

"The switch to gladiatorial cesti for the final round," Baca said matter-of-factly, panning their faces. Then an incredulous smile spread across his face. "Stark didn't tell you?"

Carl had a sinking feeling. "Tell us what?"

"Finalists wear the true cesti," Baca said, and brushed his own forearm in an upward sweep. "The wrists are wrapped in leather, but the knuckles . . ."

In the man's brief pause, Carl understood—not in words, but in image: the blocky death-dealing fists of Theogenes.

Baca smacked fist into palm. ". . . are dressed in iron."

And Carl knew with absolute certainty that the Z-Force commander was telling the truth. The Few would finish their blood sport with a fatal flourish.

This realization stunned him all over again, so that he was only numbly aware of Agbeko reasserting his intention to fight, and of Baca and his lightweight moving away.

Carl watched them go, a siren of dread wailing in his skull. He was so rattled, in fact, that he was halfway back to the apartment before he discovered the square of folded paper in his jacket pocket. He waited until he was alone in his room to open it.

Dear C, the familiar handwriting began. *Same place, same time, tonight. Please come. O.*

<hr>

A short time later, the apartment door chimed, and Kruger, seeming uncharacteristically excited, strode in, carrying two black satchels, each emblazoned with a red phoenix.

Carl wanted to hit a magical pause button and stop time. His brain had chain saws to juggle: Alexi's death, the tough talk he needed to have with Agbeko, Octavia's note—Why did she want to meet with him again?—the impending fight with Romeo, and Baca's all-too-believable claim.

"Gentlemen," Kruger said, with his trademark smile and subtle bow. He handed one bag to Agbeko and the other to Carl. The bag looked empty but felt heavy, something small but weighty inside.

Kruger asked them to unzip the satchels.

Carl opened his bag and chilled at the sight of its contents: coiled strips of leather attached to what looked like brass knuckles on steroids . . . four metal rings attached to a slightly curved plate of brass.

The championship cesti.

"Please check the fit," Kruger said.

Carl slipped his fingers through the rings. Brass covered his fist from knuckles to mid-finger in a plate half an inch thick. The back of the plate fit his hand perfectly. The face was ornamentally grooved into thirds to resemble the tri-strap design of the leather cestus. Two shorter metal ridges ran perpendicular to these, completing the facsimile.

"Amazing craftsmanship," Kruger said, again with a touch of pride in his voice. "How do they feel?"

"Deadly," Carl said, pulling the barbaric gauntlets from his hands.

"I should suppose so," Kruger said, smiling again, as if Carl had said something funny. Then Carl realized their silver-haired steward was having a difficult time containing himself.

"What are you so excited about?" Carl asked, irritated.

Kruger straightened, looking surprised, then smiled warmly. "I am excited for you, sir. Oh, I'll admit a touch of pride—being steward to *two* Funeral Games finalists—but I am primarily excited for the two of you. What a moment. You have earned your way to the final stage of the most challenging fighting tournament in the world. Such an amazing feat—and here you stand, on the eve of your destiny, prepared to secure your legacies by your strength of mind and talent, your fortitude and preparation, your magnificent bodies."

He grabbed them both by the biceps and squeezed. "Yes, you're both injured and fatigued, but you are also young and resilient. In my youth, I could march all day with a hundred-pound pack on my back, hiking up and down mountainsides, then get up and do it all over the next morning." His eyes grew wistful. "Eventually, however, one reaches an age where exercise no longer maintains the muscle, and calcium no longer strengthens the bones . . . where a slip, a fall, and a broken hip terrify a man more than the combat of his younger days. Bullets were never so frightening as the whimpering terrors of the nursing home. This is no way to live, my boys, and I'd give the world to be back inside a young body."

Kruger gave Carl's arm another squeeze and stepped away, looking almost embarrassed. "At any rate," he said, returning to his default formality, "I am terribly proud of you both. If you are satisfied with your cesti, I will return them to the officials."

"Mine are good," Carl said, thinking, *If I wanted to kill somebody*. How could he avoid ruining Romeo forever?

"Mine are also good," Agbeko said.

But there's no way I'm going to let you use them, Carl thought.

They replaced the cesti, zipped the satchels, and handed them to Kruger, who looked suddenly sad. He sighed and said, "Gentlemen, it has been my pleasure to serve you, but I am afraid that I must now bid Team Phoenix Force adieu."

"Wait," Carl said, picking up on Kruger's tone. "Like . . . forever?"

Kruger nodded. "Yes, sir. No worries, of course; my replacement, Jones, will introduce himself first thing in the morning, and should you need anything sooner, your call buttons will connect directly with him."

Agbeko nodded, stone-faced. Kruger had treated all of them like royalty, but Carl suspected Agbeko was remembering atrocities committed by Kruger's mercenary unit in Africa.

"Why now?" Carl asked. "You've been with us since day one. Why not stick out the rest of the tournament?"

"Something has come up," Kruger said, and his eyes twinkled

with excitement. He set the satchels aside. "An opportunity that I'll have but a moment—*this* moment—to scize. Timing is everything, gentlemen. That's what I will leave you with, that and the best of luck in all things, and my thanks, as well." Turning to Carl and pumping his hand with that surprising grip, he said, "Especially to you, sir. Especially to you."

Kruger squeezed Carl's hand once more, fixing him with such intensity that Carl felt not only confused but uncomfortable, and was pleased when the steward released his hand to shake Agbeko's, picked up the satchels, and departed with, "Rage in your youth, gentlemen. Strength and determination will bear you up. But when you see what must be done, don't waste a blink— jump . . . and the world will be yours."

TWENTY-THREE

HER HUG SURPRISED HIM. This time, Octavia embraced him fiercely and held him to her for several seconds before stepping back and telling him to follow her. When she led him upstairs to an abandoned locker room, he was confused. When she led him into a supply room in the back corner, he started to wonder if she'd lost her mind.

He wanted to be nice, wanted to give her the benefit of the doubt, but he still felt bitter about their last meeting, about her playing games, and how she'd spent the entirety of his hardest fight staring across the arena at the opera box, so as he closed the door behind them, he said, "What do you want, Octavia?"—and then, with an unintentional edge—"I have a fight tomorrow." He didn't bother to add, *Against your boyfriend, wearing metal cesti.*

She frowned, then said, "Look, Carl, I know you're mad. All right? And I'm sorry I was so weird last time, so secretive. I was still shocked from seeing you here."

"I thought you were in Mexico," he said, "but that didn't make me all suspicious of you."

"Not fair," she said. "I didn't show up leading Phoenix Forcers."

"No—you showed up with your boyfriend."

"He's not my boyfriend."

Yeah right, he thought, but he said, "And I'm not leading Phoenix Forcers. Not really."

She looked at him doubtfully.

"I'm not," he said. "Not the way you think." *Stop*, he cautioned himself, realizing that he had tiptoed toward some kind of confession. Despite all that had happened and all that had changed, despite her new face and boyfriend, despite everything, she still had power over him. His enduring fondness for her softened him in some subtle yet fundamental way, made him want things to be right between them and made him want to divulge everything to her, explain what he'd been doing since she'd left, what he was planning to do, and—oh, yeah—how he had surrendered his freedom to buy her safety. But this was just weakness, he knew, impatience and the need to unload his wagon. Dangerous and stupid. He couldn't afford to trust her with all of this now. For all he knew, she was working for Stark.

"It doesn't matter," she said. "I worried that you had become one of them, but when I saw your last fight, I stopped worrying. You could have knocked him out, but you didn't want to hurt him. You waited and got hurt for it, but you didn't destroy him. You haven't turned into some kind of heartless wrecking machine. I saw that and I knew: you're still *you*."

"Great," he said, and resisted the urge to ask her how she'd happened to notice all this while staring at the opera box. "I'm glad I'm still me."

"Drop it, all right, Carl? It wasn't just the Phoenix Forcers. You were so tall and big—and so vicious in the ring. The chips can cause problems—anomalies."

"That's another thing," he said. "How did you know about my chip? And what—"

"They chipped me, too," she said, and stared into his eyes.

"What? You? When?"

"Stark wanted to give you the newest generation of the chip, but *Vispera*"—she hissed the doctor's name—"worried it would ruin you, so he put you in a coma to heal and tested it on us. Me. A lab tech. Decker. I went last, because Vispera . . ." She trailed off, her jaw muscles clenching and unclenching.

Tortured you, Carl thought, remembering her horrible wounds and vacant eyes. Someday he would make Vispera suffer—and not just a broken nose this time.

"The lab tech died," she said, and snapped her fingers. "Just like that. Something went haywire with Decker's chip, too. 'An *error code*,' Vispera said. He worried that mine was messed up, too. Blabbed about it the whole time he was prepping me for surgery. Not that he was worried about *me*, of course. He was worried about you—and what would happen to him if your chip failed. I was just one more lab rat." Her eyes narrowed. "But I wasn't afraid. I just wanted the pain to stop. And then it did."

He thought he understood then. "You can turn off pain?"

"Huh?"

"Nothing—you said the pain stopped, so . . ."

"No," she said, "I—wait . . . can *you* turn off pain?"

He hesitated, feeling suddenly ashamed. The ability to mask pain was an enormous advantage in this tournament . . . the same tournament through which her "friend" was no doubt suffering.

"You *can*, can't you?" she said, a knowing smile coming onto her face. She smacked her fist into her palm. "I was right. It's just what Bleaker suspected. They gave you the sigma chip." She uttered a short laugh. "Of course—Stark wanted you as the ultimate warrior, not a remote viewer."

"Hold on," Carl said. "What's a sigma chip?"

"We both received the newest generation, but our chips are

different," she said. "Your sigma chip is designed to turn you into the ultimate soldier. Faster, stronger, immune to pain."

"And yours?"

"I'm a gamma, so my chip works on different parts of my brain. The hippocampus and the parietal lobes, mainly." She laughed. "Dr. Dougherty would flip if he heard me talking like this. He hates it when people oversimplify brain science, say this lobe does this, that lobe does that. Whatever. The gamma chip works on my spatial centers."

"Meaning . . . ?"

"I have a killer sense of direction," she said, and smiled, excitement lighting her face. "And I can do some really cool stuff. It's *amazing*."

He heard the same enthusiasm in her voice that he'd felt, discovering his new abilities. "Like what?"

"Ever hear of remote viewing?"

He shook his head.

"That's all right. I'm not there yet anyway . . . but I can *feel* stuff. Places and objects."

"With your mind?"

She nodded. "Contours and angles, relative positions. Interspatial relationships. It's like I have this three-dimensional map in my head," she said. "I can't really see it, but I can feel it . . . like a blind person touching someone's face and getting a picture of what they look like."

"All right," Carl said. What she was saying didn't make sense, but neither did the speed of his brain or rewinding photographic memories or only having to "sleep" for an hour a night.

"Most people have a touch of this—it's where our sense of direction comes from—but the chip enhances those parts of my brain. If I concentrate, I can probe areas with my mind. I can feel spaces. Edges, angles. Walls and ceilings. Furniture. People, even."

Remembering her saying something about feeling his approach the other night, he gestured toward the door. "So if somebody walked into the locker room now, you'd know it?"

"Only if I was concentrating on it," she said, "or if I knew the person. I don't know why that matters, but it does. Bleaker says I'm like a bird now, or a butterfly, something migratory that has a heightened sense of the world around it. Fly a thousand miles south for winter, then come all the way back to the same spot in the spring."

"That's another thing," he said. "You keep name-dropping, like I know these people. Bleaker. Is he your b— your *friend*?"

"Bleaker's a dorky smart guy back at the Bunker. A scientist. We work for the same agency, SI3."

"Never heard of it," Carl said, feeling vaguely stunned. It was a lot to take in.

"Few people have," she said. "Think the CIA or Cybercom, only way more secretive, way cooler, and way weirder."

"This whole time, I thought you were in some Mexican hospital."

"Like I said, I was, until a few months ago. It was so strange, waking up with no idea where I was or how I'd gotten there. I was holding a crayon, my hospital bed was covered in all these crazy drawings—maps, actually—and that guy I told you about was sitting there, staring at me."

"Stark sent an assassin," Carl said.

She gave him a confused look, then shook her head. "SI3. Apparently, I'd been in a coma for weeks. Toward the end, my hand started making all these deliberate jerking motions. One of the nurses thought it looked like writing, so on a whim, she gave me paper and a crayon. When I started cranking out map after map, one of the other nurses shot video and posted it on YouTube. SI3 showed up a few days later. Luckily, they have people surfing the Web twenty-four/seven, looking for weird stuff. SI3 focuses on the three 'SIs'—science, cyber, and psionics."

"Never heard of the third one," Carl said.

"Neither had I. Psionics is the study of superhuman brain powers. ESP, telekinesis, remote viewing, that sort of thing."

"That stuff's real?"

She smiled. "Some of it is. I am."

"What else can you do?"

Another smile. "Watch this." She grabbed a hand towel from one of the supply shelves, handed it to him, and turned her back. "Blindfold me."

He covered her eyes with the towel and tied it behind her head.

"Step aside," she said. She squared her shoulders with the open aisle and launched into a series of backward flips that carried her down the aisle like a gymnast doing a floor routine.

He grinned but then, realizing she was going to hit the block wall, he shouted, "Look out!"

She laughed as she reached the wall, springing off her hands at a different arc and bending her legs. Her feet hit the wall, and she sprung away, arching in midair. Her hands hit the floor, and she propelled herself into a series of incredible flips that carried her back down the aisle, until she planted herself in exactly the same spot where she'd been standing when she started the demonstration. Laughing, she removed the blindfold.

"That's amazing," he said, meaning it. "So you—what?—felt the wall there?"

"Yup," she said, grinning harder. "It's fun."

"And where did you learn to flip like that?"

"SI3," she said. "They're teaching me all types of stuff."

"You work for them now? Like an agent?"

"Right," she said. "They're good, Carl. Most of the Bunker Bots—that's what I call the lab types—are pretty dorky, and Bleaker has a lame sense of humor, and this one guy, Crossman, has no sense of humor at all, but they're *good*. They're constantly fighting, constantly protecting people—though the people they're protecting don't even know SI3 exists."

"Why send you here, though? What are you doing?"

"Spying," she said, "Once I get the information I need, SI3 will strike."

A new hope flickered to life. "Stark?"

"No—way bigger . . . and way more dangerous . . . the Few."

"The Few? They're just a bunch of rich jerks."

She frowned at him. "Let me guess: Stark told you that?"

"Yeah," he said, and remembered Stark saying, *A small group of enormously wealthy elitists who happen to love blood sport.* "But—"

"Well, he lied. Look, it doesn't matter if you believe me. You asked what I'm doing, and I told you—spying—but I'm almost finished. That's why I wanted to meet you tonight. We're leaving soon. Probably tomorrow, maybe before your fight." She put her hands on his arms. "Come with us."

It was his turn to stiffen. "I'm not going anywhere."

The shock was plain on her face. "What? Why?"

"I'm going back to Phoenix Island. I waited this whole time"—*suffered*, he thought—"because I knew that if I did anything . . ." He stopped himself, realizing he'd once more tiptoed up to a confession. He knew what he had to do.

She squeezed his arms. "No, Carl. You can't go back."

"Can't? I have to," he said, anger rising in him as he pictured Stark's face. "Stark has to pay for what he did to you, to me, to Ross and Campbell and everyone." All at once, ashes smoldered within his nostrils. "He's going to pay for turning me into a killer."

"You're not a killer."

"I hate to break it to you," he said, "but I am. In fact, we attended his funeral tonight."

She shook her head. "He's not dead."

"What do you mean?"

She looked up.

Carl followed her eyes over the shelf of stacked towels to the block wall painted institutional yellow and a rectangular air-conditioning vent near the ceiling.

Then she asked, "You're not claustrophobic, are you?"

TWENTY-FOUR

CARL LEANED CLOSE to the louvered vent and peered into what looked like the eerie combination of a science lab and a hospital room. From the floor-to-ceiling bank of beeping, blinking machinery, tubes and wires snaked to smaller machines that sat atop wheeled carts between the beds and gurneys. Bed-machine-gurney, bed-machine-gurney, bed-machine-gurney, on down the row, a dozen trios in total. Wires and tubes emerged from the smaller machines and coiled onto beds, where they attached to webbed caps worn by the old men lying there, their formerly silver-haired heads shaved to accommodate the caps' many electrode points. Other wires and tubes descended to the gurneys, where they plunged into younger flesh.

Fighters.

Carl recognized the Korean, one of the Argentines, and the Gypsy lightweight. Their heads, too, were shaved beneath what looked like mesh swimming caps.

These were fighters who'd died, whose boats Carl had seen burn.

But they weren't dead. Each lay upon a gurney, connected by wires and the wheeled machine to a similarly comatose man in an adjacent bed. And he recognized these men, too. They were stewards. They were all stewards.

He glanced down the row and jerked with a dull thump off the ductwork.

Octavia, who had entered the duct first, gone past the vent, and turned around so that they were now face-to-face on either side of the louvered rectangle, raised a finger to her lips.

He gave her the *okay* sign, then looked again, just to make sure he'd actually seen what he'd thought he'd seen toward the end of the row. He sharpened his vision, drawing in the unconscious boy whose chest rose and fell subtly, slowly.

Alexi.

He was alive. Alexi was alive.

I didn't kill him, Carl thought, and a wild gladness rippled through him.

But they'd held his funeral, burned his boat. Why?

They had done all that but kept him here, attached to this machine, which connected on the other side to the Zurkistani steward, in a state resembling that of Alexi, both of them sleeping . . . or comatose. Something.

What was happening to these stewards? He remembered Kruger bidding team Phoenix Force farewell, citing his big opportunity, thanking Carl, and giving his big seize-the-day speech.

What were the Few tricking the stewards into here?

A door opened, and a woman dressed in a white lab coat entered, trailed by two men dressed in green scrubs. The woman stopped briefly at the first gurney, glanced at the steward on the adjacent bed and consulted an electronic tablet. She scrolled down the screen, and said something Carl couldn't hear to the two men, who made adjustments to the machine.

The trio moved down the row, sometimes making changes, sometimes just observing. They adjusted one steward's cap.

When they reached the Argentine, the woman said, "He is nearly ready." Then she checked the tablet and leaned over the steward for a few seconds. "So is he."

One assistant checked the tubes and wires, while the other began adjusting machine dials.

What were they doing?

Octavia motioned to Carl, then started crawling backward farther out the shaft. Carl followed. They were face-to-face again.

"What's going on back there?" he whispered.

"I'm going to show you," she said.

They passed other vents through which Carl glanced.

One opened onto the largest, fanciest bathroom he had ever seen. Thankfully, despite its size and splendor, it was empty.

The next opened onto a kitchen that stretched away like the main floor of a department store. Men and women in white uniforms and cylindrical chef hats worked at stations, cutting, grilling, carving . . . and everywhere bustled hatless helpers, washing dishes and lugging stacks of plates, cleaning spills and hunching over prep stations. These helper-types moved smoothly—and had the broad shoulders and battered faces of fighters.

Then he was following after Octavia.

They shimmied around a bend in the ductwork, went a bit farther, Octavia moving as naturally going backward as someone else going forward, quickly yet never bumping into the ductwork.

"We're almost there," she whispered, looking him in the eyes. "Be very quiet."

He nodded, and then things got strange. He detected surprising smells—freshly cut grass and flowers in full bloom—and then heard a sound at once instantly recognizable and absolutely unexpected: the delighted cries of small children running at play.

The sound of children playing was so uncanny here that their laughter sent goose bumps racing over his flesh.

Reaching the vent, he peered out onto a space that made no sense whatsoever: a brightly lit summer scene, a grassy meadow with trees and a large fountain spraying water. Farther back, past an orchard of fruit trees interspersed with classical columns of white marble, a crystalline lagoon sparkled against a backdrop of dark stones, over which cascaded a shimmering waterfall, misty at this distance. Nearer, in the emerald-green meadow, several small children flitted between weathered marble statues that looked like they belonged in ancient Greece. The children wore togas cinched with golden ropes and ran barefoot upon the bright green grass, the girls with flowers in their hair, the boys with crowns of laurel, all of them wearing tiny little golden masks.

A window onto Olympus. Little godlings at play.

One golden-haired little girl squealed with glee as she tagged the shoulder of a boy with an inky mop of jet-black hair. He tumbled across the grass, rose up laughing, and shouted, "Now I'm the minotaur!"

None of it made sense. Somehow, the Few had cultivated summer here in the stony heart of this wintry volcano and populated it with playing . . .

"Children," the woman called, coming into view, her voice like a musical instrument, beautiful as the perfect body wearing only a short toga now, perfect as the blond-framed face that he recognized from the arena opera box. "Come and eat."

Some of the children protested. Some cheered. All obeyed. They flocked to the woman, who looked over her shoulder as the server appeared.

Another jolt, but Carl was ready this time—ready for anything—

and a good thing, too, because he might otherwise have shouted in surprise.

The server with the oddly shaped head stooped so that the children could reach the silver tray heaped with grapes. He, too, wore only a toga, exposing the bulk of his muscles, including the cannonball shoulder emblazoned with a bright red triangle.

TWENTY-FIVE

CARL HELPED OCTAVIA out of the vent and down to the supply room floor, where he realized an embarrassing truth: she'd let him assist her but hadn't needed any help at all. The girl could do gymnastics in a pitch-black cave.

"I told you he wasn't dead," she said.

He nodded. Alexi lived. A *huge* relief, but . . . "What did we just see back there?"

"You know what we saw."

"The Russian was dead," Carl said, remembering the vacant look in Fighter 32's eyes when they'd carried him into the locker room. "I saw him."

She spread her hands. "Maybe he just *looked* dead. Either way, he's made a pretty amazing recovery in just two days, huh?"

"What are they doing up there?"

"They're sucking the life out of the old guys and using it to heal the fighters," she said.

"Life-force isn't blood," he said. "You can't just swap it out."

"The Few are way ahead of us. They've been developing stuff in secret for a long, long time. That's how SI3 knows about them. Spend any time in the world of underground science and technology, and you start bumping into rumors. Investigate the rumors, and you uncover countless half stories going back hundreds of years. Sinister legends of a shadowy international cabal, centuries old. Their goal: to evolve, become more than human."

The pantheon, he thought.

She shivered and folded her arms. "Last night, I watched them do it."

"The swap thing?"

She nodded. "That woman and her helpers? They used a machine. Took ten minutes. They just kind of . . . dimmed the old guy down . . . drained him. Completely." She shuddered. "Then the fighter sat up and started talking. Good as new. Excited. He didn't even seem surprised."

Carl thought again of Kruger and his strange parting earlier this evening. Were the Few tricking him into surrendering his life-force, too? How could he find Kruger and warn him without raising an alarm? The old guy was fanatically loyal to his precious Few.

Octavia smiled, looking both proud and determined. "My whole life, bad people have pushed me around," she said. "Finally, I've found a way to push back . . . *hard*." She reached into her pocket, pulled out papers, and unfolded four intricately drawn sketches, each depicting a different person. Two handsome men and two beautiful women.

"You drew those?" He took them from her, studying each sketch, marveling at the incredible detail. "They're amazing . . . like photos."

"It's them," she said, her eyes hard. "The Few."

"Really? But how . . . did you see them through the vent?"

"I use my chip. Remember me saying I could feel things I couldn't actually see?"

"Like a blind person touching a face," he said.

"I can penetrate their masks and feel their faces—the contours and angles, the *landscape*." She pointed to the drawings. "Those aren't sketches. They're maps."

"So," he said, blinking at the pictures, then looking up at her, "you feel what each part of their face looks like, then copy it onto the page?"

"Yes," she said, taking the sketches from him and returning them to her pocket. "That's why SI3 sent me. The Few have been around in one form or another for a long time, but no one has ever figured out their real identities." She slapped her pocket and smiled. "Until now. I just have to get one more."

"The bearded man," Carl said.

She nodded. "I haven't been able to map him. Maybe I was exhausted—whenever I push too hard, I get these horrible headaches, like migraines with an attitude—but when I tried to probe behind his mask, there was no shape or form, just a blur. I'm hoping tomorrow, during the lightweight match, I'll have better luck."

"What if you don't?"

She looked suddenly uncomfortable, and he knew she was thinking of his fight with Romeo. "Let's just hope I do," she said.

"And if you do 'map' him . . . what then?"

"We sneak out of here. The Cauldron's shielded from satellites, all the way back to where the buses dropped us, but once I'm out of the mountains, I'll signal SI3. They're in the region, but they don't know precisely where we are. Once they pick up my signal, they'll send teams."

"Why wait? Why not go now?"

"SI3 wants the bearded guy worse than all the others put together. Julio won't leave until I finish the final sketch."

Julio, Carl thought, registering the name. *Not Romeo, Julio.* "But if you signaled SI3 now," he said, "wouldn't they catch the guy?"

"No. The Few always have an escape plan, and they wire every venue with explosives. Julio's been hunting for the explosives, but no luck so far. If SI3 showed up now, the Few would slip out the back door, push a button, and blow up this place and everybody in it."

"If the Few are so secretive," he said, "how do you know all this stuff?"

"SI3 has been chasing leads, recruiting assets, and sifting data for decades. Two years ago, they finally managed to slip three agents in the Games. One died fighting. Another, the Few caught snooping and tortured to death. The final agent fled into the forest. Just after he escaped, he saw a bright flash and watched a small jet fly away. Seconds later, the entire facility exploded, explaining why every lead they'd gotten in previous years led only to shattered ruins."

He took it all in. A year earlier, any piece of this would have seemed completely insane—the Few, a fighting tournament in a volcano, everything wired to blow . . . let alone Octavia's mapping and whatever it was they were doing in the lab upstairs—but now, standing here thousands of miles from Philadelphia with a chip in his head, he believed every word of it.

She said, "Meet me after the lightweight bout, all right?"

"Where?"

"The lake. If I can ID him during the fight, we'll leave right after."

"Take Davis with you," Carl said.

She looked at him like he was crazy. "Davis? As in the gangbanger you hate?"

"Not anymore," he said. "People change—and not always for the worse."

She nodded. "Tell him to be ready. What about the other two?"

"Not the big guy," he said, and felt a pang of sorrow. Poor, lost Agbeko. "He's one hundred percent loyal to Stark."

"And the other guy, the one with the mouth?"

Carl thought for a second. Tex had no clue about Phoenix Island, where his attitude would get him killed in a week. But still . . . the idea of Tex trying to *sneak* anywhere . . ."I don't know. Maybe. Probably."

"All right," she said, and slipped her hands into his. "Come with us, Carl."

And all at once, he felt the old connection. He sensed her there behind the disguise, sensed the *real* her, the Octavia he had known back on Phoenix Island, where they had stolen spare minutes to swap stories and laugh and just *be*. A flash flood of emotions rushed through him—fondness, sorrow, hope, doubt—but then Stark marched into his mind, attended by the things he had done to her, Ross, Davis, Campbell, Sanchez, Medicaid, and countless others.

He shook his head. "I have to stop Stark."

She growled with frustration. "Forget Stark. 313 could crush him right now. He's on an island. A *small* island."

"Why don't they, then?"

"And lose the Few? They'd cover their tracks in about five minutes."

"But think about what he did to us," he said. "Think about *Ross*."

"None of that would have happened without the Few," she said. "Don't you get it? The Few *own* Stark. They supply everything he needs to build his super soldiers. They tell him where to go and who to kill."

"Geopolitical chess," he said.

"Exactly," she said. "Playing games with the world, with people's *lives*. They're so rich, they're not even really *human* any-more. They're beyond our dreams or hopes or fears. With no connection to humanity, they can feel no love . . . only lust. And they'll drain every last one of us to get what they want."

"Stark has this fantasy," he said, "where society comes tum-bling down and almost everyone dies. He and his favorites are chipped, but for everybody else, it's back to the Stone Age."

She looked neither doubtful nor surprised. "Straight out of the playbook of the Few. The chips, the blood virus . . . they're perfecting those things for themselves. They want to be young and strong and fast, immune to pain or sickness or fatigue, with high-speed minds that can see through walls and maybe even into the future. That would leave only one fear."

It took him a second. "Death."

She nodded. "That's what they're working on upstairs: beat-ing death. They don't just want to be superhuman. They want to be gods."

TWENTY-SIX

CARL DIDN'T GET BACK to his apartment until three in the morning—*the long hour of the soul*, his grandmother, reduced now to a dark effigy in the furthermost recesses of his memory, used to call it, conjuring notions of life's very essence at low tide, a fragile, fleeting hour of fading away—but as he came through the door, his own soul was soaring. He was leaving this place, likely in six or seven hours.

Good-bye to the Cauldron, farewell to Phoenix Island. No more Stark, no more suffering. Where next? He didn't know—and it didn't matter. For now, leaving was enough. Octavia was enough. And the knowledge that together, remotely, they would ruin Stark was enough.

"My brother," said a deep voice in the darkness.

Carl jerked sideways, tucking his chin and raising his hands—the conditioned response of every startled boxer—then relaxed with a laugh. "Agbeko. You made me jump."

A massive shadow moved in the dining room. "I have been waiting for you." Something strange in his voice. "Is it true?"

Panic scrambled in Carl's chest. Did Agbeko know about Octavia? About their plans?

Impossible.

He tapped the wall mount, filling the main room with light. "Is what true?"

Agbeko emerged from the dining room, looking like he'd just left his best friend's funeral. "You will not allow me to compete in the finals?"

Davis, Carl thought bitterly, then remembered the medic's warning . . . *Either you tell him or I do*. "Yeah," Carl said. "It's true. But I sure do wish I'd been able to tell you myself."

Agbeko walked to Carl, put his big hands lightly on Carl's shoulders, and stared down with bruised and swollen eyes hollowed by grief. "Please do not do this to me, Carl."

"You fought bravely," Carl said. "You brought glory to Phoenix Island."

Agbeko's hands fell away. "There is no honor in surrender."

"You took a horrible beating today. You didn't even know you'd won."

"But I *did* win."

"Yes—but this fight is different. You saw the cesti."

"I will hit harder with them."

"So will he."

Agbeko gestured toward the dead television screen. "Come, my brother. We will watch his matches together, and you will teach me how to avoid his punches."

"You know it doesn't work like that. You can't change your style overnight."

Agbeko's eyes drilled into him. "This is the most important moment of my life. Please do not take it from me. I have worked for this many years, since the rebels came."

Not wanting to delay this anymore, Carl went straight down the middle. "I can't let you fight him," he said. "I won't."

Agbeko breathed through flared nostrils, his eyes bright with desperation. Then he dropped his head.

For a horrified second, Carl thought the hulking warrior was going to cry.

But instead, Agbeko spoke, his voice low and measured. "When I was a boy, a missionary came to my village. This was before the rebels. The missionary gave every child a Bible and a bookmark, and on the back of each bookmark, he had written a different verse, which he asked us to commit to memory. So of course I did. I was to learn the first two verses of Psalm Twenty-Three, but the man was kind, and I wanted to thank him for the Bible, so when it was my turn to go to the front of the church and recite my lines, I surprised the missionary and everyone else by reciting the entire psalm."

Carl smiled. It was too easy to picture. Agbeko's greatest strength—and greatest weakness—was loyalty.

"The missionary was very pleased," Agbeko said. "He spent more time teaching me, and I did very well, even with long division. Only one girl and none of the other boys, even my brothers who were older, could do long division, and the missionary told me that I was *smart*, something no one had ever told me. The rhino is big but not smart. But this man, he told me I was smart, and I believed him, and he told me that I would be a soldier for God, and I believed that, too. But then the rebels came."

Carl nodded, figuring he knew what had happened next and not really wanting to know.

Agbeko said, "My father was killed in the fighting that day, but my mother was not and neither were my brothers. The rebels tied the wrists and ankles of the missionary and made him kneel on the ground, and they asked the children, 'Who is his best pupil?' and the boys and girls said, 'Rhino,' and the rebels pointed their guns at me and gave me a pistol and told me to shoot him or they would shoot me."

"That's horrible," Carl said.

"I did not want to shoot him," Agbeko said. "I was very afraid. But the missionary looked me in the eyes and told me not to be afraid. He said to do what they told me to do. He said that no matter what they made me do, I would remain a soldier of God. He was not afraid because he was a man of God."

Agbeko lifted his hand, his eyes staring through Carl now, into the past. "I raised the gun, and the missionary smiled at me, and I knew that I was forgiven, and then he said to me, 'Recite it with me,' and then he said, 'The Lord is my shepherd . . . ,' and so we said together . . .

> " 'The Lord is my shepherd; I shall not want.
> He maketh me to lie down in green pastures,
> He leadeth me beside still waters,
> He restoreth my soul.
> He leadeth me in the paths of righteousness
> for His name's sake.
> Yea, though I walk
> through the valley of the shadow of death,
> I will fear no evil,
> for thou art with me;
> Thy rod and Thy staff,
> they comfort me.
> Thou preparest a table before me
> in the presence of mine enemies.
> Thou anointest my head with oil;
> My cup runneth over.
> Surely goodness and mercy shall follow me all the days
>   of my life,
> and I will dwell in the house of the Lord forever.' "

Agbeko looked Carl in the eyes. "And then I shot him, and he was dead. It was a clean kill, and he did not suffer."

"I can't imagine," Carl said. He wished there was something else to say, but there was nothing. What could anyone say about the horror Agbeko had endured?

"Next they brought me my brothers and told me to kill them, and I killed them," Agbeko said, and his face showed no emotion, neither sorrow nor regret nor even bitterness. "The rebels were very drunk, and they were laughing, but I was not afraid, and then they brought me my mother, and they told me to kill her, and I killed her, and then I went different places with them and killed many people until Commander Stark rescued me and brought me to his camp."

Carl nodded. No wonder Agbeko worshipped Stark.

"To many people, I am a monster," Agbeko said, "but they have not lived my life. My path is not their path. They would not want my path. And yet they judge me. Only God can judge me."

These thoughts were very familiar to Carl, but he couldn't let them blur the facts. "Fighter 47 has killed everyone he's faced."

"I am not afraid to die," Agbeko said. "I would sooner die than forfeit this fight."

"That's not the point."

"No disrespect, my brother, but yes—it is. My blood is my own. My life is not yours to save."

Something wobbled inside Carl. Agbeko was making sense— his blood, his life—and yet Carl couldn't allow it. He didn't want his friend to die and refused to spend the rest of his own life wishing he had saved him.

Agbeko said, "I have lived my entire life in the valley of the shadow of death. It does not matter how I die. Only how I live."

"It does matter," Carl said.

Agbeko's voice throbbed with emotion. "God gives us our

strengths *and* our flaws. We are not judged on these—only on the paths we choose. God sent Commander Stark into my life and rescued me from the devils who forced me to do evil things. It was then that I chose my path. Through dedication to Commander Stark, I have once more become a soldier of God, and I believe that when I die, God will forgive the evil I have done, so long as I do not leave my path. So you see, my brother, we are talking not only of victory but redemption . . . perhaps even salvation. You must please allow me to fight this match."

Carl struggled to keep his face as emotionless as possible, remembering Stark's advice about dealing with impassioned subordinates. He felt awful, but if Agbeko refused to protect himself, Carl had to do it for him. "You can't."

"I *must*," Agbeko said. "Commander Stark told me to fight, to win."

"I'm mission commander," Carl said. He had to put an end to this. "It's my call, and I'm telling you: you're not fighting tomorrow."

"You forbid it?"

"I do."

"Is this an order?"

"It is."

For a moment, Agbeko just stared at him, and Carl could see the end of something in his friend's eyes. A painful uncoupling and moving apart.

Then Agbeko himself was moving away, heading for his room. "I am sorry," he said as he drifted into the darkness. "Know that I am sorry."

"That's okay," Carl said, watching him go.

It wasn't until much later that it occurred to him to wonder *why* Agbeko was apologizing . . . and by then, of course, it was too late.

TWENTY-SEVEN

AFTER THE LIGHTWEIGHT CHAMPIONSHIP, Octavia hurried upstairs, then paused outside the apartment door, shaking with the pain, sick with it.

She had failed.

She had tried her hardest to map the bearded man, pushing through the pain, *into* it. Now she felt like someone had split her skull with an ax. Leaning against the apartment door, she squeezed her eyes shut and breathed deeply, battling nausea.

Almost as bad as the pain was the frustration.

Mapping the others had been easy. Sure, she'd earned a whip-cracker of a headache, but she'd mapped them. Until the bearded man. Scanning his face was like trying to see her own reflection in a river of rushing black water . . . no features there whatsoever, just a sense of formless motion.

Her failure gutted her. To come all this way, to get this close, only to fail. Crossman had been clear about her mission. Map the Few—but most important, map the bearded man. Julio knew this—and probably more, given his obsession with her success. To him, mapping the bearded man was second in importance only to deactivating the explosives . . . which he still hadn't located.

Some dynamic duo we turned out to be, she thought.

When the pain in her head dulled to mere migraine level, she opened her eyes. Her vision was still blurry at the edges. Had she gone too far? Blown something out?

Oh well, she thought. *Nothing you can do about it now.*

She needed to convince Julio to leave . . . before his fight with Carl.

Otherwise, Julio would stick with his plan. Win the finals and take her to the champions' dinner. At that range, mapping would be a cinch.

Only there was a serious problem with Julio's plan.

Carl.

Julio could never beat Carl. Never, ever, ever. Even if he wasn't hurt so badly, even if he wasn't exhausted from staying up night after night searching for the explosives and from fighting devastating matches back-to-back, even if he was fresh and well rested, he couldn't beat Carl. He probably couldn't win even if Carl hadn't gotten the chip.

And Carl *did* have the chip. That not only ensured victory. It also meant risks. She had downplayed these to Carl, not wanting to repel him, but they terrified her.

To his credit, Bleaker had shown her the video only after making certain that her chip was functioning properly.

"Skiddy before implantation," he had said, narrating the video of several white rabbits hopping around a tidy hutch.

"Which one?"

He pointed to a pair of nose-to-nose rabbits that looked like they were sharing an Eskimo kiss. "Skiddy's on the right."

"But how can you tell them apart—oh . . . I see it." The rabbit on the right wasn't *all* white. A short black stripe ran between his ears.

"That's why we named him Skiddy," Bleaker said with a sad smile. "Short for Skid Mark."

She laughed. The little black stripe did look like a miniature tire burn.

"Other than his marking, Skiddy was perfectly average," he said, stopping the video. "Just a ten-pound rabbit with a warmer-than-average social adjustment that made him seem like a stuffed animal come to life. Later, we implanted a chip in each of the six rabbits."

As he spoke, he avoided eye contact and moved things around, stacking papers and relocating pens, as if cleaning his desk, which was so heaped and messy he'd need a flamethrower to really clean it.

"Unfortunately," he said, "most of the rabbits were functionally lobotomized when we activated the chips." He drew up a clip time-stamped three days later than the previous video. "Not Skiddy, though. Fair warning: this isn't pretty."

Octavia winced at the sight of the hutch: blood and fur and body parts everywhere—a severed rabbit's paw lying in the pink depths of the water dish, looking like anything but a good-luck charm. "Ugh," she said.

"The chip changed Skiddy *dramatically*."

The camera dipped into the hutch, peering into the covered half, where—

"Oh," Octavia said, and put a hand to her mouth. "That's Skiddy?" He was *huge*. He filled the space, white fur stretched over rippling muscle.

"An error in the code caused rapid mutation. His muscles swelled overnight."

As Skiddy registered the intruding camera, the muscles beneath his white fur rippled like those of a prize steer.

"And he became extremely aggressive," Bleaker said.

When the head came around—and yes, she saw the black

stripe between the ears—Octavia leaned away from the screen. The head wasn't big enough for the body. Its face was misshapen and masked in blood. The eyes flared, utterly insane, the mouth opened and launched at the camera, snapping.

The film cut.

"We were forced to euthanize him," Bleaker said. "His autopsy weight was eighteen pounds." Bleaker had gone on to explain that Skiddy hadn't just grown. The architecture of his muscles had changed, making them much denser and stronger.

Carl had shot up in height and packed on an enormous amount of muscle since she had last seen him. His muscles were well formed and proportional, unlike Skiddy's deformed monster-mass, but he had nonetheless gained an awful lot of size in so short a time. There was something different in his bearing, too. A guarded darkness in his eyes.

Watching his first two fights, she'd been terrified. His speed, his power, his viciousness.

The third fight, when he'd obviously put himself in danger to avoid hurting his opponent, had given her hope, but Carl was no rabbit. An error code in his chip might manifest differently. What rage simmered at his core, awaiting its trigger?

She had to stop Carl and Julio from fighting, had to get them both out of the Cauldron before it was too late. Drawing up her strength, she opened the door and went inside.

Julio sprawled on the couch like a murder victim, one arm thrown over his forehead, its broken hand twice its normal size and badly discolored. His mouth hung open, a gaping hole in a swollen face crisscrossed in bandages that looked too bright against the dark bruising. His chest rose and fell, rose and fell.

He deserved better, she thought. *He deserved a real trainer, someone who could have offered real help in the corner, someone who could have provided better medical attention.*

She went to wake him, then caught herself. *How could you be so stupid?*

But she knew the answer, didn't she? Brain-splitting headaches had a way of messing up a girl's thought processes. Luckily, she'd stopped herself. She needed to draw before waking him.

She started for her room . . . but then Julio called to her, sounding groggy. "Rita?"

She turned. *Time to improvise.* "You're awake." She tried to feign enthusiasm, but the pain foiled her.

He sat up. "Did you get it?"

"I did," she lied. "Grab your things. I'll get the other sketches. We have to get out of here." She attempted a smile.

He didn't smile back, just beckoned with his good hand. "Let's see it."

"No time," she said, and drifted toward her bedroom. "Come on, sleepyhead, we need to get out of here, before—"

"Show me the picture," he said. She could hear the suspicion in his voice, but he was polite enough to lie, too. "I want to see what he looks like."

A red-hot bullet of pain ricocheted inside her skull. She didn't have the strength to play this game. "You can't fight him."

He stood. "You didn't get the sketch, did you?"

"You look like an old man trying to stand up," she said. "Look at your hand. Look at your face."

He lifted his broken hand, but his eyes never left hers. "One more fight, then the champions' dinner. You need to map him. I refuse to go back empty-handed."

"You can't beat him," she said.

He glared at her, suddenly angry. "I will win. He's only here for money."

You have no idea why Carl is here, she thought—and knew that telling him now would be disastrous. Early on, she had considered explaining but decided against it. Snooping at night, Julio might be caught. No matter how macho he was, they would make him talk. If that happened, and he knew about Carl . . .

So she hadn't.

Well, he would know soon enough. She would have some explaining to do when Carl joined them on their escape flight.

"Money won't be enough when we're wearing the metal cesti," Julio said. "I am not here for money. I am here for justice."

"Don't be an idiot," she said. The bullet in her head burned hotter, bounced faster. She grabbed him by the shoulders and tried to shake him. It was like trying to shake a building. *A stone mausoleum,* she thought. But she had to get through to him. "What, you feel ashamed that you can't find explosives, so you have to get yourself killed? We had a job here, and we did as well as we could. Don't turn this into some stupid *honor* thing."

"What would you know about honor?" he said, and shoved her away. Hard.

She almost fell—would have fallen, she realized, if it weren't for her new balance and body awareness.

He pointed, jabbing the air between them. "You know nothing about why I'm here."

"Whatever it is, it's not worth getting yourself killed."

"That's where you're wrong," he said. "But I'm not going to die. I'm going to *win.* And you're going to come with me to the dinner and do your little magic trick. We're going to unmask *El Jefe.*"

She just stared, her vision still blurry around the edges. It was pointless. He wouldn't listen. And he was right—she had no clue why he was really here. She didn't even know his real name.

There was only one person here who she *really* knew . . . and it was time to go meet him at the lake.

Oh, Carl, she thought, and wished there was some other way to fix this—but watching Julio turn his back, she knew there wasn't.

She would hate herself forever for what she had to do to Carl now.

TWENTY-EIGHT

AS SOON AS OCTAVIA stepped off the elevator onto the black sand, Carl knew there was trouble. She showed up fifteen minutes late, wearing a forced smile and walking stiffly.

"How did it go?" he asked.

She frowned and shook her head.

"Oh no," he said, and drew her into a hug. "Bad headache?"

He felt her nod against his chest.

"What happened?" he asked.

"Distance happened," she said, stepping back. "The closer I am, the easier it is to map."

"But the others . . ."

"I know," she said. "He's different, though. I need to get closer."

"Forget it," he said. "You got four out of five, Octavia. That's great. SI3 will be— What?"

"They want the bearded man. He's not just the head of the Few. He's the only *true* member. In fact, they shouldn't even be called 'the Few.' They should be 'the One . . . and his guests.'"

"Guests? You said they formed a powerful global network."

"They do," she said, "but he's the only permanent member. They're more like sponsors. They come and go. Only he remains. All of this," she said, and spread her arms, twisting at the waist, then tilting back, indicating the lake, the arena above, everything, "is *his* doing." She took a step toward him. "There's something else, something I didn't want to tell you before. . . ."

Carl tensed. "What?"

"I didn't want you to flip out or something." She reached out, cupping his elbows. "He created Phoenix Island. His idea, his money, his connections."

"What about Stark?"

"Just a soldier," she said. "The bearded man recruited him, paid for everything, and shielded it from the world. He ruined our lives, Carl."

"He's the one?" Carl said, his knuckles suddenly throbbing.

She nodded, looking sad. "I can't look at him without thinking of Ross."

At the mention of his dead friend's name, Carl felt the old ache in his chest. *Ross.*

"Remember Ross?" she said.

"Remember him? He was my best friend."

"Remember how brave he was?"

"He was too brave," he said. "I keep thinking how, if it wasn't for me, he'd still be alive."

"Don't think that way," she said. "You didn't make that place. The bearded man did. He destroyed Ross."

"And Campbell," he said.

She pulled up her sleeve, displaying flesh mottled in old burn marks. "All because of him," she said, her voice full of bitterness. "Thousands of kids tortured, killed, or turned into monsters. Now this place, his pleasure dome."

He gritted his teeth, picturing the bearded man laughing in the opera box, the devil enjoying his theater of pain.

"To him, we're just gladiators and guinea pigs." She took his hand and lifted it to her neck, pressing his fingertips to her throat.

Beneath the soft skin, her pulse fluttered like a butterfly trapped under warm silk.

"Carl," she said, her eyes wide and glistening, "he would slit my throat just to warm his hands in the blood."

He pulled his hand away, horrified by the thought. "Don't say that."

"You know it's true," she said. "We have to stop him."

He felt himself nodding—they *had* to stop him—and pictured his fist encased in the metal cestus, blasting through the golden mask, caving in the bearded face.

"We can't leave until I've mapped him," she said. "I have to get closer."

"How? He'll never come near us."

"You're right," she said. "I have to go to him."

"Impossible," he said. "His guards will stop you."

"After the awards ceremony, he hosts the champions' dinner. From that distance, I'll map him in about thirty seconds."

"Sure," he said, "but he only invites the champions."

"And their guests."

"Wait . . . are you saying I should take you as my date? Don't you think they'd find that a little suspicious?"

She paused, her eyes never leaving his, then shook her head. "Not *your* date, Carl."

"Not mine?" His mind flashed over the possibilities: the Zurkistani lightweight, who'd won this morning? Or the ape-like Z-Force heavyweight to whom Agbeko would forfeit this evening? She wasn't making any sense. . . .

She took his face in her hands and smoothed her thumbs along his jawline in a caress. "Let him win."

Understanding hit him like a right cross, and he leaned away from her touch. "Julio?"

"I'm sorry," she said, tears streaming from her eyes. "I'm so sorry."

He just looked at her. Let Julio win? Throw the fight?

Strangling a sob, she threw herself forward, hugging him hard and burying her face in chest. "Don't hate me. I wouldn't even want to live if you hated me."

"Hate you? I could never hate you, Octavia." He held her close and rubbed her back.

"You know I wouldn't ask you if there was any other way," she said.

"I know," he said, rubbing her back. "I know."

"Tell me you'll do it," she said, "and then we can run away together."

They stood that way for a long time, two throwaway kids holding each other at end of the earth, before he answered her. . . .

TWENTY-NINE

WRAPPED IN THE DEADLY CESTI, Carl's fists felt hard and heavy.

". . . representing Phoenix Island, Fighter 19," the announcer said.

He threw three punches in the air—all with his right hand, of course, making a show of how he kept his injured left arm close to his body, just as he'd made a show of limping into the octagon, favoring his broken toe as if it were a busted ankle. He lifted his right hand overhead.

Phony applause roared.

"This is it," Agbeko said, rubbing his shoulders. "You must win."

No "my brother" anymore, Carl thought. At least Agbeko was talking again. He'd sulked in his room all day. It was unfortunate, their friendship ending this way—once Carl went AWOL, Agbeko would hate him forever—but at least they could come together for this moment.

The announcer introduced Julio, who bowed toward the opera box, his bronze muscles shining with sweat. Beside him, Octavia talked and nodded. She never even glanced in Carl's direction.

He felt a surreal blend of fondness and sickening jealousy that tightened the knot of anxiety in his gut.

Better to not even look at her.

This was it. He'd never thrown a fight in his life, would rather have died than taken a dive. But now . . .

"Here we go, boss," Tex said, slapping his shoulder. "Knock him out fast so I can get back to the pad. I got a hankering for fried chicken."

Davis eyed Carl with suspicion, having apparently noticed something in his demeanor that the others had missed. Better not to look at him, either.

Fighters and trainers lounged in the bleachers. A handful clapped. Across the arena in the opera box, the Few offered polite golf claps—save for the bearded man, who smiled down from his throne, not bothering to clap at all.

Hope he bet billions on me, Carl thought. *Hope he bet his kidney.*

Then the ref was calling them to the center. Carl took a deep breath and started forward.

Julio's hard eyes stared from a bruised and swollen face coming apart with lacerations. The guy had guts. Carl had made it clear to Octavia that he couldn't just lie down. With the Few watching and wagering, they had to make this look real. He would pull his punches, but he had to hit the kid hard enough to make it look real, and that meant Julio would take more damage. But he didn't look afraid, only determined. Good.

Octavia kept her head down.

Then Julio was holding out his gloves, and Carl realized the ref had told them to touch it up. They knocked cesti with a metallic *clack*—Carl careful to avoid hitting Julio's broken right hand, as he'd promised Octavia, just as she'd guaranteed that Julio would avoid striking Carl's broken arm. Polite savagery . . .

"This is for the middleweight championship of the Funeral

Games," the ref said—as if they needed a reminder—and then spoke in Spanish, likely saying the same thing. Then he split them and ordered the teams out of the octagon.

Carl limped back to his side of the ring and swiveled into a southpaw stance. This put his right side forward, kept his left arm farther from the action, and sent a clear message: he was badly hurt and fighting one-handed.

Across the octagon, Octavia gave Julio a hug, kissed his cheek, and exited.

Just an act, Carl reminded himself, smacking down the jealousy that rose in him as automatically as a knee-jerk reflex. *Besides, she's not even your girlfriend. Never has been, really.*

The bell rang.

Julio came straight at him.

Good, Carl thought. *Just as planned.*

Also as planned, Carl moved laterally, tripping a little on his feigned injury and jabbing with his right hand.

To Carl, Julio moved in slow motion, feinting with a leg kick and then pushing out a one-two, which Carl slipped with ease. He slid out to the right and jabbed Julio's gloves, thinking, *You're going to have to do better than that, buddy. Throw the head kick.*

Julio tore after him.

Carl flicked another jab, which clattered off the kid's cestus and glanced off his forehead, splitting the skin and opening yet another cut. *Oops*, Carl thought, and slipped away again.

He was aware of his corner shouting, calling for the quick knockout—even Davis's voice in the mix, the medic seeing how easily Carl could clip the kid, could knock him out and finish this nightmare tournament—and he heard Octavia's voice, too, calling not to him but to Julio, not in English but in Spanish. Her

cries throbbed with urgency. One word he did understand—
cabeza—and that was good.

Cabeza meant *head*, and that was the plan. *Come on, Julio.
Kick me in the* cabeza.

And here it came, a rear roundhouse that Carl watched swing
in his direction, angling upward—though not upward enough, he
realized—and at the last second, he pulled his battered left arm
out of the way, and Julio's kick slammed into his ribs, knocking
the air from his lungs.

Julio followed up with hooks upstairs, left-right-left-right.
With superhuman speed, Carl whipped his right hand back and
forth, blocking the attacks. Anger roared up through him, filling
his nose with smoke and his skull with flames. What was this guy
doing?

Julio dropped back downstairs and drove his cesti into
Carl's arms.

Both arms.

Carl spun off the cage, grabbing and turning Julio, and
slammed him against the mesh. "What are you doing?" he said,
his words garbled by his mouthpiece and his rage.

He had agreed to something he'd thought he would never
do—take a dive—and asked only *one* thing in return: no strikes
to his broken arm. None. Octavia had guaranteed it.

Julio jabbed at Carl's head—a pitiful feint—then swung a
wild right . . . again at Carl's broken arm. The jerk was *targeting* it.

Carl locked him up, swung his right leg between them, and
hip-tossed the kid.

"No!" Agbeko called, no doubt remembering the Brazilian.
"Stay on your feet!"

But Carl followed him down, wanting to get things straight.

Julio grunted with the impact, then struggled wildly as Carl wrapped him up. Even this—exerting the necessary force to restrain this thrashing liar—was torquing his injured arm . . . and his temper, which he very much needed to control. "What are you doing?" Carl said into the struggling fighter's ear, working to form clear words through his mouthpiece. "Stick to the plan." He released him and stepped away.

It took Julio a second to get to his feet. This display of weakness only enraged Carl further—how dare this third-rate wannabe come at him hard?—but he kept his head and faked a wince, leaning away from where the kick had smashed into his ribs.

Back on his feet, Julio looked at Carl with confusion—and something like fear. What was wrong with this guy?

Julio bulled forward with hooks—again at the body.

Carl picked off one with his lead elbow, then lifted his fractured arm and sucked in his gut to avoid the second.

Carl tied him up in a standing position. Maybe Julio was too excited. Maybe he'd forgotten the plan. Maybe he hadn't understood Carl's reminder through the mouthpiece. Carl jammed a knee attack, spat out his mouthpiece, and dodged a stomp kick, all with the ease of a parent patiently avoiding a toddler in a tantrum, then whispered into Julio's ear, "Kick me in the head, you idiot. *Not* my broken arm. Stick to the plan, Julio."

He freed the tugging, grunting fighter, and almost laughed at the look of shock on the Julio's face. What was he, mad that Octavia had told Carl his name?

Carl glanced in her direction then, saw her standing just outside the cage, the cords in her neck standing out as she screamed, urging Julio forward, "*¡Cabeza! ¡Cabeza!*"

Yeah, Carl thought, cabeza. *Throw the stupid head kick, so we can get this over with.*

He hated the passion in her face, the hope and desperation in her voice.

And the kick slammed into Carl's broken arm.

He'd spent one fateful second looking at her, and Julio, despite Octavia's promise and Carl's two reminders, had driven a hard kick right into Carl's fractured arm, a direct hit that shoved Carl sideways and made him wince—not out of pain, of course, but from the awful feeling of his arm breaking clean through, the bones separating into halves.

When his bones snapped, so did Carl. Stoked by Julio's brazen treachery, the beast in Carl roared flames, incinerating its cage, and engulfed him in white-hot rage, into which Octavia's cries splashed like gasoline.

One-handed, he batted away Julio's ridiculous attacks and shoved him—hard.

Julio flew backward, banging into the cage.

"Look what you did," Carl said, and held up his arm, which flopped loosely halfway to the elbow. He walked straight at Julio—no bouncing, no blading away of the upper body, with his hands at his sides. "I was going to go easy, but now . . ."

He deflected a laughable kick.

Julio covered up—a pitiful sight that stoked Carl's rage.

Carl hammered the coward's thighs with powerful Thai kicks, swept his guard aside, and stunned him with a short, sharp head butt.

Julio wobbled, but Carl pinned him to the cage, keeping him on his feet. *No falling down now, pretty boy. You had your chance. I offered to walk away, and you stabbed me in the back.*

He was a conflagration of fury.

He drove a knee into Julio's ribs. Split his cheekbone with an elbow. Stomped down hard on his feet, loving the feel of bones breaking beneath his heel.

Julio flailed weakly, but Carl bumped him up against the cage, grinning at Octavia's shrieks as he dragged his cestus up Julio's face, opening a long cut. The sight of fresh blood spurred the beast in Carl. Again and again he struck his stunned opponent, raking away with his leather-wrapped palms, ripping open long furrows in Julio's face.

You will remember me by these scars, Carl thought. He cupped Julio's chin in his bloody hand, jerked the dazed fighter's head toward him, and at the same time whipped his own head forward in a vicious head butt that melted Julio's bones and sent him spilling to the ground, completely unconscious.

Then the fight was over, and the canned applause roared, and his team was all around him, cheering and slapping his back and calling him *champion*, and Octavia was crouched beside Julio, cradling his bloody head and trying to wake him up.

THIRTY

ONLY WHEN CARL REACHED the end of the tracks, having sprinted uphill for miles, did he consider what, exactly, he was doing. Barely out of breath, he paused there, remembering Octavia's hateful glare and the exuberance of his team and how, in the locker room, as Davis set, splinted, and wrapped Carl's broken arm, his rage had cooled and the terrifying recognition of what he had done settled over him like a killing frost. He'd fled the locker room, running away from his team, away from Octavia and Julio, away from the bearded man and the Few, away from the arena, out miles of track and tunnel, not running *to* anything, only away . . .

Bringing him here.

There were no guards, of course. Why guard an exit that led only to a frozen death?

He pressed the arrow-up button in the wall, and the heavy gate groaned open. Stepping from the tunnel, he squinted into the wind and sleety rain.

He stood atop the severe, unforgiving peak from which the jagged ridge of stone and ice plunged straightaway to the formidable coastline. Mountains without lowland, sheer stone cliffs falling to a brief beach of jagged talus booming with the crush of black tides, the vast ocean spreading away beneath dark skies to where, in the distance, lightning flashed, like a battle of gods unseen at the edge of the world. He stood in the howling wind, his clothes fluttering about him, sleety rain lashing down. By something approaching instinct, he dimmed further down his sense of cold and the stinging bite of the sleet, but then he thought, *No . . . feel it.*

The object of life was not avoidance of pain. Stark had said that. All this time, all this change, and Stark was still in his head. So be it. Sometimes, Stark was right.

He dialed his temperature awareness back to what he felt to be normal—it wasn't so easy to tell anymore—and reveled in the spasm of discomfort that shuddered through him, the sudden, saturating chill, the assault of wind and icy rain upon his face and exposed flesh, the cold rivulets within his hood, draining down his neck, onto his chest.

Yes. Cold. Discomfort. Reality.

Exactly what he needed now that he'd fled the false world of the Cauldron, where subversion and sublimation ruled, action defied intention, good destroyed good, and he had become a monster of rage.

Forget the Cauldron, he told himself, shuddering with cold. *Focus on reality; fixate on the now. . . .*

An unforgiving, uninhabitable place. The farthest reach of the world. Cruel and hard. Unsustainable. A land beyond all questions of hope. No life, nor even any soil in which to sow it. A bleak, untenable country that knew only stone and crashing surf, ice and blustering wind.

He stood at the base of the world, its lowest ring, as frozen and as devoid of hope as Dante's Judecca, the very bottom of the abyss to which were exiled the most vile of all sinners: those who had betrayed their benefactors.

He belonged here. He had only hosts and patrons—no benefactors—but knew he had betrayed everyone. Not just Stark but Octavia and even his father. Somehow, he had betrayed even himself.

Now, in this land of penance, there could be no more fitting punishment than reality.

For it was unreality, not just the lies and secret agendas but the *chip*, that had undone him. The chip had weakened him with strength. He had let it ruin him slowly, from the inside out, surrendering to one small concession after another, avoiding discomfort, blocking pain, coddling himself until the soft rot of comfort had hollowed out his core, leaving him empty.

Relying on the chip, he had exaggerated his own capabilities, had absorbed too much damage, and then overreacted when his body had finally broken, as of course it would . . . given the treatment to which he'd subjected it.

Already shaken by the cold, he dialed the awareness of his broken body back to normal—and growled, hit at once by the pain of his shattered toe, battered wrists and ribs, and badly broken arm. His entire body throbbed until he could barely breathe or see or think, until the pain made him a dull beast, a draft animal whose only burden was pain.

Eventually, thought returned and discomfort ebbed. Pain remained but did not wholly rule. This time, it was not the chip at work but him. For years, he had suffered bravely, endured. He hadn't needed heart for a long time, but here it was, coming back to him.

He straightened . . . hurting, sure, but feeling. That was the thing. This wasn't about punishing himself. He needed to feel the world, to understand. He had let the chip run off with him.

Where did you go when you reached the end?

He glanced out at the trail that they'd hiked to reach this

place and knew that to retrace those steps now, without proper clothing or direction, would mean suicide.

He turned back around.

The mountain ridge plunged away to the crashing sea out of which rose the Cauldron itself, a cone of dark stone steaming like a gateway to hell.

The Cauldron was the *real* Devil's Pocket, he realized then, not his neighborhood back in Philly. The devil—with his beard and smile and carnival of blood—used that pocket of steaming stone to tuck tortured souls away from the world. Temptation and torment, lies and ruin.

Have I ruined myself? Carl wondered . . . and instantly thought, *No*.

He'd been tempted and tormented. He had lied and transgressed and laid ruin, but he was not ruined. He remained. And it was he—not the chip—standing here, bearing up, swallowing the pain and gutting out the cold and thinking with sharper clarity than he'd summoned in weeks.

For too long he'd been apart from the world, shielded from pain—which was, to him, life. Now he had returned.

Into this renewed clarity came the voice of his old mentor. *You all right, son. Control the breathing and control the mind.*

Carl closed his eyes, breathed deeply, and channeled Arthur James.

You're at where you're at, Arthur's voice reminded him—as it had so many times in the past, whenever things had gone south. *Now what you going to do about it?*

He didn't know. He honestly did not know. He had broken everything, even himself, had lost not only his way but also his destination. He no longer knew who he was or what he wanted or where he belonged.

Man ends up in the dark, Arthur's voice said, *first thing to do is find a light switch.*

What was his light switch? What was his way out of the dark, out of the abyss, his way back to himself?

He waited for more of Arthur's wisdom, but it was Stark who returned to him then, repeating those words Winston Churchill was said to have uttered during Britain's darkest hours of World War II: *"If you're going through hell . . . keep on going."*

Yes, sometimes Stark was right.

But I've already ruined everything, Carl thought. He'd destroyed Julio, stealing Octavia's vital ticket to the champions' dinner.

He pictured the dinner and realized that, with Alexi out of the picture, the two Zurkistani champions would have only one guest to invite: Baca, who would grin and gloat as Carl choked down his bitter meal . . . attended by whom?

Agbeko would be ashamed, Davis would be afraid, and Tex would be . . . Tex. Better to simply go alone.

Unless . . .

And that's when Carl at last returned to himself. There is an almost supernatural sharpness of mind possessed solely by wild things that live nose to ground and to a few feral humans, who dwell fearlessly as wolves amid chaos, relying not on assurances and guarantees but on instinct and intuition and a fluidity of thought in sync with circumstance. It comes to the long-haul prisoner, strolling into the yard and reading threats where none should exist, and to the street-corner hustler, smelling opportunity where others see only danger and loss, and it came then to Carl, who had some time ago surrendered this oneness with the world when it seemed that his chip and coveted apprenticeship had lifted him above it all.

I'll take Octavia.

An absurd idea . . . a champion taking the girlfriend of the fighter he'd beaten.

The Few wouldn't be suspicious. They would be *shocked.*

Never underestimate the power of audacity, Stark often told him. Carl would have preferred the wisdom of Arthur James during this moment of need, but once again, Stark supplied truth.

Seeing Octavia, the Few would reel, searching blindly in the darkness of their ignorance . . . and Carl would flip the switch for them. He'd *won* her.

It would certainly be easy for Octavia to play the part of the resentful date. Then, up close, she could pull her mapping trick.

And then?

He didn't know—and didn't want to. Not because he was afraid she would never talk to him again but because he understood now that wanting to know too much, looking for guarantees, and calculating certainties had only set him up for failure.

He needed to fight this one in the pocket, roll with the punches, and look to counter.

That being said, he thought, *no reason to be stupid*, and he dimmed his pain down—way down . . . but not all the way. He left a whisper of cold and a hint of pain. He needed discomfort. Pain tied him to the world, to reality, and kept hope and overconfidence at bay. Suffering kept his heart strong and his mind sharp.

Time to take the fight to the Few.

Before him yawned the mouth of the tunnel that would carry him back into the hell on earth that was the *real* Devil's Pocket. He smiled, seeing something he hadn't noticed when he'd first passed this way. Chiseled into the stone overtop the tunnel's shadowy maw arched an ancient Latin warning— LASCIATE OGNE SPERANZA, VOI CH'INTRATE—which he recognized instantly from his recent readings with Stark: *Abandon all hope, ye who enter here.*

He began his descent.

The world had already taken everything from him. He had nothing left to lose . . . and that made him the most dangerous person in Devil's Pocket.

THIRTY-ONE

CARL JOGGED OUT OF THE TUNNEL and down the hall, passed the statue, and rounded the corner, heading for the elevators—until he heard booming music and the roaring of the canned applause.

A fight?

That made no sense. The tournament was over. The lightweights and middleweights had fought it out, and Agbeko had agreed to forfeit.

I am sorry, Agbeko's voice echoed in his mind. *Know that I am sorry.*

Oh no, Carl thought, and sprinted down the hall, the music and applause swelling louder and louder as he raced forward. He stumbled onto the bleachers, where a crowd of fighters and trainers stared down, looking shocked.

"No!" he cried.

Down in the octagon, Fighter 47, a blur of rippling, blood-soaked muscle, spun and launched Agbeko through the air. For Carl, panic downshifted the moment into excruciating slow motion. An uncanny sight, his huge friend drifting through the air, and Carl's eyes sharpened, drawing in Agbeko's look of stunned disbelief. Then the fighter crashed into the wire mesh—perhaps six feet up—rebounded, and dropped hard to the mat.

Agbeko! He'd broken his promise to Carl, jumped in for the

honor of Phoenix Island, and now—oh, now he was getting himself killed.

All because you weren't there to stop him, Carl thought.

He pushed across the bleachers and leaned over the rail, screaming, "Stop the fight!"

That's when he noticed Tex and Davis on the ring apron just outside the octagon, Tex shaking the mesh and shouting, Davis straining against the door, trying to get in. White towels littered that side of the ring. They had been trying to stop the fight.

Fighter 47 scooped Agbeko off the ground, lifted him overhead, and dropped him onto his knee. Agbeko rolled away, flailing weakly.

No!

Carl rushed back up the bleachers and into the hall, where he slapped the call button and waited what seemed an eternity for the elevator to arrive.

A minute later he was on the ground floor, racing into the arena. He bolted across the black bridge, barely aware of the purple lightning bolts shooting from his feet as he shouted, "Stop the fight! I'm team captain! Stop the fight!"

Inside the octagon, Agbeko wobbled forward, throwing clumsy punches, looking like a drunk trying to catch a fly. Fighter 47 advanced in a crouch, his freakish muscles bunched as tightly as a coiled spring. His face, which was a mask of scar tissue upon scar tissue, leered in a predator's grin.

As Carl topped the stairs, Davis turned with wild eyes. "Where you been? He's getting killed!"

Carl yanked at the locked door, shouting at the referee, "Stop the fight!"

The ref half turned, sneered at Carl, and dismissed him with a wave.

Fighter 47 clapped his hands high, then shot low—jarring a dark fragment of memory in Carl that felt more like a bad omen than a true remembrance—and scooped Agbeko's legs out from under him.

I have to stop this, Carl thought, and scaled the cage wall, shouting, but he was too late.

Holding the stunned Agbeko in a chest-to-chest bear hug, Fighter 47 bent his thick legs, sprung into the air, and flipped backward, hauling Agbeko with him. They arched in nightmare slowness—Carl screaming, "No!"—as Fighter 47 executed the suplex that smashed Agbeko headfirst into the ground.

Fighter 47 swaggered away from his crumpled victim, raised his fists overhead, and roared an inhuman bellow.

Carl leapt into the octagon, hit the floor running, and knocked the ref aside to crouch next to his friend. Agbeko shook with convulsions, then stiffened. One eyelid lifted, and Carl watched in terror as the eyeball rolled loosely in its socket, then drifted to one side and stopped moving. Agbeko shuddered, sighed, and went still.

Davis pushed Carl away and slid his fingertips under Agbeko's jaw. "He's alive," he told Carl. "Barely." Then he shouted for a stretcher. "Stat!"

Carl stood and watched, feeling helpless, as Davis worked.

All your fault, Carl told himself. *This is all your fault.*

But then he thought, *No—not* all *your fault*, and he turned toward the opera box, where the Few, drunk on their blood circus, chatted excitedly among themselves, and the bearded man smiled down, the devil presiding over his pocket.

Carl didn't bother to change, didn't bother even to wipe the blood from his hands. He went straight to her apartment and pounded on the door until it slid open. Octavia, also bloody, glared at him. "Stay away from us!" She slapped the button, setting the door into motion, but Carl stepped forward, jamming the sliding door with a shoulder, and it shuddered to a stop.

He stepped into her apartment.

Rage burned in Octavia's eyes. "I told you to get out of here."

He stepped toward her. She stood her ground. Suddenly they were against each other, both of them shaking with emotion.

"Be quiet," he said. "You need to listen."

Then he felt a sharp point pressing into his stomach and knew she had a knife.

"Feel it?" she said. "Get out or I gut you."

"I know how to get them," he said. "I know how you can map him."

"It's too late for that," she said. "Now get out." The knife moved forward, biting into Carl's skin a fraction of an inch.

He didn't flinch. "You're wrong."

"We had a plan," she said. "You promised, Carl. You were going to take it easy, let him win. Then you flipped. You let the chip take over, and you hurt him. You ruined everything."

"I had *one* request—don't hit my broken arm—but he went straight for it. Yeah, I got mad. I was giving up everything, letting him knock me out, and he couldn't do the one thing I asked? What's his problem? Winning wasn't enough? What, does he get off on pain?"

She stared into his eyes for a second before saying, "I never told him."

"What do mean, you never—"

"I didn't tell him about your arm, okay? There was no way to tell him."

"But you said—"

"I know what I said. I lied, all right? I told you what I had to tell you to get you to throw the fight. If I'd told you the truth, you wouldn't have helped—just like if I told him about you, he would have flipped. So no, I didn't tell him about your arm. I just told him to go for the headshot."

He stared down at her blond hair and brown contact lenses and angry face and realized he didn't know her at all. "Forget it," he said. "We have to take care of business. Agbeko's dead—or they're hooking him up to one of those machines."

She looked confused. "But you said he was forfeiting—"

"He said he was forfeiting, but he still went in there and fought."

Her face softened. He felt the knife's point leave his belly. "Oh, Carl. I'm so sorry."

He shook his head. "You and I, we don't have time for pity or the past or anything except nailing the bearded man."

"You ruined everything," she said. "It's too late now."

"No, it's not," he said. "You're coming with me. You're my date."

Her laughter was terrible, full of disdain. "You can't be serious. They would never believe—"

"They *will* believe," he said. "Never underestimate the power of audacity."

"They know I would never go anywhere with you. I can't stand you."

"Right—which is why they'll be so shocked when they see you walk in with me," he said. "They'll see your hatred and my cocky grin, and they'll think, *What are they doing together?* And right then, when they're primed for an explanation, I'll tell them the answer."

"Which is?"

"To the victor go the spoils," he said, aware that he was quoting Stark yet again. So be it. "Julio and I had a bet, I'll tell them. He lost, and I got you for the night. What an insult, huh? How does it feel to be loaned out to the guy who busted up your boyfriend?"

"You think it could work?"

"It will work . . . as long as you glow with hatred for me."

"No problem there," she said, but didn't put much into it. Her eyes shifted as she thought.

"This is our only shot," he said. "These guys have to pay."

"What are you doing here?" a weak voice said, and Julio limped into view, with one hand wrapped across his ribs. His face was a bloody mess, the cheeks flayed from eye to jaw.

It turned Carl's stomach to see what he'd done—but then he remembered his broken arm and his sense of guilt waned. They were even, as far as he was concerned. Turning to Octavia, he said, "I'm not dealing with him."

"Just wait there," she told Julio, who staggered forward, growling in Spanish now.

"Have fun explaining everything," Carl told her, and stepped into the hall, "but don't let it make you late for dinner."

THIRTY-TWO

THEY SAT AT A LONG TABLE at the center of the surreal slice-of-summer meadow he and Octavia had spied from the ductwork, everything warm and green, the air redolent of fresh-cut grass and flowers. Standing between classical marble statues, a woman in a red toga strummed an enormous golden harp. The music was soft and subtle, barely audible against the gurgling of nearby fountains. Servers in red togas—all of them with the scarred knuckles and whipcord muscles of former fighters—came and went, replenishing water and filling slender glasses with champagne that the bearded man asked them not yet to drink.

Stark would love this, Carl thought. *Straight out of ancient Greece.*

Though it wasn't really like ancient Greece, he thought, spotting the electronic speakers meant to look like rocks. The place felt like some weird theme park, where everything looked old and classical but was actually constructed with cutting-edge science and technology. Whatever. He just wanted to get this over with. He hated the toga, which made him feel like he was wearing a dress, and loathed nearly everyone at the table, Z-Force and the Few. That left only Octavia, and she hated him now. *Oh well*, he thought, sprawled back in his chair like the world's cockiest jerk, *at least they're buying our act.*

Her toga was longer, reaching almost to the floor. A circlet of flowers rested atop her blond hair—almost comical, given her convincing scowl—and twists of ornamental silver encircled her bare arms.

Playing his part, he put a hand on her leg. She cursed in Spanish and batted it away—but not before Carl felt the knife she'd strapped to her inner thigh.

Why had she brought a knife? He hoped she wasn't planning some insane attack on the bearded man. That would get them both killed.

Seated at the other end of the table, the Few wore golden half masks. By their exposed arms and shoulders, mouths and necks, he saw that they were younger than he had expected. Far younger. Not much older than him, actually.

The bearded man was the oldest, but still not *old*—late twenties?—and, like the other members of the Few, incredibly fit. He had the square jaw and trim black beard of an ancient hero. Unlike the others, he wore not a toga but a loose-fitting purple robe open at the chest, displaying the chest and neck muscles of a bodybuilder. He raised his champagne glass and spoke—not in the deep, modified voice he'd used in the arena—but in his real voice, which struck Carl with its warm, almost musical sound, the lyricism of which was only magnified by his English accent. "I would like to propose a toast."

Everyone raised their glasses—except Octavia, whose eyes bored into the table. Was she mapping the bearded man?

I hope so, Carl thought. *This is our last chance.*

But he didn't want her drawing the wrong kind of attention, so he nudged her. She came out of her stupor, blinking, then raised her glass as the bearded man said, "To victory."

Along with the other guests, Carl echoed their host's words. Then he sipped his glass—the stuff tasted awful, like the world's worst soda—and set it back on the table.

"I would like to propose a toast as well," the blond-haired woman said, and everyone took up their champagne flutes again. This woman had been giving Carl looks all night—strange, eager looks, like she wanted to eat him or something—and now she looked directly at him, saying, "To champions."

They completed the toast, Carl uncomfortably aware of the woman's lingering gaze, and the bearded man started talking about their accomplishments, winning the Funeral Games— "and," he reminded them, grinning wolfishly, "ten million dollars apiece."

Directly across from Carl, Fighter 47's toga looked ridiculous draped across his misshapen muscles, as did the crown of laurel tilted atop his boxy, bald head. With his hairless mask of reddish scar tissue and deformed features—his nose was a stunted snout of gnarled flesh with slits for nostrils—he looked like a burn victim who had subsequently sliced every inch of his melted face with a straight razor. Carl glared, hating him, his stupidity, his brutality, his leering stare, and the rank animal smell of him wafting so pungently across the table. Registering Carl's glare, he smiled, revealing a jagged range of broken teeth. His uncannily bright blue eyes, so unsettlingly familiar, lingered a second on Carl before swinging back toward Octavia.

"I hope the champagne meets with your approval," the bearded man said, and smiled. "Juglar cuvée," he said slowly, as if savoring the name. "Eighteen twenty."

"A very good year," one of the masked men said, and the Few laughed.

"Sixty thousand dollars a bottle," the bearded man said.

Sixty thousand dollars for a bottle of booze? Carl thought. *A quarter of a million going around the table right now?* It made no sense—or *wouldn't*, rather, anywhere but here.

"Divers rescued these bottles from a shipwreck in the Baltic," the bearded man said, "at a depth that provided ideal consistency of temperature and light, perfectly preserving them for nearly two centuries." He raised his glass again. "Ladies and gentlemen, if you would, please hold your glasses to the light. Observe the bubbles."

No matter what it costs, Carl thought, staring at his glass, *it still tastes like crap*.

"Now," the bearded man said, "if you'll further indulge me, hold the glass close to your ear."

Carl leaned close and heard the snapping of effervescence.

"Each of these bubbles," the bearded man said, sounding reverent, "was trapped inside a bottle for two hundred years. Now, as we watch, they race to the surface and burst, gone forever. This is their moment in time . . . and ours, as well." He looked around the table, then raised his glass. "To impermanence, then. . . . Let us savor its terrible beauty."

"To impermanence," the blond-haired woman said, and the phrase echoed around the table.

Carl pretended to sip his, then set it down.

"Tonight, we share a most excellent feast," the bearded man said, "cuisine even kings and queens would covet."

Good, Carl thought. Maybe once everybody started feeding their faces, this guy would shut up. He wanted to get out of here.

Straightening in his throne, their host said, "Before we summon the celebratory meal, however, we must first ensure that the Funeral Games have, indeed, concluded."

What did he mean? The tournament was over. . . .

"Each year," the bearded man said, "we give the champions the opportunity to challenge one another."

Challenge another champion? Carl thought, and pictured his ironclad fist smashing Fighter 47's disfigured face.

"If challenged, you may accept or decline," the bearded man said. "If one accepts and loses, he will retain his prize money. You fight only for honor."

Do it, Carl told himself. *Challenge him. Punish him for what he did to Agbeko.*

But that was ridiculous. He couldn't fight again, not with a broken arm.

"Fighter 45, you first," their host said. "Would you care to issue a challenge?"

Baca translated.

The Zurkistani lightweight, who'd been scowling at Carl all evening, leaned forward eagerly, but Baca shook his head, and the little hammerhead declined, then leaned back in his chair, regarding Carl with simmering contempt.

"Fighter 19?" the bearded man said. Both he and the blond-haired woman stared expectantly at Carl. "Do you issue a challenge?"

Carl hesitated. Fighter 47 needed to pay for what he'd done . . . but now wasn't the time. As soon as dinner was over, he and Octavia would join Julio and Davis and maybe Tex—Carl still hadn't decided—and escape the Cauldron. He couldn't hang around to fight another match. But there was something else, wasn't there? Another reason not to issue the challenge, a reason he didn't want to admit to himself . . .

With his pride screaming, Carl shook his head.

The bearded man gave an as-you-will nod and turned to Zurkistan's heavyweight. "And you, Fighter 47?"

The apelike fighter grunted and turned toward his host with his mouth hanging open. From this angle, he had no discernible neck, only massive shoulders of humped muscle.

The bearded man asked, "Would you care to issue a challenge?"

Fighter 47 just stared.

Baca leaned close to his fighter. "He's asking if you'd like to fight again," he said, using English, not Zurkistani, Carl was surprised to notice.

Fighter 47's head bobbed up and down. "Hah-ee-wuh," he said, his voice low and garbled, like gravel in a blender.

Baca chuckled.

Hah-ee-wuh? Carl thought, feeling unexpectedly jarred. Some Zurkistani phrase?

Fighter 47 fixed Carl with his icy blue eyes, pointed a thick arm across the table, and growled, "Holly-wuh."

Carl jolted out of his slouch.

Hah-ee-wuh.

Holly-wuh.

Suddenly, in a moment of bright terror, he understood everything—the unsettlingly familiar eyes, the brutality, the impossible muscles and insane aggression . . .

He was saying *Hollywood.*

"Decker," Carl said, feeling like he'd plunged into a pool of ice water.

Fighter 47 showed his broken teeth again.

Vispera had chipped Decker, and something had gone horribly wrong, as it had in Octavia's story about the mutated psycho rabbit, and turned the redneck he'd fought back on Phoenix Island into a monster.

"A challenge," the bearded man said, his voice suddenly excited.

The Few leaned in, bright-eyed. The blonde stared at Carl, tracing the rim of her goblet with a manicured fingertip.

"And how do you respond, Fighter 19?" the bearded man said.

Carl was so shocked by his realization—*Decker!*—that it took him a second to unstick his thinking.

He had never backed down from a challenge in his life . . . and this was *Decker*, the guy who'd ruined Agbeko, the guy who'd pushed Carl back on Phoenix Island, causing all the trouble with Parker, the guy who'd hunted Ross, the guy who'd killed Medicaid and blamed it on Octavia . . . who sat beside Carl now, oblivious, still staring at the table. Lost in her secret world, she couldn't interfere. Decker had challenged him, and this was his chance to set things right.

But his arm was broken, and they had immediate escape plans, and there was the other reason, the thing he didn't want to admit to himself.

His mind replayed a painful clip: Agbeko sailing across the ring like a man stuffed with straw.

You're afraid, he thought bitterly. For the first time in his life, he was terrified of someone. A wave of self-loathing washed over him—*coward!*—but his broken bones throbbed, reminding him of his limitations. He couldn't let hatred for Fighter 47 or contempt for himself goad him into a fatal mistake.

"Well?" the host asked.

Hating himself, Carl shook his head.

The bearded man frowned. "Are you certain? The match promises *singular* spectacle."

"Yeah," Carl said, burning with shame. "I'm certain."

Decker laughed—a sound like a dog vomiting—and pointed at him.

Baca smiled, his dark eyes glittering.

Seeing their faces, Carl felt like an emotional piñata, simultaneously beaten by bewilderment, rage, fear, and self-loathing. . . .

The bearded man sighed dramatically. "Our loss," he said, "but never let it be said that I forced opponents into the octagon. And so we conclude another Funeral Games." He smiled, then gestured toward the other end of the meadow, where dozens of servers in red togas appeared, laden with trays heaped with food. "Let the feast begin."

THIRTY-THREE

OCTAVIA WAGED WAR.

Outwardly, she slouched, appearing sullen, but inwardly, she attacked.

Several courses came and went. When nudged, she emerged from her private world to sample food, actually tasting none of it, consumed as she was by frustration and burgeoning fear and the steady salvo of artillery rounds thumping and bursting inside her skull.

Something was wrong.

In the arena, the bearded man's features had simply evaded her, rapidly shifting beneath the probing fingertips of her mind. At this range—if she were much closer, she could reach over and rip the frigging mask off his face—she'd expected to map him with ease, but no . . . every time she penetrated the mask, her mind's hands sunk *into* the target, at which point she would feel a subtle drawing inward, as if the face were made of quicksand.

Carl elbowed her again, breaking the connection and bringing her back as a server leaned close, placing a blurry plate before her. Booming howitzers bloomed flame in her brain. She gritted her teeth, bunched her toga fabric in white-knuckled fists, and nodded to the server, who spoke softly and stepped away. When the food came into focus—meat smothered in sauce, other stuff on the side—she sawed off a small corner, put it into her mouth, chewed mechanically, swallowed, and dropped back into herself . . .

Where she *finally* made contact.

With a surge of excitement, she felt resistance, an actual surface, the hidden topography unfolding beneath her sweeping perception. She felt skin and bones, the rise of a nose—long and thin and unexpectedly feminine—and her touch slipped away over smooth skin, crossing a high cheekbone that gave way to a slightly upturned eye, over which arched an eyebrow trimmed to a fine line.

Bewildered, she realized that she knew this terrain. It was the face of the blond-haired woman.

Had she misfired, targeting the wrong person?

It didn't seem possible, stress or no stress, headache or no headache. She'd never missed a target, not even when she was new to mapping and thought Bleaker was a complete madman and didn't yet understand that this was science, not mysticism.

She sipped her water, trying to still her trembling hands.

Forget it, she told herself. *You can wonder what happened later, after you map him.*

She remembered her role, cast a withering glance in Carl's direction, and went back in.

This time, the sucking liquid formed quickly beneath her probing . . . and seconds later, feeling a familiarly crooked nose, she realized that she was mapping not the bearded man but Carl.

Again and again she tried, passing through puzzlement to frustration, from frustration to fatigue, and finally from fatigue to fear, not just fear of failure, which loomed large in her now, but fear of the moment itself. She was in the grips of that most ancient bogeyman—ignorance—for with each attempt, she encountered a different face, cycling through everyone at the table, save for the bearded man, until, at last, in a moment so terrifyingly unnatural that it filled her with revulsion, she was mapping her *own* face.

She jolted upright in her seat, shocked and nauseated.

The humongous fighter across from her snorted laughter, and she was thankful that her unsteady vision kept her from having to see his incomprehensibly ugly face.

In her skull, countless fireworks detonated simultaneously in a grand finale of pain.

Carl stared at her with concern. Even reeling as she was with pain and confusion and terror, she knew she had to scowl him back into his all-important act, but her face tingled with numbness, and her mouth didn't seem to want to cooperate with her mind.

Someone said something, and people laughed, and then someone in a red toga was leaning over her, apologizing in Spanish as he dried the table where, exiting her nightmare moment with a spasm, she had apparently tipped over her water goblet.

Dinner's nearly over, she realized, smelling the untouched cup of coffee not quite steaming before her. *My last chance* . . .

But the idea of what she'd just felt stopped her cold.

How had she mapped her own face?

Did the bearded man's golden mask contain some kind of high-tech defense that reflected psionic probing?

"And finally," the bearded man said, his voice distant and strangely dislocated in position, seeming to come from the left . . . then the right . . . and then farther off at an angle, anywhere other than his actual location, "we wish each of you safe travels and a fortuitous future."

He's sending us away, she thought, and her unwillingness to fail surged. For years, other people had ruined her life, abused her, turned her into a loser. This was her one shot at erasing all of that, her one opportunity to stick it to the organization that had tortured her, killed her friends, and turned her into a freak, her one chance to strike back at everyone—not just the Few, Stark, and Vispera but even her stepfather and her mother, who, despite loving Octavia, had made a series of horrible choices, failed to protect her, and then left her in the lair of a monster. Succeed here, and she would wipe away the past, save countless people, and start a new life not as a loser on the run, some shadow-dwelling fugitive one traffic stop away from incarceration, but as an agent for good, someone with an incredible talent that would only grow more impressive with SI3's help.

Do this, she told herself. *You're in control of your own future.*

She dove back in . . .

Where she found not the bearded man's face but Carl's, only this time, something was horribly, horribly wrong.

She was suddenly terrified.

Oh, Carl . . .

His face was badly disfigured and *lifeless*.

Covering it was a thin membrane engulfed in flame. Carl was gone—beaten or tortured to death—and wrapped in a burning shroud. . . .

She slammed backward in her chair with a scream, toppled to the grass, and crawled frantically backward several feet before realizing the face had vanished.

Around the table, people gawked. Carl was coming toward her, leaning to help. Seeing his face—his real face, his *living* face—she nearly cried out in relief.

Gathering her wits just in time, she slapped his hand away

and shouted at him in Spanish to keep his filthy hands off or she would kill him.

Carl froze, plainly too shocked to pick up his side of the act, so she hauled herself to her feet before he could do something stupid—like show concern or courtesy.

Brushing angrily at her toga, she shouted, "*¡Cabrón!*" Then she turned toward the Few and said, "*Tocador de señoras, por favor.*"

The bearded man smiled knowingly, then turned to her server. "Please assist the lady to the powder room."

She forced a polite nod and shot Carl another glare for good measure.

What had just happened?

Shortly after her arrival at the SI3 Bunker, Bleaker had explained the ultimate goal of remote viewing: not just global projection that disregarded space—but also temporal projection that ignored the obstacle of time. According to some theorists, a full-blown remote viewer could scout not only across distance, locating and observing someone halfway around the world, but also across time, locating and observing a target hours, days, or even years in the future. *Time and distance are inextricably linked*, Bleaker had said, and he'd laughed and confessed his serious doubt that remote viewers would ever conquer chronology. She, of course, had agreed. Psychic stuff was cool for comic books, but in the real world, it seemed utterly ridiculous.

Until now.

Now, with the feel of Carl's battered and lifeless face fresh upon her mind's fingertips, the concept of prescience was utterly terrifying.

Had she glimpsed one possible future? Had her mind shot

forward along hypothetical trajectories and bounced back with this grisly warning?

When the server offered his arm, she declined, following alongside him as he headed for a break in the hedges.

"No," the bearded man said, bringing them to a halt. "Show her to the other powder room." He pointed to a tall archway of carved marble at the opposite end of the glade, beyond which, she knew, comatose pairs lay in unholy union facilitated by tubes and wires and circuitry.

THIRTY-FOUR

CARL ROSE TO FOLLOW OCTAVIA, but the bearded man insisted he stay. "She'll be fine," he said, his voice light and friendly. "The feast was apparently too rich for her." He beckoned to a server, who leaned close, nodding as the bearded man whispered, and then hurried off through a side door.

Dinner broke up, and the bearded man bade Z-Force good night. Decker showed Carl his broken teeth one more time before he swaggered after his departing teammates.

"Prepare the evening ritual," the bearded man told the Few. "I will join you shortly."

They bowed and left, the blond-haired woman pausing to look Carl up and down one more time before saying, "I do hope to see more of you, Fighter 19."

Carl said that would be nice, thinking, *Thanks, but no thanks, lady*, and lingered beside his chair, glancing across the glade to the arch through which Octavia had disappeared. Why had she screamed and fallen? What had gone wrong with the mapping? Was she okay?

"Each year, the ancient Incas selected a child to symbolize the sun god," the bearded man said—a strange statement that brought Carl around. He replayed the man's words in his mind, just to be certain he'd heard them correctly, and realized yes, he had. *Each year, the ancient Incas selected a child to symbolize the sun god.* Huh?

The man gestured. "Please, have a seat."

"Thanks," Carl said, "but we'll be out of your hair as soon as she—"

"I insist," the man said.

Carl sat. *Come on, Octavia. Let's get out of here.*

"Being chosen as the symbolic sun god was a tremendous honor. Parents groomed their children and displayed them before the emperor, who chose only one—the *perfect* child." With the other guests gone, the man seemed far away in his throne at the end of the table, and Carl was even more aware of their surroundings, the bright green grass and gurgling fountains and guards almost but not quite hidden here and there among the trees and topiaries.

"Imagine," the man said, and snapped his fingers. "Peasant to godling in an instant."

Carl raised his brows, trying for *wow.*

"From abject suffering to absolute splendor," the man said. "Worshippers paraded the child from village to village, holding decadent feasts in its honor."

Carl nodded, pretending interest, and glanced again across the meadow. Nothing.

The man regarded him, looking amused, then sipped his wine. "Finally, when the feasts ended, the parade wound up the mountain, where priests sacrificed the beautiful child."

"That's awful," Carl said.

The man shrugged. "Is it? Would you prefer thirty years of misery and squalor, or ten years of grooming ending with feasts and crowds of adoring worshippers?"

"Look, I don't want to hold you up," Carl said, and hooked a thumb toward the archway. "I'll go wait for her over there, and you can go do your ritual or whatever."

"Oh no," the man said, waving dismissively. "Do you really think me so poor a host?" He gave a short whistle, and a patch of darkness detached itself from a nearby tree—one of the muscular Krebs hawks, Carl realized—swooped down and landed on the table, where it tilted its head and stared at up the bearded man with bright yellow eyes.

"Amazing creatures," the man said, and signaled a servant. "Observant and highly trainable." He reached out and stroked the bird's head.

The bird's beak vibrated rapidly, producing a chittering sound.

"That's neat," Carl said, just to say something, and turned toward the arch again. His stomach churned. *Come on, Octavia.*

A servant brought the man a silver plate topped in strips of red meat oozing blood.

"Tell me, Carl," the man said. "Are *you* trainable?"

"You know my name, then," Carl said, not bothering to feign surprise.

"Of course," the man said. He pinched a strip of meat between thumb and forefinger and dangled it before the bird. The Krebs hawk gently pulled the bloody offering into its beak. "I research all guests. Can't be too careful these days. Wouldn't you agree?"

Carl nodded, trying to seem relaxed. He didn't like the bird's yellow eyes, the blood on its beak, or the way it bobbed its head back and forth, choking the meat down whole.

"Carl Freeman," the man said, "age seventeen, orphaned son of a fallen Philadelphia police officer, sentenced several months ago to Phoenix Island on repeated charges of assault. Now . . . tell me about the chip."

The request sucker punched Carl, but his mind fired quickly—no sense playing dumb; this wasn't some wild guess, after all; Stark must have told him—so he rolled with it, saying matter-of-factly, "What about it?"

The man offered a smile nearly as bright as his golden mask. "I know you were holding back in the ring. How fast are you really? How strong?"

"Pretty fast," he said, deciding to admit the same basics he'd given Stark, figuring the guy already knew anyway. "I'm faster than I am strong, but I can hit pretty hard. Speed is power."

"Indubitably," the man said, and fed the bird another strip of raw meat. "What a shame it is we weren't able to see a full display of your powers. Stark's *golden boy* . . ."

Carl just looked at him.

"You're not entirely dissimilar to him," the man said.

"To Stark?" Carl said. Whatever this guy knew about him, he was *way* off on that one.

"Warrior poets, brains *and* brawn. Stark and Freeman." The man chuckled. "Stark and Freeman . . . sounds like a moving company, doesn't it?"

Carl forced a smile. "I guess."

"When Stark came to me, he had one foot on this side of the Styx and the other in Charon's raft to Hades." The man paused, seeming to expect questions. When Carl asked none, he continued. "In Afghanistan, the shot callers dropped Stark and his men into a region they'd all but resigned to the Taliban. Stark saw the situation there for what it was and understood that his two directives—the rules of engagement and his mission to stabilize the region—were in direct opposition. He reacted logically, ignoring the rules and prioritizing the mission . . . with fantastic success.

"Enemy activity in the region dropped to near nonexistence. The rear echelon brass celebrated Stark as a hero. He was incredibly charismatic, and they used him to stir morale across the theater and to win favor with politicians at home. Then reports of atrocities surfaced. Torture. Villages burned. Mass graves filled with noncombatants. Heads displayed on spikes as warnings. He was winning the war—but at what cost?"

Carl shifted in his seat. It was all too easy to picture Stark doing these things.

"Suddenly, Stark presented a problem," the man said. "Their golden boy had been up to some very dark business in the hinterlands. Not exactly winning the hearts and minds. They couldn't allow him to continue—the scandal, if they were discovered!— and yet they also couldn't afford to publicly acknowledge his war crimes. To troops in the region, he was more than a hero. He was a legend. If the brass persecuted Stark, they would spark an unwinnable PR war on two fronts: outraged media around the world and outraged troops in the field. In the end, unwilling to ignore or condemn, they made a decision so coldly pragmatic that even Stark might condone its savage utility. They directed his convoy straight into an enemy ambush."

"That's horrible," Carl said.

"Indeed," the man said, feeding the bird another strip of meat. "After the IED overturned his Humvee and the Taliban hammered it with RPGs and AK-47s, American artillery obliterated *everything*. The Taliban *and* the Americans. Later, investigations were launched, apologies were tendered, and a few low-level heads rolled. The brass had solved their problem. Or so they assumed. . . .

"But Stark not only survived, he understood. Even as the American bombs were crashing down, he told his soldiers what was happening. That's why, after the column had been reduced to smoking ruins, Stark's two surviving troopers—both of them grievously wounded yet fueled by fanaticism—did not wait for American support to arrive. They understood that if their warrior king ended up in an army hospital, the brass would never allow him to survive surgery. So they hauled him across the desert on foot—one of the men hobbling on a broken leg—and brought him to a village, where a pair of private contractors, German brothers who specialized in delivering armored vehicles across Afghanistan, delivered him to frankly the only place on earth capable of saving him, a medical facility within a laboratory compound owned and operated by yours truly."

"You saved his life," Carl said.

"More than that," the man said. "I rebuilt him. I personally oversaw each step and used every resource at my disposal. Over time, he healed. Then became *more*. And as I guided his rehabilitation and facilitated his education, he became more than a patient to me. He became a son."

Carl sipped his water. The story went a long way in explaining Stark—and dovetailed into Octavia's claims about the Few and the bearded man.

"As I said, I see similarities between the two of you," the man said, "but watching you in the ring, I recognized differences, as well. You're merciless enough when you decide to destroy an opponent, but unlike Stark, you harbor a curious restraint."

Nodding toward his bandaged arm, Carl said, "Well, I broke my arm."

The man's eyes twinkled. "You *let* him break your arm. This hesitation of yours is a mystery to me. Strange, almost charming . . . like a gap between the front teeth of a beautiful girl."

Carl shrugged. "I guess I don't like wrecking people if I don't have to."

"Stark would have decimated his opponents, though, don't you agree?"

"Yeah, I guess probably he would."

The man tossed a piece of meat into the air, and the bird snatched with a sharp *clack*. "And tonight, at dinner, would Stark have challenged the other champions?"

"I don't know," Carl said. "I mean, if he had a broken arm? I don't know."

The man touched one bloody finger to the tip of his tongue. "Yes, you do know. He would have challenged them both, and he never would have declined a direct challenge . . . but *you* did."

"*You* want to fight that kid?" Carl said.

The man looked at him for a second, saying nothing, then pushed the meat plate forward. The bird plunged its beak into the red mess. "In my pantheon," the man said—and the word *pantheon* jabbed Carl like a thumbtack—"I am Zeus. Stark is my son . . . Ares, god of war. Brash, fearless, savage, an unprecedented wonder of destruction. I know that you are a like a son to him, and he describes you as a young Apollo—the sun god, bright and bold and handsome, but with a terrible temper, the oracular god of Delphi, god of prophecy and truth." He held up one finger. "But, of course, Stark's missing the point. Apollo wasn't the son of Ares. The god of war had two sons, both by his sister-wife, Discord: Phobos and Deimos. Which are you, Fear or Terror?"

"Neither," Carl said, not liking the guy's tone, which had gone from jovial to accusatory. "Look, I appreciate you sitting with me, but I'm going to go check on Margarita."

"*Margarita*," the man said in a disgusted voice. He slammed a fist on the table, toppling goblets. The bird squawked and flapped away. "You're no Apollo—and certainly no god of truth.

You're Hermes. Not just messenger to the gods, but conveyor of souls to the underworld. Patron of thieves and *liars*. Tell me, O trickster god, who is she, and what are you doing here?"

"What are trying to say?" Carl said, buying time now, urging Octavia to hurry up. Things were falling apart. . . .

"Do you really think I rose to power through stupidity? I know all about your chip and the one in *Decker*." The man smiled, seeming to savor Carl's surprise. "You recognized him during dinner, didn't you? Delicious, watching that unfold. I know everything. Stark's promise of promotion, your midnight meetings with the girl—oh, you didn't know I was watching, eh? What did the two of you discuss?"

Carl shrugged, his mind racing. His own temper was rising—this guy, who had caused everything, Phoenix Island, the death of Ross, everything, coming at him now—but he had to keep it in check, had to play stupid long enough to get Octavia and get out of here. No sense denying the meeting. The Few must have cameras down there. "I told her she was pretty."

"Lies!" the man bellowed, and struck the table again. He hunched forward, making the light glint off his golden mask, and pointed at Carl. "There is no record of you and *Margarita* sharing a placement . . . and yet as soon as you arrived here, the two of you arranged your midnight rendezvous."

Carl faked a smile. "Guess she thought I was pretty, too."

"This wasn't some clumsy make-out session. The two of you talked—argued, by the looks of it—and then surveyed my boats. Strange first date, wouldn't you agree?"

"So she showed me the boats. Big deal. They're weird."

"*Weird*," the man said, drawing it out. "Not so weird, I assure you, as feeling your little friend trying to peek behind my mask tonight."

Carl shifted in his chair. He'd *felt* her mapping him? "What do you mean?"

"No more games," the man said. "Out with it. Stark reported no successful chipping of a female, yet she's clearly a gamma. Stark's up to something—some *power play* at last—and you're obviously one more acolyte in his cult of personality. Who is the girl?"

"I told you—"

"Your spotter?"

"What?"

"Spotter—the sniper's eyes . . . that's the correct term, isn't it? She verifies the target, and the assassin strikes. Is that what you've become, Carl Freeman? An assassin? Did you come here to kill me?"

Carl scrunched up his face. "No . . . this is crazy. I don't know what you're talking about, but whatever it is, I'm done listening. Thanks for dinner." He stood.

"Sit down," the man said.

Carl just stood there, glaring back at him. "You want to know about Margarita, ask her. You got a problem with Stark, talk to him. I came here to fight. That's it. And yeah, the promotion. You wanted a show, and I gave it to you."

"Not yet, you haven't," the man said, and snapped his fingers overhead.

Burly servers in red togas stepped from behind trees and fountains and statues. Now, instead of bearing trays or ladles, they carried short batons of coiled steel.

Turning to the bearded man, Carl pretended confusion. "Take it easy. I'll talk. I just don't know what to tell—"

"Too late," the man said. "What I want from the girl, I'll take, and I'll have Stark groveling at my feet before you can say *Et tu,*

Brute? As to you, perhaps now we'll see how well you can *really* fight."

That's it, Carl thought. *I'm out of here.* But as he twisted, he saw red togas stepping through doors, from behind hedges, and at least a dozen double-timing it out of the distant archway. No way out—and no way to fight all of them. That left only one option.

He swept a fork into his fist. "Call them off, or I'll drive this straight through your heart."

"Fascinating," the man said. He stood, a smile coming onto his face. "The wolf at bay."

Carl started around the table, thinking, *Get to him now, before it's too late. Get the fork under his jaw. Take him hostage and get out of here.*

The man raised his arm, and a dark cloud rushed from his sleeve straight at Carl's face.

Carl closed his eyes and raised his hands, but the cloud engulfed him. Electricity flooded through him with the force of a dozen Tasers, and his skin burned as if he'd been dipped in acid. A gagging stench like road-killed skunk filled his nose and mouth, choking him. He fell to the ground, screaming and convulsing. Retching, unable to control his muscles, he tumbled into a confusion of panic. He had to get away from the electricity and the burning and that awful stench, but he couldn't move. . . .

By the time the pain, spasms, and nausea abated, guards had shackled and surrounded him. He sagged, muscles spent and twitching, between two red togas. His burning eyes streamed tears, and his nose streamed mucous.

"Hose him off, dress him in fighting trunks, and throw him in a cell," the bearded man said, sounding almost bored. "We'll give him a little time to recover, and then we'll announce the exciting news: he has accepted the challenge of Fighter 47."

THIRTY-FIVE

OCTAVIA DIDN'T BOTHER trying to replace the louvered vent grate. Sooner or later—and the answer was *sooner*, she believed—they were going to quit pounding on the bathroom door and either find a key or shoot off the lock. Right now, speed mattered more than stealth.

Fear sharpened her senses. This was not the tentative and cluttering fear of worry; this was *real* fear, *survival* fear, and she moved through the dark ductwork as surely as she might navigate a well-lit corridor.

Reaching the vertical duct, she slid deftly into its shaft, pressed her feet and back into its walls, and shimmy-walked down to the next floor.

She swung into the horizontal shaft that flanked the main hall but paused before crawling toward her apartment. She couldn't afford to burn five minutes traveling to an empty room.

Julio was in the room—she felt him there as soon as she pushed in that direction—but he wasn't alone.

Oh no.

Others—three, four . . . six . . . eight—were also there. Three surrounded him. The others were scattered through the apartment, moving things, searching.

The sketches . . .

She hustled along the ductwork in the direction of the apartment. By the time she rounded the corner into the hall, she no longer needed to map the unfolding situation. She could hear it.

The door banged open, and someone—Julio, she thought—shouted. She heard grunting and thumping—a scuffle. Reaching the grate overlooking the hall, she hissed with fear. A team of red togas was carrying an unconscious Julio toward the elevator. At the rear of the pack, the gigantic Russian with the red triangle tattoo lumbered after them, her sketches gripped in one cannonball fist.

Her emotions spun over a pit of terror, but she called upon courage and logic. She could do nothing for Julio now. The sketches were lost. All she could do was run. She had to get out of the Cauldron and off the mountain range, where she could signal SI3.

She needed her parka and boots, some water, and a flashlight. There wasn't time for much else, and she already had the knife, which she unstrapped from her leg. She popped the vent free, dropped to the hallway floor, hurried to her room, started to reach for the ID pad, and—almost as an afterthought—used her mind to scan beyond the door.

Her heart jumped.

Someone was inside her apartment, just beyond the door, waiting . . . for her, no doubt. And not just someone, she realized, but *two* someones.

Cursing herself for not thinking to count the people in the hall—so stupid!—she gathered up the long fabric of her dress and sprinted back to the ductwork. She tucked the knife into her teeth like a pirate, jumped, grabbed the ductwork opening, and kicked her way up the wall and into the shaft.

Minutes later, she was two floors down, hustling along the horizontal pipe. When she'd fled the bathroom, she'd expected shrieking alarms, but she'd heard none, and the hallways appeared empty . . . which all made sense, really. Where would she go? Where could she go? They would expect to apprehend her as she reentered her apartment or to find her lying broken at the bottom of a vertical shaft.

Arriving at a vent, she peered out through its slats—all clear—popped off the grate, dropped into the luxurious hall, and started running, hiding the knife blade alongside her forearm in case she passed anyone *not* looking for her. To the casual observer, a girl might run past in a toga for any number of reasons . . . but a girl running with a steak knife tended to arouse suspicion.

She flitted along the tapestried hall, turned the corner, and sprinted past the massive statue of the seated fighter, thankful once again for the way they'd changed her blood on Phoenix Island. She had always been a good runner, but now she could run faster than anyone she knew and could keep running for hours without tiring.

She turned another corner, and there, at the end of the hall, was the mouth of the tunnel, where the train sat, still as a sleeping beast.

Yes, she thought, *I've made it*.

An icy breeze sighed from the dark mouth of the tunnel, chilling her enthusiasm. She was going into a blizzard wearing only a dress and sandals?

Yes, you are, she thought, *because there is no other option*.

Explore the train, look for clothes or blankets . . . something?

No. She couldn't afford the time. She hoped SI3 reached her before she froze to death.

She was almost to the tunnel when someone stepped from the shadows.

She lurched to a stop, started to bring the knife around, and then stopped, recognizing Carl's friend, the one with the big mouth. *Tex*, she thought, remembering the name easily because it was so strange, short for *Texarkana*, which was even stranger. She relaxed. Carl must have told him and Davis to meet them here.

"Hey," Tex said, smiling. "Where's Carl?"

"Something happened," she said. "He can't come yet."

Tex looked past her. "You got people chasing you?"

She glanced over her shoulder. "I don't think so. Not yet, anyway. Where's Davis?"

He shrugged. "That boy's moodier than a pug." He grinned, walking toward her. "Know what I mean? Little dog, built like a toaster, got a pushed-in face? Moody little things . . ."

She started to say, *Isn't Davis coming with us?* but then noticed something that chilled her more deeply than had the icy wind. "Where's your parka?"

He stretched out his hand. "I don't think we ever *really* met. I'm Texarkana Reginald Dubois."

She stepped backward—this wasn't making sense—and even that small retreat set her internal alarms clanging. Something was wrong here. . . .

He dropped his hand but kept walking slowly forward. "You're Octavia, right?"

"Margarita," she said, and gripped the hidden knife, thinking, *Carl would never have told this guy my name. . . .*

"I'm not talking code names, honey," he said. "I'm talking your real name . . . the one you used back on Phoenix Island."

Okay, she thought. *That's it. Get around this guy, run fast, and leave him in the dust.* She glanced right and left.

"Don't bother," he said. "You're not going anywhere." Suddenly, his voice was completely different . . . cold and flat as a knife blade, no hint of his trademark twang. "I must say, your English has improved remarkably."

So has yours, she thought, but what she said was, "Who are you?"

He spread his hands, and his smile changed, too, losing its goofiness. "Maybe it's easier to say who I'm *not*," he said, still creeping forward. "I am not, as you seem to be realizing, some brick-witted hick. Honestly, I'm surprised it took you so long. I mean, didn't it ever strike the two of you as strange that Stark would send a green recruit to the Funeral Games?" Then his voice did twang. "Y'all're slower than a turtle with a limp."

"I don't know what you're talking about," she said, terrified now. She didn't care who this guy was. She just wanted to get away from him . . . but she'd been backing in the wrong direction, away from the tunnel.

"Turns out, I'm not so green after all," he said, and chuckled. "I'm no cage fighter. But Stark didn't send me to fight. He sent me to watch."

"Watch the fights?" she said, talking to talk, trying to figure her next move. She couldn't run backward—alarms or no alarms, guards would be hunting her, and as soon as they spotted the vent covers, they would charge in this direction—but she couldn't run forward, not with him blocking her.

He shook his head. "Stark sent me here to watch for *you*. I suspected you were Octavia when I saw you two together that night down by the lake, but you made me second-guess myself when you got so angry after Carl beat up your fighter. I didn't really know for sure until Carl asked you to dinner tonight. Little reckless, don't you think?"

"You have me confused with someone else," she said, angling left.

He mirrored her, stepping to his right, cutting her off. "Who got you out of the hospital, anyway? SI3, right? That's what Stark thinks . . . and the man is seldom wrong. He's the one who said if you two got together, you'd likely duck out before the mass exodus, so I figured I ought to come down here and make sure that didn't happen."

"You could never stop Carl," she said, moving to the right. He mirrored her again, blocking her way. She couldn't slip past him and certainly couldn't go through him. As one of Stark's mercenaries, he wouldn't even blink at her steak knife. So that meant . . .

He took a step forward. "Oh, I would have stopped him. See, I know his Achilles' heel. He's too nice. Good old Tex would have put on a puppy-dog face and said, 'Please don't leave me behind, boss,' and Carl would've taken me. Then I would have pushed both of you off the mountain and seen which one hit first. Where are you going?"

She ran back the way she came, away from the tunnel, but not *too* quickly. She heard him laugh, heard his footsteps coming after her, but more importantly *felt* him drawing nearer. Once again, fear and adrenaline sharpened her sixth sense, and as she slowed her retreat and twisted her wrist, she could feel him—all of him, every plane and angle and its exact relation to her own planes and angles—so distinctly that even without looking, it was nothing for her to swing her arm backward and plunge the blade handle-deep into the meat of his thigh.

He grunted but still grabbed her, one hand digging into her shoulder, the other yanking her hair. She swung into him, scared witless yet not needing her wits, needing only the courage to fight and the amazing awareness that flooded her mind and body as she shook her shoulder free and drove her knee into the knife handle.

He jerked and howled and clubbed with a thumping blow that hit her somewhere—the shoulder or the neck . . . she didn't know, didn't care, just had to fight now, fight and run—and she screamed, raking his face, scratching at his eyes.

He cursed and hit her again, but she twisted her body away from him.

Growling, his face streaked with bloody scratches, he yanked her long braid, trying to haul her back to into his grasp, but at the same moment, she gritted her teeth and thrust her head in the opposite direction.

A hard tug, a painful tearing away, and she snapped free, turning and sprinting for the tunnel.

Feeling his distance behind her, she risked a glance and saw him limping in pursuit, twenty feet behind, thirty, with blood draining from the handle jutting from his thigh. He shook his fist, still clutching what looked like blond roadkill. "I'll kill you!" he shouted, staggering doggedly after her.

Entering the tunnel, she ran along the narrow gap between the tunnel wall and the train itself until she passed the final car, where she hopped over the rail and started sprinting up the center of the tracks.

Stark had known about SI3, anticipated her coming here, and sent along an assassin.

Should've buried the knife in his gut, she thought. *One less killer hunting me.* Since joining SI3, she'd mistakenly assumed she'd escaped Stark's reach—but she understood now that SI3 had underestimated him. Worse still, despite everything she had seen and endured on Phoenix Island, *she* had underestimated him. Vastly. No matter how this ended, could she ever be safe again?

Forget it, she thought. *Just run. Get away from this psycho and you can ponder life's mysteries later . . . if you live that long.*

Yet as she pounded uphill, thoughts tortured her. What were they doing to Julio and Carl? Were the Few slipping out some back door, flying to safety? Was the Cauldron about to explode?

She imagined a thunderous boom and a wall of flame rushing up the tunnel, burning her to ash, the idea so terrifying that she could almost feel . . .

No . . . *could* feel.

No explosion, no flame, but a faint rumbling.

The tracks were moving.

Shaking.

Then, in a moment of dawning terror, she understood . . . the train.

No!

In the bright screaming clarity of that nightmare microsecond, she heard and felt the onrushing train—the soft purr of its approach, the vibration of the ground—and then light panned around the corner behind her, growing brighter.

There was no safe place, no walkway or platform on either side. Sure, she could flatten herself against the wall, but with such a narrow gap, the train's vacuum would suck her straight under the metal wheels and chop her in half.

She sprinted uphill, wild with fear, running like she had never run before, throwing every fiber of muscle into the effort, pounding up the incline, growling with effort, but there was nowhere to run, no way to escape, and she could *feel* the train, could feel its massive, undeniable bulk hurtling inexorably closer, bearing down on her, louder now, the light breaking fully into the tunnel, the ground shaking beneath her, and suddenly, flight seemed so pointless that hopelessness filled her legs, making them heavy, slowing her until it felt like she was being sucked backward into the train.

She cast her mind forward, scanning the tunnel walls for some recess or alcove or door, anything into which she could duck, but found nothing, nothing at all to save her from the mass of approaching steel that filled the tunnel. . . .

Or rather, *almost* filled it.

And in that second, she *felt* the crucial difference defined by this *almost* in a way she never could have perceived, had she relied simply on her eyes and brain, which prior to the chip would have analyzed the moment in a three-dimensional myopia of objects and absolutes. Yes, cowering in the gap between train and tunnel wall, she would never escape the suction of the passing train, but she didn't just feel the gap. In a flash approaching Bleaker's coveted prescience, she felt the static and the dynamic—gap, train, wall, herself—felt everything simultaneously and four-dimensionally, not just the objects in relation to one another but the objects in relation to one another *in time*.

She stopped running, turned downhill, and ran straight at the train, which roared into view, rushing toward her.

Within the illuminated engine cabin, Tex—or whatever his real name was—hunched over the controls, leering at her with wild eyes and the toothy smile of a crazed clown. He pounded the dashboard, blasting her with the banshee wail of the train whistle, then threw his head back with grotesque laughter.

The train raced toward her—thirty feet away, twenty, ten . . .

At the last second, she jumped.

Not at the train but at the wall, which she hit just as the train whooshed past. Before the deadly vacuum could seize her, she sprung up and away, kicked off the train, rebounded off the wall again—higher this time—climbing as she ricocheted back and forth, train to wall, wall to train, *feeling* the necessary timing, until she kicked off the wall once more, harder this time, and dove stomach-first onto the roof of the train.

"Yes!" she shouted, her voice a mad shriek of triumph, and for several seconds, she just lay there, insane with adrenaline and the surging joy of having so narrowly escaped death. Then she shuddered out a prayer of thanks and started crawling forward, inching toward the engine.

THIRTY-SIX

CARL PACED THE CELL, scanning for weaknesses or resources but finding nothing. No cot, no sink, no window, no toilet. Only a cement floor with a recessed drain—the drain bothered him for reasons he couldn't quite untangle—three walls of solid concrete, and the sliding wall of thick plexiglass that served as a floor-to-ceiling window onto the empty corridor.

Where was Octavia? What were they doing to her?

He lashed out with a powerful kick. The plexiglass didn't even wobble.

Would Decker wobble? He had certainly wobbled when they'd fought back on Phoenix Island. Carl had head butted him into La La Land, then knocked him clean over the cot with an uppercut.

But they weren't forcing him to fight *that* Decker. They were forcing him to fight the mutant, Fighter 47. Why? Less for sport than spectacle.

Stark had told him about the ancient Romans, who, when glutted with blood sport, infused excitement by importing unlikely opponents from around the world: boars against hyenas, wolves against apes, tigers against bulls. Tens of thousands of animals killed, whole species going extinct, all for the twisted novelty of a crowd desensitized to human suffering.

Now the bearded man had slated an exotic finale certain to

delight even the jaded Few . . . two chipped opponents fighting to the death.

So be it, Carl thought. *He might be stronger than me, but I can out-think him*. He put his back to the wall, slid into a crouch, and did what he hated to do, replaying the memory of Agbeko's fight with Decker. *Agbeko*, he thought, watching his friend fade again, and felt a sinking sensation in his chest, sorrow and guilt weighing down his heart.

If only he had stayed with his team, Agbeko would be alive and well. But that was a foolish and pointless line of thought, like saying if only his father hadn't been shot or cancer hadn't killed his mother. Fate dealt you cards, and you had to play them, not waste time wishing for aces.

Make Decker pay, he told himself. *Don't waste time feeling sad. Get it together*.

Easier said than done, he found, wrestling with remorse as he replayed the memory again.

Focus on Decker, he told himself, and played it again. And again. And again . . . on and on, for an hour, two hours, pausing and rewinding the clip to analyze every second of its grisly footage, paying special attention to Decker's position throughout, studying him for even the slightest vulnerability . . . until he realized that, like this cell, Decker would reveal no weakness, leading Carl to the ultimate conclusion . . . he couldn't beat him.

Shouldn't, he corrected himself, *not couldn't*—for no boxer dealt purely in absolutes. In a fight, *everyone* had a chance.

Carl might have an edge in speed—might—but his only definite edge was brains. The error code had stacked Decker with muscle, making him incomprehensibly, irrepressibly strong, but it had also punted his brain back into prehistoric savagery. Carl expected no subtlety or surprising strategy. Decker would charge straight at him.

He's the bull, Carl thought, *and I'm the tiger*. A troubling analogy . . .

In the Roman Colosseum, he had been shocked to learn, bulls beat tigers every time. It didn't seem possible that a tiger, with its speed and strength and variety of attacks, could lose to the bull's straightforward charge, but it did . . . without exception.

But of course tigers, despite their terrible strengths, were limited to instincts, locked into a style dictated not by what they *thought* but by what they *were*.

He was not so limited. The chip in his head did not define him the way instincts defined a tiger. The chip would not carry him to victory—only his mind could do that.

He had to blind Decker or crush his windpipe or break his knees—but understanding these tactics was not the same as seeing a way to make them happen.

Think, he told himself, and shut his eyes. *That's your only shot. Think.*

But there was nothing. Only the undeniable reality of the thing Decker had become, the same unsolvable riddle.

Maybe there is no answer, he thought, *and even if you do win . . . what then?* Sooner or later, he would float and burn. He had no illusions that they would revive him as they had the others.

Yet he felt no fear. A wonderful gift, the absence of fear, and he said a prayer of thanks for the calm that had settled over him. Ironically, when he'd had the opportunity to challenge Decker, a panic of possibilities had seized him, but now, out of choices, with the fight set, he feared neither Decker nor death.

The fact that victory ultimately meant nothing—for he had

no illusions concerning his fate, should he miraculously defeat Decker—might have crippled the resolve of some fighters, but in Carl, it only served to strengthen. Nothing to gain, nothing to lose, nothing to distract or weaken, should the tide turn against him. He would fight to win, to destroy.

And as to his inability to find a workable plan, so be it. After all, wasn't that what he had learned atop the mountain . . . to stop clinging to guarantees? Yes, he would need to think to win, but he had to trust himself to do that thinking on his feet, in the moment, during the fight.

To fight his hardest, he needed rest—not sleep, but the deeper, more efficient rest afforded by the chip. Kneeling upon the hard floor, he downshifted his systems, slipping quickly into his inner darkness, where respiration and circulation practically ceased.

When he opened his eyes again, someone in a red toga stood on the other side of the plexiglass, staring in at him.

Carl jumped to his feet. "Agbeko!" They must have sucked the life-force from some poor steward in order to save him. A repulsive thought, but Carl was *overjoyed* to see his friend standing there before him.

Agbeko smiled strangely, looking sheepish, almost embarrassed. "I'm sorry, sir. Things aren't precisely as you're perceiving them," Agbeko said, and his voice was odd—still deep but . . . different. A new accent?

Carl crossed the cell and flattened his palm against the glass. "Get me out of here, man. There's a button on the wall."

Agbeko placed his own hand against the glass in an almost–high five. "I am afraid I can't do that, sir."

Carl slapped the glass. "Is this about the tournament, me telling you not to fight?"

Agbeko tilted his head, clearly not understanding. "Perhaps it was a mistake, visiting, but I just wanted to thank you."

Then Carl had the accent. Under normal circumstances, he would have identified it straight away, but you don't expect your African friend to start speaking with what sounded almost—but not quite—like an English accent. . . .

"You dealt me quite a kindness when you eliminated the Zurkistani middleweight," Agbeko said. "It feels absolutely amazing to be back in a young body again." He offered a quivering smile, his eyes wet with tears. "Thank you, sir."

Carl withdrew his hand, relief at seeing his friend alive again crumbling away. "Kruger?"

"Indeed, sir," the thing beyond the glass said, neither in Agbeko's voice nor Kruger's but in some unnatural hybrid of the two. It stepped back, spread its arms, and glanced at its own body. "If my mates back in the regiment could see me like this . . ."

In a nightmarish rush of revulsion, Carl understood. Though Agbeko's body stood before him, his friend was gone . . . evicted to make room for the consciousness of Kruger. That's what they were doing in that lab: not draining the life of stewards to save injured fighters, as he and Octavia had supposed, but eradicating injured fighters and giving their bodies to loyal servants.

The Agbeko-Kruger-thing laughed. "But of course my mates are all dead now, aren't they? Not I . . . no . . . 'Kruger,' as you call him, lives on. You've given me a second lease on life. That's what really matters."

No, it's not, Carl wanted to say, but he was used to parleying with monsters, and this creature before him was his only hope, so he disguised his disgust and horror and said, "If you really are grateful, let me out of here."

The thing shook its head. "It is unfortunate that you have run afoul of the Few, and I do hope you will be able to reconcile, but unfortunately, I cannot assist you. I'm terribly sorry, sir, but as much as I appreciate your contribution, it's the Few to whom I owe my principal debt. You could even say that my debt to them is *eternal*." He started drifting away, down the hall.

Carl slapped the plexiglass. "Wait! I'm not going to hurt them. I just want to escape. You of all people must understand. I just want to keep living."

The thing turned back to him then, smiling. "But you *can* still live on, sir. Just don't die in the octagon. They can fix nearly anything, even a broken neck"—he demonstrated, rolling his big head in a smooth circle—"but dead is dead. True death cannot be reversed. What a waste that would be. Death ruins the vessel, makes it a sieve—and any life runs out. Lose without dying, and your body will make a wonderful home for someone else . . . perhaps even one of the Few. Rumor has it that one of them already covets your body."

With that, the thing disappeared.

Carl, gripped by fresh terror, remembered the blond-haired woman's long and longing gaze. *No matter what*, he thought, *I will not become a vessel*. Like a Spartan warrior of old, he would accept only victory or death.

THIRTY-SEVEN

WHEN THE TRAIN REACHED the end of the tracks and slowed to a stop, Octavia dropped to the ground alongside the engine. Seconds later, the train clunked, shook, and started rolling slowly back down the tracks.

She charged forward into the lobby and saw two large buttons on the wall, one with an arrow pointing up, the other with an arrow pointing down. She slapped the up-arrow, and the front portion of the wall shuddered and started groaning upward.

Yes!

Then she recoiled as a frigid wind blasted in under the rising door, covering her in goose bumps and dusting her sandaled feet with snow so cold that it burned.

Glancing over her shoulder, she saw the engine rolling away around the corner. Tex, who had undoubtedly assumed that she'd died on the tracks, stood in the illuminated cabin with his hands pressed to the window, shouting furiously. The train disappeared around the corner, and the tunnel filled with an awful squealing sound.

Brakes, she thought. *He's figured out how to stop the thing, and any second now, he'll hop out and come after me.*

She slipped under the door and onto the frozen mountaintop. When a thousand needles of windblown sleet bit into her, she screamed involuntarily and twisted to a stop, applying her own brakes. Her body didn't want to go any farther.

Freezing wind rushed over her, tugging at her toga and making her squint. Her muscles tensed, as if rebelling against her madness. And it *was* madness. How could she possibly descend over miles of rocky ground slick with ice and treacherous with drifting snow, through gusting wind, sleet, and absolute darkness . . . wearing only sandals and a toga?

You have no choice, she told herself again and struggled forward.

A short time later, she glanced back uphill at the snow-blurred pane of light that was the mouth of the tunnel. It didn't seem possible that she had covered only this short distance. Her teeth chattered, and her eyes streamed tears from the cold. For several seconds, she stared longingly at the tunnel, drawn like a moth to its light and warmth.

But Tex would come for her—with the bloody knife not in his leg but in his hand.

Better to die out here, trying, she thought, and stumbled downhill, moaning against the cold, which burned her skin and stole her breath. She shut her eyes to block the sleet—what good would they do her in the dark, anyway?—and patted her lead foot tentatively before each advance. This slow pace terrified her. How long would it take to freeze to death under these conditions?

Her sandal hit an icy patch, and she fell hard to the rocky ground. At least *most* of her hit the ground. Her left arm landed on nothing at all. . . .

It dangled in the freezing air, touching nothing, and she realized with a chill that this time had nothing to do with temperature, that she'd nearly fallen off the path. She remembered the hike up, the long views and sheer cliffs.

She wouldn't freeze to death. She'd fall to her death first.

Stop, she told herself. *Think*.

She shuffled ahead on all fours. Her hands and feet screamed with the cold, but it was reassuring in the darkness to feel the path beneath her.

With that thought, she jerked to a stop and cackled wildly.

That was it!

Feel the path.

How could she have been so stupid?

Because you were running for your life, she thought. *The cold stunned you, and the dark terrified you.*

She stood, and despite the long odds and bitter cold, a warm thought rose in her. *You don't have to fear the dark ever again.* She walked confidently forward, her eyes still closed against the stinging sleet. She could feel the terrain unfolding before her just as clearly as she might see it during broad daylight. Ice and snow and loose stones still demanded caution, but she nonetheless built speed and soon moved downhill in a sliding shuffle nearly as fast as a jog.

Uphill, a murderous scream ripped the night.

She turned and opened her eyes and saw Tex's shape silhouetted against the light of the tunnel. She could *feel* him up there, too, could sense his insignificance and vulnerability against the great mountains and the howling wind. She clenched her chattering teeth in a satisfied grin.

"Come and get me," she taunted, "unless you're *afraid*."

The wind gobbled his response, but her taunting had obviously worked, because he tottered into the darkness after her.

Good, she thought, and started downhill again, shuffling along the slippery path with her eyes closed, bent forward into the icy wind that assaulted her exposed flesh and flattened her flapping toga to her straining body. In all her life, she had never been so cold, but she couldn't risk going any faster, not shaking like she was and navigating with numb feet over slick rocky ground. Making matters worse, her increasingly clumsy muscles jerked with the cold, and her breathing had become rapid and shallow. Still she struggled forward. She would not surrender to the darkness or cold or wind—and certainly not to terror.

She would not quit. From personal experience, she knew how pain could dilate one's sense of time, turning seconds into minutes, minutes into hours, hours into not just days or weeks or months but a seeming eternity, so she dismissed her sense of time, scouted forward with her mind, and focused on the terrain ahead and the sense of herself as an object dropping steadily toward the coast.

She persevered, struggling through darkness and Antarctic cold, filled with tough hope.

She hoped to make it downhill past the jammers; hoped to find a cave and escape the wind; hoped a satellite would detect her and send help before she froze; and hoped with delicious bitterness that she would hear Tex scream as he fell to his death. . . .

THIRTY-EIGHT

THIS IS IT, Carl thought, coming into the octagon. *Kill or be killed*.

But that wasn't really true, was it?

Glancing up at the opera box, he saw the Few chatting it up. The blond-haired woman eyed him hungrily, and the bearded man smiled down from his throne.

No, this wasn't kill or be killed—at least not for Carl, who harbored no illusions about his fate. In the unlikely event of his emerging victorious, it would be kill *and* be killed.

Or rather, killed and be killed . . . and then serve as what Kruger called a *vessel*. A terrifying notion . . .

So be it, he thought, and ripped the air with a right uppercut. He would fight to the end—not in hopes of saving himself, but to destroy Decker. He would show neither mercy nor hesitation— and least of all fear, which he wouldn't sell to the Few for every penny of their staggering wealth.

With luck, his own death would be absolute, a true and irrevocable death, and he would burn upon the black lake. His charred bones would sink into the murky depths, where they would join the bones already cluttering the bottom of the lake, until the Few departed, triggered the explosives, and blew the Cauldron into oblivion.

That was okay.

Anything to avoid becoming a vessel.

Either way, this was the end.

The past was gone. The future would never arrive. All he had was now. This. A final moment in time. The fight.

Bound in leather and metal, his right fist felt hard and heavy. Now they would see what the cestus could *really* do.

His left hand, which had carried him to many victories, would do him no good now. The arm was badly broken. Both bones. They had removed his splint, and only the leather of the cestus kept the wrist from flopping forward. He couldn't punch with that hand—doing so might send broken bones tearing through his arm—but he could still strike with his left elbow. Of course, if he got that close, Decker would finish him.

With Davis kneading his shoulders, Carl scanned the bleachers. Their near emptiness suggested that half the fighters had already headed home, but of course they hadn't left. They'd died . . . or nearly died, only to be used, like Agbeko, as vessels. He saw no sign of Octavia or Julio. Were they both strapped onto gurneys alongside stewards? No sign of Tex, either. Davis hadn't seen their teammate since the previous night, just after Carl left for dinner. That didn't bode well for Tex, but Carl couldn't worry about his missing teammate now.

The music died, and the announcer's voice said, "Welcome to a most special occasion, a battle between champions. In the red corner, this year's Funeral Games middleweight champion, representing Phoenix Island, Fighter 19."

Canned applause rose and fell.

Rather than taking a bow or waving to the crowd, Carl showed the opera box his middle finger. The bearded man smiled down as the others laughed or feigned shock.

The announcer said, "And in the blue corner, this year's Funeral Games heavyweight champion, representing Zurkistan, Fighter 47."

Across the ring, Decker roared, thumping his chest with a fist wrapped in leather and iron. He was no longer human. The chip hadn't vaulted him forward, hastening post-human evolution; it had pitched him backward into a brutal subhuman age.

The lightweight bounced beside Decker like an excited puppy. Baca, on the other hand, paid no attention to his fighter. He swept his eyes back and forth, scanning the bleachers.

The referee called them to the center.

Here we go, Carl thought, and as they came together, he smelled Decker's rank animal odor. They stood inches apart, Decker shorter than Carl but far larger, the unnatural muscles radiating heat and vibrating with superhuman strength. His blue eyes stared from the mask of scar tissue with the same dark interest Carl had seen back on Phoenix Island, backlit now with savage rage.

Carl looked through him.

Decker chuckled—a hissing, burbling sound like lava bubbling to the surface. The lightweight rattled at Carl in his ugly language. Baca said, "Any last words for Stark?"

"Yeah," Carl said. "Have him say hi to your mom for me."

Then the ref told the fighters to touch gloves.

Carl turned without touching gloves and headed across the ring. Time to get down to it.

Davis hung at the center for a moment, watching the other team. Then he joined Carl with a look of concern. "What I said before, about getting behind him, hitting him in his neck?"

"Yeah," Carl said, remembering how the medic had surprised him with terms like *occipital artery* and *cervical vertebrae*. "Hit him hard enough, I can paralyze him."

"Forget it," Davis said. "Too much muscle back there. He's got muscle where there shouldn't be muscle."

"Thanks," Carl said, and laughed. He felt oddly calm, almost excited. There was nothing now but the fight. And he knew how to fight.

Within him, the rage-beast paced in its cage, growling like a tiger at feeding time. It would be so easy to open its cage and embrace the fury, but that, like relying solely on the chip or some carefully calculated plan, would blind him, would doom him. No shortcuts. No pat answers. He had to live in the moment and trust himself to make the necessary adjustments as the fight unfolded. Time for Stark's self-efficacy. His wholesale commitment to and confidence in his mission—destroying Decker—would allow him to dispense with worry and focus each second solely on the task immediately at hand. Stick and move, hustle and flow.

"Seconds out!" the ref called, meaning it was time for Davis to leave.

"Eyes and throat," Davis said. "Especially the throat."

Carl nodded.

"Here," Davis said, and pressed a finger into the little dip beneath Carl's trachea and above where his collarbones met, "or here," and touched him alongside his Adam's apple.

"Got you," Carl said. He knew Davis meant well, but nailing those targets would be *tough*. Decker was short and kept his chin tucked.

"Out of the ring, red corner!" the ref hollered.

Davis opened the door but paused to give Carl's shoulder a squeeze and look him in the eyes. "Do me a favor and kill this mo—"

The bell rang.

Decker charged with uncanny speed. Carl pivoted away, jabbing with his right hand, hitting only air, and backpedaled toward
the center. Watching Decker whirl in full speed, he thought, *They
sabotaged my chip.*

The world hadn't slowed down for him.

Decker lunged low with speed that made no sense.

Carl scooted to one side but felt Decker's hand close like a pit
bull's jaws around his ankle. He tried to pull free, but Decker
shoved forward, bulled him off-balance, and yanked on his ankle.
Just like that, Carl was off his feet.

Decker swung him around by the ankle and let go, and then
Carl was flying across the ring. In that suspended moment, he realized that his chip was working fine. Decker was just so fast that
it didn't seem that way. Then he slammed into the cage and rebounded straight at Decker, who was rushing him again.

Years of boxing experience saved Carl. Coming off the cage
felt like bouncing off the ropes, and he instinctively launched a
right. His metal fist caught Decker between the eyes. It wasn't a
hard punch—he was off-balance and unable to twist his body—
but it landed cleanly, ripping a gash in the scarred face. Decker
kept coming, completely unfazed.

Carl ducked, heard Decker hit the cage, and had just enough
time to regain his feet before the monster wheeled and shot for
his legs.

Carl stomped out with a kick that pounded Decker's
face—but did nothing to slow him. Instantly, he understood
his mistake—kicking demanded too much commitment against
such a fast and aggressive opponent—and then Decker had
him again.

Panic filled Carl as Decker lifted him from his feet and tossed
him into the air. He flew in a high arc, turning a slow-motion

cartwheel, and fell not to the mat but into Decker's punting kick, which exploded into his stomach, knocked the air out of him, and pitched him halfway across the ring.

He hit the mat hard and struggled into a crouch, fighting for breath, certain his ribs were broken, and Decker charged straight at him.

Like a bull, he thought, *a bull killing another tiger*, and the wall of muscle slammed into him, bowling him over and pitching him into the cage.

He struggled to his knees just as Decker loomed over him, smashing downward with his metal fist. Carl tucked his chin and lifted his guard, and the strike slammed like a sledgehammer into his broken arm, which folded back sickeningly. Decker's cestus plowed through, grazing Carl's face and opening a long cut on his cheekbone. Decker took half a step back and launched a flurry of savage hooks. Carl had never seen such incredible hand speed, but the redneck telegraphed every punch, drawing his fists back too far and swinging too wide, and Carl slipped these blows, slid out to the side, and got to his feet.

As Decker turned, Carl faked a jab and popped him with a short Mexican uppercut. He hoped to snap the sharply angled punch into Decker's throat, but it only clipped the chin, and then the monster scooped him up and slammed him to the floor again.

What a lousy way to die, Carl thought. Decker wasn't even a good fighter. He was just strong and fast, impervious to pain and relentlessly aggressive. Carl couldn't get set, couldn't time him, couldn't work combinations. There was no chance for strategy, only for single tactics delivered from disadvantageous positions.

Over and over, Decker charged, sometimes swinging his heavy shoulders side to side like a gorilla and launching attacks from angles that made no sense in Carl's experience. Carl ducked and dodged and managed to land a few retreating jabs, none of which had any real effect on his irrepressible opponent, whose speed, size, and ferocity overwhelmed him again and again. Decker tossed him, slammed him, flipped him, and steamrolled over him. Decker was toying with him, humiliating him, and slowly but surely breaking him down.

And yet Carl refused to quit, just as he refused to surrender to panic. The rage-beast within him gnashed at the bars of its cage, but he fought that down, too, knowing he couldn't afford its red temptation. Against this opponent, the reckless stupidity and overconfidence of anger would only get him killed.

His own punches were clipping Decker, cutting him, but doing no real damage. If anything, the streaming cuts excited the mutant. He stalked Carl, eyes gleaming with amusement, and showed his broken-toothed grin. Blood everywhere.

Didn't even bother to wear a mouthpiece, Carl observed. Then he was airborne again, and during this slow-motion flight, he realized he had to double down.

From the opening bell, he'd been trying to fight smart— sticking and moving, playing defense, avoiding Decker's power, and hoping for an opening that he knew now would never arrive in time . . . because well before he had a clean shot at Decker's throat, he'd be dead.

He couldn't wait for opportunity. He had to *make* opportunity. And to do that, he had to take risks.

Fighting smart was getting him killed.

Time to fight *dumb*.

Get his respect, he thought. *Catch him hard. Make him think twice before rushing in.*

Decker charged.

This time, rather than ducking or dodging, Carl sacrificed de-

fense, stood his ground, and *drilled* him with a punch. This was
no flicking jab or sneaky uppercut. For the first time in the fight,
he surrendered mobility and defense, standing his ground and
twisting every ounce of power into a blasting right cross that
slammed into Decker's onrushing face like a metal bat cracking a
fastball encased in scar tissue.

Thock!

Decker didn't so much as blink—not even when blood from
the new cut poured into his insane eyes.

Then Carl was in the air again, tumbling across the ring,
thinking, *You are going to die.* No dissenting voice spoke up in
his mind. This was the end. He could not beat this freak.

He landed not just hard but awkwardly, posting his leg at a
bad angle and crashing into himself with his own weight. His
ankle rolled, and he felt it pop, something cracking, giving away,
and then he spilled to the mat.

Decker hovered over him, grinning down with broken teeth.

Carl scooted back to the cage and used it to haul himself up
yet again.

Decker's icy blue eyes sparkled, as remote and merciless as
frozen moons. "Hollywood," he said, and slapped his own face,
laughing. "Punch, Hollywood, punch."

Carl jawed him and hobbled away.

Decker laughed harder, a new cut draining blood, and walked
straight at Carl again. "Good," he growled, nodding and slapping
his bloody face. "Punch."

Carl let him have it again.

More laughter. "Punch."

He's just having fun before he finishes me off, Carl thought.
He drew back his fist one more time but never threw the punch—
firing a surprise kick at Decker's knee instead.

A mistake.

Decker caught the kick, drove Carl backward, slammed him into the cage, and blasted him with an elbow that filled Carl's head with sparks and turned his muscles to dough. His legs buckled, but panic brought him back to consciousness as he felt Decker's arms wrap him into a bear hug that pinned his own arms to his sides. The crushing arms had him not around the chest but the waist, squeezing, lifting Carl from his feet.

The suplex, Carl's mind screamed, *his killing move.*

Decker squatted and leapt. Carl rushed upward, then tilted as Decker, still squeezing, arched beneath him, driving Carl head-first at the mat.

At the last second, Carl rolled his head, and the mat slammed into him like a speeding truck. Blackness pulsed as he flashed into unconsciousness. Half a second later, he came rushing back and lay there, feeling broken. *Should've killed me*, he thought, but knew his shoulder had taken a good deal of the impact.

Decker jumped up, roaring, hands held overhead.

Get up, Carl thought wearily. *Get him while he has his back turned*, but he was still half-stunned, and it took every ounce of willpower to hoist his battered body from the mat. He stumbled after the mutant, drawing back his fist.

But then Baca was yelling and pointing, and Decker turned—too far away, too far—and raced at Carl again, one metal fist cocked to the shoulder, ready to fire the killing shot.

The bell rang, ending round one.

Carl staggered back to his corner, shaking the cobwebs from his fuzzy mind, confused by the white towels there . . . then realized Davis, who was through the door now, helping him onto the stool and taking his mouthpiece, had been trying to stop the fight.

There could be no surrender, of course. No appeal, no mercy.

The ref, the Few, Decker, Baca—even the canned applause, it seemed to Carl—would demand not only his blood but also his life. He refused to allow the Few to recycle his flesh. This struggle could only end with his death . . . and that dark slumber beckoned to him now.

Davis was talking. ". . . hear me, Carl?"

"Yeah," Carl said, slumped on the stool.

Across the ring, Decker hadn't even bothered to sit. He hopped side to side, hyped for the bell.

What's the point? Carl thought. He was going to die. Decker knew it. Davis knew it. Baca, the bearded man, the ref . . . everyone knew it.

Just dial down and be done with it, he thought. *Go to sleep forever.* It would be so simple to give everyone what they were waiting for. Just go out there, stretch out, and—

It hit Carl like smelling salts, bringing him up straight in his seat. That was it! He knew what he had to do, what *they* had to do. . . .

"Don't go back out," Davis said. Tears—real tears, not tattoos—streamed from his eyes.

"I have to," Carl said, "and you have to help me."

"You go back out, you're going to die."

Carl nodded. "You're right. I *am* going to die. And you're going to make sure I'm dead."

Davis shook his head. "I'm sorry, man, but I can't do it. Not after Sanchez—"

"No," Carl said, and had just enough time to explain before the bell rang, drawing him out to his fate.

He struggled off the stool and limped toward the center with exaggerated exhaustion.

Decker took the bait, throwing him only twice before scooping him once more into the bear hug and flipping into the terrifying suplex that was his signature killing move.

Now, Carl thought, and once more tucked his head into his shoulder at the last second. He exploded into the mat, and force jolted through his body, which jerked and went limp. Lying there, he felt his consciousness dim, felt his heart skip, stutter, and stall. As the world faded, he was vaguely aware of Davis crouching beside him, pressing fingers to his throat, and wailing. Carl's breath shuddered free, and he faded to black. . . .

THIRTY-NINE

CARL AWOKE TO FLAMES, *in* flames, burning . . . not in hell or as a rendering phoenix but lying on his back, wound in a shroud of burning fabric melting into his skin, lighting him afire . . .

Simultaneously, he heard loud music—and instantly understood.

This was his funeral. He lay, wrapped in his burning burial shroud at the center of a boat engulfed in flames.

It had worked.

Everyone had expected him to die, and he had died. At least that's what it had looked like, and that's what Davis had told them. The referee had both expected and found the evidence he'd needed to confirm the death—no pulse, no respiration.

He gasped, but there was no air, only heat and flame. He uncrossed arms, spread them like wings, ripping through the burning fabric, and emerged into the airless heat at the center of a raging ring of fire. Overhead, the flaming sail and rigging made the mast a fiery cross. Burning fabric still clung to him, but there was no time even to brush it away. Instead, he drew his fist back—happy to see it still capped in metal—and smashed it into the bottom of the boat, cracking the wooden hull. He swung again and again, smashing through the planks, which gave with a rush of black water. Then, with water filling the boat, he pushed at the damaged planking, snapping it away, and the boat sunk like a stone in the dark lake.

He dove.

The water was shockingly cold, but it extinguished the flaming shroud, which fell away as he swam from the sinking boat, heading away from the dim shore of funeral-goers toward the deeper darkness of the far shore. His body was wrecked, stiff and badly out of alignment, his left arm no good at all as he pulled through the dark depths with an awkward underwater sidestroke, pulling and pulling until he thought his lungs would burst. He needed air, but even more, he needed to get as far away from the boat and funeral shore as possible before surfacing.

When at last he could hold his breath no longer, he broke the surface, expelled charred air, filled his lungs, and slipped underwater again. A short time later, reaching a shoreline, he pulled himself into the shallows—the lake bottom strangely soft, like clay beneath his fingertips—and he swiveled, bringing his head around to face the lake but keeping his body mostly submerged in the manner of a crocodile.

He'd done it.

The music—the Phoenix Island anthem, Carl realized—died, and the voice of the bearded man, modified once more into inhuman deepness, boomed, "We honor Fighter 19. May we all die such an honorable death."

Yes, Carl thought, picturing the masked devil. *And may you die soon.*

"And now," the deep voice said, "ascend, warriors. Join us for the closing ceremonies of these historic Funeral Games, so that we might honor the dead and laud the living before sending you on your way back into the world, where you will walk like giants among the timid masses." Far above, light returned to the arena, illuminating the Cauldron and brightening the lakeshore from pitch-blackness to dim gloom.

At the center of the lake, the last scraps of burning flotsam flickered and faded. Along the opposite shore, dark figures grouped mostly in twos and threes trudged away up the slope of black sand toward the waiting elevator. Only one figure remained, a tall, gaunt silhouette that stared out into the lake until the last flames died.

Davis, Carl thought, and wanted to call out to his friend, his magnificent friend who had saved his life by pronouncing him dead . . . but no, he couldn't risk that, not with the straggling crowd clustered around the elevator and not with the security cameras he was all but certain were rolling now, somewhere in the subterranean darkness.

He floated there in the shadows, his right hand absently dragging grooves in the sloping lake bottom, which was not only soft but slick. Strange. He would have expected a rough floor of volcanic rock, not this substance that felt like Silly Putty.

Across the shore, Davis and the stragglers climbed aboard the elevator.

Overhead in the bright arena, music started. From his hiding spot, Carl could see people filing onto the bleachers.

As he lay there, he twisted the pain dial quickly, winced, and dialed it most of the way back down. Whether he could feel it or not, pain filled his broken body. By its echo, he estimated damages—his broken arm and ribs and toe, severe damage to his ankle and shoulder, and something wrong with his neck, which didn't want to straighten. Cuts throbbed on his face, and his whole body pulsed with the damage of having been slammed again and again by Decker. Sharpest of all, however, was the pain he had glimpsed in his scorched arms, legs, and side, where tattered sections of the black fabric that had enshrouded him still hung from his burned flesh like flaps of charred skin. Stitched into a larger piece of the cloth dangling from his seared thigh was a triangle of red, and beneath it, slightly recessed, another red point.

Wingtips, he thought. *They wrapped me in the flag of Phoenix Island.*

He was glad to have survived—and even gladder not to have died wrapped in that particular standard, which to him represented all the evil in his life.

As he peeled away the black-and-red fabric, actual wings rustled in the darkness, and a flock of Krebs hawks burst from the shadows and rushed upward, as if hurrying to catch the opening ceremonies. A lone bird remained, hunched upon the stones. Dark and miserable looking, it regarded him with yellow eyes.

Overhead, the voice of the woman who had announced the fights said, "Ladies and gentlemen, welcome one and all to the closing ceremonies of this year's Funeral Games."

He turned over and lay in the cold water with his back on the soft incline, resting and listening to the announcer thank and congratulate the brave competitors. Sharpening his vision, he drew in the faces of those competitors and their trainers, most of whom looked far from brave. They looked haggard and confused and terrified.

"The Few have entered the arena," the announcer said. "Please rise and pay tribute to our most generous hosts."

Canned applause roared. Music blared. Along the bleachers, teams stood and bowed.

Carl was pulling himself along the soft bottom for a better look at the opera box, when his fingers dragged across something strange running from the Silly Putty bank up onto the shore . . . what he first mistook as a braid of roots or vines, and then recognized as a bundle of thin wires. Squinting in the gloom, he examined these thin wires sheathed in multicolored plastic. Red, white, and green, they reminded him of stereo wires. Was that what they were, wires to the hidden speakers? Or were they, perhaps, wires to whatever surveillance cameras had allowed the Few to spy on the conversations he'd had with Octavia?

Hoping these hidden cameras were locked solely on the mourning shore and not this side, he rose dripping from the water, and traced the lines out of the water and up the shore.

These weren't speaker wires. Why would speaker wires run underwater?

Overhead, the announcer, who had been blabbing on, said, "The grand champion, also representing Zurkistan, Fighter 47."

Triumphant music filled the volcano, and Carl turned to watch as, five stories overhead, Baca escorted Decker over the black bridge to the octagon.

He turned his attention to his discovery. The main shore was comprised not of soft putty but of rough stones that scratched his bare feet as he followed the wires out to the back wall, where, behind a dark boulder, they attached to a heavy black box, out of which rose a black antenna. On the face of the black box, a yellow light winked at Carl, as if to say, *Get it?*

He got it, all right.

He'd seen the same sort of thing back on Phoenix Island, during one phase of his endless training with Stark. The winking light, the antenna, the box, and the wires . . . this was the receiver/detonator unit, and—he shuddered with the realization—he'd been lying upon a shore of C4 plastic explosives, enough putty not only to blow this entire complex to dust but also to unleash the volcanic activity bubbling just beneath the surface. These were the explosives Julio had been hunting.

Unfortunately, Stark had taught him only to detonate, not deactivate. He looked again at the wires. Red, white, and green. What did each do? Would severing the incorrect wire set off the explosives, or was that just a movie thing?

He started to conjure the memory clip of a not-so-recent demolitions training session, when a terrible squawking started. He jerked—*I've triggered them!*—and something hit him from behind.

He stumbled across the rocks, and something black rushed screeching out of the gloom.

The Krebs hawk was attacking him.

With a mad chitter, it swooped at his head, circled, and dipped at him again.

"Get off," he said, batting it away. Go figure . . . he'd discovered the detonator, and this thing apparently had a nearby nest of eggs to defend.

He blocked his face, and the crazed thing raked its razor-sharp talons across his forearm, spattering him with blood.

What was going on?

The hawk fluttered up and dove again. Once more, he blocked, and claws sliced his arm, the bird insane and vicious and determined. He had to stop its loud racket and couldn't just let it tear him to shreds.

The thing chittered madly, flapped away, and raced at him again—only this time, Carl was ready. Once more, he held out his forearm, but this time he snapped his hand forward and grabbed the thing. Huge and muscular, the hawk screamed, flapping its powerful wings and slashing him with its claws. Craning its neck, the crazed bird snapped at his face with its beak and glared at him with its bright yellow eyes.

Feeling its talons digging into his flesh, Carl swung his arm and slammed the insane creature into the volcanic boulder.

It *crunched* . . . and emitted a shower of sparks in the darkness. It fluttered on the rocks, whistling and hissing. Carl backed away, horrified, as the broken bird flapped and twitched and sparks sputtered from its torn body, within which Carl could see meat and metal, vein and wire.

The thing shuddered, its yellow eyes faded to black, and Carl winced at a foul smell that combined singed feathers, scorched meat, and fried electronics.

The Krebs hawk hadn't been a real bird but some kind of cyborg—part animal, part machine, a franken-bird—and it hadn't been protecting a nest. It had been protecting the detonator. *And filming you,* he thought, suddenly studded in goose bumps.

Somewhere, recycled fighters in red togas were seeing this footage, sounding alarms . . .

Across the lake, the elevator *ding*ed.

Carl turned to the box. No time for memory clips or caution or anything but action.

People spilled from the elevator, shouting. They were all the way around the lake, but escape was impossible. It was too late to save himself. All he could do now was jam his thumbs into the eyes of the Few's grand plan.

He grabbed the wires and yanked, but they wouldn't come free.

"There he is!" an all-too-familiar voice—deep, not quite English, not quite African—hollered.

Carl pulled frantically at the stubborn wires, but they wouldn't come loose. He needed to sever them—all of them, regardless of the dangers, real or imagined—but he had no cutters, no knife.

As the shouters raced around the shore, coming for him, Carl searched for something sharp. He picked up a stone, tossed it away, and saw the bird, lying twisted at the base of the boulder, its wings fanned out at strange angles, its feet flexed, clawing even in death.

That was it!

He swept the shattered thing from the rocks, gripped a talon between his thumb and forefinger, slashed the bundled wires . . . and the Cauldron *erupted*.

FORTY

LOUD EXPLOSIONS shook the volcano. Alarms shrieked overhead, where Carl heard shouting and gunfire. Debris hurtled
down, splashing into the lake and pitching geysers of black water.

What had he triggered?

He tossed the severed wires out into the water, then dodged a
chunk of falling stone that cracked loudly off the rocks where
he'd been standing.

Across the lake, the red togas, having evidently abandoned
him for whatever was happening upstairs, raced back into the elevator.

Hope the thing falls in on you, Carl thought, watching the
doors slide shut.

Overhead, smoke clouded the air, but he could see the empty
opera box, people fleeing the bleachers, and three figures—
Z-Force—standing on the black bridge, looking up . . . where
dozens of soldiers in black uniforms and gas masks were rappelling down out of the smoky upper reaches, firing machine
guns as they descended. Someone in a red toga came hurtling
down, splashed into the center of the lake, and did not rise.

Red togas fired machine guns from the bleachers.

Carl saw one rappelling soldier twitch, spin, and go limp, like
an abandoned puppet, but the others—so many of them!—
blasted away, some mowing down red togas, others firing at tar-

gets unseen, and still others contending with a far stranger threat.

Dark shapes cut the smoky air, dive-bombing the dangling soldiers. The Krebs hawks had joined the fight. They tore into the men, pecking and slashing and flapping their muscular wings. Muzzles flashed flame, and mechanical birds folded and spun, raining from the above like a bad omen.

A sequence of rapid pops patter-rattled somewhere up there, and mist joined the smoke.

Tear gas, he thought, and then another large explosion rocked the mountain, and someone fell, screaming, from the bridge.

Carl watched in slow motion as the Z-Force lightweight plummeted not into the water but onto the shore of black sand, where he lay in a motionless heap.

Above, Baca dangled from the bridge, having been knocked from his feet by the explosion. A soldier rappelled onto the bridge, seemed to hesitate, then offered his hand to Baca, who swung up to safety. A second later, Decker felled the soldier with a vicious blow to the back of the neck. Baca scooped up the soldier's machine gun and went to work, firing in short bursts as he retreated across the bridge, followed by Decker. Then Baca jerked and fell out of view. Decker grabbed Baca in one hand, snatched up the machine gun in the other, and swung the weapon one-handed, blasting away. Then the hulking boy-thing jerked once, twice, three times, and Carl saw wounds open in the overmuscled legs and shoulder.

Still holding Baca, Decker jumped from the bridge. This was no hop-and-drop. His tremendous leg muscles crouched and sprung, launching him out and away from the bridge, with Baca fluttering behind him like a flapping cape. Thanks to Decker's mighty leap, they arched out over the sand and splashed into the lake.

Carl smelled a sharp and unmistakable chemical smell misting down from above. At the same second, his eyes began to sting, and he felt the muscles of his face beginning to twitch and spasm. Tear gas raining down . . .

He winced, ready to dive into the lake, and then saw the elevator doors open. Red togas emerged first, waving machine guns.

Carl crouched in the shadows.

The Few hurried from the elevator—or rather, four of them did, followed by the masked children Carl had seen in the upper levels—with the bearded man leading the way. He shouted at the red togas, who nodded and took up defensive positions, covering the retreat of the Few, who sped across the black shore to the far end. They had just reached the boat ramp when Decker rose from the water, Baca draped over one shoulder. The bearded man raised an arm, obviously ready to fire the curious cloud weapon with which he had incapacitated Carl, then hesitated, seeming to think, and beckoned to Decker, who followed the Few as they disappeared up the ramp and into the huge room filled with the remaining funeral boats.

Across the lake, the red togas opened up on soldiers firing down from the bridge.

All at once, Carl understood. He hadn't caused the explosions. Those had come either from the defenders or the soldiers . . . who he now realized were agents of SI3. Somehow, Octavia—brave, amazing Octavia—had managed to signal them, and they were assaulting the Cauldron full force, fighting and dying to stop the Few from escaping.

At the other end of the lake, something groaned loudly, as if the Cauldron itself were voicing its pain.

Determined to help SI3, Carl pointed himself in the direction of the groaning and hauled his damaged body along the darkened shore opposite the firefight, lurching and hitching toward the boat room. He couldn't stop the Few, but it was in his nature to join the fight, and since, as Stark often pointed out, *information wins wars*, he chased after his enemies in hopes of seeing something—*anything*—that he could later share with the soldiers.

He had expected a telltale blood trail, a secret door slamming shut, or perhaps funeral boats rocking as the Few settled into hiding spots, but nothing could have prepared him for what he saw when he topped the ramp.

The floor of the boat room was gone, having spread apart to reveal a vast pool of water, at the edges of which, tilted like broken toys, bobbed the last of the funeral boats. At the center of the pool floated a dark blue submarine perhaps fifty feet in length.

Overhead, more explosions shook the Cauldron, raining down debris, but the gunfire slowed, coming now only intermittently, in short, controlled bursts.

The CS mist drifted past, and Carl watched with stinging eyes as the sub sunk, disappearing into the pool, and the boat room floor groaned, rumbling slowly shut again.

FORTY-ONE

CARL CREPT FROM THE BOAT ROOM to see the red togas retreating across the sand, backpedaling in his direction, firing at the soldiers rappelling onto the opposite end of the lake. In the same instant, the Agbeko-Kruger-thing turned in slow motion, saw Carl, and fired.

Carl dropped.

The bullet snapped overhead, so close he could feel its slipstream on his scalp. He scrambled back into the room and hunched, awaiting the next volley . . . which never came.

All at once, the shooting stopped. Then came a rapid string of splashes on the lake and a muffled pattering on the sand, what sounded like a final round of debris raining down.

After several seconds of silence, Carl risked a glimpse. Krebs hawks, dead or deactivated, littered the beach and lake. Near the elevator, several soldiers gathered around the red togas, who lay motionless on the beach. *Shot them all*, he thought, and felt a pang of sorrow. That hadn't been Agbeko firing at him, but it had been Agbeko's body. . . .

Carl rose and limped from the shadows.

Soldiers raised their weapons and shouted, "On the ground! On the ground!"

Carl flattened out, a smile coming onto his face. A curious

moment—feeling *happy* to have guns pointed at him. The good guys were finally here.

All gunfire had stopped. Not just down here. Everywhere.

Five SI3 shooters approached in a fan—maintaining good form, Carl noted—two weapons trained on him, the others covering a full 360. In their black jumpsuits, gas masks, and body armor, they looked like they had rappelled straight out of some black-ops shooter game.

Two flanked him. The others raced into the boat room.

Carl tried to tell them that the Few had left, but no one would listen until the forward team returned from the boathouse. Then it was hurry-up-and-go. This place was going to explode any minute now.

"No," Carl told them, "it's not." And he explained what he'd done around the shore.

Things relaxed slightly once they verified his story. Surprise rippled through the men when he reported his name.

"Sigma," someone said.

"Lock it up," the leader, a burly guy with a superficial bullet wound to his shoulder, said. Turning to Carl, he peeled off his gas mask, revealing a square jaw and piercing eyes. "Sergeant Cutter, SI3," he said, and looked Carl up and down. "We're happy to see you, kid. You did one heck of a job, deactivating those munitions, and you also happen to be one of the things we came here to find. Maybe this mission isn't completely hosed after all. Put those cuffs away, Slade. Kid's got a broken arm."

After all Carl had been through, even this small kindness felt like the warmest of welcomes. But he couldn't relax until he knew the truth, no matter how much it frightened him. "Where's Oc—Margarita?"

Cutter frowned. "Advance chopper did an emergency evac."

He shook his head. "That girl saved this mission. How she did it, I'll never know. Running all those miles over mountain trails in the snow and dark, only wearing sandals and a toga. Time we reached her, she was hypothermic, but she wouldn't let herself pass out until she'd told us what we needed to know."

Carl swallowed with difficulty. *Emergency evac, hypothermic.* "Is she . . . all right?"

"She will be," Cutter said. "She's with the medics now."

"And Davis?"

"Don't know who that is," Cutter said. "Let's head upstairs and sort all this out."

As they led him across the sand, Carl told them about the sub and the moving floor, about Decker and Baca, and how he'd only seen four of the Few, one of the women missing, the blonde, he thought.

Cutter nodded. "She's . . . upstairs," he said, and Carl understood by the man's tone that she, too, was dead.

Agbeko lay beside the other togas. Carl looked at him and then looked away, feeling sick and sad and angry. Agbeko's eyes were open yet empty, their whites as red as his toga. Blood pooled at the corners. Red tracks ran down his face into the black sand. The others' eyes were the same.

"They all dropped at once," Cutter said, and snapped his fingers. "Like somebody flicked a switch."

Looking at the tears of blood, Carl figured he knew exactly what had happened. The bearded man had indeed flicked a switch—or maybe pressed a button. The red togas, just like the Cauldron, had been wired to explode. It didn't take C4 to ruin a brain. All it took was a tiny explosive wired into a neural chip . . . and a remote detonator. A similar arrangement would explain the rain of ruined birds.

Despite his grief over Agbeko, Carl's brain rushed forward. He needed to get upstairs, needed to know what had become of Davis.

They ascended to the main floor, where lingering CS gas stung his eyes and tickled his nose. At least his facial muscles had stopped doing the two-step. The fighting had ended, but the devastation was incredible. Carl scanned the scene, looking for his friend.

Smoke poured from the upper levels and huffed out the volcano's chimney. The track and bridge were covered in thousands of brass casings, broken glass from the shattered television screen, and the dark corpses of countless birds, one of which sparked at the feet of a fascinated soldier. The trooper watched for a second, then stomped the sparking mess with his combat boot.

Bodies littered the track and bleachers. Most of the dead wore red togas, but Carl was sad to see dead tournament fighters and SI3 troopers, too. He said a silent prayer that Davis wouldn't be among their number.

"Watch it," a soldier said, guiding him around a random puddle of blood. A drip splashed at its middle, and Carl looked up. A soldier hung twenty feet overhead, obviously killed by gunfire, spinning slowly back and forth from his rappelling line, looking like a half-finished meal a spider had left for later.

SI3 had taken heavy casualties.

Then Carl's heart surged. "Davis!"

His friend didn't hear him. He was busy helping a fallen trooper. Davis's hands were bloody, but he moved with confidence, tightening a tourniquet around the man's injured leg, then called across the floor to a medic. The medic handed something to a soldier, who ran it to Davis. In that instant, Davis looked up, saw Carl, and beamed—then went back to work saving a life.

Carl swelled with pride, seeing his friend in action. It occurred to him then that Davis might go on to become the first doctor in history with tattooed tears—only to spend the rest of his life trying to erase them.

He started to step around the corpse of another red toga and lurched to a stop. Alexi lay at his feet, staring up lifelessly, the tracks of crimson tears now pink against his pale flesh.

"Someone you knew?" Cutter asked.

"Sort of," Carl said, and discovered that he didn't know exactly how to feel about this. No, he hadn't ended Alexi's life—not in the fight, and certainly not by flipping some remote kill switch—but he had crushed him in the ring, and based on this, the Few had recycled the Zurkistani. Now Alexi would join the ranks of Ross and Drill Sergeant Parker, neither of whom Carl had killed but who had both died *because* of him.

Not far away, the beautiful blond woman sprawled indignantly on the arena floor directly beneath the opera box from which she had undoubtedly fallen. Her look of shock suggested disbelief that Death would *dare* come calling someone of her status.

"She's one of them," Carl said, "one of the Few."

Cutter crouched and retrieved the golden mask from the ground beside her. "Not anymore," he said. He radioed forensics and told them to send a team immediately. Then, to Carl, he said, "If we can ID her, it might help us identify the ones who got away." He glanced up to where smoke billowed from a hallway high above. "I wish we'd been able to rescue Margarita's sketches." He shook his head. "But they're long gone."

Carl offered a weary smile. "No, they aren't."

FORTY-TWO

"THAT'S IT," Carl told the sketch artist. He shifted on the hospital bed, checking the drawing from different angles, then nodded. "It's perfect."

"Amazing," Crossman said. The SI3 director stood, hands on hips, just inside the door.

It had taken several hours, given Carl's endless refinements, but the artist had finished the fourth and final sketch. Carl had simply rewound his memory of Octavia's maps and directed the artist's efforts until the new sketches were mirror images of the original drawings.

The artist, a willowy middle-aged woman with long, slender fingers, smiled wearily. She looked both happy and exhausted. "You did great," she told Carl, patting his shoulder. Then Crossman dismissed her, and she left the two of them alone.

It was still difficult, even after a day of being back in America, tucked away in the SI3 Bunker, for Carl to believe that he, Octavia, and Davis really were safe at last. Octavia would need time to heal—as would he—but doctors expected both of them to recover fully. Davis was ecstatic. He'd received a hero's welcome at the Bunker for having saved soldiers' lives, and the medical staff had already offered him a full-time apprenticeship. Julio had made it out, too, though the Few had beaten him severely in their attempt to extract information.

Search-and-recovery teams had never found Tex, so his death couldn't be verified. By choice, Carl imagined the traitor frozen in a kind of Judecca at the bottom of some icy gully, abandoned for eternity.

"We can't thank you enough," Crossman said. "You've saved the mission."

Carl shrugged. "I couldn't have done it without Margarita"

"I'm certain this news will be great medicine for her. These are the best leads we have."

"What about the blond-haired woman?"

The SI3 director shook his head.

"You couldn't ID her?" Carl asked.

"Oh, we ID'd her, all right," Crossman said. "It's just that we can't make any sense of her identity. We'd been expecting someone rich and powerful—a young CEO or heiress or duchess . . . something like that—but we were *way* wrong. Her name was Ada Boros, and she was a poor farm girl from rural Hungary."

"A farm girl? You're positive?"

"One hundred percent. She disappeared from the fields six months ago. Authorities listed her as abducted but had no real leads."

"But that doesn't make any sense," Carl said, yet even as the phrase left his mouth, he understood. "She was a *vessel*."

"What?"

"A vessel," he said. "The Few used her body. They're riding in other people."

Carl had expected shock, confusion, or doubt, but the SI3 director merely leaned forward, staring at Carl with those intense blue eyes.

"Tell me," he said. "Take your time. I want to hear everything."

The next day, Crossman visited again, this time with Dr. Bleaker in tow. By this time, they had more to share.

When SI3 had run the faces against an international data-base of suspects, they had come up empty. Then, based on Carl's vessel theory, Crossman had changed his investigative approach, and SI3 soon matched the sketches to missing persons, one from Greece, one from Singapore, and one from Bulgaria. Like Ada Boros, these three were simply regular people who'd gone missing.

"So we're back to square one," Carl said, feeling dejected. All that work, all that sacrifice . . .

"Not at all," Crossman said. "We have leads, and thanks to you, we have a much better idea of what we're up against."

"I would love to have a look at the technology they're using," Dr. Bleaker said. Unfortunately, the Few had wired the Cauldron labs with smaller yet adequate demolitions—the explosions Carl had first heard and mistaken as his own work—and had destroyed anything that might have helped SI3 better understand how, exactly, they were swapping consciousness from one body to another. "We conducted autopsies on the *vessels*," Bleaker said. "They all had neural chips, but they'd been destroyed." Inside the Krebs hawks, the Bunker Bots uncovered revolutionary cybernetic structures, but detonation had also destroyed their neural chips, along with what looked like the remnants of cameras.

"We owe you," Crossman said, giving Carl's shoulder a squeeze. "You saved hundreds of lives by deactivating the main explosives, and you saved the entire mission by recovering those sketches."

"Give me Stark, then," Carl said. "Shut down Phoenix Island and save the orphans." Earlier that day, he'd given them everything, going over SI3's satellite images and detailing practically every square foot—Stark's quarters, Camp Phoenix Force, the armories, everything—for one half of the island. The other half, the *here are dragons* side, remained as mysterious to Carl as it was indefinite in satellite images, which showed only a few buildings, some clearings, and a lot of jungle.

Crossman shook his head, looking sad yet stern. "We can't tip our hand. If we raid Phoenix Island now, the Few will go deep underground."

Carl's fists ached.

"As soon as the time is right, we will capture it. You have my promise," Crossman said. "But for now, something else. Tell me what you want, and I'll make it happen."

Carl thought for a moment. What did he want, other than to save Campbell and see Stark and the Few brought to justice? It was hard to even think in those terms. He wracked his mind and memory, trying to dredge up something he'd wanted before his world had been reduced to high-stakes goals like life and death and stopping a madman bent on global destruction. . . .

And then he had it.

Smiling, he said, "There is something. . . ."

SEVERAL WEEKS LATER . . .

Carl stood at the edge of the cliff and spread his arms wide, as if embracing the ocean. Below him—far, far below—waves boomed and boiled, crashing against great exposed rocks that rose like monster's teeth from the terrible waters that the fishermen of this

Caribbean island called *La Boca de los Perdidos*: The Mouth of the Lost.

Only the dead dive here, they told him the first day, *only the suicides.*

He'd made the dive every day since.

Now the locals called him *El Fantasma*: The Ghost.

If only they knew how close he'd come to being a ghost. . . .

But he hadn't died—or stayed dead, at any rate. For the second time, he had descended into a kind of death only to rise again.

Behind him, the little children who each day gathered to watch him dive laughed and cheered and called, "¡*Fantasma!* ¡*Fantasma!*"

He curled his toes over the edge of the cliff, closed his eyes, and smiled, feeling the bright sun on his skin. He muted the cheering children, drew his lungs full of the good, salty air, and focused on the roll and thunder of the tide. Selectively filtering his senses—hearing the surf yet not the children, for example— was one of the skills that Dr. Bleaker and the Bunker Bots had helped him to develop during the weeks he'd spent recuperating there. Now, standing with his eyes closed, he slowed the moment and opened himself to the air and water, letting the rhythm of the tide enter him. Its push, its pull, the way it broke and curled around the stones like wind blowing through a winter forest . . . he could hear it all, smell it all, feel it all. And then, feeling the heave of the tide, feeling the way the water curled up the cliffs and wrapped round the exposed stones, feeling the vastness that was the sea inhale again, he matched himself to it all: his breathing, his heartbeat, his energy . . .

And he dove.

He opened his eyes in flight, not to see whether he would cut the water safely—he knew he would—but to enjoy the rush of the wind on his open eyes. It was like flying. No . . . it *was* flying. Rushing free through the open air, he whooped with laughter and accelerated his senses and perception, slowing time, savoring this perfect moment.

He cut the water within an arm's length of the largest stone, just as the waves crashed into the cliff beyond. His body arched instinctively, and he gave himself to the water, riding a long-curving inner tide that pulled him back toward the base of the cliff wall even as the broken wave receded once more toward the open water. *This*, he thought, *this is freedom*, and the current whipped him away, out into the bay again. As the current carried him, he allowed his body to twist and turn, rise and dive, and so passed through the water like a bird through the air. All those years, he had dreamed of the ocean, of how wonderful it would feel, yet he'd never anticipated anything half as magnificent as this: the blue-green Caribbean all around him, warm as a bath, stripping him clean of dirt and pain and darkness.

Then he swam, cutting the water with strength and grace, kicking smoothly and staying underwater all the way to shore, where he walked onto the sand, paused to wave at the small shapes of the cheering children atop the cliff, and walked farther around the sea wall, out of their sight, onto the isolated beach where he and Octavia had spent the last week and where he wished he could spend the rest of his life.

"Show-off," she said, smiling up from her blanket. It had taken a long time for her to heal, but she looked well now, tanned and happy, well rested and well fed, beautiful. Her hair was growing out again, the forelock very white in the bright sun, and she looked at him not through colored contacts but with her own gray eyes, which had always reminded him of wet stones.

He leaned over her and shook his head, shedding water like a dog, sprinkling her long, sun-darkened legs with sparkling beads.

Her laughter was music.

They had spent their days walking the beach and swimming and lying there, basking in the sun and talking and just enjoying each other. Even the supervision of their "parents"—two pairs of SI3 agents, who huddled now beneath a sun umbrella down the beach—hadn't damaged this amazing vacation.

"No matter what happens in the future," Octavia said, "we'll always have this."

"It's been perfect," he said, and plopped down onto his blanket.

She sat up and slid her hand into his.

He smiled, but within him, something cold and hard shifted, waking: dread . . . always there, always waiting. Despite his great happiness here, dread had become a part of him, like an unwanted internal organ that periodically pumped ice water into his heart and dark memories and darker visions into his mind. It whispered to him in the night, when he woke from dreamscapes painted with blood and pain, and told him what he knew to be true: Stark and the Few were still out there in the world. . . .

His fight wasn't over.

But at least he wouldn't have to fight alone.

Crossman had invited him to join SI3, and he had accepted . . . under two conditions: that they set things right on Phoenix Island as quickly as possible, and that Crossman wouldn't separate him from Octavia.

Separate you? Crossman had said, offering a rare smile. *Why would I separate my best team?*

"I can't believe we head back tomorrow," Octavia said.

His first instinct was to reply with one of those tired responses hammered into everyone from birth—*I know! It seems like we just got here!*—but that would be a lie. Time doesn't actually fly when you're having fun. It expands. And sometimes, when you're diving off a cliff or swimming in the currents or laughing with a beautiful girl, time stops altogether. It's only later, looking back, when you don't want the moment to slip away, that time seems to have flown.

And yet the past is never really gone. As you push forward, it remembers you and your debts to it. Some nights, during silent moments here on the beach, when the wind would blow off the sea, and the campfire flames would gutter low, and Octavia would lean close to him and shiver, it seemed to Carl that he could feel the weight of his friends' absence in the air around him, as if the loss of Ross and Agbeko and others was stitched into the wind, written upon the world. Whenever this happened, he thought of telling her but only tightened his arm around her small shoulders instead. It was easier to dive off cliffs than talk about your dead friends, and it would be time soon enough to repay the living and the dead.

"Carl?" Octavia said. She smiled uncertainly and touched a hand to his chest. "Are you all right?"

He forced a smile. "Yeah. I'm fine."

She lifted his hand to her lips and kissed his scarred knuckles. "I know that look," she said. "You're thinking about Stark."

He nodded. "Among other things."

She gave him a hard look. "Well, stop it."

"Stop thinking about Stark?" he said, knuckles throbbing. "How can—"

She put a finger to his lips. "Let's just live for a little while longer, all right? We'll deal with the future when it gets here, okay?"

He kissed her finger and felt some of the tension go out of his shoulders. "Okay." She was right. Why let the hell they'd been through ruin this momentary heaven?

It was time to be happy, if only for a little while longer. It's what they had.

She popped to her feet and held out her hand, and when he took it, grinning, she hauled him up. Then she pointed toward the tilted mast of the sunken ship two hundred yards out in the water. "Come on," she said. "Last one to the shipwreck is a rotten egg!"

Then she was off, sprinting across the sand with a squeal of laughter.

He tore after her, his laughter joining hers, and together they dove into the warm waves.

And as they raced happily through the turquoise water, they freed this moment from the grasp of time. The past fled like ashes in the wind, and the future faded and vanished like constellations before the dawn. All that remained was this perfect *now*, incorruptible and whole unto itself, with the two of them ensconced in its heart, together at last, safe and well and very, very happy.

ACKNOWLEDGMENTS

FIRST OF ALL, thanks to my family and friends for your love, support, and enthusiasm.

Thanks to the incredible team at the Jane Rotrosen Agency, especially my wonderful agent, Christina Hogrebe, for constant assistance in anything and everything and for talking me off the ledge time and time again.

Thanks to Adam Wilson, the coolest editor on the planet, for believing in me, for guiding me when I needed help, and for letting me run when I needed to sprint. You have been such an unbelievable advocate with this book, from the conception of its premise all the way through the finishing touches. I'm absolutely blessed to have you as my editor.

Thanks to John Vairo, for creating another knockout cover, and the whole team at Simon & Schuster/Gallery Books, especially Liz Psaltis in marketing, the delightful Princess of PR, Stephanie DeLuca, and copyediting superheroine Erica Ferguson, who once again spotted roughly ten thousand errors, saving me from looking like an idiot.

Thanks to crit partner and tough guy Don Bentley, for your constant help with this book, from my early struggles all the way through the final touches.

Thanks to Dr. Gary Della'Zanna and Dr. John Dougherty, both of the National Institutes of Health, and combat medic

Horace Jonson, for lending me your brains and for making research so much fun.

Thanks to cage fighter cool cats Kelly Lasseigne and Randy Pogue, for helping a boxer understand the octagon.

Thanks to my bud and constant counselor, Matt Schwartz, for keeping me safe and sane.

Thanks to author pals Melissa Marr, Lissa Price, Douglas Clegg, Tim Waggoner, and Craig DiLouie, for answering so many questions.

Thanks to the ITW, HWA, and SFWA, the OneFours, the Inkbots, the Brandywine Valley Writers Group, my Necon family, and Seton Hill University's WPF program.

Thanks to Pete Aragno, Kimberley Howe, Brent Foehl, Jeff Wood, Joyce Wolfe, Elaine Prizzi, Bill Fay, Peter Klawitter, and the Briglias.

Obrigada to Caroline Freitas, and *obrigado* to my Brazilian readers, for your enthusiasm and for helping me with Portuguese.

Thanks to Metallica, for *Ride the Lightning*, which I listened to a few hundred times in a row writing this book.

My deepest thanks go once again to my best friend, first reader, and beautiful wife, Christina. When this book had me up against the ropes, you cheered me on, giving me the strength I needed to keep fighting . . . and that made all the difference.

Finally, thank *you* for reading this book. Without you, the reader, all of this is nothing. Without you, Carl, Octavia, Davis, Stark . . . they're just thoughts, exiled to my head.

Thank you.